• MURMANSK

• NIVSKY

• ALAKURTTI

RUSSIA

• ST. PETERSBURG

6/19

★ MOSCOW

BACKLASH

BACKLASH

A THRILLER

Brad Thor

EMILY BESTLER BOOKS
—
ATRIA
New York   London   Toronto   Sydney   New Delhi

For Robert C. O'Brien
Patriot. Diplomat. Friend.

An Imprint of Simon & Schuster, Inc.
1230 Avenue of the Americas
New York, NY 10020

First Emily Bestler Books/Atria Books hardcover edition June 2019

EMILY BESTLER BOOKS / ATRIA BOOKS and colophon are trademarks of Simon & Schuster, Inc.

For information about special discounts for bulk purchases, please contact Simon & Schuster Special Sales at 1-866-506-1949 or business@simonandschuster.com.

The Simon & Schuster Speakers Bureau can bring authors to your live event. For more information, or to book an event, contact the Simon & Schuster Speakers Bureau at 1-866-248-3049 or visit our website at www.simonspeakers.com.

Manufactured in the United States of America

10 9 8 7 6 5 4 3 2 1

Library of Congress Cataloging-in-Publication Data

Names: Thor, Brad, author.
Title: Backlash : a thriller / Brad Thor.
Description: First Emily Bestler Books/Atria Books hardcover edition. | New York : Atria/Emily Bestler Books, 2019. | Series: The Scot Harvath series; 19
Identifiers: LCCN 2019018645 (print) | LCCN 2019019228 (ebook) | ISBN 9781982104054 (Ebook) | ISBN 9781982104030 (hardback) | ISBN 9781982104047 (mass market)
Subjects: LCSH: Political fiction. | BISAC: FICTION / Political. | FICTION / Thrillers. | GSAFD: Suspense fiction.
Classification: LCC PS3620.H75 (ebook) | LCC PS3620.H75 B33 2019 (print) | DDC 813/.6—dc23
LC record available at https://lccn.loc.gov/2019018645

ISBN 978-1-9821-0403-0
ISBN 978-1-9821-0405-4 (ebook)

There will be killing till the score is paid.

—HOMER, *THE ODYSSEY*

CHAPTER 1

The transport plane, like everything else in Russia, was a piece of shit. For years, mechanics had swapped out its worn scavenged parts with even older parts. Cracks had been filled with epoxy. Leaking tubes and frayed wires had been wrapped with tape. A crash had been inevitable.

A booming noise, like a horseshoe thrown into a dryer, had been coming from the left engine. The pilot had throttled back, but the noise had only gotten worse.

He and the copilot had scanned their instruments, searching for clues, but hadn't found any. Everything, right down to the cabin pressure, had appeared normal.

But suddenly, the interior had begun filling with smoke. Seconds later, the left engine died, followed by the right.

As the pilot restarted them, an explosion erupted from the right engine. Seeing the exhaust temperature spike, he immediately ordered the copilot to activate the extinguisher. They had to keep the fire from spreading to the rest of the aircraft, even if it meant shutting the right engine down permanently.

The copilot pulled the fire extinguisher handle as ordered, but they had another problem. The left engine, which had successfully been restarted, wasn't producing enough thrust. They were falling at a rate of more than one thousand feet per minute. Over the blaring of cockpit alarms, the pilot put out a distress call.

They were flying in bad weather over one of the most remote, most inhospitable regions in the country. It was unlikely anyone would receive the transmission.

The pilot never got a chance to repeat his Mayday. The avionics and electrical system were next to go.

After trying to get the auxiliary power unit back online, the pilot instructed the crew to prepare for the worst. They were going down. Hard.

All this risk, he thought, *all this danger, just to deliver one man—a man chained in back like an animal.*

A Russian Special Forces team had boarded him with a hood over his head. No one had seen his face. The entire crew had assumed he was a criminal of some sort; maybe even a terrorist. They had been informed that he was dangerous. Under no circumstances were any of them to speak with or get anywhere near the prisoner.

But that was before they knew the plane was going to crash.

Moving quickly to the rear of the aircraft, the plane's loadmaster approached the large Spetsnaz soldier sitting nearest the prisoner.

"You need to put an oxygen mask on him," he said in Russian.

The operative, who *already* had *his* mask on, looked at the hooded prisoner, adjusted the submachine gun on his lap, and shook his head.

"*Nyet*," he stated. *No.*

Career Russian Air Force, the loadmaster was used to transporting elite operators. He was also used to their bullshit.

"I'm not asking you," he replied. "I'm *ordering* you."

The soldier shot a sideways glance at the intelligence officer sitting nearby.

The plane was losing altitude. The smoke in the cabin was getting worse. The officer nodded back. *Do it.*

The ape reached over, snatched off the hood, and affixed a mask over the prisoner's face. Then he replaced the hood and, satisfied, leaned back in his seat.

"Now unshackle his arms so he can brace for impact," the loadmaster continued. It enabled only a minor altering of the body's position, but in a crash it could mean the difference between life and death. Whatever the prisoner had done, surely he didn't deserve to die, at least not like this.

Pissed off, the soldier glanced over again at the intelligence officer. Once more, the man nodded.

Producing a set of keys, the Spetsnaz operative reached down and opened the padlock securing the prisoner's handcuffs to his belly chain. Grabbing the man's arms, he raised them and placed them against the seat in front of him.

"His feet as well," the loadmaster ordered. "He must be able to rapidly evacuate the aircraft."

The soldier didn't need to look to his superior a third time. The intelligence officer answered for their entire team.

"The only way that man walks off this plane is with one of us," he said from behind his mask.

The loadmaster gave up. He had done what he could and knew it was pointless to argue any further. They were out of time.

"Make sure your weapons are secure," he directed, as he turned to make his way to his jump seat.

Suddenly, the plane shuddered and the nose pitched forward. The crewman lunged for the nearest seat and buckled himself in as anything not locked down went hurtling through the cabin like a missile.

With no instruments and no visibility, they were flying blind. The pilot and copilot fought to regain control of the aircraft.

Fifteen hundred feet above the ground, the pilots managed to pull the nose back up and slow their descent. But with no thrust from the remaining engine, they were still falling. They had to find someplace to land.

Peering through the weather, the pilot could see they were flying over a dense forest. Ahead was a clearing of some sort. It might have been a field or a frozen lake. All he could tell was that it appeared to be devoid of trees.

"There," the pilot said.

"There's not enough length. It's too short."

"That's where we're landing," the pilot insisted. "Extend the landing gear. Prepare for impact."

The copilot obeyed and engaged the emergency landing gear extension system. With no electricity with which to activate the PA, he turned and shouted back into the cabin, "Brace! Brace! Brace!"

The command was acknowledged by the loadmaster, who then yelled over and over in Russian from his seat, "Heads down! Stay down! Heads down! Stay down!"

Only a few hundred feet above the ground, the pilot pulled back on the yoke to lift the aircraft's nose in an attempt to slow it down, but he misjudged the distance.

The belly of the plane scraped across the tops of the tall snow-laden trees. The left landing gear was snapped off, followed by the right.

Just before the clearing, one of the wingtips was clipped, and the plane went into a violent roll.

CHAPTER 2

Police Chief Tom Tullis had seen plenty of dead bodies over his career.

But this was a record for him at a single crime scene.

During the height of the summer, the popular resort town of Gilford could swell to as many as twenty thousand inhabitants. Off-season, like now, the number of full-time residents was only seventy-three hundred. Either way, four corpses were four too many.

Pulling out his cell phone, the tall, crew-cut-sporting cop texted his wife. They were supposed to meet for lunch. That was impossible now. He told her not to expect him for dinner either. It was going to be a late night.

Returning the phone to his duty belt, he focused on the bodies—two men and two women. They had all been shot, either in the head, the chest, or both. Judging from a quick scan of the walls and windows, no rounds had missed their targets. That told him the shooter was skilled.

Interestingly, three of the four victims were armed. One of the women had a Sig Sauer P365 in her purse, the other a Glock 17 in her briefcase. One of the two men carried a Heckler & Koch pistol at his hip. No one had drawn their weapons. That told Tullis something else. Either the victims had known their killer, or they had all been taken by surprise. Considering who the victims were, he doubted it was the latter.

The woman with the Sig Sauer had credentials identifying her as a former Boston Police Detective, eligible to carry concealed nationwide.

The woman with the Glock had no such credentials, but in the "Live Free or Die" state of New Hampshire it was legal to carry without a permit. Not that she would ever have had trouble getting one.

Seeing the name on her driver's license, Tullis had instantly recognized her. She had made a lot of headlines when the President had elevated her to Deputy Director of the CIA.

The gun-carrying male victim had ID that claimed he was an active military member. United States Navy.

What the hell were they all doing here? the Chief wondered. *And who had killed them?*

He suspected the key might lie with the final victim.

Just off the dining room, facing a large TV, a hospital bed had been set up in the den. In it, shot once between the eyes, was a man who appeared to be somewhere in his eighties. He was the only victim Tullis and his team hadn't yet identified. The Chief had some decisions to make.

Judging from the postmortem lividity of the bodies, they had been dead for at least two days, maybe more. The killer's trail would already be going cold.

As a seasoned law enforcement officer, Tullis knew the importance of doing everything by the book. He needed to secure not only the house but also the grounds.

Going the extra step, he decided to shut down the lone bridge that connected the 504-acre Governors Island to the mainland and to request Marine Patrol units to cover the shoreline.

This wasn't some murder-suicide where the husband had shot the wife and the pool boy before turning the gun on himself. And it wasn't some drug deal gone bad. This was a high-profile case; exactly the kind of case no town ever wanted—especially a tourism-dependent town like Gilford.

Getting on the radio, the Chief told the dispatcher to send the entire shift. He then instructed her to call in all available off-duty officers. They were going to need as much manpower as possible.

The next step was to alert the State Attorney General's Office in Concord. Per protocol, they would mobilize a Major Crime Unit team from the State Police to come up and lead the investigation. Before he made that call, though, he decided to place another.

It wasn't a by-the-book move. In fact, Tullis was way overstepping his authority.

But if it meant protecting Gilford and the town's hardworking men and women who so depended on the tourist trade, that was one scenario in which the Chief was willing to bend the rules.

CHAPTER 3

When the call came in to Langley, the Director of Central Intelligence, Bob McGee, happened to be in a meeting with the Director of the FBI, Gary Militante.

Though the DCI's assistant was hesitant to interrupt, she knew she had to make her boss aware of the call. McGee put it on speakerphone. He and Militante were stunned by what they heard.

The FBI Director introduced himself, gave Tullis his personal cell phone number, and asked to be texted as many pictures from the crime scene as possible—pictures of the bodies, the IDs, the weapons, all of it. Minutes later, his phone began vibrating.

As the photos poured in, McGee kept his emotions in check. With professional detachment, he narrated who and what they were looking at, right down to the body in the hospital bed—retired CIA operative Reed Carlton, the man who had founded the Agency's Counter Terrorism Center.

Militante had the same questions as Tullis. "What were they all doing in New Hampshire, and who would have wanted them dead?"

It was a long story, which McGee promised to explain in-flight. He wanted a look at the crime scene for himself—and the only way he'd have any legal access to it was if the FBI was attached.

Before he and Militante could leave, though, there was an additional person he needed to reach.

He tried three times, but his calls all ended up in voicemail. *Why the hell wasn't he picking up?*

After sending a quick text, McGee grabbed his jacket and headed downstairs with the FBI Director and their security details for the two-minute ride to 84VA, the Agency's helipad a mile west of Langley.

Once they boarded their respective helicopters, it was a short flight to Joint Base Andrews, where an Embraer Praetor 600 was fueled and waiting.

The jet was a recent addition to the CIA's fleet. Fast and able to take off using less than five thousand feet of runway, it was perfect for the trip to Gilford.

When they landed, a phalanx of SUVs was waiting for them. The detail leaders hated movements like this—no warning, no planning, and little to no coordination with elements on the ground. Nevertheless, both directors had insisted that the trip was necessary and that time was of the essence.

From Laconia Municipal, it was only four miles to Governors Island. They were met at the airport by Gilford PD and given an escort through town and over the bridge to the crime scene.

Stepping out of one of the SUVs, McGee took a deep breath. The air was cold and smelled of pine. A hint of wood smoke drifted from a chimney somewhere unseen.

McGee looked like a marshal from an old Western. He was a tall man in his late fifties with gray hair and a gray mustache. A testament to his Army career, his shoes were shined, his suit was immaculate and his shirt was crisply pressed.

He wore no jewelry other than a Rolex Submariner—a gift to himself when he left Delta Force decades ago and signed on with the CIA's paramilitary branch.

McGee was old-school, known for being tough, direct, and unflappable. He hated politics, which had made him a good choice to head the CIA.

The nation's once proud intelligence service was being choked to death by bureaucracy. It was packed with talented people willing to give everything for their country, but they were being held back by risk-averse middle managers more concerned with their next promotion than with doing what needed to be done.

Familiar with the Agency from the ground up, the President had put McGee in charge of cleaning out the deadwood. And he had gone after it root and branch.

But McGee had quickly realized that mucking out the Agency's Augean stables was indeed a Herculean task—one that was going to take much longer than any of them had envisioned.

In the meantime, the threats against America were growing— becoming deadlier, more destabilizing, and more intricate.

As red tape slowed Langley down, America's enemies were speeding up. Something needed to be done—something radical.

With the President's approval, McGee had agreed to a bold new plan, as well as a major sacrifice.

The plan was to outsource the CIA's most clandestine work. It would go to a private intelligence agency outside the bureaucracy's grasp. There, safe from government red tape, sensitive operations could receive the support and commitment they deserved.

It was viewed as a temporary fix while Langley was undergoing its gut rehab—a rehab that would have to go all the way down to the studs.

The private intelligence agency charged with taking over the darkest slice of the CIA's pie was The Carlton Group, founded by the aforementioned, now deceased, Reed Carlton.

And as to McGee's sacrifice, it was personified by another victim at the scene.

With his blessing, Lydia Ryan had left her position as CIA Deputy Director in order to run The Carlton Group.

That was the backdrop against which Bob McGee stepped out of the SUV, breathed in the chilly New England air, and prepared himself for the horror he was about to see inside.

Tullis met the two directors at the front steps and solemnly shook their hands. Then, after having them sign into the crime scene log, he distributed paper booties and latex gloves. The protection details didn't get any. They would have to wait outside—the fewer people coming in and out, the better.

The Police Chief was about to show the two men inside, when one of his officers came up carrying a clear plastic evidence bag.

"We found something back in the trees near the end of the driveway," the patrolman said, holding it up. Inside was a phone.

McGee recognized it immediately. Or, more specifically, he recognized its case.

Made from a rigid thermoplastic, the distinct Magpul cell phone case was popular with military operators. Its styling mimicked the company's rugged rifle magazines. On the back, a distinct Nordic symbol had been customized. The Chief stepped off the porch for a closer examination.

As he did, the FBI Director saw the look on his CIA colleague's face. Slowly, he mouthed a name. *Harvath?*

McGee nodded.

Their bad situation had just gotten worse.

CHAPTER 4

When Scot Harvath regained consciousness, his ears were ringing. There was the distinct, metallic taste of blood in his mouth, probably from having bitten his tongue during the crash. *The crash.*

Slowly, he opened his eyes, but he couldn't see anything. The hood was still over his head. Reaching up, he began to pull it off, half-expecting one of his captors to knock his hand away. No one touched him.

His sandy-brown hair was matted, and his blue eyes struggled to focus.

Removing the oxygen mask, he looked around. The aircraft's fuselage had been severed into three pieces. In some places, seats were missing. In others, entire rows had disappeared.

He glanced to his right, but the soldier who had been next to him was gone, along with the seat he had been sitting in.

A strong odor of jet fuel filled the air. It was mixed with the smell of smoke and melting plastic. Some part of the plane was on fire.

Under normal circumstances, he would have moved slowly—assessing the damage and making sure that he didn't have a spinal injury—but these weren't normal circumstances. He needed to get out.

Planting his feet, he stood. But when he tried to step into the aisle, he couldn't. His Spetsnaz minder had locked his ankle chain to the leg of his chair.

Sitting back down, he attempted to jerk himself free, first by kicking out his legs and then by reaching down and trying to pull the chain loose. It didn't work.

Searching around his seat, he looked for anything he could use to help him escape. There was nothing. Without a key, he was fucked.

Though he had been sedated on and off over the last several days, images began to flood his mind. As they did, an unbearable pain began to build in his chest and his heart rate started to climb.

Taking a deep breath, his training kicked in, and he forced himself to relax. There was no question that unspeakable things had happened. Worse things, though, were on the horizon if he didn't get control of the situation.

As one of America's top intelligence operatives, he had been a prime target for the Russians. His knowledge of spy networks, covert operations, and classified programs was invaluable. But that wasn't the only reason they wanted him.

Year after year, he had been behind some of the most successful operations against the Russian military and Russian intelligence. As such, he had ranked very near the top of a little-known, clandestine kill list maintained in Moscow.

But as badly as the Russians wanted him, and as much as they had risked to grab him, he knew the United States would risk even more to get him back. He just had to remain alive and one step ahead until then.

Scanning the cabin, he saw one of the crew pinned beneath a nearby cargo container that had broken free. The legs of his uniform were stained with blood. Over the ringing in his ears, he could hear the man moaning.

Harvath recognized him. It was the loadmaster who had insisted that he be allowed to brace for impact. When his hood had been removed to put his oxygen mask on, he had only caught a quick flash, but he remembered the man's face. Without his help, Harvath might not have survived the crash.

Pinned next to the loadmaster was the body of his missing Spetsnaz minder. He was neither moaning nor moving.

From everything else he could see, he and the loadmaster were the only two survivors in this section of the plane. That was the good news. The bad news was that the temperature was rapidly dropping.

Looking through one of the ruptures in the fuselage, he saw nothing but snow and ice outside. Wherever they were it was cold. *Really* cold.

Harvath had no clue as to his location. He'd had a bag over his head since being taken in New Hampshire. He assumed, though, that they were somewhere in Russia.

Nevertheless, he hadn't made it into his forties and survived a plane crash only to turn around and freeze to death. If he and the loadmaster were going to make it, they were going to have to work together.

Harvath called out to get his attention. "I can help you," he said in his choppy Russian.

For a moment, the airman stopped moaning and looked over at him. He then just shook his head.

"Hey!" Harvath yelled. "Hey!"

When the man turned his agony-stricken face back in his direction, Harvath sniffed the air around him in an exaggerated fashion.

It took the loadmaster a moment, but he finally realized what the prisoner was trying to draw his attention to—*fire*.

The man strained against the cargo container pinning his legs, but it was beyond his ability to move.

"I can help you," Harvath repeated.

"You?" the man replied in Russian. "How?"

Pointing at the Spetsnaz operative crushed by the container, Harvath searched for the word, then held up his shackles and said, "*Klyuch*." Key.

Toss me the key and I'll help you. The loadmaster considered the offer. Of course, the prisoner could be lying, but the Russian airman didn't have much choice.

Patting down the soldier, he found the keys and, using what little of his strength remained, tossed them in the prisoner's direction.

The throw came up short. Harvath leaned out as far as he could into the aisle, the shackles tearing into his ankles, but he missed it and the keys landed on the floor several feet away.

"Damn it," he muttered under his breath.

"*Prahsteetyeh*," said the loadmaster. *I'm sorry*.

Glancing around, Harvath saw a nylon tie-down strap with a heavy metal clamp. He couldn't tell if was within reach or not.

Getting down onto his stomach, he lengthened his body to its max, struggling to create every millimeter of reach possible, but the strap remained just inches beyond his grasp.

He searched for something handy—a screwdriver, a pen or pencil, anything—even a rolled-up magazine. Then an idea hit him.

Returning to his seat, he grabbed his oxygen mask and pulled out the hose. Tying it to his hood, he attached the two together. They weren't long enough to reach the keys, but they might be long enough to reach the tie-down strap.

Kneeling, he took aim and tossed the hood toward the buckle. It landed right on top of it. Slowly, he retracted the oxygen tube and pulled it in.

With the buckle in hand, he began gathering up the strap, which turned out to be much longer than he needed.

He had reeled most of it in when he noticed something else. The opposite end was stuck.

"Damn it," he repeated.

When the strap went taut, he began yanking on it, twisting and pulling from every possible angle. When that didn't work, he started flipping it like a whip.

"Let loose, *motherfucker*," he cursed as he cracked the strap, sending a ripple down its length, and then yanked it backward with all of his might.

It turned out to be the right combination, as the buckle on the opposite end was freed from its entrapment and came screaming backward like a bullet. If Harvath hadn't ducked, it would have hit him right in the face.

Realigning himself, he pitched the strap into the aisle and pulled back the keys the loadmaster had thrown.

Finding the one he needed, he unlocked his wrists and then bent down and unlocked his feet. He was almost free.

Removing the remaining chains, he made his way over to where the loadmaster was pinned. But before he could even think about helping him, he needed to make sure the soldier lying next to him was dead.

Harvath placed two fingers where the man's jaw met his neck. There was no pulse.

In his holster, the soldier carried a nine-millimeter Grach pistol.

It now belonged to Harvath. After checking to make sure a round was chambered, he put his shoulder against the cargo container and pushed.

The metal box barely budged. He was going to need a fulcrum and a lever of some sort to lift it. And judging by how much the loadmaster's left leg was bleeding, he was going to need to find a tourniquet as well.

But before he could help him, he had to sweep the rest of the wreckage. If there were any threats remaining, those would need to be dealt with first.

Grabbing a thick rag, he folded it several times and pressed down on the wound. He was searching his mind for the correct words to say to the man in Russian about keeping the pressure on, when he saw a flash of movement outside.

CHAPTER 5

Harvath only had time to react. Bringing the pistol up, he applied pressure to the trigger and fired three shots, just as he had been trained—two to the chest, one to the head. The Spetsnaz operative outside fell dead in the snow.

Sliding behind the cargo container, Harvath took cover. The loadmaster stared at him, wide-eyed. Harvath didn't know if it was from the shock of the gunfire or from the blood loss—probably both.

Ejecting the Grach's magazine, he looked to see how many more rounds he had. There were fifteen, plus one in the chamber.

Leaning over, he pulled a spare magazine and a flashlight from the dead soldier next to the loadmaster. Dressed in hospital-style scrubs, he didn't have any pockets, nor did he have a tight-enough waistband to tuck them into. He would have to carry them in his hand.

If any of the other operatives had survived, and were even partially ambulatory, the sound of the gunshots was going to draw them in like a tractor beam. There was only one thing Russians liked more than drinking or fucking, and that was fighting.

Harvath had gotten lucky. Seeing the operative outside first had been a gift. He didn't expect to get another one. He needed to go on the offensive. But to be successful, he needed information.

Looking down at the loadmaster, he asked, "How many men?"

The man's condition was worsening. "Four crew," he replied weakly in Russian. "Six passengers."

That sounded right. A pilot, a copilot, the loadmaster, and maybe a navigator or flight officer of some sort would have composed the crew. As for the six passengers, Harvath had been traveling with the same group since being taken. There were four Special Forces soldiers accompanying him, plus one intelligence officer—*Josef*.

At the thought of the man's name, his rage again began to build. It was like acid eating away at him. He wanted to let it loose, to vomit it out in every direction and kill every Russian in sight. But instead, he warned himself, *Not now. Keep your shit together.*

Laboring to remain calm, he focused on the situation and ran a count. Two of the soldiers were down—one had died in the crash and the other he had just shot outside. The loadmaster was pinned beneath the container. That meant six potential threats remained. Each had to be accounted for and, if necessary, neutralized. Raising his pistol, he slipped out from behind the container.

The fuselage was difficult to traverse. It was on its side and strewn with debris. There were sharp, jagged pieces of metal everywhere.

As he picked his way through, he kept his eyes peeled for survivors, as well as warm pieces of clothing. He found neither.

At the front of the tail section, he had to step outside to get to the next portion of the plane. Carefully, he leaped down onto the ground.

Immediately, he was hit with a blast of razor-sharp snow. It was driven by one of the coldest, bitterest winds he had ever felt.

As the crystals raked his exposed skin, he knew he would have only minutes in this temperature—five tops—before numbness would commence and the cold would begin to overtake him.

In the fading light, the crash wreckage was scattered as far as the eye could see. It looked to Harvath as if they were in the middle of a snow-covered field, surrounded by forest. He could make out where the plane had torn through the trees. A long scar of burning debris and snapped pines led back into the woods.

Hip-deep in the snow, he crossed to the next section of fuselage and climbed inside. Because this section faced upwind, the freezing air blew through with a vengeance.

With the spare magazine clenched between his teeth, he held the flashlight away from his body in case anyone saw the beam and wanted to take a shot at him. A few moments later, he found another Spetsnaz operative.

The motionless man was still strapped into his seat. His head hung at an obscene angle, his neck probably broken. Harvath grabbed him by the hair and lifted up his head so he could look into his face.

He didn't know the soldiers' names. They had only used call signs around him—words in Russian he didn't understand. What he did understand, though, was what they had done.

After handcuffing him at the house on Governors Island, this Spetsnaz operative had delivered a searing blow to his kidney. Harvath's knees had buckled. No sooner had he hit the floor than the Russian had grabbed a fistful of hair. Yanking his head up, he had forced him to watch as Josef had murdered Lara, Lydia, Reed, and the Navy Corpsman.

Harvath had thought they were going to kill him, too. And for a moment, he had wanted to die—right there with Lara, whom he loved more than anything in the world. But then he had been jabbed with a needle and everything went black.

When they brought him back around, it was obvious that he had been moved. They were in a dank, cold basement someplace. He didn't know where, or how long he had been out.

He had a splitting headache, his clothes had been removed, and he had been tied to a chair. A video camera had been set up. Half an hour later, Josef had come down the stairs and the interrogation had begun.

Whenever he hesitated, whenever he refused to answer a question, it was the man with the broken neck who had struck him. In the beginning, Josef was playing good cop; trying to build rapport. It wasn't until they boarded a private jet that things had gotten really ugly.

Letting the dead man's head drop, Harvath placed his fingers against his neck, just in case there was a pulse. There wasn't. "You got off easy," he said, sizing up the Russian.

The other two soldiers had been monsters—barrel-chested thugs, well over six feet tall. This one was closer to his height and build of a muscular five feet ten.

Wearing nothing but scrubs and the equivalent of prison slippers, Harvath had already begun shaking from the cold. He needed to conserve whatever heat he had left and quickly stripped off the Russian's uniform.

Snatching an American, especially one of Harvath's stature, was an act of war—particularly when carried out on U.S. soil. It would have been a completely black operation.

If Harvath had to guess, everything they needed—civilian clothing, fake IDs, credit cards, even weapons—had been arranged via Russian mafia contacts in the United States.

Once the private jet had touched down, the soldiers had changed out of their American street clothes and into cold-weather military uniforms. The man with the broken neck was wearing long underwear, wool socks—the works. Harvath took all of it.

The only thing the Spetsnaz operative wasn't wearing was a coat. They had boarded with them, though, so there had to be at least one somewhere.

Buttoning up the clothes with stiffening fingers, he pulled on the man's boots and laced them up. Then he continued his search.

Picking his way through the wreckage, he came upon a small crew closet.

It had been jammed shut by one of the rows of seats that had come loose during the crash. Harvath had to burn precious calories to shove the seats out of the way, but it was worth it.

Inside was a thinly insulated Russian Air Force jacket with a faux fur collar. He pulled it on and zipped it up. There were no gloves in the pockets, but there was a beret. It wouldn't keep his ears warm, but it would help retain some heat and was better than nothing.

He was about to close the closet when he heard a noise from the other side. Without hesitating, he put two rounds through the door. The plane's flight officer fell down dead on the other side.

Closing the door, Harvath saw what he had done. He hadn't intended to kill any of the flight crew unless absolutely necessary. Though Russian military, they weren't directly responsible for what had happened. That responsibility lay with Josef, his Spetsnaz operatives, and whoever had tasked them with kidnapping Harvath and murdering the people he cared about.

But after everything that had happened, he had zero capacity for remorse. Russia, and every Russian in it, was his enemy now.

Pushing forward into the wind, he cleared the rest of this section of the fuselage. There were no additional survivors.

Trudging through the snow, he arrived at the final section of the plane—the nose. It included the badly damaged cockpit, which was consumed by flames. From what he could see, the pilot and copilot were both dead and still strapped into their seats. The fire was too hot, though, for him to get any closer. Getting his hands on a map, a radio, or some sort of flight plan was out of the question.

Staying in this part of the plane was also out of the question. As much as he needed the warmth, the thickening toxic smoke forced him out.

Stepping into the snow, he pushed back toward the tail section, making sure to keep his eyes open for Josef and the remaining Spetsnaz operative.

He had no idea where they were. For all he knew, they had been torn from the plane during the crash.

Sweeping back through the center segment of the aircraft, he hurriedly gathered up anything he could safely burn to keep warm, including a heavy aircraft manual the size of a phonebook and two wooden pallets.

When he returned to the tail section, he checked on the loadmaster. The Russian's pulse was thready. His eyes were glassy and his skin was ashen. He had lost far too much blood. Nevertheless, Harvath was determined to do what he could to save him.

Dragging over a sheet of metal, he set it as close to the loadmaster as he dared and used it to build a fire on. There was a shovel clamped to the wall. After breaking down the pallets, he found a small piece of flaming wreckage outside, scooped it up, and brought it in to get the wood burning.

Tearing the dry pages out of the technical manual, he crumpled them into balls and tossed them in to stoke the fire higher. As soon as it was burning good and hot, he set his attention to helping the man who had saved his life. He had to stop the bleeding.

None of the soldiers had been carrying tourniquets, so Harvath was forced to improvise. Grabbing two carabiners from the vest of the

Spetsnaz corpse nearby, he collected several strips of cargo netting. It was a spit and baling wire solution, but it was all he had.

Using one of the carabiners as a windlass, he applied the improvised tourniquet to the man's left leg, cinched it down, and employed a length of wire and the other carabiner to hold everything in place. Then, adding even more fuel to the fire, he moved in closer to warm up.

Because of the angle of the tail section, the wind here wasn't blowing straight through, but that was a small blessing at best. Outside, the temperature continued to plunge. Harvath needed to figure out some way to help better wall them off from the cold. He also needed to find blankets and a way to get IV fluids into the loadmaster. There had to be some sort of medical kit on the plane. Whether it had survived the crash was another question entirely.

In addition, he still needed a lever and fulcrum to raise the container off the man's crushed legs, to gather up any food and water he could find, and come up with some sort of a pack in which he could carry as many supplies as possible that would aid in his escape.

It was a long list. The sooner he got started on it, the better—for both of them. He had no idea how soon a rescue team would arrive.

"I return," he said, in his limited Russian.

The loadmaster didn't respond.

It was a bad sign. Even so, Harvath had promised the man that he would help him.

Further back, near the cargo ramp, he opened a series of metal cabinets. Each contained a range of equipment, but none that he needed. If there was a med kit on board, it wasn't in this part of the plane. Maybe it was kept up near the cockpit. And if so, it was a lost cause.

Harvath did, though, find what resembled some kind of moving blanket. His luck, at least in part, was holding out.

Removing it, he turned to hurry back to the loadmaster. But as he did, he came face-to-face with the remaining Spetsnaz soldier. The man was bleeding from a gash above his left eye and had a suppressed ASM-Val rifle pointed right at him.

"*Zamerzat!*" the man ordered, blood dripping down his face. *Don't move.*

CHAPTER 6

"Whoever the killer was," said Chief Tullis, "he or she knew what they were doing."

"You think this was done by one person?" asked McGee.

"Not necessarily. Based on the footprints outside, there were likely multiple assailants. The victims, though, were all lined up, on their knees, and shot execution-style. Judging by the wounds, we believe it was done by the same shooter with the same weapon."

Pointing at the bodies, he continued, "Based on the shot placement, specifically rounds being directed to the head, the chest, or both—the killer appears to have training. None of the shots went wide. We didn't dig anything out of the walls, the ceiling, or the floorboards. No rounds went through any of the windows. Cool, calm, and collected. If I had to guess, I'd say the killer had probably done this sort of thing before.

"Then there are the cameras. Most of the seasonal properties up here have them in case of burglary or vandalism. This house has four and should have showed us anyone coming or going."

"But?"

"We can't review any of the footage."

"Why not?"

"It was recorded to a DVR in a crawl space above the front hall closet. It has been smashed, and the hard drive is missing."

Before he had even landed, there was no doubt in McGee's mind that this was a professional hit. His two most pressing questions at this point were *Who was the hitter?* and *Where was Harvath?*

"How about the adjoining properties?" he asked. "How many of them have cameras?"

"Several," the Chief answered. "I already have officers working on accessing the footage."

"How soon will your team start in on hair, prints, and fibers?" asked Militante.

"All of that gets handled by the AG and the State Police. Our job is to secure the crime scene and preserve all possible evidence."

"If there's any assistance the FBI can give, all you have to do is ask."

"Thank you," Tullis responded. "I'm sure the Major Crime Unit will appreciate that."

While McGee knew that forensics were often key in solving homicides, they didn't have that kind of time. Whoever did this already had a big head start. In fact, if it was a professional, he or she was probably already out of the country. Time and distance were two of their biggest impediments—and those would only grow.

"What else have you found?" he asked.

"The shooter," the Chief stated as he held up another evidence bag, "appears to have policed up all of the brass, except for one."

McGee accepted the bag from him and, along with Militante, studied the shell casing.

"Nine millimeter," the FBI Director concluded. "Popular round. Likely consistent with the gunshot wounds of the victims."

The CIA Director nodded and handed the bag back to Tullis, who set it back on the table.

"Now it's your turn," replied the Chief.

Militante knew the police officer wasn't speaking to him. He glanced at McGee, who had turned away and was staring out the window at the flat, gray lake.

"This was supposed to be a safe house," the DCI revealed.

Tullis wasn't surprised. With what he knew of the CIA, anything was possible. "Who were you keeping safe?"

"The man in the hospital bed."

"Who was he?"

"One of the best our business ever saw."

It was evident from his voice that the DCI held the man in high esteem. Out of respect, the Chief allowed a moment of silence to pass before continuing. "What was his name?"

McGee turned to face the den, and with it, the hospital bed. "Reed Carlton."

"Was he CIA?"

"He was. Served decades as a case officer, ran stations around the world, and helped establish the Counter Terrorism Center. They broke the mold with him. No mission was ever too tough or too dangerous."

Tullis looked at the body lying in the hospital bed. "Whom were you protecting him from?"

The DCI grinned. "Everyone."

The Chief raised an eyebrow. "So he had enemies."

"Lots of them."

"Why the hospital bed? What was wrong with him?"

"He had Alzheimer's."

"My mother had Alzheimer's," Tullis responded. "It's a terrible disease. Why wasn't he in a hospital or an assisted living situation?"

"Part of the disease," the CIA Director explained, "can involve the brakes coming off. Patients can say things they shouldn't."

Remembering his own ordeal, the Chief mused, "Tell me about it."

"Reed had a lot of very sensitive information stored in his head. Some of those things, if they fell into the wrong hands, could have been harmful to the United States."

"The CIA could have hidden him anywhere in the world, though. Why Governors Island?"

It was a reasonable question, but it hadn't been the CIA's call. It had been Harvath's. He had been not only Reed Carlton's protégé but also his heir apparent and in charge of all of his affairs.

"Reed summered here as a boy," the DCI recounted. "His grandparents had a cottage on the island. The hope was that he'd be comfortable here—maybe even relive some of his oldest memories."

"I wish you had let us know," said Tullis, the compassion evident in his voice. "We could have looked in on him. Added extra patrols. My officers would have taken a lot of pride in helping to protect a man like Mr. Carlton."

The DCI turned to face him. "I don't doubt it. Thank you. In the end, we felt the fewer people that knew he was here, the better. It's how we do things."

"In secret."

McGee nodded.

Chief Tullis regretted causing more pain, but he needed additional information. "I know it's difficult, but what can you tell me about the other victims?"

The knot in McGee's stomach hadn't gone. In fact, it had only tightened. "Lydia Ryan worked for me at the CIA. She was one of the best field operatives I have ever known."

"Any idea what was she was doing here?"

"She worked for Reed."

"As in *used* to work for him? Back at the CIA?" Tullis asked.

McGee shook his head. "When the time came, Reed retired from the CIA. He gave it a good try. He played golf, took a couple of cruises, even joined a group of ex–case officers who got together weekly for lunch, but the lifestyle didn't agree with him. He missed being in the game.

"By the time he tried to come back, though, the things he disliked about the Agency—particularly the bureaucracy—had only gotten worse. So, he decided to see what he could do from the outside and started his own company, The Carlton Group.

"Things went well for several years until he was diagnosed with Alzheimer's. When that happened, he recruited Lydia to become the company's new director."

"What kind of company was it?"

"It's a private intelligence agency."

The Chief looked at him. "Is that like private contracting?"

"Kind of," the DCI acknowledged. "They hire ex-intelligence and ex–special operations people to assist CIA missions."

Tullis was intrigued. "What kind of missions?"

"I'm not able to discuss that."

"Why not?"

"The operations that The Carlton Group were involved with are classified."

That didn't surprise the Chief. "What can you tell me about the other two victims?"

Gesturing toward the male corpse, McGee said, "Navy Corpsman. He was part of a rotating team. There was always someone in the house with medical expertise, keeping an eye on Reed."

"Were they always armed?"

"Just in case."

Tullis made a mental note of that and then, gesturing toward the final victim, inquired, "Do you recognize her?"

"I do. Her name was Lara Cordero."

"She was carrying credentials identifying her as ex–Boston PD. Did she also work for The Carlton Group?"

The DCI shook his head. "No."

"Any idea what she was doing here?"

"She was friends with Reed. And with Lydia."

Tullis hadn't handled a lot of murders, but he had conducted a lot of interrogations. He could tell when someone wasn't being fully truthful.

"So, just up for a visit, then?"

"I guess so," replied the CIA Director.

"Huh," said Tullis as he removed a spiral notebook from his pocket. Flipping several pages in, he scanned his notes. "Based on the suitcase and clothing in the guest room, we assumed the Corpsman was staying here in the house. Lydia Ryan and Lara Cordero, though, had key cards for rooms at a nearby hotel.

"Ryan's room was single occupancy, but Lara Cordero checked in with a man, a man whose clothes are still in their room and who hasn't been seen for at least the last two days. Any idea who that might be?"

The knot in McGee's stomach ratcheted ten degrees tighter. Pointing at the evidence bag containing the cell phone, he asked, "Is it on?"

The Chief nodded. "It is. It even has some battery left, but it's locked."

The CIA Director didn't care. He had people who could open it. Though he had recognized the case, he just wanted to be certain it was Harvath's.

Taking out his own cell phone, he pulled up his call log and redialed the number he had been calling and texting before leaving Langley.

It took only a moment for the call to connect.

As the phone inside the evidence bag began to vibrate, one of McGee's worst fears was confirmed.

CHAPTER 7

The CIA Director was no stranger to death, but identifying the bodies of three close friends had taken a toll. He needed to get some air and clear his head. Until he did, he wasn't going to be able to think straight.

Tullis could sense the DCI needed a break and suggested they all step outside. One of his officers had just made a run into town for coffee.

"Hope black is okay," he said as he handed him a cup.

McGee, who was leaning against one of the patrol vehicles and studying the house, thanked him.

The pair stood in silence for several moments as the steam rose from their cups.

"What can you tell me about this Scot Harvath?" Tullis finally asked.

McGee chose his words carefully. Harvath was one of the country's most valuable intelligence assets. "He's one of the good guys. And tough as hell. He reminds me a lot of Carlton."

The Chief let that sit for a moment. He didn't want to ask his next question, but he had to. "Is Harvath capable of what happened inside?"

"Absolutely not."

"You sound pretty certain."

"I'm *positive*," McGee declared. "And if you knew him, you'd be positive, too."

"Then help me out. Who is he? Tell me about him."

The only reason McGee was here was that Tullis had extended him a professional courtesy. The CIA had no jurisdiction. And short of some as-yet-undiscovered federal nexus or an official request for help, neither did the FBI. The least McGee could do was cooperate. "Where do you want to start?" he asked.

"How about we start with his full name?"

"Scot Thomas Harvath."

Tullis had his spiral notebook back out, along with his pen. "And what was his relationship to the victims?"

"He worked for Reed Carlton."

"At The Carlton Group?" the Chief asked.

"Yes."

"In what capacity?"

McGee raised his cup and took a sip of coffee. "I believe he was Director of Operations."

"You don't know for certain?"

"It's complicated. Harvath wasn't big on titles. All I know is that Lydia carried out the day-to-day business, while Harvath took care of the ops side of the house."

"Which entailed what?"

"He dealt with the assignments. Staffing them. Executing them. That sort of thing."

Tullis took a few notes and then asked, "Tell me about his background."

"He was a Navy SEAL for many years."

"Which team?"

"If I remember correctly, he started out at Team Two—the cold-weather specialists—and ended up at SEAL Team Six. He caught the eye of the Secret Service and did some work for them, then ended up at the CIA doing contract work before joining Reed's operation."

"What kind of contract work?"

"I can't discuss that."

The Chief made several more notes. "Any PTSD?"

McGee shook his head. "The joke in our industry is that guys like Harvath don't get PTSD, they give it."

"So no issues that you are aware of."

"Zero."

"Any medications?"

"None that I know of."

"What was his relationship with Cordero?" asked Tullis. "Were they romantically involved?"

"Yes."

"Married?"

McGee shook his head once again.

"Engaged?"

"Not that I know of."

"So were they boyfriend-girlfriend?" the cop probed. "Or was it more casual? A friends-with-benefits sort of thing?"

"They had been dating for a while. In fact, Lara had recently moved in with him."

"Where was that?"

"Virginia, right on the Chesapeake. Just down from Mount Vernon."

"Any problems? Any stress in their relationship that you knew of?"

McGee looked at him. "No."

"How about at work? Any problems between him and Carlton?"

"No."

"Any problems between him and Lydia Ryan?"

"No."

"Was there anything beyond business going on between him and Lydia Ryan?"

"Absolutely not," the CIA Director asserted, getting annoyed. "I'm telling you, Harvath's not the killer."

Tullis looked up from his notebook. "I have to ask these questions. I'm just doing my job."

McGee took another sip of his coffee. He needed to remain professional. "I know. I'm sorry."

"You've lost people. I understand. But what I need *you* to understand is that until we're able to rule him out, Harvath is going to remain a person of interest in this case. Based on everything you've told me, you must want his name cleared as soon as possible."

"I do," McGee replied. "Absolutely."

"We have that in common, then."

"What else can I do to help?"

The Chief trailed backward in his notes until he found what he was looking for. "When Harvath checked into the hotel with Cordero, he listed the make, model, color, and tag number of the car he was driving. It was a rental, picked up from Hertz at Manchester-Boston Regional Airport, about an hour and fifteen minutes south of here. It hasn't been seen either.

"The AG's people will likely issue a subpoena for the rental agreement. In the meantime, if you can provide a photo of Harvath, as well as his Social Security number, a copy of his driver's license, as well as any credit card and banking information, you'd be giving the investigation a huge leg up."

McGee's mind, partially cleared, was already two steps ahead. "By law, I can't give you anything from his file, not without a subpoena. But as a private citizen, concerned over his whereabouts, I might be able to get you a photograph."

"That'd be very helpful."

"In the meantime, how thoroughly have you searched the area?"

Tullis pointed to the K9 SUV parked halfway down the drive. "We secured a piece of his clothing from the hotel. So far, our canine unit hasn't had any luck."

McGee knew that detecting viable scent differed from dog to dog. It normally depended on the handler and how the animal had been trained. The longer the scent was in the wild, though, the harder it was for most dogs to pick up, much less track.

"Any blood or sign of a struggle outside?" he asked.

"None," answered Tullis.

"Have you checked the shoreline?"

"I have two Marine Patrols working the water. So far, nothing there either."

McGee wasn't quite sure how to process that information. On one hand, it sounded as if Harvath hadn't crawled off somewhere and was lying in the woods dying. On the other hand, how the hell had he been able to walk out of a situation like this? Either he was in pursuit of the killer, or he himself was the killer, which was absolutely a nonstarter.

There was, though, a third possibility: that everyone inside the cottage had been killed as part of an operation to snatch Harvath.

But why kill them? Why be so heavy-handed, so excessive? As the question entered McGee's mind, he was reminded of the North Korean dictator having his half-brother assassinated in plain sight, in the middle of the Kuala Lumpur International Airport. Then there were Russia's high-profile assassinations of former spies living in the UK. The Saudis had been arrogant enough to send a fifteen-man hit team, complete with their own forensic pathologist and a bone saw, through Turkish customs to murder a dissident journalist at their embassy in Istanbul.

None of the perpetrators had been afraid to operate on foreign soil, and none had chosen to be understated with their methods. Subtlety and the dark arts no longer seemed to go hand in glove. The world was indeed a dangerous place—and getting more so all the time.

McGee was confident that he had heard and seen enough. He was ready to leave. The sooner he was on the jet, the sooner he could begin relaying instructions back to Langley. Wherever Harvath was, he was going to find him. He only hoped that when he did, Harvath was still alive.

Looking over to where the FBI Director had been chatting with one of the detectives, he saw both men approaching.

"Good news," the detective said. "We finally made contact with the owners of the home across the street. They have a hide-a-key in back and have given us permission to enter and review their security footage."

"That *is* good news," Tullis replied. "Maybe we just caught a break."

CHAPTER 8

"Hands!" the Spetsnaz soldier shouted in Russian.

Harvath was cradling the moving blanket, and underneath it, out of view, his pistol. Instead of dropping the blanket, he dropped to the floor, repeatedly pressing the trigger as he did.

The rounds struck the Russian in the stomach and in the chest. And as he fell, he fired back.

Harvath rolled as the bullets tore up the fuselage around him. They came dangerously close, but fortunately none found their target.

When the shooting stopped, Harvath stood up and, keeping his pistol pointed at the soldier, approached.

The man was in rough shape. Bleeding badly, he had dropped his rifle when he'd hit the ground. Harvath now kicked it away.

This soldier was the worst of the muscle from New Hampshire. He was the one who had forced everyone, except the Old Man, who was bedridden, onto their knees, in advance of being executed.

When Lara had reached out to Harvath, this Spetsnaz operative had punched her in the gut. Helpless, his hands cuffed behind his back, Harvath had watched in agony as she doubled over in pain.

The Russian then grabbed her by the throat and yanked her to her feet, only to body-slam her to the ground. When she tried to get up, he viciously kicked her in the ribs.

Next to Josef, this was the man Harvath had most wanted to get his hands on—and not in a gentle way.

He could have just put a bullet in his head, ended it, and walked away. But he didn't. Harvath wanted revenge.

Drawing his boot back, he kicked the man in the side harder than he had ever kicked anyone in his life. Then he did it again, and again, and again, knocking the wind out of him and shattering his rib cage. It was only the beginning.

Kneeling down as the man gasped for air, Harvath wrapped his left hand around the Russian's throat and began to squeeze, slowly cutting off his oxygen supply.

A bloody froth appeared at the corners of the soldier's mouth as he fought to suck in air. Harvath kept applying pressure.

He dialed it up until the man's eyes began to bulge and his skin started to turn blue. Once that had happened, he pushed down as hard as he could, crushing the man's windpipe. But his bloodlust wasn't satisfied. Not yet.

Grabbing the man by the hair, he gave in to his rage and pistol-whipped him with the Grach.

Back and forth he swung the weapon, harder and harder with each blow. He struck him for Lara. He struck him for Lydia. He struck him for Reed Carlton. Even the Navy Corpsman.

Totally out of control, he went from pistol-whipping to bludgeoning.

He didn't stop swinging until he couldn't lift the pistol anymore. By then, he had beaten the soldier to death.

With his body trembling, his lungs heaving for air, and every ounce of his strength gone, he collapsed against the wall.

Rivulets of sweat ran down his face. Part of him wanted to throw up. Another part of him wanted to revive the Russian, just so he could beat him some more.

Revenge was a bitter medicine. It didn't cure suffering. It didn't provide closure. It only hollowed you out further.

Harvath didn't care. In his world, you didn't let wrongs go unanswered—not wrongs like this, and especially not when you had the ability to do something.

Vengeance was a necessary function of a civilized world, particularly at its margins, in its most remote and wild regions. Evildoers, unwilling to submit to the rule of law, needed to lie awake in their beds at night worried about when justice would eventually come for them. If laws and standards were not worth enforcing, then they certainly couldn't be worth following.

The Russians wanted to enjoy the peace and prosperity of a civilized world, without the encumbrances of following any of its laws. They wanted their sovereign territory respected, their system of government respected, their ability for self-determination respected, and on and on.

What they didn't want was to be forced to play by the same rules as everyone else. They fomented revolutions, invaded and annexed other sovereign nations, violated international agreements, murdered journalists, murdered dissidents, and strove to subvert democratic elections and other democratic processes throughout the Western world.

If the Russians were allowed to sit at the global table without adhering to any international norms, why would the totalitarian regimes of the Middle East, Africa, or Asia bother to comply? It was much easier to amass wealth and hold on to power by subverting rather than by respecting the rule of law.

But bad behavior, be it by an Osama bin Laden, a Saddam Hussein, or a Muammar Gaddafi, couldn't simply be wished away. There was no moral equivalence among systems of government, their leaders, or cultures. Any society that did not respect human rights or the rule of law could not consider itself the equal of those that did. Cancer was cancer. Only by tackling it head-on could you hope to beat it.

And in a sense, that had always been Harvath's job—going after cancer. When everything else failed, he was called in to kill it, by any means necessary.

Sometimes he was given a strict set of rules by which to operate. Other times, things were so bad that his superiors agreed to look the other way, as long as he got the job done. And he always got the job done, just as he would get *this* job done.

With his strength returning, he reached down and unsheathed the man's knife. Then, leaning forward, he grabbed him by the hair and began slicing.

When rescuers eventually showed up, Harvath wanted it to be clear what had happened here. The Russians were not only superstitious but also congenital gossips. The tale would make its way through their military and intelligence services. By the time it was done being told, he would be credited not only with killing some of their most elite operators but with bringing down the plane as well. If nothing else, they would think twice about ever coming for an American like him again.

After swapping out the magazine in his pistol, he checked the man's wrist. This was the asshole who, on top of everything else, had also stolen his watch.

Sure enough, there it was—his Bell & Ross Diver. Removing it, Harvath put it in his pocket and finished patting down the dead soldier, helping himself to anything of value, including his rifle. Gathering up the blanket, he then returned to the loadmaster.

Though he hadn't been gone long, he found the man worse than when he had left him.

In his hand, the loadmaster held a tattered picture of his family. Even if Harvath had found something to use as a lever, he wasn't going to make it. All he could do at this point was make him comfortable.

Draping the blanket over him, he stoked the fire and sat down next to him. It was bad enough he was going to die; he shouldn't have to die alone. His to-do list could wait.

As he listened to the wind howling outside, he kept one hand on his pistol, one hand on his flashlight, and both eyes on the ruptures in the fuselage. There was one last passenger still unaccounted for: the one in charge of the operation, the man who had given everyone else their orders, the most important passenger of all: Josef.

As he sat there, all the horrific images from New Hampshire began to flood back into his mind, but he didn't have the energy for them. His focus needed to be on staying alive. The biggest part of that strategy depended on information.

Reaching over to the loadmaster, he gently put his hand on the man's shoulder. "I'm sorry," he said to him in Russian, and he meant it.

The man opened his eyes halfway and looked at him. "*Spasiba*," he responded. *Thank you*. He knew the prisoner had done all he could for him.

"Where are we?" Harvath asked in Russian.

In response, the loadmaster simply shrugged. He had no idea.

Harvath held out his hand and pantomimed an airplane taking off. Pointing at the imaginary ground beneath it, he asked "Where? What city?"

"Murmansk," the man mumbled. Fortunately, it was loud enough for Harvath to understand.

Pointing his pretend airplane down, he repeated his question. "Where? What city?"

"Loukhi."

Harvath had a basic grasp of Russian geography, but didn't know Loukhi.

He repeated the name to make sure he was pronouncing it correctly. The loadmaster nodded in response.

Resetting his airplane, Harvath pantomimed taking off and then crashing. Once again, he asked the same question. "Where? What city?"

The Russian shrugged, his eyes shutting.

Harvath gently squeezed his shoulder to get his attention. "Where?" he repeated. "What city?"

"*Ja ne znaju*," the loadmaster replied, struggling to open his eyes. *I don't know*.

"Direction?" Harvath asked, pantomiming the plane taking off and landing. "Murmansk to Loukhi. Which direction?"

"*Yug*," the man whispered. *South*.

Pantomiming the plane's takeoff to its crash, he bracketed the distance with his fingers and said, "Distance. How many?"

The man's eyes had closed again.

Harvath was losing him. "Time," he stated. "How many?"

There was no response.

Applying pressure to his shoulder, Harvath tried to rouse him once more, but without any luck. He tapped him lightly on the cheek. Nothing. The loadmaster had lost consciousness.

Opening each of the man's eyelids, Harvath used his flashlight to test his pupils. Neither constricted. His brain was shutting down.

"You're going to be okay," Harvath lied. "Don't fight it. Just relax."

He had no idea if the man could hear him, much less understand what he was saying. It didn't matter. Harvath kept talking, watching as the Russian's breaths became shallower and farther apart. He didn't have much longer.

Unable to do anything but await the inevitable, Harvath's mind turned to a checklist of things he needed to accomplish in order to survive.

In the SEALs, he had undergone extensive SERE training. SERE was an acronym for Survival, Evasion, Resistance, and Escape. If you were caught behind enemy lines, the goal was to keep you alive and help you get to safety. If Harvath hoped to survive and get back home, he was going to have to remember every single thing he had ever been taught in SERE school. And even then, there were no guarantees.

At the moment, his primary focus was survival. Having eliminated the immediate human threats, his most pressing environmental threat was the cold.

Even with the fire, the temperature inside the cabin was continuing to drop. He needed to find a way to seal it off from the outside.

Using his flashlight, he did a quick scan of his surroundings, but nothing presented itself. Heavy tarps or plastic sheeting of some sort were what the situation called for. But unless some were hiding in one of the remaining lockers he hadn't opened in the tail, he was screwed.

He could stack wreckage until his strength gave out, but it would never act as an effective barrier. Like water flooding a leaky boat, the cold would exploit every single opening until it overwhelmed him. He had to come up with a better plan.

Looking down at the loadmaster, he watched him exhale, and then waited for him to take another breath. It never came. He had expired. And with him, so had any moral responsibilities Harvath had left.

Taking the blanket from the man, Harvath wrapped it around himself and got busy trying to survive.

CHAPTER 9

It turned out that the solution to his most critical problem had been staring Harvath right in the face. He didn't need to seal the cabin off from the cold. He only needed to seal *himself* off from it. The cargo container that had crushed the loadmaster's legs would provide the perfect shelter.

Opening the doors, he discovered it was filled with mining equipment. Like most everything else he had come across on the plane, it was totally useless. He dragged pieces out until there was enough room for him to comfortably fit inside.

Tearing loose insulation from the walls of the cabin, he packed as much into the container as possible, creating a nest.

Next, he moved the fire closer to the opening and propped up a couple of sheets of metal behind it to help direct the heat toward him.

As the icy wind blasted the exterior of the aircraft, he conducted one last sweep for supplies. The entire time, though, he kept one hand on his weapon. There was that one final passenger, the man in charge of the operation, whom he assumed to be an intelligence officer—likely Russian military intelligence, also known as the GRU—still unaccounted for.

Searching the loadmaster and the dead Spetsnaz operative next to him as he had done to the one in the back, he pocketed anything of value that he found—cash, watches, jewelry, and even a couple of condoms.

There was no galley area, but he did find a coffee station. The pot must have gone missing in the crash, so he opened the condoms. Using them as bladders, he filled them with as much of the water as he could and tied them off at the top. Like the missing pot, there wasn't any coffee either. There was, though, a tin with some loose tea, which he took, along with a metal canteen cup.

The most significant discovery came in the final locker. It was just wide enough for the loadmaster to have hung his winter parka. There was a knit cap and a pair of gloves in one of the sleeves.

As Harvath hurriedly put them on, he looked down and saw a gray sling pack. Pulling it out, he realized that it was a Russian Air Force survival or "ditch" kit. Underneath was a portable emergency locator transmitter—ELT for short.

Carrying everything back to the cargo container, he piled it all neatly inside. Now, there was only one more thing he had to do.

With several lengths of wire he had scrounged, he rigged random pieces of debris and laid a series of trip wires. If anyone else was still alive and was thinking about coming for him, he wanted as much notice as possible. Once that task was complete, he returned to his improvised shelter and the warmth of the fire.

Despite the hat, gloves, and new parka he had just donned, his body was still trembling with cold. He needed to get something warm into his system.

Filling his metal cup with water, he set it as close to the fire as he could and then turned his attention to the ELT.

The first thing he noticed was that it was pretty old. It probably didn't even operate on the current frequency for distress signals. Based on the tag taped to the side, it hadn't been serviced in a long time. The battery was almost certainly dead.

The best thing about it was that it was a portable, manually activated unit. That meant the chances of there being an additional ELT, automatically activated by the crash and currently broadcasting their exact location to COSPAS—the Russian Space System for the Search of Vessels in Distress—were next to zero. Despite how unreliable their technology was, the Russians weren't into redundancy. Any rescue team was going to have to find the crash site the old-fashioned way—they were going to have to hunt for it. Just to be safe, he broke off the ELT's antenna and set the equipment aside.

Next, he checked out the contents of the ditch kit. Inside was a flare gun case, as well as four olive drab, vacuum-sealed pouches covered in Cyrillic writing. His ability to read Russian was almost as bad as his ability to speak it. At best, he could make out only the most basic words.

From what he could understand, the two largest pouches were individual food rations called Individualnovo Ratsiona Pitanee, or IRPs for short. They were the Russian military's version of American MREs—meals ready-to-eat.

These were Cold Climate/Mountain Operation versions, which were calorie-dense, and meant to see a soldier through an entire twenty-four-hour period.

Harvath couldn't remember the last time he had eaten. It had been at least three days.

All he wanted to do was rip open the packaging, but he had been trained better than that. In a survival situation, every item you came in contact with could be potentially life-saving or life-threatening. Nothing should ever be taken for granted.

Slow is smooth, and smooth is fast went a popular SEAL mantra, which he now heard echoing in his brain.

Taking off his gloves, he felt along the edge of the packaging, looking for a notch or someplace to tear back the cover. There wasn't one.

Removing a folding knife he had taken off the dead Spetsnaz operative next to the cargo container, he carefully made an incision in the packaging, closed the knife, and returned it to his pocket. He then peeled back the plastic.

It was sharp in spots, and he took care not to cut himself. He remembered a buddy of his growing up in California who had sliced his hand opening a tin of coffee. It resulted in an infection that was so serious, doctors had wanted to amputate the hand to stop the infection from spreading to his heart.

Luckily, he had been at one of the best hospitals in the world, and they had ultimately discovered the right combination of antibiotics.

That kind of luck, though, wouldn't be in the cards for him. Not as a fugitive on the run inside Russia. If he got sick, he couldn't just walk into some hospital, much less one on a par with anything to be found in the United States. No, it was critical that he stay healthy. His health and his training were his two greatest assets.

Sitting cross-legged, he removed the food items and laid the amazing array of provisions on the ground in front of him.

There were six sleeves of crackers or some kind of shortbread-style cookies, with about ten in each. There were also five bars of dark chocolate, a small tin of processed cheese, a pudding-sized cup filled with a chocolate-hazelnut spread, two bags of hard candies that appeared to be caramel, a cherry-flavored drink mix, one multivitamin, two servings of instant coffee, a tea bag, two pouches of dried muesli with dehydrated milk, a nut-and-fruit bar, and a packet of applesauce.

In addition, there were three Army-green plastic spoons, six antiseptic wet naps—half were formulated for cleaning utensils and the other half for cleansing human skin—three paper napkins, paper sleeves of pepper and salt, and six rather large packets of sugar with twenty grams in each.

An ingenious piece of lightweight machined metal, no bigger and not much thicker than a playing card, was included and could be bent into a tiny camp stove that stood on three legs. Along with it came three hexamine fire tablets, five stormproof matches, and a striker.

Assembling the stove and placing a hexamine tab in the center, Harvath ignored the stormproof matches and used a lighter he'd taken off one of the dead soldiers to ignite it. He used his glove to draw his canteen cup back from next to the fire and placed it atop the camp stove in hopes of bringing the water to a quicker boil.

Turning his attention to the tin filled with processed cheese, he grabbed the tab and carefully pulled back the lid. He then raised it to his nose and inhaled. It smelled delicious. Picking up a spoon, he dug in. It was one of the best things he had ever tasted.

Licking the spoon clean, he opened a sleeve of crackers and tackled the chocolate-hazelnut spread next. He was ravenous. Everything tasted so good.

Though he assumed the water from the coffee station was potable, he didn't want to take any chances. He let the water in his cup come to a good, rolling boil for several minutes before removing it from the flame, adding the tea bag, and setting it aside to cool.

There were six purification tablets, each individually wrapped in foil, and each good for purifying a liter apiece. Popping one out, he untied the larger of his two water-filled condoms and dropped it in. He didn't expect to tap that water source until he left the plane. By then, any potential contaminants would be neutralized.

Two thermostabilized entrees, one pork and one beef, as well as flameless ration heaters, were also included. The heaters were something the U.S. military used too, but they had come a long way from the water-activated systems Harvath used to know. Because they gave off highly flammable hydrogen gas, the old versions had been forbidden on planes and in submarines.

Like their predecessors, the new, air-activated flameless ration heaters allowed precooked food to be warmed up, in its pouch, via heat from a chemical reaction—the idea being that if a campfire wasn't advisable or available, soldiers could still enjoy a hot meal. There was, though, something else the heaters could be used for.

Their chemical reaction was identical to that of disposable hand and foot warmers. That was because they all used the same main ingredient—iron powder.

When exposed to air, and assisted by sodium chloride, activated charcoal, and vermiculite, iron powder produces iron oxide—rust—and, most important, *heat*. How much heat depended upon how much iron powder was used. Hand and foot warmers used less and could reach 163 degrees. MRE heaters used more and could reach 200 degrees.

The point here was that Harvath had stumbled onto two, albeit temporary, portable forms of instant heat. There were likely two more in the other IRP. In the end, even one of them might end up being the difference between life and death once he struck off from the wreckage. They weighed next to nothing, and he knew he would never regret having them along.

In addition to the entrees, there were two pâté appetizers, both pork, apparently. One appeared to have been made with pig brains, the other with pig's liver. Harvath opted for the liver. Pulling open the pouch, he went after the salty protein with his spoon.

He had to force himself to go slowly. His stomach would have shrunk over the past three days, and eating too much too quickly could make him throw up.

By the time he was done with the pâté, his tea had cooled enough to drink. He took that slowly as well. As soon as he began drinking, his mind began flashing back to what had happened on the private jet.

CHAPTER 10

W hatever drug his Russian abductors had been using to knock him out, they had an equally powerful antidote to return him to consciousness.

It produced an instant migraine and was like having red-hot coat hangers rip your brain out through your eyes. There was no pain he had ever experienced anywhere near it. That was only the warm-up, though.

His interrogator was a Russian in his late fifties who had introduced himself simply as Josef. Tall and fit, Josef had gray hair that was cut in a trendy, long-on-top, skin-tight-fade-on-the-sides style that was more appropriate for a man in his twenties. He looked like a douchebag, and Harvath had told him so.

What made the insult even funnier was that despite his impressive command of English, Josef was unfamiliar with the term. Harvath had to explain it to him, and did so in such a way that the Spetsnaz operatives understood it as well.

When Josef finally clicked on the equivalent word in Russian and mumbled it aloud, his men chuckled. So did Harvath. It was, without a doubt, a terrible haircut.

For a moment, Josef appeared to have a sense of humor and laughed right along with everyone else. Nothing about his demeanor suggested what was about to happen next.

In a flash, the Russian pulled out an electrical cord and started beating Harvath with it. The blows fell again and again, lashing his chest and shoulders, stomach and thighs. Secured to a chair, he had no way to fend off the painful attack.

It was meant to show dominance and sow fear. Josef was making it perfectly clear who was in charge and who wasn't. He intended to break his captive, by any means necessary.

For his part, Harvath had already made up his mind back in New Hampshire that he was going to kill Josef. The only question was how badly he would make him suffer first. The beating with the cord only strengthened his resolve and lengthened the pain he would make the Russian endure.

And that went double for whoever, higher up the chain, had tasked Josef. Harvath didn't care if the trail led right to the President of Russia himself. Anyone and everyone involved would pay, *dearly*.

Over the last three days, Harvath hadn't had much time to piece things together. Most of the time, he had been drugged. When he wasn't drugged, he was being beaten and interrogated. They had even water-boarded him.

It was a tactic he had used on prisoners himself. He knew how effective it was. Even though he had undergone it in training, it was still a horrible procedure to be on the receiving end of.

Upon being placed inside the private jet, he had hoped that part of the nightmare was over. But when he saw the four-liter water jugs stacked in the galley, he knew that it had only just begun.

The flight to what he now knew had been Murmansk was brutal. He had blacked out several times. And, on at least one occasion, he had lost more than just consciousness. Judging by the pads stuck to his chest, the automated external defibrillator, and the vial of epinephrine nearby, he had flatlined.

His memories were fuzzy. What he remembered best was how it had all started.

Josef and his men had shown up at the cottage in New Hampshire out of the blue. Harvath had gone there with Lara to visit Reed Carlton, whom he affectionately referred to as the "Old Man."

He was also there to wrap up some loose business ends with Lydia, one of which involved a meeting with a diplomat from the Polish embassy in D.C.

Artur Kopec was a double agent, working for his own country's foreign intelligence service as well as the Russians. He was a drunk, nearing the end of his career, who had lied, cheated, manipulated, and schemed to get one final, plum posting.

Early on, he had actually been a capable intelligence officer. But as his star had risen, so, too, had his opportunities for corruption. Unfortunately for him, and for Poland, he had chosen self-enrichment over patriotism.

He and Reed Carlton went way back—back to the days of the Cold War. They had undertaken great risks together, bled together, and buried friends together, all in the name of defeating Communism and advancing the cause of freedom.

But once Carlton learned that his old ally had been co-opted, he was left with only three choices: kill him, report him, or use him. He opted for door number three.

Kopec was so sure of himself and so confident in his tradecraft that he believed no one would ever find out he was working for the Russians on the side. He might have been able to fool everybody else, but he hadn't been able to fool Carlton.

Instead, the American spymaster had decided to use the cocksure Pole to America's benefit. Over the years, Carlton fed him a steady diet of quality intelligence—"one old friend to another."

It was stuff that, if the Russians didn't already know it, they would eventually.

The quality of it, plus his access to such a renowned, well-connected CIA officer, made Kopec a star back in Moscow. That had all been part of Carlton's plan as well. The more they believed the veracity and reliability of Kopec's reporting, the easier they were to manipulate. That was how Carlton had used him.

In addition to feeding him a diet of grade-A intel, when it suited the United States, he'd mix in some things that were absolutely false, things he knew the Russians would believe to be true.

The reasons were myriad. Sometimes, the CIA just needed the Russians to be confused. Sometimes, they needed them to act. Sometimes, Carlton just wanted to fuck with them.

When his health began to fail, the Old Man handed the reins over to Harvath. He explained what a valuable asset Kopec had been but allowed Harvath to make up his own mind about what to do with him. Harvath chose door number three as well—using the unwitting Polish intelligence officer in ways even Carlton hadn't considered. All of that, though, was over now. It had ended with the assault on the cottage on Governors Island.

When it came to intelligence gathering, the Russians ran a brutish operation that somehow succeeded despite itself. They were not thoughtful, meticulous savants. They were rats with terrible eyesight and even worse noses. Luck and bravado, more often than talent or hard work, usually carried the day.

Despite their failings, they had eventually caught wind that Reed Carlton was ill. They wanted Kopec to confirm it for them. So did Harvath.

He wanted them to believe that Carlton was so far gone that he was of no value and no threat to them whatsoever. His hope was that if Kopec reported back to Moscow that Carlton didn't have much time left, and had lost his mental faculties, they would write him off. The last thing Harvath wanted was for the Russians to uncover his whereabouts and attempt to snatch him. But little did he know that Carlton wasn't the only person the Russians were interested in.

Playing the distraught former comrade-in-arms, the flabby, white-haired Kopec had kept asking to see his old friend. Once Harvath had felt the time was right, Lydia Ryan had set it up. Never in a million years would he have believed the Russians could set up a snatch operation that quickly. But that was what had happened, and Harvath should have been ready for it.

Kopec had flown up from D.C. on a commercial flight into Portland International Jetport in Maine. A private car service was waiting for him at the airport and had driven him the rest of the way to the island. The car waited for him in the driveway.

When his visit with Carlton was over, he and Harvath chatted, and then Kopec got into the car and drove away, presumably back to the airport.

Harvath had watched him drive off and then returned inside to chat with Lydia. They discussed a couple of items before Harvath saw Lara through the window outside. She had been on a hike and had just gotten back.

Pausing his conversation with Lydia, he had stepped outside to join Lara, and that was when all hell had broken loose.

CHAPTER 11

Having seen the Russians before he did, Lara had yelled for him to "Run!" but by then it was too late. They quickly surrounded her, and Josef put a gun to her head.

In retrospect, maybe Harvath should have gone for his weapon. Maybe he should have tried to shoot his way out. If they had taken him down, perhaps he could have taken a couple of them with him.

Maybe Lydia and the Corpsman would have joined in. Maybe neighbors would have heard the shots and called the police. Maybe his taking a risk would have saved the others. They were questions that would haunt him for the rest of his life.

The one question he didn't need answered was why he had acted as he did—why hadn't he pulled his weapon and risked everything?

Years before he had met Lara, there had been someone else, someone as near to perfect as he had ever known. But because of him, she had taken a bullet to the head.

An assassin, looking to settle a terrible score, had targeted her out of revenge. Miraculously, she had survived, but in almost constant, unimaginable pain. Her one last act of love for Harvath was to leave him, so he could start over again with someone who could give him what she knew she never could—a family.

He had been racked with guilt and heartbroken on top of it. He would have done anything to ease her suffering. He would have taken it all upon himself if he could have, but that just wasn't possible.

Instead, all Harvath could do was relive over and over again what had happened to her, finding new ways each time to blame himself. It was a terrible form of self-torture.

Slowly, though, his pain at losing her began to dissipate, though the guilt for what he had caused would never fully go away.

As a kind of perverse therapy, he threw himself into his work. He became more brutal with those who had committed evil, blurring the line between him and them. It wasn't healthy. And although he told himself he could compartmentalize anything, this thing he couldn't.

To compensate, he had done what everyone else he'd ever known in his line of work did—he had retreated further into himself, shrinking his circle of friends, drinking more, and playing it all off with a graveyard humor common in men who stared death in the face and kicked it in the balls for a living.

"Better to be lucky than good," he would crack, echoing a flippant saying in the Special Operations community.

All the while, though, he knew that he was taking greater risks and that at some point it was going to catch up with him.

But Lara had changed that. His relationship with her had calmed his recklessness. She had given him something worth living for.

Now, though, his guilt was back. The more he thought about what had happened in New Hampshire, the deeper he spiraled.

Whether outside the house or in, Josef was always planning to kill Lara and everyone else. Harvath knew that. There was nothing he could have done to change it. But even so, he blamed himself.

He blamed himself for being the beacon that had drawn Josef there. He blamed himself for bringing Lara along. And most of all, he blamed himself for not thinking more quickly, for not finding some way to protect her.

The stew of rage and recrimination was eating away at him, now opening the door wider to his vengefulness and darkening his heart.

The more he fanned the flames of hate, the greater the threat to his humanity grew. If he allowed that part of himself to be extinguished, there was no coming back. He would become the abyss he was staring into.

He needed to snap out of it and turn his mind to something else—most important, getting the hell out of Russia alive.

Setting down the tea, he reviewed the remaining items in the ditch kit. Picking up the bag marked with a first aid cross, he sliced it open and dumped out the contents.

It contained a suture kit, more water purification tablets, Russian aspirin, blood-clotting gauze, an Israeli-style wrap bandage, tweezers, six Russian-style Band-Aids of varying sizes, two antibacterial wipes, a small tube of antiseptic ointment, and an electrolyte drink mix.

The fourth and final pouch in the ditch kit was emblazoned with words Harvath didn't know. Opening it up, he looked inside.

As soon as he saw the signal mirror, he knew exactly what this bag was—a SERE kit.

In addition to the mirror, there was a compass, a whistle, more stormproof matches, more water purification tablets, a small notebook and pen, a silk scarf printed with panels containing survival instructions, more hextabs, a flint and striker, a packet of sunscreen, and some mosquito wipes.

Opening the flare gun case, he examined its contents. In keeping with similar setups from the Soviet days, the kit included the pistol itself and four flares, beneath which was a conversion tube. When inserted into the barrel, it allowed for firing of .45 or 410 ammunition. Two cardboard boxes with five rounds of each were also included.

It was a clever piece of equipment, but not something Harvath anticipated needing. Thanks to the Spetsnaz operatives onboard, he had access to much more effective firearms.

That said, the flare gun might come in handy, so he set it aside. Opening the aspirin container, he popped two in his mouth, picked his tea back up, and took a sip to wash them down.

As he took another sip, he gazed at all of his supplies. They didn't seem to be nearly enough, but they were much better than nothing. He was alive, and aside from the beatings he had suffered, he was walking away from a major plane crash unscathed. For all intents and purposes, he was ahead in this game. *But for how long?*

It was the number-one question in his mind at this moment. Had the pilot's Mayday been received? How long until the plane was missed? And after that, how long until a search was launched? That was the equation Harvath was most concerned with. How long should he stay with the wreckage, getting warm and assembling his escape kit, before fleeing?

The light was completely gone now and the storm was howling outside. If he struck off before morning, he was as good as dead. The only thing he had going for him was that there was no way the Russians would launch a rescue operation in weather like this. They wouldn't risk losing more aircraft. They would wait until the storm had passed.

For the moment, Harvath was safe. But the sooner he got moving the better.

After stoking the fire, he wrapped himself tighter in the blanket, his pistol in one hand, his flashlight in the other. Closing his eyes, he told himself he was only going to grab a few hours of sleep.

He was exhausted and instantly drifted off.

CHAPTER 12

"Pause it," Bob McGee said, pointing at the TV screen. "Right there."

They were at the house across the street, reviewing security footage.

"Whose vehicle is that?" he asked.

"The caretaker's," said Chief Tullis.

"And he's the one who found the bodies?" Militante asked.

The police officer nodded. "The lease your man Harvath signed requires the owners to maintain the property. We've had a lot of weather up here, so he was bringing by extra salt for the driveway. According to his statement, he was checking the gutters around the house for ice damming when he saw the victims through one of the windows."

"Which is when he called 911?"

Tullis nodded. "Six-eighteen this morning," he stated, reading from his notebook.

"Okay," replied McGee. "Keep rewinding."

They watched footage from the past two days. Only a handful of cars passed the security camera. None of them drove into or out of Reed Carlton's driveway.

Then a silver four-door Chevrolet was seen leaving the property.

"Stop," said the CIA Director.

The Police Chief complied, pressing the Pause button once again. Checking his notes, he read off a series of letters and numbers.

McGee peered at the screen and studied the car leaving Carlton's driveway. "I can't make out the plate."

"Or the driver," Militante added.

Tullis rewound and advanced the footage, pausing at different spots, trying to get a good view. From the vantage point of this camera, shooting across the street, the image just wasn't sharp enough. "Maybe they can enhance this at the lab in Concord. For now, though, what we can see is that the make, model, and color of the vehicle we're looking at are a match for the one Harvath registered at the hotel."

"Keep going backward," the CIA Director ordered. "Slowly."

Chief Tullis activated the remote. Based on the condition of the corpses, they were looking at footage from the day of the murders.

"Stop!" McGee ordered.

Onscreen, they could see that the driver's window of the silver sedan had been rolled down and the driver's arm was sticking out.

"Roll it back a few more frames and then push Play."

Tullis did as he was asked.

From across the street, they could make out only the bottom of Reed Carlton's driveway. But it was enough.

As the Police Chief hit Play, they all watched as the car appeared in view, the driver thrust his arm out the window, and then snapped it back in.

"What side of the driveway did they find the cell phone on?" asked Militante as Tullis paused the feed again.

The Chief walked up to the TV, rewound the video, and pressed Pause. Everyone could see the driver throwing something. Tullis put his finger on the object and drew a line from it into the trees.

Leaning in, the CIA Director saw that the driver was wearing what appeared to be a chunky, rubber-strapped diver's watch, similar to the one that Lara had given Harvath for his birthday. Sport watches were common among military types and fitness buffs, but Harvath's was different. Made by Bell & Ross, it was square with a blue face and a thick blue strap. But at this distance, without magnification, it was impossible to be certain.

Nevertheless, seeing Harvath's cell phone being chucked out the window of Harvath's rental car by a driver wearing the same kind of watch shook him. He tried to keep the exclamation to himself, but the word still escaped his lips. "Fuck."

Without needing to be asked, Tullis activated the DVR and scrolled back even further.

When a black Lincoln Town Car was seen exiting the driveway, he pushed Pause and examined the time code. The vehicle had left the property just before Harvath's car. There was less than an hour between them.

"Any idea who that was?" Militante asked.

The Chief shook his head. They shuttled back and forth through the immediate footage without luck. The vehicle had tinted rear windows and its license plate was blurry. It appeared to be a livery of sorts.

McGee signaled to continue rewinding.

They scrolled back far enough to see the Town Car arrive. It appeared to have been at the cottage for a few hours. The only other activity was Harvath's car arriving, preceded by the vehicle Lydia Ryan had rented and registered at the hotel. Other than those, no one else entered or left the driveway.

"What other footage do you have access to?" Militante asked. "What about red light cameras? Speed cameras? That sort of thing?"

"In New Hampshire," Tullis responded, "the government isn't allowed to spy on citizens."

It was a good policy—the *right* policy in a free country. Nevertheless, in a world obsessed with surveillance, it seemed out of step.

"There is one exception," he clarified.

"What's that?"

"Our EZ Pass tolls."

"Where, I'm assuming," said McGee, "you capture a photo of the driver as well as the vehicle license plate as they pass through?"

The Chief nodded.

"Can you get us a copy of that footage?" asked Militante.

The lead detective, who was standing near the fireplace, shook his head. "We don't have access to it."

"Who does?"

"It all goes through the State Police."

"Fine," said the FBI Director. "Let's put in a request. In the mean-time," he added, removing a thumb drive, "I want to download all of the footage of those vehicles coming and going from the property."

The detective looked at his boss, who was reading a text that had just come in on his phone. Looking up, Tullis nodded his approval on the footage. Then, turning to McGee, he motioned for the CIA Director to follow him back to the kitchen.

Once there, he opened the sliding glass door and the two men stepped out onto the rear deck so that he could have a smoke.

Tullis pulled out a pack of Marlboros and searched for his lighter. As he did, he noticed McGee looking at the cigarettes. Shaking one out of the pack, he offered it to him, but the CIA Director waved it away.

"I don't smoke," he said.

"Suit yourself," Tullis replied. Removing a cigarette, he placed it be-tween his lips and lit it.

McGee watched as the Chief took a long drag and drew the smoke deep down into his lungs. He could almost see the stress leaving his body. He remembered the sensation.

Even though he had gone cold turkey years ago, the cravings had never completely gone away. That said, he hadn't wanted a cigarette this badly in a long time.

Exhaling a cloud of smoke, Tullis stated, "The Major Crime Unit team is going to be here in forty-five minutes. The AG and the Investiga-tive Services Bureau back in Concord will want to review the evidence, but a decision has already been made regarding Harvath."

"What kind of decision?"

"They think he snapped."

"They what?"

The Chief held up his hand. "They're naming him as their lead sus-pect. A BOLO is going to go to law enforcement. An APB has already gone out on the vehicle."

"Damn it," said McGee.

"It gets worse," Tullis went on. "There's talk about a press confer-ence. They want to share some of the details with the public in the hope of apprehending him as quickly as possible."

"I *told* you. He isn't the guy. This is an unbelievable waste of resources. Not only that, but consider the damage you'll be doing to this man's good name. He has given everything to this country. And then some."

"It's out of my hands. This is the AG and the State Police we're talking about. And besides, you need to see it from their side."

"Actually," the CIA Director countered, "I don't. The only side that matters is the truth."

"That's what they're trying to get to."

"By outing this guy on TV? Claiming, without any proof, that he's got some sort of PTSD? And that he went on a killing spree? That's bullshit."

"So you keep telling me, but the evidence is what the evidence is," said Tullis.

"It's not good. I'll give you that. But right now it's all circumstantial."

"But it places him at the scene at the time of the murders. And now we have footage of him leaving the scene and ditching his phone as he does."

"We can't tell it's Harvath in that vehicle," McGee argued, defending his friend.

"You think it's somebody posing as Harvath?"

"Maybe."

The Chief took another puff of his cigarette. "Let's say you're right. Why throw the phone into the trees?"

"To set him up. To make it look like he had ditched the phone so he couldn't be tracked."

"But what if that's exactly what he did?"

McGee shook his head. "That's not Harvath. And it's *definitely* not how he was trained."

"I don't understand."

"If he was worried about being tracked, he would have used the phone as a decoy to send you on a wild goose chase."

"How?" asked Tullis.

"All he'd have to do is select a vehicle going in the opposite direction. He could have found one at any gas station or truck stop. While there, he might overhear a conversation, or start one up himself and discover a driver headed to Texas or California. It wouldn't be hard to hide a phone so that its signal could continue to ping passing cell towers."

"And send law enforcement chasing a bogus trail of bread crumbs."

"Precisely," replied McGee.

The Chief took another drag of his cigarette. "Or . . ." he said, his voice trailing off.

"*Or* what?"

"Or maybe he wasn't willing to go to all that trouble. Maybe he thought he already had enough of a head start. Or, after he snapped, realizing what he had done, he just ran."

"Is that what you think?"

"What I think doesn't matter," Tullis remarked, exhaling another cloud of smoke. "What matters is what the AG's team thinks. And I guarantee you, this is high on their list."

Tullis was right. He wasn't the person McGee needed to convince. If he wanted to help Harvath by heading off a news conference or anything else, he was going to have to deal with the AG. Or, more specifically, he was going to have to convince Militante and the FBI to deal with the AG. Absent the Federal nexus, though, it was going to be a very difficult, if not impossible, case to make.

Thanking the Chief, he stepped back inside to brief Militante. As he passed through the kitchen, his mind was going at full speed. There had to be something they could use as leverage.

Then, just as he set foot in the living room, it came to him.

CHAPTER 13

Konstantin Minayev glared at his deputy for a solid ten seconds without responding. He was a terrifying man, given to fits of anger and extreme violence. Delivering bad news to him was never pleasant. Doing so any time after midmorning, when he began his drinking, was a nightmare.

The deputy stood uncomfortably on the worn carpet in front of his boss's scarred wooden desk. The large office smelled like stale cigarettes, cheap counterfeit American cologne, and dog shit. Of course it wasn't really dog shit, it was worse. It was a dog shit *sandwich*.

Minayev was an old-school Russian, proud of his peasant lineage and how he had risen through the ranks. He prided himself on his work ethic and was famous for eating at his desk, never once having set foot in the GRU cafeteria.

Each day he arrived at headquarters with a sack lunch consisting of two thick slabs of farmer's bread and one of the worst-smelling cheeses ever produced.

The scent fell somewhere between rotting human flesh and roadkill. It was so bad that it was banned on all public transport in Russia.

Though none would ever have had the courage to say so to his face, being summoned to Minayev's office was referred to as paying a visit to the "devil's asshole."

The joke had been around for so long, no one could say whether it was in reference to the odor or to the General's temperament.

"What do you mean the plane *fucking* vanished?" he bellowed.

His deputy had learned early on to stick to facts. He wasn't paid to give analysis. "It disappeared from radar somewhere over Murmansk Oblast."

"Where exactly?"

The deputy removed a printout from his briefing folder, stepped forward, and placed it upon his boss's desk.

Minayev reviewed the report. "Is this a mistake?" he asked, pointing to the attached map—a large portion of which was covered with a thick red circle.

"No, sir."

"This is the fucking search area?"

"Yes, sir."

The General rubbed his meaty face with his even meatier hand. "Are you kidding me?"

It was a rhetorical question. The deputy knew better than to respond.

"Wasn't the aircraft outfitted with an emergency locator transmitter?"

The young man checked his notes. "Yes, a portable version that must be manually activated by survivors."

"And?"

"And there has been no activation."

Minayev was not happy. "What about search planes?"

"They can't take off until the weather improves."

"Fine. How about one of our satellites with infrared?"

The deputy drew in a sharp breath of air between his teeth.

The General cocked a bushy eyebrow. "What's wrong with satellites?"

"Nothing. But the Air Force would have to request it. Technically, that flight never happened. And, as far as anyone is concerned, our people had nothing to do with it."

His deputy was correct. It was a black flight. There was no record of it, or of its passengers. The Kremlin had been crystal clear.

They wanted all knowledge of the operation kept to as few people and as few agencies as possible. Plausible deniability for Russia was paramount.

As head of the GRU's special missions group, Minayev had had the idea to snatch Scot Harvath in New Hampshire, smuggle him out of the United States, and render him to Russia.

A festering, debilitating thorn in their side for years, he had interrupted countless critical operations and had been responsible for the deaths and suspected disappearances of untold numbers of operators.

The plan was to wring as much intelligence out of him as they could and then kill him.

The order had come from the Russian President himself. In fact, it was he who wanted the honor of *doing* the killing. That was why Minayev had told Josef to leave Harvath's face unmarred.

He could abuse his body, break his bones—pretty much whatever he wanted—but when the GRU handed him over to the President, he had to be recognizable.

The General wanted there to be no mistake in what he had accomplished and whom he had delivered to the President. This would be a high point in his career, and he was going to take it all the way to the bank.

When pleased, the President could make men's wildest dreams come true. Minayev had watched lesser men deliver lesser achievements and be handsomely rewarded.

Having just turned sixty, he had spent more than forty years in the Russian military. No one could argue that he hadn't served his country. Now, he wanted it to serve him.

He needed investors and government approval to launch a timber company, which would exploit the rich forests of Siberia. This was a dream that the President could make a reality, if he was so moved. The General had every intention of "moving" him. This news about the plane vanishing from radar, though, threatened everything.

Everything on the aircraft was replaceable: its crew, the Spetsnaz team, even Josef—one of the absolute best operatives the General had ever trained and put in the field. They were all replaceable. The only person on that plane who wasn't replaceable was the American—Harvath.

If this operation went south, the closest Minayev would come to becoming a timber baron was being beaten to death with an axe handle and buried in a shallow forest grave. In that regard, the Russian President had also been very clear. He was not a man you disappointed—ever.

"We also don't have a satellite with infrared capabilities on station," his deputy explained. "I checked."

The General could feel his blood pressure rising.

"Retasking one," the deputy continued, "would raise a lot of questions, and not only in Russia. With the Chinese, the Europeans, and especially the Americans all monitoring the positions of our satellites, altering an orbit would draw unwanted attention.

"What's more, we'd be pulling in an additional agency from which there'd be pushback. They'd want to know what was so important about a transport plane that it required such valuable and immediate attention."

His deputy was right. They couldn't risk it. "How long until the storm is forecast to pass?" he asked.

"A day. Possibly two."

"What are the chances of anyone surviving in that weather, provided they even survived the crash?"

It was another rhetorical question, but the deputy answered anyway. "Not very good."

Minayev agreed. But if anyone could survive something like that, it was Josef.

He was a man of extraordinary focus. He would kill and eat his own men if that's what it took to complete the mission.

"How many search teams are standing by?" the General asked.

"Four. As soon as they can get airborne, they will. Each one will take a section of the search area. Once the aircraft is located, a rescue team will be sent in to—"

"No rescue team," Minayev interrupted. "We will send our own people in."

"Understood. Whom did you have in mind?"

"Wagner."

The deputy blanched. Wagner was the call sign of a former Spetsnaz commander, Kazimir Teplov.

A twisted devotee of the Third Reich, Teplov was alleged to have selected the call sign himself—an homage to one of Hitler's favorite composers.

The private mercenary company Teplov created bore the same name and was shot through with Nazi symbolism and ideology. Many of its members subscribed to Rodnovery, a brutish, cultlike religion that paid homage to Nazi paganism in general and the Nazi Schutzstaffel, also known as the SS, in particular. It had sprung up during the collapse of the Soviet Union and its logo was reminiscent of a highly stylized swastika.

As private military corporations were technically illegal in Russia, they were referred to as "ghost soldiers." The deputy preferred the term "shock troops," since there was no barbarity they weren't willing to carry out. And as such, they were useful, especially when it came to off-the-books operations where plausible deniability was paramount.

They were the Kremlin's "little green men," multitudes of highly paid former special forces officers sent abroad to places like Syria, Ukraine, and Crimea to carry out Moscow's bidding without leaving any direct fingerprints.

In fact, when Minayev had first discussed his plan with the Kremlin, the President had suggested he use Wagner for the operation, but the General had politely demurred.

Having been repeatedly pitted against less capable adversaries, Wagner's people had begun to believe in their own invincibility. That kind of arrogance bred carelessness.

Minayev wanted men he knew and whose training he had personally overseen. He wanted men he trusted and who were loyal to him. His future was riding on this operation.

He also hadn't wanted to give up the prized intelligence asset he was coordinating with in the United States—not to a cowboy like Wagner.

Minayev had been correct to keep the entire operation within his own control. It had been perfectly executed. Harvath had been grabbed, exfiltrated, and brought to Russia.

But despite all of his careful planning, the operation had now fallen short. Never in a million years would he have foreseen the flight from Murmansk to the GRU interrogation facility as being the weak link that would unravel it all.

If there were survivors, though, the operation might still be salvaged. The key was getting to them as quickly and as quietly as possible. Like it or not, Wagner was his best option.

"Should we update the Kremlin?" the deputy asked.

"Are you out of your mind?" the General replied. "Absolutely not. Until we have more information, we tell them nothing. Do you understand?"

The deputy nodded.

"Good," said Minayev. "Now go track down Teplov. I don't care where he is or what he is doing. I want him on a secure line within the next twenty minutes."

CHAPTER 14

MURMANSK OBLAST

Harvath awoke with a start. There had been a *crash*—like the sound of a heavy piece of debris falling over. *Was it one of the pieces he had rigged with a trip wire? Had someone crept into the tail section? Was it Josef?*

Throwing off the blanket, he leaped to his feet and stood near the opening of the container, listening. It was dark and the storm was still howling.

He had blown well past the "couple of hours" he had allotted himself to sleep. Instead, he had been out for most of the night. His body was repairing itself, but he had lost precious time.

Like the wreckage outside, his fire had burned down. It was nearly pitch black.

Suddenly, he regretted not having dragged a little more of the mining equipment out of the container—just enough to create a space where he could have taken cover in case he had to fight from inside.

His ears strained to pick up any sound that might explain what he had heard.

Had it just been the wind? It seemed stronger than when he had gone to sleep. Maybe a gust had knocked something over.

That was the most logical assumption. But he had been trained never to assume anything.

For a moment, he wondered if maybe his mind had played a trick on him. Maybe he hadn't heard anything at all. Then there was another sound.

This time it was unmistakable. It was a *thud* and sounded as if something had struck the exterior of the fuselage.

But how could something be both inside and outside his section of the plane? In a fraction of a second, he had his answer.

Instantly, the hair stood up on the back of his neck, and his grip tightened around his pistol.

They had probably been out there for hours, circling the wreckage, studying it, as they waited for the fires to die. Now, there was nothing holding them back.

Leaning out of the container, into the darkness of the tail section, Harvath activated his flashlight.

Eight pairs of yellow eyes stared back at him. They had come to feed on the dead.

The dead, though, were frozen solid by now. Not much of a meal. Harvath, on the other hand, was warm. Nice and warm.

Russian wolves were fearless predators and had no qualms about taking down humans. While they preferred women and children, they would take a man if hungry enough.

The fact that Harvath's presence, much less the bright beam from his flashlight, hadn't frightened them off told him that they were hungry enough. They were only feet away and, in unison, began to growl.

Their lips were pulled back, revealing long, sharp teeth. Saliva dripped from their mouths.

None of them moved. They all stood together, staring at him; staring into the beam of his flashlight. He was no stranger to wolves and knew what they were planning.

Their job was to keep him occupied, distracted, so that the alpha could flank him and take him down. That wasn't going to happen.

Raising his pistol, he began to fire. The wolves attempted to scatter, but there was no place for them to go except back the way they had come in.

The only other breach in the fuselage was to his left, where he had seen the Spetsnaz soldier earlier and shot him.

He expected the alpha to charge at him from there, but the attack never came. Possibly, the gunfire had scared him off.

Stepping out from the container, he moved forward to where he had lit up eight sets of eyes.

Two wolves lay dead, another lay dying, and at least three trails of blood led out of the wreckage and into the snow.

It wasn't exactly shooting fish in a barrel, but having them bunched up inside the fuselage had given him an advantage. In an open space, if they had set upon him all at once, he wouldn't have been so lucky.

The question that remained was how many of them were still out there.

Harvath hoped not to find out. As long as they left him alone, he'd return the favor. Right now, he needed to make up for lost time.

His plan had been to leave at first light, storm or no storm. There was still much to do.

After restarting his fire, he went down his list. First was to fashion a pair of snowshoes, which he did over the next hour via metal tubing, cargo netting, wire, and duct tape.

They weren't pretty, but they didn't have to be. All they had to do was distribute his weight evenly so he could stay on top of the snow rather than sinking down into it.

Once the snowshoes were complete, he packed up the ditch kit with all the supplies he had gathered.

Under his parka, he wore a chest rig with extra magazines for the rifle. He tucked one of the pistols into the outer pocket of his parka and slid the other into the holster on his thigh.

In his other pockets he carried the folding knife, batteries, an extra flashlight, and as much additional ammo as he could find. No matter what might get thrown at him, he didn't intend to go down without a fight. A *big* one.

With everything set, he drained the last of the water from the coffee station into his depleted condom, added a purification tablet just to be safe, and then cooked himself a hot breakfast.

He pulled the blanket tightly around him as he alternated between spoonfuls of warm muesli and sips of hot coffee from an additional cup he had found. He knew all too well that the rest of the day was going to suck. Right now, at this moment, was the warmest he was going to be. He took breakfast slowly, savoring every bite and sip.

Getting to safety was going to be a massive undertaking. It would be like trying to solve a blackboard-sized equation, where three quarters of it had been erased. The key was in starting with what parts you knew to be true.

Though he wasn't certain exactly where he was, he knew that they had taken off from Murmansk. He also knew the geography of Russia well enough to know that the nearest friendly country was Finland.

It was all he had to go on, so he had decided to head in that direction— due west. He would course correct as circumstances dictated. In a survival situation, it was important to have a goal.

Staying put in hopes of a rescue by American forces was out of the question. They likely didn't even know he had been kidnapped, much less that he had crash-landed in Russia. The only person who could save him was him.

So, once his breakfast was finished, he packed up his gear and made ready to leave, but not without taking care of one last thing.

Starting with the Spetsnaz operative behind the cargo container, he took out his fixed-blade knife and set about collecting the rest of his scalps.

The body of the dead soldier outside, as well as the man with the broken neck in the center section of the fuselage, had been torn apart by the wolves, but there was still enough left for Harvath to get what he needed.

He hung all four scalps on a piece of wire in the tail section.

Then, just as first light was breaking, he strapped on his snowshoes, picked up his pack and rifle, and headed out into the storm.

CHAPTER 15

The arrival of daylight did little to improve the weather. It was still freezing. But if there was one thing SEALs were taught to withstand, it was the cold.

Harvath had spent more time in the frigid water of San Diego Bay than he cared to remember. After that, he had gone to the U.S. Navy's facility in Alaska, where he endured extensive training in winter warfare and cold-weather survival.

It was no wonder to him that so many Navy SEALs moved to warm climates once they left the service. By then, they had seen more cold than most people do in a lifetime.

Sometimes, he wondered where he'd be if he hadn't chosen a career that kept him glued to D.C. He was a big fan of the Florida Keys and the Greek islands. He also loved Park City, Utah, and the Swiss Alps. He didn't have a "special" place he saw himself in. He had even moved to Boston for a time simply to be closer to Lara and her little boy, Marco.

Just the thought of her sent a wave of remorse through his body. He couldn't believe she was gone. And not only was she gone, she was gone because of him. Once again, someone he loved had been marked for death, and it had been his fault. He vowed never to let that happen again.

Struggling through the snow, the visibility next to nothing, he made it into the trees at the edge of the clearing. Pushing Lara from his mind, he concentrated on his most important priority—putting as much distance between himself and the crash site as possible.

When a rescue team finally did show up, and when they realized the plane was carrying a prisoner who had disappeared, someone was going to start doing some math. Average speed per hour of a healthy adult male in snow would be multiplied by the estimated hours that had elapsed since the crash. A circle would be drawn on a map, and the hunt would be on.

Scenes of a Russian Tommy Lee Jones from *The Fugitive* telling his men to conduct a hard-target search of every "gas station, residence, warehouse, farmhouse, henhouse, outhouse, and doghouse" within that radius played across his mind.

He figured that at best, in the current conditions, he was making three miles an hour on his improvised snowshoes. How long he could keep it up was the question. At some point, he was going to have to stop to rest.

Then there was the issue of where he'd spend the night. He needed not only someplace where he could keep warm but also someplace from which he could defend himself. The image of the pack of hungry wolves wasn't far from his mind. He had imagined something on his six o'clock ever since leaving the crash site. Even in this storm, he was keeping his eyes and ears open. The idea that they could be only feet behind him, ready to pounce, wasn't very comforting.

The upside to the weather, though, was that wind and blowing snow would help to cover his tracks. Without a visible trail, any manhunt would be forced to spread its resources in all directions, leaving more gaps for him to slip through. But Harvath hoped to be long gone before any search even started.

To do that, first he needed to find a road. Then he needed to find a vehicle. From there, everything else would work itself out. All he had to do was get to the border. *Goals*, he reminded himself. *Stay alive. Stay ahead of the Russians. Don't freeze. Make it to Finland.*

Being careful not to drop it in the snow, he checked his heading on the survival compass and pressed on.

Snowshoeing had one big plus and one big minus. The minus was that it burned a lot of calories. The plus was that burning that many calories was like carrying an onboard furnace. In fact, he had to unzip his parka to vent some of the heat.

The Russian gear he had on wasn't nearly as high-tech as American cold-weather clothing. If he got soaked from too much sweat, he might not be able to get dry. Even being slightly damp would accelerate heat loss if he was forced to remain outside without a shelter.

Harvath checked his watch. Moving through the forest, he tried to keep his pace consistent. After two hours, be began encountering hills, some much steeper than others. Though his hips and legs were aching, he pushed on. An hour after that, it was all he could do to keep going. He was forced to take a break.

Pausing under a large pine, he propped his rifle against his pack, took off the snowshoes, and gave them a quick inspection.

They had held up remarkably well and needed only a few minor adjustments, which he made before attending to anything else. That was something else he had learned in the SEALs. The instructors had been fanatical about it. Even when returning from a grueling mission when all you wanted was a hot meal and an even hotter shower, you always took care of your gear first. It was a lesson that had become a part of him.

With the snowshoes taken care of, he gave his weapons a quick once-over and wiped down the rifle. Only then, with all of that complete, could he see to everything else.

Under the pine, he was able to get out of the weather, which was a welcome relief. Walking for hours with icy crystals being blown into your eyes was a special kind of torture.

From where he sat, he could see that the intensity of the storm had begun to lessen. Visibility was starting to improve. He knew better than to tempt the fates by celebrating, but inside he allowed himself a quick thought that maybe things were breaking in his direction.

Removing his tiny, foldable camping stove, he ignited a hextab and scooped up some snow in his canteen cup. He needed to rehydrate, as well as to replenish the water in the condoms. In addition to burning a lot of calories, snowshoeing also depleted a lot of fluids.

As the first batch of snow began to melt, he added some of the cherry drink mix from the IRP, along with some of the electrolyte powder from the med pouch, to form his own version of survival Gatorade.

Making sure the liquid wasn't too hot, he stirred it with a spoon and then raised the metal cup to his lips.

It tasted better than he had expected, and he quickly drank it down.

He was convinced that the reason sports drinks were referred to as "thirst quenchers" was that the moment their salts and sugars hit your taste buds, your body knew the relief it had been begging for was on its way. That's what this felt like to Harvath.

After chugging it down, he quickly whipped up another batch. Judging by how much he had been sweating, it was no surprise that he needed to replenish himself.

He took the second cup more slowly, savoring it as he had his breakfast. There was no sound other than the wind and the occasional clumps of snow falling through the boughs of the trees. In any other circumstance, it might have been peaceful, beautiful even.

Removing his compass, he marked which direction was west and then finished off his drink.

Packing his cup with snow again, he placed it on the little stove and stood up to take a leak.

His urine, no surprise, was dark, and proved what he already knew—he hadn't been hydrating enough. It was a luxury he couldn't afford at the moment. Though it wasn't healthy, he had to push himself in order to stay ahead of anyone who might be coming after him. The alternative—getting captured—wasn't an option.

Sliding back under the tree, he spent the next fifteen minutes melting snow and refilling the condoms. Before tying them off, he added what was left in the drink mix and electrolyte packages to each, along with some of his sugar and a little bit of his salt.

Steadily consuming that mixture would allow him to go harder, longer. It would also reduce the likelihood of cramps and headaches. He had to start thinking of it as a marathon, not a sprint. There was no telling how far he'd need to travel before he would feel safe enough to stop.

With his makeshift bladders topped off, he extinguished his fire and repacked his gear. Putting the snowshoes back on, he checked his compass one last time and then headed out.

As the storm continued to recede and the curtains of snow parted, he began to notice signs of life throughout the forest. A couple of blue hares came into view, as well as a red fox. Then, half an hour later, he spotted a lynx, and suddenly, it was decision time.

Fresh meat was a godsend in a survival situation. It also came with a certain amount of risk.

Topping Harvath's risk list was that the shot from his rifle could give him away. The odds that anyone was going to hear it, though, seemed pretty remote, especially as the weapon was suppressed and its retort would be considerably reduced.

He had a day's worth of food left, two if he stretched it. He was going to need every single calorie to stay alive, and to stay ahead of his pursuers. The moment he stopped putting fuel in his tank was the moment his mileage would start to drop.

What's more, there was no telling if the weather was going to continue to improve, or if what he was seeing was the precursor to something even worse. This part of Russia was renowned for terrible storms that could bring both bitter cold and mountains of snow.

He decided the risk was worth it.

Unslinging his pack, he lay down in the snow, picked up his rifle, and balanced it on top.

Without even thinking, his mind went into marksmanship mode, focusing on the big three: breath control, sight alignment, and trigger press.

He wasn't going to take the animal back to a taxidermist, so he didn't care where his shot landed as long as it did the job.

Wanting the easiest target, he abandoned a head shot and focused on a lung shot, just behind the cat's shoulder.

Sucking in a deep breath, he tried to oxygenate his blood and get his respiration under control. Because of how strenuous the snowshoeing had been, his heart was thudding in his chest. It was like running in a marathon and abruptly having to stop in the middle of the race to perform surgery.

The conditions weren't terrible. The animal was in range; visibility—at least for the moment—was decent; and the wind was in his favor.

Lining up the front and rear sights, he took one more breath, exhaled, and applied pressure to the trigger.

CHAPTER 16

The subsonic, 9x39 mm round didn't produce the loud "crack" most people associated with gunfire. It was designed to be quieter, especially when coupled with a suppressor. The tradeoff, though, was less muzzle velocity—the speed with which the bullet left the gun.

But while it was moving more slowly and packing less punch, it still had an effective lethal range of more than five hundred meters, perfect for Harvath's purposes.

Still peering through his sights, he watched as the bullet struck the lynx and the animal went down.

Then it got back up and took off.

Harvath was confused. It had been a clean shot and should have dropped the cat right there.

He prepared to fire a second time, but the voice in the back of his head said "No."

As a kid, he had read, and watched, everything he could get his hands on about the great American mountain men. Jim Bridger, Jedediah Smith, Jeremiah Johnson, and Jim Beckwourth were some of his favorites. He remembered even asking his father if there'd been a rule that only men whose names started with J could be mountain men.

He also remembered something else—and it was that something else that stopped him from taking a second shot. In one of those books, or in one of the many movies he had seen, some grizzled old mountain man had passed on a key piece of survival information to a newcomer: Only shoot once. If you shoot again, the Indians will be able to find you.

So, instead of taking a second shot, Harvath decide to track the animal. It had gone down pretty hard, and he was relatively certain it couldn't have gotten too far away. He just hoped it hadn't scrambled up a tree.

Flicking the lever above the trigger guard, he rendered the weapon safe and got to his feet.

Dusting the snow off his pack, he put it on, and then slung his rifle across his chest. He wanted to be able to get to it quickly, just in case the cat had any fight left and decided to come at him. If that happened, Indians be damned, he *would* fire again.

Slogging through the snow, he arrived minutes later at the spot where he had shot the lynx. There was a bright patch of blood on the ground and a trail leading off into the distance. It wouldn't be hard to track.

Harvath took a quick check of his compass. The animal was headed south. He needed to be going west.

He wasn't crazy about having to divert, but he not only needed the food, it was also the right thing to do. If you wounded an animal, you tracked it and finished the job. You didn't let it suffer.

His father, a SEAL instructor, had drummed that into him. It was not only the morally correct thing to do, but there was this notion that if you left the animal to die, you were inviting a host of bad things to happen.

What those things were, his father never explained. It stemmed from an American Indian belief that if you were worthy, the Great Spirit would provide. And as it did provide, you should take only what you needed. The land and all things in it and on it should always be respected.

His father had been a fascinating font of wisdom. A rugged individualist, he probably would have made a good mountain man. A lover of American Westerns and standing up for the underdog, he also would have made a great gunslinger—riding into town, righting wrongs, and then riding off into the sunset.

All of those things were what likely had drawn the elder Harvath to the SEAL community. They were unquestionably what had developed his son's character and path in life as well.

It was a shame that the two men hadn't realized how similar they were before the elder Harvath had died in a training accident. Perhaps it was because they were so similar that they had often been so at odds.

Following the blood trail, Harvath made sure to constantly scan the area around him, as well as look up into the trees. Lynx were highly intelligent predators. They were known for ambushing their prey and could take down adult deer weighing more than three hundred pounds. The last thing he needed was to miss that the cat had doubled back. He had no desire to be attacked.

Soon enough, he noticed that the blood spatters had changed direction and were heading uphill. He raised his gaze toward the top of the ridge, but there was no sign of the lynx.

Adrenaline and an animal's will to live notwithstanding, it was starting to look as if Harvath's shot hadn't been that well placed after all.

Ready for any even deeper burn in his legs, he leaned into his snowshoes and began to climb. It was like scaling the back of an icy wave.

Several times during the ascent, he was overcome with the feeling that he was being followed—convinced that someone or something was on his tail. But each time he stopped and turned around, there was nothing there.

Once at the top, he noticed more blood and that the spatters were coming closer together. Based on the length of the lynx's stride, he could tell that the animal was slowing down. It wouldn't be long now.

When he finally caught up to it, the majestic cat was an incredible sight to see. It was a healthy, full-grown male, at least sixty pounds in weight. Black-tipped ears and a short, black-tipped tail offset its dappled, silver-gray fur.

Short clouds of labored breath escaped from its mouth and rose into the cold like puffs of steam from a dying locomotive. The wound, which Harvath had been sure was a lung shot, had been off by several inches.

While only a bad carpenter blames his tools, he assumed the sights on the rifle had been damaged in the plane crash. It would explain what had happened to the lynx and, fortunately, why the Spetsnaz operative's bullets had failed to hit him inside the wreckage.

He watched as the cat's breathing continued to slow. Its eyes appeared fixed on him, yet they seemed to look right past him at the same time. The animal didn't hiss or growl as they were known to do.

Harvath hadn't thought much about what he was going to do once he found his quarry. Would he take that second shot? Or would he find some other way to humanely finish the animal off?

In the end, the lynx made the decision for him. The cat exhaled one final time, releasing its spirit with its last breath.

After making sure the animal was dead, he took out his knife and went to work.

Lynx was a lean meat that was alleged to taste like pork or chicken. Harvath couldn't say for sure, as he had never tried it. What he did know was that, like rabbit and squirrel, it didn't have a lot of fat. In a survival situation, that could be a problem. You could actually get too much lean protein.

Splitting the animal open, he worked quickly. The only internal organs he was interested in were the liver and kidneys. Everything else went into a guts pile. It was messy work, but he was grateful for the food.

He was about to skin the carcass when the hair on the back of his neck stood up, just as it had at the wreckage. He didn't need to turn around to know why. The growling of the wolves was all he needed to hear.

CHAPTER 17

Gray wolves were the greatest predators of the lynx. Whether the pack had come for Harvath or for his kill didn't make a difference. He wasn't going to let them have either.

Grabbing the rifle, he spun and began firing.

He was amazed at how close they had gotten before his Spidey sense had kicked in. He was also amazed by how many of them there were. He had never seen a pack this big. It was a sea of teeth, and claws, and fur.

As he had back at the crash site, he kept his shots controlled, moving back and forth, focusing on the wolves closest to him. And all the while expecting to be flanked.

Though the suppressor dampened the sound of the rounds leaving the rifle, it was still loud enough to scare most of the wolves into halting their advance.

The other great thing was that the bullets he was firing had an air pocket in the tip that caused them to tumble when they hit soft tissue.

At this range, not only was he able to hit his targets without relying on the screwed-up sights, but it was as if each wolf he shot had been hit with a mini buzz saw. The rounds chewed right through them.

Standing his ground, one snowshoe on the lynx to prevent it from being dragged away, he waited to see if the wolves would regroup and come back at him. As he did, he unzipped his parka, indexed a thirty-round magazine from the rig on his chest, and reloaded. Never once did he take his eyes off his surroundings.

He tucked the depleted mag into his outer pocket, breathing a little bit easier now that he was topped up on ammo.

Scanning the dead wolves that littered the snow in front of him, the same question from earlier popped back into his mind. *Where was the alpha?*

He had a feeling he'd know soon enough.

In the meantime, he needed to make a choice—wait the pack out and see if they dispersed, or run his ammo down by taking out as many of them as possible.

If he didn't make a stand against the pack here, they'd keep coming for him. But every round of ammo he expended now was a round he might wish he had later, especially if the Russians ended up coming for him.

As the wolves glared and growled only yards away, he made his choice and opened fire.

He dropped three and was trying to line up a fourth when the pack turned and disappeared into the trees.

Their sudden retreat was followed by an unsettling quiet. Next to the ringing in his ears, the only thing he could hear was the blowing of the wind.

While he couldn't see them, he knew better than to assume they had completely given up. If this was the same pack, they had been stalking him for hours. He needed to find some way to put distance between him and them.

Removing his snowshoe from the carcass, he slung his pack. Then, with one hand on the pistol grip of his rifle, he reached down with his other hand and grabbed the lynx.

Dragging the cat next to him, he sidestepped up to the very top of the ridge and looked over the side. It was steep, which might be a plus, or could be a minus.

It would be a plus if it was too steep, or the snow too deep, for the pack to follow him. It would be a minus if it turned out to be too difficult for him to traverse and he ended up injuring himself. Or worse.

Because of the limited visibility, it was impossible to see how far the slope descended and where it stopped. But as Harvath didn't have the luxury of any alternative routes, this was it.

Swinging the lynx over his shoulders, he took a deep breath and stepped over the edge.

The blowing snow had significantly built up on the opposite side and was quite deep. The incline was also much steeper than he had anticipated.

As soon as he put his snowshoe down, a large sheet of icy snow cracked and broke away.

This whole thing was a deathtrap, but so was going back the way he had come. Avalanche versus wolves—his own Scylla and Charybdis.

Adopting a technique called "side-hilling," he pushed the uphill side of each snowshoe into the slope as he traversed across its face in a zigzag pattern.

It was monotonous, but he didn't have a choice. He couldn't go straight down. It was too steep.

What he really needed to help maintain his balance was a pair of poles. He kept his eyes peeled and eventually found two sturdy branches that would do the trick.

Tying the legs of the lynx together, he continued, stopping every so often to glance behind him, while constantly listening for any danger.

The good news was that the wolves seemed to have given up, and the snowpack was holding. Half an hour later, the slope leveled off.

Though the snow was still blowing, some of it had tapered off at this elevation. He appeared to be in a valley of some sort with a frozen river running through it.

The ice, where patches of snow had been blown away, was clear, and he could see water moving beneath it. Confirming with his compass that the river ran somewhat westerly, he decided to follow it, hoping that it would lead to civilization.

As he drove his legs forward, he looked for possible places to build a shelter. There were only a few more hours of daylight left. If he had to dig out a snow cave, he wanted the job done before dark. Engineering a fire in such a way that it would keep him warm while also keeping predators at bay and not giving his position away to any search-and-rescue aircraft was going to be an undertaking.

It was a good thing to keep his mind occupied. Too often his thoughts had drifted to Lara, Lydia, and the Old Man, and the rage would threaten to overtake him. One foot in front of the other, he'd remind himself, drawing his focus back to what he needed to accomplish simply to stay alive.

He was fortunate that he had food and water covered. That meant heat and shelter could be at the very top of his to-do list.

As far as what kind of shelter he might create, there were several options. If he wanted to carve blocks of packed snow, he could build an igloo. He could also dig out a snow cave or snow trench. There were enough evergreen trees around that he might build a lean-to with a fire in front if he chose.

The problem with lean-tos, though, was that they were largely exposed. They could be nice and toasty with a fire going in front, but if the wind shifted or a storm intensified, they could become rather inhospitable.

No matter what shelter he chose, he was going to have to hoist the lynx carcass, along with any garbage from his IRP, into the trees, to keep predators away.

The best scenario would be to find an empty cave that he could move right into. So far, though, the topography wasn't cooperating. He hadn't seen so much as a rocky overhang that he could shore up and spend the night beneath. It was pretty clear that wherever he ended up overnighting, he was going to have to build his shelter from scratch.

Up ahead, the river looked as if it took a ninety-degree turn before disappearing from sight. If he hadn't found a good spot by the time he got there, that was where he'd dig in for the night. He simply couldn't go any farther. It was only by sheer force of will that he had made it this far.

One of the hardest things about snowshoeing was the wider stance. Even if you were as fit as Harvath, hadn't had your body abused by Russian captors, and were pushing only a fraction as hard, the first day out was brutal on your body.

He knew that the pain he was feeling now was nothing compared to what he was going to be feeling in the morning. Overnight, as the lactic acid built up in his muscles, things would only get worse.

It wasn't a pleasant thought, but he had been sore and tired and cold enough times to know he could handle it. It was why SEALs were put through Hell Week. The idea was to push them past the breaking point so if—God forbid—they were ever in this kind of situation, they would persevere.

And that was exactly what Harvath intended to do. Failure was not an option. The *only* option, no matter how bad things became, was success.

It was the mindset that had been drilled into him in the SEALs, and especially at SERE school. He needed to set small, achievable goals—a shelter, a fire, a meal—and then appreciate and build upon his successes. *Everything* was about state of mind and how he chose to perceive his situation. The people who felt powerless were the ones who wouldn't make it.

Coming around the bend in the river, Harvath needed a moment to realize what he was looking at. As soon as he did, he froze in his tracks.

CHAPTER 18

It was when Chief Tullis had mentioned the Investigative Services Bureau of the New Hampshire State Police that the piece McGee needed had fallen into place.

In December of the prior year, a disturbed man had contacted the CIA via its website and had threatened to shoot the Governor of New Hampshire.

In addition to reaching out to the Governor's office and the FBI, the Agency had also gotten in touch with a little-known division of the Investigative Services Bureau known as the Terrorism Intelligence Unit. Working with officers there, the CIA was able to keep the New Hampshire authorities informed of their investigation, which found that the suspect had no known connections to international terrorism. The FBI had also come to the same conclusion on the domestic front.

The investigation had been given high priority, and had been conducted thoroughly, professionally, and quickly. It also, as it turned out, had earned the CIA and FBI a favor from the Governor. He agreed to put the press conference announcing Harvath as their prime suspect on hold.

He insisted, though, that a notice be put out to law enforcement. If Harvath had snapped and then turned around and shot a cop, he didn't want blood on his hands. McGee understood, and Militante helped the State Police draft the alert.

With that task complete, they had convoyed back to the airport with their security details, boarded the Agency's private plane, and flown back to Andrews Air Force Base.

In flight, McGee had contacted the White House and had requested an emergency meeting with the President. He would need to be briefed. And after being briefed, he would need to authorize what the CIA Director wanted to do next.

The FBI's Hostage Recovery Fusion Cell was a multiagency task force, based at FBI headquarters, that pooled resources, data, and intelligence in an effort to recover Americans who had been kidnapped abroad.

There were obvious reasons he needed the President's approval to activate this cell, most glaring among them that there was zero evidence that Harvath had been kidnapped.

But that's exactly what McGee's gut was telling him—this had been a snatch operation.

The question, though, was who was behind it. Harvath had a list of enemies longer than his arm, all of them extremely violent.

It could have been Islamic militants, organized crime, even the Russians, all of whom Harvath had tangled with on behalf of the United States.

The Russians had the most skill, and a particular axe to grind with him, but McGee was skeptical. Even though Harvath had foiled their ambitions more than once, they would have known grabbing him on American soil like this would be an act of war. The reprisals they had already suffered for their prior bad actions would be nothing in comparison to what the U.S. would do in response to something like this.

The CIA Director felt certain that an undertaking this brazen, with such an incredible downside, had to have been carried out by a nonstate actor. It was the only thing that made sense.

Nevertheless, before the plane had even landed, he had pulled together a trusted team at Langley to comb through Harvath's past assignments, all the way back to his SEAL days, to see if anything jumped out at them.

Accessing Harvath's jobs for The Carlton Group was another matter.

They had other clients besides the CIA. McGee was going to need somebody inside whom he could trust, someone with access to all of the files. There was only one person who filled that bill.

In any other situation, the request could have been made via a secure teleconference or an encrypted email. Today, though, it needed to be made in person. No one at The Carlton Group was yet aware of the murders. It was going to hit the entire organization hard, but no one harder than the man McGee was about to meet.

The man known in international intelligence circles as "The Troll," The Carlton Group's Chief Technology Officer, met the CIA Director at the elevator. Because of primordial dwarfism, he stood barely three feet tall.

With him were his ever-present guardians—Argos and Draco—a pair of white two-hundred-plus-pound Ovcharkas, also known as Caucasian Sheep Dogs. In the dangerous, cutthroat world he inhabited, the dogs were both a bulwark against attack and a reminder of the powerful enemies he had made.

Before joining The Carlton Group, the little man had enjoyed an extremely lucrative career trafficking in the purchase and sale of highly sensitive black-market intelligence. He was a hacker and IT specialist par excellence. What he lacked in physical stature he had more than made up for in brainpower and ambition. He was also a man of particular appetites whose predilections would put some of the world's grandest bon vivants to shame.

His given name had been abandoned to a past fraught with heartache, pain, and abandonment. A quiet supporter of orphans and orphanages in far-flung corners of the world, he had taken for himself the name of the patron saint of children, so his small circle of friends and colleagues at The Carlton Group knew him as Nicholas.

When the CIA Director and his retinue stepped out of the elevator, the little man could read the expression on his face. Something very bad had happened.

McGee suggested they conduct their meeting in Lydia Ryan's office, as it was more comfortable than the Sensitive Compartmented Information Facility, or SCIF, that Nicholas called his own.

Agreeing, the little man led the way.

When they arrived at Lydia's office, McGee's security detail did a quick sweep and then retreated into the hall.

"Take a seat," Nicholas said, gesturing toward one of the long leather couches. "Can I get you something to drink?"

"Coffee," McGee replied, as he scratched Argos and Draco behind the ears. He had gotten to know them quite well since Nicholas had joined the firm.

There was the sound of ice cubes being dropped into glasses, followed by bourbon being poured.

Putting the cork back in the bottle, Nicholas turned from the liquor cart and waddled over to the couch with two tumblers. "We're out of coffee," he said as he handed them over.

Once he had climbed up onto the couch, he took one for himself and asked, "Why do I get the feeling I'm going to need this?"

McGee had already decided he wasn't going to pull any punches. "Lydia has been killed. So has Reed. And so has the Corpsman who was on duty."

Nicholas was in shock. "When? How?" was all he could manage to say.

"As best we can tell, a few days ago. They were all shot inside the cottage in New Hampshire. Lara Cordero was there, too. She's also dead."

The blood drained from the little man's face as he braced for what he was certain was coming next.

The CIA Director's following sentence, though, surprised him. "There was no sign of Harvath."

Emotion overcoming him, Nicholas fought it back and took a long sip of his bourbon. As he raised it to his small mouth, the large glass trembled in his hand.

McGee wasn't good at consoling people. There were a bunch of things he could have said, but he was afraid they might sound hollow, or, worse, phony. Instead, he kept his thoughts to himself.

He knew that Harvath and Nicholas shared a special bond. They were kindred spirits. Once on opposite sides of the fight, they had been drawn together somehow. Theirs was an extremely unlikely friendship, but it was a friendship nonetheless. And it was deep. Harvath reserved for Nicholas an esteem that he had extended only to men with whom he had been in combat. For Nicholas, Harvath represented something he had never truly enjoyed—family.

Having dribbled a little of the liquor down his chin, Nicholas reached up with the back of his hand and wiped it off. Then he raised the glass again and drained what remained. McGee followed suit.

Handing over his empty tumbler, the little man motioned to the bar cart and asked, "Do you mind?"

The CIA Director didn't. Getting up, he took both glasses over, filled them up, and then returned to the leather couch, handing Nicholas his.

"Who did it?" Nicholas asked.

McGee leaned back, exhaled a tired breath, and shook his head. "I don't know."

"Who do you think did it?"

Again, he shook his head. "I don't have any idea."

Nicholas took another long sip of bourbon before asking, "He isn't a suspect, is he?"

The CIA Director nodded. "According to local law enforcement, he is. Their working theory is that Harvath has some kind of PTSD and snapped."

"That's ridiculous."

"Of course it's ridiculous."

"No," Nicholas replied, lowering his glass. "I mean it's *fucking* ridiculous. Do you have any idea why he and Lara went up there?"

"I assume to see Reed."

The little man looked at him, his eyes wide in disbelief. "They didn't tell you?"

"Tell me what?"

"Of course not," said Nicholas, shaking his head. "Nobody was supposed to know. At least not right away."

"Nobody was supposed to know what?"

Setting his glass down, he filled his guest in. "Scot and Lara had gone up there to get married. They hired a local minister to do the ceremony. Reed had been getting worse, and they wanted him to be part of it. The plan was to have a proper wedding with Lara's parents and everyone else a few months down the road."

"Jesus," said McGee, leaning forward. "Who else knew?"

Nicholas shrugged. "Only Lydia. She had to be up there already to see Carlton. Afterward, she was going to take a few days off. I assumed that's why I hadn't heard anything from her."

"Who else might have known that they were going to be at the cottage?"

The little man thought for a moment. "I heard them talking about an old intelligence asset that Reed used to run. The asset knew that Reed was sick and wanted to see him one last time. Lydia was trying to put something together, but she wanted Harvath to be there for it too."

"Did this asset have a name?"

"Just a codename," Nicholas replied. "*Matterhorn*. Does that ring a bell?"

Very slowly, as the color in his face drained, McGee nodded.

CHAPTER 19

Kazimir Teplov, the man known as Wagner, stood atop an armored personnel carrier, a rifle hanging at his side, and yelled to his team. "Let's go! Hurry it up. I want the plane loaded this year!"

He had handpicked his best men, all seasoned special operations veterans, and all winter warfare experts.

The call had come directly from Minayev. The head of the GRU's special missions group had made it crystal clear that this assignment was a top national priority. And by *top national priority*, it was automatically understood to mean that it was a top Kremlin priority.

The mission parameters, though, were interesting, if not downright unusual.

Whenever the government had used Wagner before, it had always been for assignments outside the country. This was an operation *inside* Russia.

The Russian military, though, had its own elite soldiers. There could be only one reason that the Kremlin wanted mercenaries: deniability.

But with all the active military and intelligence personnel devoted to the Russian state and its President, it was hard to imagine what could require such extraordinary measures.

Even over the encrypted line, Minayev had been reluctant to say. He would meet the plane at Alakurtti Air Base and explain everything there. He had provided only broad brushstrokes—expected terrain, weather conditions, size of force required, and equipment suggestions.

If Teplov had to guess, there was some sort of coup afoot. Though hard to imagine, it wasn't an impossibility. The fact that a mercenary team was being called in suggested that the Russian military couldn't be trusted.

He ran through a potential list of plotters in his mind, men in the Army's high command capable of such a thing. There were more than a few of them.

The plotters, though, couldn't have had much support, because Minayev wanted the operational footprint kept small. His request had been for two dozen men. More than that, he claimed, would be unnecessary.

Teplov didn't like it. Assembling and equipping a team without knowing all the details was dangerous. These were his men, not Minayev's. The ultimate responsibility for a successful outcome would fall to him.

By the same token, Teplov respected the General's experience. The man had not risen to where he was by accident. He was both tough and highly intelligent. And despite Teplov's success in the field, the older man had seen more action in a lifetime than he would see in two. He would defer to the GRU chieftain's judgment. For now.

In addition to twenty-four of his best men, he had marshaled his best equipment, and then doubled the amount of ammunition they might need. Everything else would be up to the gods.

He had then briefed his team on what he knew. They were flying to an air base north of St. Petersburg for an operation of indeterminate length, the objective of which had yet to be revealed.

The men were professionals. They had worked on countless missions where the details were unknown until the last moment. Even now, none of them questioned why they were being deployed on Russian soil. They were almost fanatical in their loyalty to their leader, and would follow him anywhere.

Teplov hoped he wasn't making a mistake.

CHAPTER 20

It was as if God himself had set down a tiny jewel in the middle of the vast, unforgiving Russian wilderness. And while it tore at his painfully frozen skin, Harvath smiled.

The question of where he would shelter for the night had been answered.

On the opposite bank sat a small, weather-beaten cabin.

No smoke rose from its chimney. Drifts of snow reached up to its windows. There were no signs of life anywhere. It appeared uninhabited.

Now all Harvath had to do was get across the ice.

Fording an unfamiliar river was dangerous enough. Fording a frozen one took the danger to another level.

The fact that he had been able to see water moving under the surface concerned him. It was practically guaranteed that the thickness wasn't anywhere near what he'd like it to be. His options, though, were limited.

He could take his chances and cross here. He could keep walking, hoping to find the "perfect" point to cross. Or, he could give up altogether, stay on this side of the river, and get to work building a shelter.

Compared to sleeping outside in subzero temperatures, the cabin was the Ritz Carlton. It would provide shelter not only from the elements but also from predators. And though it didn't look like much, there was no telling what supplies he might find inside.

There was also the possibility of a road, which he could trace back to civilization. His choice was clear. He needed to cross. The only question was where—upriver or down?

Based on the abrupt right angle the water took, he decided that was the worst place. The water was being forced around a corner, which meant there'd be a lot of churn and the ice would be at its thinnest. He decided to push farther down the bank.

A few hundred yards later, he stopped. This seemed as good a place as any.

Dropping the lynx carcass and his pack, he took a good look around and listened for any sound of danger. All he could hear was the sound of the wind, accompanied by the groaning of the frozen river, and beneath it, ever so faintly, the rushing of the frigid water.

Glancing at it, he was suddenly reminded of a fly-fishing trip he'd been on years ago. They had been working a fast-moving stream with a strong current they had to lean into. One of their party had slipped and fallen. Despite the belt meant to cinch them tight, his waders quickly filled with water as he was swept away.

They barely made it to him in time. The man had almost drowned. It was something Harvath had never forgotten.

Looking across the ice to the opposite bank, he decided to repack his gear. He wanted the most critical pieces on his person. Everything else— the pack, the rifle, and the lynx—he would tow behind him via a piece of cord he had salvaged from the wreckage.

If he fell through, he wanted as little as possible weighing him down and, God forbid, dragging him under the ice with the current.

Within moments of removing his gloves, his hands began to stiffen. He worked as fast as he could, stopping only to take short breaks to warm them.

When everything was ready and he had his gloves back on, he stepped carefully out onto the ice and stood there listening.

The wind still howled, the frigid water still rushed, and the ice still groaned, but no more so than before. *Good sign.*

He had strapped the pack to the lynx carcass and now set the bundle down on the ice next to him. He had about five feet of cord left over to use as a towline. He would have preferred more, but it was better than nothing.

The problem was whether to tie it around his waist with a quick-release knot or pull his gear along by hand.

He still had his makeshift poles and wanted to hold on to them. Most of the river was covered with snow, and he could use them to probe the ice as he moved forward. He decided to tie the cord around his waist.

Once it was in place and the knot secure, he began lightly placing one snowshoe in front of the other.

The farther he got out across the river, the harder his heart pounded. The ice felt as if it was flexing underneath him. His decision to make the crossing was going to be either really smart or really stupid. He'd know in less than fifty feet.

Like a dentist examining a mouth full of decaying teeth, he used his poles to cautiously pick his way toward the opposite bank.

With each step he took, he reminded himself to breathe. Everything was okay. He was almost there. He was going to make it.

That was when he heard the crack.

CHAPTER 21

It wasn't a particularly loud crack. It was more like someone had snapped a piece of kindling. Nevertheless, it stopped him in his tracks, and he stood stock-still.

As his eyes swept the area around him, his ears struggled to pick up any further hints of danger. It took only a moment.

The sound resembled a string of lightbulbs being crushed, as if they were being driven over by a heavy truck. It was quiet at first, but was quickly growing louder. He didn't need to see through the snow to know the ice was spiderwebbing.

His mind panicked and urged him to run, but he ignored it. Instead, he listened to his training.

Casting his poles away, he quickly flattened himself on top of the ice, arms and leg spread wide in an effort to distribute his weight as evenly as possible.

The cracking stopped. All he could hear now was his heart hammering inside his chest.

He tried to kick off his snowshoes, but it was no use. They were too firmly affixed. Instead, he had to turn both of his legs out at uncomfortable angles in order to belly-crawl the rest of the way across the ice.

Using his forearms to pull himself along, he dared move only inches at a time, but at least he was moving, and fortunately, the ice was holding up.

Arm over arm he crawled, dragging his equipment behind him. The snow piled up in front of it like a plow, making it harder and harder to tow.

He was doing everything with his upper body. With his feet off the ice because of the sides of the snowshoes, all he could do was drag his legs behind him. It only added to the pain he was already feeling in his hip sockets, but he pushed it from his mind and forced himself on.

Less than twenty feet from the bank, he had to stop. His lungs, seared by the arctic air, were burning. His body was out of adrenaline. He needed to catch his breath and regain his strength.

Spreading his arms and legs like a starfish once more, he lay back down. As he did, a wave of fatigue swept over him.

He was beyond tired. What he was feeling now might have been even worse than what he had felt in Hell Week. All he wanted to do was close his eyes.

Instead, he forced himself to look at his objective. Even with the snow, he could see the edge of the riverbank. It was so close—only fifteen feet away. He was almost there.

You can do this, he told himself. *Just a little bit more. You've got to get off this ice. It isn't safe here. Start moving.*

Coming up onto his right elbow, he reached his arm out and pulled himself forward. But as he did, the ice cracked and gave away beneath him.

Before he knew what had happened, he was fully submerged under the freezing cold water.

Don't lose the hole! Don't lose the hole! his mind screamed.

As his arms pulled in wide, powerful strokes, trying to help him resurface, the cord around his waist went taut and pulled him back down.

His gear had fallen in too and was acting not only like a heavy stone but also like a sail that had caught the wind of the current and was now threatening to drag him downriver, *beneath* the ice.

Cut it loose! his mind yelled. *Hurry!*

Reaching down, he yanked the short end of the knot, and instantly the water ripped his gear and the lynx away.

He kicked and stroked for the surface, the hole still within his grasp.

The snowshoes and his heavy winter boots, though, acted like cement blocks tied to his ankles.

Pull, damn it! Pull! his mind shouted.

Summoning one last burst of strength, he pulled as hard as he could and broke the surface.

Grabbing the edge of the ice, he latched onto it with a death grip. He knew that if he lost hold, he'd slip back down and drown.

Now, all he had to do was get out—something much easier said than done.

His snowshoes, though a latticework of cargo netting, had caught the current's attention and were threatening to pull him back under. There was no way he could unlace his boots and slip out of them in time.

Adding to his predicament, his clothes were soaked through. He simply didn't possess enough strength to fight against the current and pull himself out of the hole. Something had to give, and he knew immediately what it was—his parka.

It felt as if it had taken on an additional fifty pounds of water. He needed to get rid of it. It was the only way he was going to survive.

Terrified of what might happen when he let go, he managed to get one arm fully up onto the ice. Wedging himself against the edge as tightly as he could, he released his opposite hand, unzipped the parka, and struggled out of the sleeve.

As soon as he did, the current caught it and began pulling at it, trying to drag him under.

He wanted to take a breather, to muster what little strength he might have left, but the current was relentless. He had to switch arms and let the rest of the coat free—*now*.

Repeating the process, he pinned himself against the ice and allowed the river to rip the parka the rest of the way from him.

In an instant, it was sucked down into the water and disappeared beneath the ice. He knew that if he didn't climb out of the hole immediately, it was only a matter of seconds before he followed.

With the current firmly gripping his snowshoes, he clamped both his forearms onto the ice and pulled.

An excruciating pain tore through his back and shoulders—a pain that, once again, he ignored.

He pulled and kept on pulling until he could feel his chest on the ice, then the middle of his abdomen, followed by his waist.

Once his thighs had cleared the opening, he tried to pull himself the rest of the way out, but he couldn't get enough purchase.

Risking a further fracturing of the surface and the very real possibility he would end up back in the river, he rolled over onto his back and used the momentum to pop his legs out of the water.

The gamble paid off.

His legs, followed by his boots and snowshoes, came shooting up in an icy spray and landed hard on the ice.

He thought for sure the force with which they struck had done him in, but nothing further happened. The ice held.

Without energy enough to roll back onto his stomach, he started inching backward, using the palms of his waterlogged gloves to propel him.

He didn't stop until he reached the bank.

Once there, it took every ounce of discipline he had not to close his eyes, even for just a moment, and rest. He knew that if he did, he would never wake up. Soaking wet, with no coat in the bitter cold, he would die from exposure right there. He had to get up and get moving.

He could see the cabin. There was only one way he was going to make it.

Rocking up into a sitting position, his frozen hands no better than crude clubs, he hammered away at the bindings of his makeshift snowshoes. He kept it up until the first came loose, and then the second.

Kicking them off, he rejected a lotus-laced voice enjoining him to close his eyes, just for a moment—just long enough to regain his strength. Rather than succumb, he forced himself to stand.

Though he had no strength left whatsoever, he still managed to stumble forward. The snow was deep, but free of the snowshoes, his steps felt wonderful. It was a minuscule relief, but reward enough to keep him going. At this point, anything that got him to the cabin was welcome.

Based on the feeling in his extremities, coupled with his collapsing vision, he knew hypothermia was setting in. Part of him was beginning to doubt that he could make it to the cabin at all, but he shut that part right down and banished it from his consciousness.

He told himself that his mission was to make it to that cabin. His life depended on it. He had come too far to fail. He would *not* fail. He would make it. Success was the only option.

Gritting his chattering teeth and wrapping his arms around his shuddering body, he picked up his pace.

As the cabin got closer and closer, he spun wild fantasies of what was waiting for him inside. The first thing he imagined was a roaring fire. Next was a warm bed. After that, he saw a long wooden table set with all kinds of food. At its head, he saw Lara—sweet, beautiful Lara, wearing a sundress, with a glass of white wine in her hand, just like his favorite picture of her, taken on his dock and kept in a silver frame in his bedroom back in Virginia.

He was well aware that he was losing his mind. But the image of her kept him going, so he allowed it to continue.

Nearing the cabin, he saw Lara standing at the front door, smiling. Her hair was tied back, showing her long neck. He wanted so much for this vision to be real.

He felt the ground rising beneath his boots. The cabin was uphill from the riverbank. It made the trek even more difficult. He struggled to stay upright, not to lean too far in any direction and topple over into the snow. He knew that if he did, he no longer had the energy to get back up.

Keeping his eyes on Lara, he battled forward. She looked so gorgeous. And just beyond her, through the open door, he could see that she had a big, beautiful fire going. She had been cooking as well. He could smell it. It smelled like roast beef.

There was also music. She was an opera fan. It sounded like "Nessun Dorma" from *Turandot*, which she played over and over at home.

As he arrived at the entrance, Lara stood back and beckoned him in. The table was fully set. A bottle of wine had been opened. She loved fresh flowers, and in the center was a pitcher filled with irises. He assumed she had picked them herself from someplace nearby.

Stepping up to the threshold, he paused for a moment to lean against the door frame and catch his breath. She stood patiently and waited for him. *He had made it.*

She smiled in that way that drove him crazy. She could have been a model—tall, with a beautiful body and the most captivating eyes he had ever seen.

She beckoned him to join her and get out of the cold. Placing his hand upon the door handle, he pushed it open and stepped inside.

The wind rushed in behind him, chasing away the scent of cooking and extinguishing the fire. It blew away the flowers, the table settings, and the wine.

All that remained was Lara, sitting by the hearth, wrapped in furs. He closed the door behind him to seal out the cold and went to her.

"The fire has gone out," she said from her chair. "You need to re-light it."

He watched as she pointed to an old metal box. Inside were matches. From the stacks next to the fireplace, he gathered up tinder and kindling. When he had them going, he added several logs to the fire.

"Take off your clothes," she commanded, in that voice that drove him wilder than her smile.

He didn't want the dream to end, so he obeyed.

As he removed his wet clothing, she pointed to the cot against the wall. "Wrap yourself in the blankets."

Doing as she asked, he wrapped them around his body and joined her at the fire.

"More logs," she ordered, and once again he obeyed.

With the fire burning hot and bright, she gestured for him to sit down in front of it.

The warmth of the flames felt good—almost as good as having her so close.

"Close your eyes," she told him.

He looked up at her but couldn't see her face.

"You're safe now," she whispered. "Sleep."

He didn't want to sleep. He wanted to pull her to him and breathe her in. But she had cast a spell on him, and, powerless to resist, he felt his eyelids begin to close.

The last thing he remembered was Lara helping him lie down as he fell into a dark pit of deep and dreamless sleep.

CHAPTER 22

When Harvath awoke, it was to the fading echo of Lara's voice. "Don't let the fire die," she warned.

Shaking the cobwebs from his head, he allowed his eyes a moment to adjust to the darkness.

The only light in the cabin came from the glowing embers in the fireplace. He had no idea how long he had been asleep.

Glancing to the left of the fireplace, he saw the seated figure wrapped in furs. Even without sufficient light, he could tell it wasn't Lara, although they both had one very big thing in common. They were both deceased.

It was probably the cabin's owner. Based on the way the man was dressed, as well as the rusty devices hanging on the walls, he was a trapper.

He appeared to be somewhere in his seventies, although appearances in Russia, especially when it came to age, were often deceiving. He looked to be one of the Sámi, the collection of indigenous people sometimes known as Laplanders, who inhabit northern Sweden, Norway, Finland, and this part of Russia. Under the Soviets, they had been very badly treated, even forcibly removed from their lands. The resentment and hostility lingered to this day.

Getting up from the floor, Harvath moved in for a closer look.

There was no apparent trauma. The man had probably died from a heart attack. How long ago was anyone's guess. The subzero temperatures would have helped to preserve the body.

Turning his attention to the fire, he threw on a couple of logs. They were well seasoned and caught instantly. With the increasing heat and additional light, he could reconnoiter the rest of the space.

The first thing he noticed were his boots and the pile of wet clothes nearby. He remembered falling through the ice, but not much after that. It was as if he had witnessed it at a distance, as if it had happened to someone else.

He knew what hypothermia and severe cold could do to a person. He was incredibly fortunate not only to have survived the river but also to have made it to the cabin. How he'd had the presence of mind to get a fire going and get out of his wet clothes was beyond him. Somebody, somewhere, he figured, was watching out for him.

In a space that appeared to be used for preparing food, he found a bucket of water almost completely frozen. What small portion had thawed had probably done so in response to the gradual warming of the cabin from the fireplace. Until this moment, he'd had no idea how thirsty he was.

Raising the bucket to his mouth, he drank all of the liquid water. Then he took the bucket over and placed it near the fire so the rest of the ice could melt.

Returning to the food prep area, he opened its lone cupboard and did a quick inventory. There wasn't much. A few cans of what looked to be vegetables, plus a little tea and coffee, sat on the shelf. He'd lost more in the river than what was stored here. There had to be more.

Propped next to the front door was an old pump-action shotgun known as a Baikal, along with a box of shells. He placed both down on the table and kept looking.

He found a small toolbox, an old flashlight, kitchen items, and a few pieces of clothing, including some heavy wool socks. Tossing the blankets back on the cot, he put on the clothes and spread out his wet items to dry in front of the fire. He was almost beginning to feel human.

Removing a hammer from the toolbox, he knocked off a piece of the ice from the pail, placed it in a saucepan he had found, and stuck it directly into the fire to boil. After everything he had been through, hot tea would be a welcome luxury.

Setting the hammer down, he examined the rest of the odds and ends in the toolbox. There was a small container of oil, as well as some twine, screws, nails, pliers, duct tape, an adjustable wrench, and a screwdriver with multiple heads. What was missing were many of the tools necessary for the fur trapper to ply his trade—including skis or snowshoes.

By the looks of the cabin, he didn't skin any game inside. There had to be an outbuilding of some sort. At first light, Harvath would take a look around the property. In the meantime, he continued his tour of the interior.

The one thing he hoped to find, though, eluded him. There was no map, nothing that would tell him where the hell he was. The only printed materials he turned up were two vintage Russian paperbacks and a stack of out-of-date magazines. He tried not to let his disappointment get him down.

Glancing at his watch, he tried to estimate how much more time he had before daybreak. His best guess was that there were a couple of hours left. Once the sun was up, and he had done his quick look around outside, gathering whatever additional supplies there were, he would head out. Staying any longer was out of the question. He had to keep moving. Sitting still meant capture. And capture meant death.

In order to keep moving, though, he needed heavy outerwear. Not only was his coat gone but there was no way his boots were going to be dry by sunrise. The trapper, on the other hand, was fully outfitted.

By all appearances, the man had either been on his way out of the cabin or back in when he sat down by the fireplace and died. He was wearing an anorak, hat, mittens, leggings, and boots, all of them made from reindeer fur.

As respectfully as possible, Harvath lifted the trapper from the chair and moved him to the bed. There, he worked quickly.

While he didn't mind stripping dead Spetsnaz soldiers, this felt different. It felt wrong somehow.

Be that as it may, he didn't have a choice. This was about survival—something no longer relevant to the deceased trapper.

After removing the man's clothes, Harvath solemnly wrapped him in one of the remaining blankets and, after observing a moment of silence, placed him outside.

"Thank you," he said before closing the door. "I owe you."

Returning to the fireplace, he saw that his water had come to a boil. Using a thick piece of cloth to protect his hand, he removed the saucepan by its handle and set it aside. Filling an infuser with loose leaves of black tea, he placed it in an enamel mug and poured the water over it.

The tea had a distinctly smoky aroma, which was popular across Russia. It was referred to as *Caravan* tea.

It was originally imported from China via camel train, and the smokiness was caused by exposure to caravan campfires over the tea's eighteen-month journey. In the modern era, drying the leaves with smoke created the flavor.

The closest comparison was Chinese Lapsang Souchong—a tea Lara loved, but whose name Harvath had always felt sounded too pretentious for him to say. Literature professors could order Lapsang Souchong. Navy SEALs? Not so much.

That didn't mean he didn't enjoy drinking it. Whenever Lara made it at home, he was happy to have a cup, especially in fall or winter. The rest of the time, though, he was strictly a coffee guy.

Lara loved to tease him about it, often when they were out with friends. Reluctantly, he would admit to drinking tea, but only the "chai" popular in the Muslim world, and only because it was part of Islamic culture and therefore part of his job when overseas.

As the steam rose from his mug, he closed his eyes and could see Lara standing in his kitchen. She had a row of hand-painted tins lined up on his counter, each with a different kind of tea. Making him close his eyes, she liked to hold different ones under his nose to see if he could guess what they were. The only one he ever nailed consistently was the Lapsang.

Remembering her frustration brought a smile to his face. But it was immediately wiped away by a tidal wave of guilt.

Never again would he be able to tease her, or hold her, or tell her how much he loved her. She was gone, and it was *his* fault.

Looking down into his tea, he wished the cup was filled with something stronger—much stronger. Something that would allow him to forget, if only for a little while, what had happened.

"How does a Russian," he wondered aloud about the dead man, "even in the middle of nowhere, not have a bottle of vodka?"

He waited, but of course the man outside didn't answer.

Walking over to the cupboard, Harvath attempted to identify the cans of food.

As best he could tell, there were carrots, beets, potatoes, and something that might be pickled cabbage. They offered some nutritional value, but not much. He tried not to think of all the food he had lost in the river.

Instead, he worked on being thankful for what he had—the cabin, a fire, and dry clothes immediately came to mind.

Looking over at the corpse, he also realized that he was thankful to be alive. He wasn't out of the woods, not by a long shot, but he was alive. And as long as he was alive, there was hope.

But hope for what? *Escape? Revenge?* Were those the only things worth living for?

He neither knew nor cared. It was his training and his instinct to survive that were pushing him, dictating what should be done next.

There was a kerosene lamp hanging from one of the rafters. Taking it down, he gave it a shake and sloshed the liquid around inside. *Full.*

He set it on the table next to the shotgun and walked over to the fireplace for the matches. *Small tasks,* he reminded himself. *Small victories.* That was the key to staying positive and staying alive in a survival situation. Everything came down to attitude. With the right attitude, anything was possible.

Adjusting the wick, he lit the lamp and lowered its glass chimney. It was amazing how much light it produced. Out of caution, he decided to drape the blankets over the windows. Even the flame from a lone, flickering candle could be seen from miles away.

Returning to the table, he emptied the box, as well as the shotgun, and examined each of the shells. They were the correct gauge, and all appeared to be in good shape.

After placing them aside, he fieldstripped the shotgun, cleaning and lubricating it as best he could with the materials he had available.

It didn't require much work. The Baikal's owner had taken good care of it. Reassembling the weapon, he loaded it and leaned it up against the wall.

Brewing another cup of tea, he dumped a can of potatoes into the saucepan. And as he got to work on breakfast, he tried to keep his mind on being thankful.

Once the sun was up, there was no telling what his day was going to bring.

CHAPTER 23

WASHINGTON, D.C.

Spies who stayed in the game too long tended to make mistakes. Artur Kopec had been in the game too long.

The old spy was on his last posting. It was a plum assignment for the Agencja Wywiadu, Poland's foreign intelligence service. Based in the Polish embassy, he enjoyed official cover and diplomatic immunity, which was why Bob McGee had put Nicholas in charge of snatching him.

To his credit, Kopec didn't fight. He was too old, too tired, and too out of shape to put up any resistance.

To *his* credit, Nicholas had done the deed himself and had shown up in person. Along with him, of course, were his dogs, as well as several of The Carlton Group's top operatives.

It was a sign of respect, something Kopec appreciated. Why, though, the little man had gone to such extremes was beyond him. He was old friends with Reed Carlton, quite enamored with Lydia Ryan, and fond of Scot Harvath. A call suggesting any of them needed anything would have brought him to their offices posthaste.

Nicholas, though, had a shockproof bullshit detector. And now that he knew who Kopec was, he knew he was full of it.

Yesterday, when McGee had asked to meet with Nicholas in Lydia's office, it wasn't just so they could be more comfortable. In case anything ever happened to her, she had given her former boss and mentor the code to her safe. Inside was an array of sealed envelopes, hard drives, paper files, journals, and binders full of information.

Removing one such binder, McGee had handed it to Nicholas as he explained who the Polish intelligence operative really was.

Codenamed Matterhorn, Artur Kopec was one of America's greatest weapons against the Russians.

He was a double agent. He worked for Poland, but his deeper loyalty was to his paymasters in Russia. Over the years, he had grown rich feeding Moscow sensitive intelligence, particularly about NATO and its member states.

Reed Carlton had uncovered him, but instead of turning Kopec in, he had convinced the United States to turn the Polish spy to their advantage.

The two had worked together on multiple allied assignments and had developed a strong affinity for each other. There was even trust between them. But once the Pole's duplicity had become known, all of that was over.

Carlton being Carlton, the experienced spymaster had figured out a way to use their friendship to his advantage. Not only did he maintain his relationship with Kopec but he also continued to share information with him.

For the plan to be successful, though, the information had to be authentic and, at times, even damaging to NATO and the West. It was the only way to ensure that Moscow continued to place high value on the intel the Pole gave them. Which was exactly what had happened.

Kopec was considered a source of such high quality that eventually his reporting was briefed directly to the Russian President himself. He was their "golden bird." Carlton had built a covert pipeline right into the Kremlin.

It was quite a feat. But Carlton hadn't stopped there.

In an effort to rattle the Russians and to erode confidence in their sources, he had leaked the existence of Matterhorn. It wasn't anything in great detail, simply that a high-level Western asset being run by Russian intelligence as a double agent was actually a triple, feeding them bogus information.

It drove the Russians crazy. None of their intelligence operatives knew who had the rotten source. They wasted countless man-hours interrogating their assets, fraying relationships, and creating an all-around toxic environment of distrust and suspicion.

The best thing about it was that Kopec didn't even know he was being used. No matter how many times his handler had quizzed him, his answers had never wavered. No one in Russian intelligence had any reason to distrust him.

So, having survived the crucible, Matterhorn had become even more valuable to both Russia and the United States.

This meant that whatever Nicholas decided to do with him, he had to be very careful.

"Wait," the little man had said, confused. "How is this my call?"

In addition to the binder on Matterhorn, McGee had removed one additional item from the safe—an envelope with McGee's name on it.

Inside was a cover letter from Ryan, along with a sheaf of legal documents signed by Reed Carlton.

Nicholas had always assumed that if anything happened to Lydia Ryan, leadership of the organization would pass to Scot Harvath. And if anything happened to Harvath, control would pass to the company's Chief Financial Officer.

Based on the documents McGee now showed him, he had been right on the first two candidates in the line of succession, but when it came to the third, Carlton had someone much different from the CFO in mind.

Nicholas was stunned. "He wanted me to take charge? Of all this?"

"He obviously thought you were up to the task."

Nicholas didn't know what to say. He didn't actually need to say anything. Carlton had shown tremendous faith in him. McGee knew Nicholas wouldn't disappoint any of them—especially Harvath, whose life depended on the decisions they needed to make.

The moment Nicholas had revealed that Kopec had been at the safe house, McGee had his answer to who had been behind the attack. It was the Russians. He was certain of it. But before he could move forward, they needed proof, and Kopec was the key.

Nicholas and McGee had then discussed strategies, some more radical than others. Each posed considerable risk.

In the end, Nicholas chose the least elegant but most direct path.

They didn't have time to screw around. Harvath was worth a thousand Matterhorns.

Now, here he was, face-to-face with Kopec—two master craftsmen, skilled in the art of deception.

Nicholas, with his short, dark hair and close-cropped beard, stared at the jowly, clean-shaven Pole, with his white hair and bulbous nose.

Physically, they couldn't have been more different, but appetite-wise, they had much in common, which was exactly how Nicholas had lured him out into the open.

As a diplomat, discretion was top of the list for someone like Kopec. With only a couple of hours of hacking, Nicholas had been able to learn that in addition to being overweight, the Pole suffered from alcoholism and cataracts, and had a two-pack-a-day smoking habit, high blood pressure, high cholesterol, and symptoms indicative of the onset of diabetes.

The only reason the Polish government didn't know this was that he was bribing a doctor to keep all of it out of his official file and away from the attention of his supervisors.

Artur Kopec was a man with many secrets—exactly the kind of target Nicholas liked. Secrets were vulnerabilities, points upon which pressure could be applied and, if necessary, into which blades could be thrust.

For the moment, though, they wanted Kopec to believe that despite the manner in which he had been picked up, he was safe, among friends.

"I don't understand," said the Pole as he was shown into Lydia's office. Nicholas then commanded the dogs to lie down, and the guards were dismissed.

"Neither do we," the little man responded, walking over to the bar cart. "Vodka?"

Kopec nodded. "Neat."

Nicholas prepared their drinks and, as he had done with McGee, handed both to his guest as he leaped up onto the couch to join him.

"I'm sorry for the drama," said the little man as he reached out and accepted his glass. "You were being watched."

"I was? By whom?"

"*By whom*? Everybody. Do you not know what has happened?"

Kopec looked at Nicholas, completely clueless. "I have no idea."

This time, the little man believed him. "Reed and Lydia are dead."

"*Dead?*" he replied, shock written across his face. "What happened?"

"We don't have all the details yet. I understand you went to visit Reed not too long ago?"

"Is that why I'm here?"

Nicholas took a sip of his drink and nodded. "There's video of you leaving his cottage in New Hampshire shortly before the murders took place."

"*Murders?*" he replied, even more agitated.

"Along with his nurse and Harvath's wife."

"Harvath was married?"

Nicholas nodded. "They had gotten married earlier that day, before you arrived. Harvath wanted to do it before Reed had fully slipped away."

"He didn't mention it."

The little man smiled. It was good to have Kopec on record as having been there. "Harvath isn't much of a talker," he replied. "More of a doer."

Kopec sat expressionless, drink in hand. "What happened to him? To his wife?"

"The wife is dead. Reed's nurse is also dead."

"Oh my God. I'm so sorry. What about Harvath?"

"We don't know. That's what I was hoping you could tell us."

The Pole looked at him, confused. "Me?"

"Like I said, *everybody* is looking for you, Artur—the FBI, CIA, DSS, all of them. But they didn't find you. I did."

"Is that good?"

Nicholas smiled again. "I think you can end up being the hero in all of this. There could even be a White House visit and possibly a Presidential Medal of Freedom."

It was an attractive offer, and one that appealed to his vanity, but it would take a lot more than a medal and a visit with the American President to pay for the villa he wanted in the south of France.

That required cash, and lots of it—which was where the Russians came in. As long as he continued to do what he was told, they would continue to keep the money flowing.

Those payments were his retirement plan. He had no intention of taking a flamethrower to the goose that laid the golden eggs.

"There's no need for a medal," he replied. "All I want to do is help."

For an intelligence operative, Kopec was a terrible liar. Nevertheless, Nicholas played along. "Who knew you were going up to New Hampshire?"

The Pole pretended to think for a moment. "Everything was coordinated through Lydia. I assumed she and Harvath were the only ones who knew."

"Did you tell anyone else about the trip?"

"No," Kopec replied with a shake of his head. "Not a soul."

More lies.

Nicholas wanted to put a bullet in him. Or, better yet, he wanted to set the dogs on him, wait for his confession, and *then* put a bullet in him.

But that wasn't what he and McGee had agreed to. If nothing else, Nicholas was a man of his word. It was time to stop playing games.

Removing a folder from behind one of the cushions, he handed it to Kopec and said, "There's something we need to talk about."

CHAPTER 24

The Alakurtti Air Base was located near the southern boundary of the Murmansk Oblast, fifty kilometers from the Finnish border. It was home to Russia's Fourth Naval Bomber Regiment and the 485th Independent Helicopter Regiment.

General Minayev was already waiting for Teplov when his enormous cargo plane from Ukraine touched down and taxied into the hangar.

Though it was a highly secure military airfield, Minayev preferred to keep the presence of the Wagner mercenaries as quiet as possible. Not even a ground crew had been allowed inside.

When the aircraft's loading ramp dropped, the first thing the General saw was Teplov.

He was the picture of an elite Russian commando—tall and muscular, with thick veins that snaked under his skin like ropes. His body was marbleized with scar tissue, a testament to his years of combat.

Calling out orders to his men, he stepped down the ramp and greeted Minayev. "What's the latest?"

"Follow me," the General replied, returning the mercenary's salute.

At the rear of the hangar was a large ready room that had been temporarily converted into an operations center. It was staffed by a handful of trusted GRU personnel Minayev had brought along from Moscow.

Tacked to one of the walls was a large map of the Murmansk Oblast. A grid, marked out in red grease pencil, defined a search area. Teplov helped himself to a cup of coffee and then stood back to study the map.

"What are we looking for?"

"One of our transport planes," said Minayev, picking up a picture of the Antonov An-74 aircraft and taping it to the wall next to the map, "took off from Murmansk two days ago and disappeared in bad weather."

"No emergency beacon?"

"It carried a manual beacon. Never activated."

"What was this plane transporting?"

The General picked up another photograph, this one of a man in restraints, and taped it beneath. "An American intelligence operative."

Teplov looked at the name under the photograph. "Scot Harvath. Should I know him?"

"The Kremlin knows him. That's all that matters."

"What can you tell me about him?"

Minayev handed over a file. "It's all in there. Most important, he's a former U.S. Navy SEAL with advanced winter warfare training."

"So is this a rescue or a recovery operation?"

"You won't know until you get there."

Eyeballing the search area again, the mercenary replied, "If that's your haystack, I'm going to need a lot more men."

"Our biggest problem has been the weather. All aircraft have been grounded, but now the storm is beginning to pass. We expect the search to start within the next couple of hours. Once the plane has been located, you and your men will be sent in.

"Your job is to ascertain the situation on the ground, report everything back to me, and then await further instructions."

Teplov nodded as he skimmed through Harvath's file. "Out of curiosity, who was accompanying the prisoner?"

"A four-man GRU Spetsnaz team."

"Led by whom?"

"Kozak."

The mercenary looked up from the file. "*Josef* Kozak?"

Minayev nodded. He knew that the two had not only served together but were also good friends. In fact, it was a rather poorly kept secret that when Teplov had started Wagner, he had done all he could to woo Josef away from the GRU to come work for him. "I'm sorry," the General offered.

"Don't be sorry," he replied. "Josef Kozak is one of the toughest, meanest bastards I have ever known. You don't write off a man like that without a corpse. Trust me."

Minayev agreed. Josef was one of his best operatives. The chances, though, of surviving a crash, much less the brutal conditions in the Oblast, weren't very high. "I have two helicopters standing by—Arctic Mi-8s. One will be for cargo, the other for personnel. As soon as we get word, I want you and your team in the air. I don't want to waste any more time."

"Yes, sir."

"And no matter what you encounter on scene, there is only one objective: *Harvath*. Everything and everyone else is secondary. If he's alive, bring him back alive. If he's dead, I want the body. Is that clear?"

"Completely."

Minayev paused to make sure he had the mercenary's undivided attention. He even addressed him by his call sign. "Understand me, Wagner. There is absolutely no room for error. When you reach for a tool, it had better be a scalpel and *not* a fucking hammer. This isn't Syria, Ukraine, or Venezuela, where you're being sent in to spill blood and break things. This is Russia, and this assignment is a national security imperative. Work quickly, work quietly, and above all else, do not fail. Because if you do, I personally guarantee that it's the last thing you will ever do."

CHAPTER 25

First light found Harvath fed, dressed, and caffeinated. After his breakfast of potatoes, he had indulged himself in a cup of coffee before putting on all of the dead trapper's outerwear. The clothing was snug, but warm.

Outside, it was still windy and snowing, but less so than before. Visibility was improving.

Harvath had walked only a few feet from the cabin when he began to make out the contours of another structure set farther back. From it, he could hear a faint rattling that resembled wind chimes.

He was careful to maintain his bearings. If the weather took a turn, he didn't want to lose his way back. His survival training had been replete with tales of people who had gotten lost in the snow, only to freeze to death feet away from their shelters.

The drifts were deep and difficult to trek through. It was hard to know how much had fallen since he had arrived, but it had to have been several feet.

As he neared the structure, he could finally take it all in. It was more a shed than anything else. Long, narrow, and leaning to one side, it was constructed of the same wooden planks as the cabin.

Hung from the roofline at the front were strings of bleached-white bones and broken antlers. The wind banged them into each other, like some sort of haunted xylophone.

The rough-hewn double doors were unlocked. Pushing one open, he ducked beneath the low frame and stepped inside. Just as he had suspected, it was the trapper's workshop.

It was cluttered with junk, the floor stained with blood. Even in the deep cold, the space smelled earthy and stale.

In addition to a small cast-iron stove, there were two workbenches, one under each of the shed's dirty windows. Upon them were all manner of tools, traps, and skinning accessories. Underneath were crates and boxes. A pile of animal pelts sat stacked in the corner.

Harvath took out the old flashlight he'd found in the cabin and began searching the place in earnest.

Halfway through, hanging on a peg, he made an incredible discovery—*snowmobile keys*. He didn't waste any more time in the shed. If there was a snowmobile somewhere outside, he didn't want to wait to find it.

Tucking the keys into his pocket, he put the fur mittens back on and stepped back outside.

Next to the shed was a lean-to. It was nothing more than an additional piece of roofing supported by poles. It was open to the elements and a large drift had piled up beneath it. Harvath began scooping away the snow, most of which was powder.

A couple of moments later, he hit a blue plastic tarp. Working the edges, he kept digging until he had removed enough of the snow to peel it back. Underneath was the trapper's sled—a Finnish brand of utility snowmobile known as a Lynx Yeti.

After fully removing the tarp, he straddled the machine and unscrewed its gas cap. He rocked the sled from side to side and listened to the fuel sloshing around inside. It sounded like about half a tank, maybe less. Replacing the cap, he made sure the kill switch was engaged, inserted the key, and attempted to turn it over.

Snowmobile technology had come a long way. The Yeti had a four-stroke engine with grip-warmers, a two-speed gearbox—which included reverse—a twelve-volt power outlet, and an electric starter. Unlike sleds of old, there was no pull cord.

Under optimal circumstances, push-button starters were a breeze. When circumstances were less than optimal, though, you started having problems.

No matter what Harvath did, he couldn't get the machine to start. In fact, he couldn't get any signs of life out of it whatsoever.

Opening the front housing, he made sure nothing was missing and that everything was connected. It all looked good. The only thing he could think of was that the battery was either too cold or was completely out of juice. As with the body of the dead trapper, there was no telling how long the snowmobile had been sitting here.

Removing the battery, he took it back to the cabin to warm up, and then returned to the workshop to continue his search.

The effort turned out to be more fruitful than he had hoped. Hidden in all the junk were some real finds. In addition to spools of wire for snare traps, there was a container of smoked bear meat, a pair of old wooden snowshoes, and a small, plastic bin containing electronics.

Popping the lid, he removed a small Russian GPS device, a portable battery booster, a flexible, portable solar panel, and several different cords.

He tried to power on the GPS, but it was dead. The battery booster was dead, too. Taking a look out the window, he tried to ascertain how much power he'd be able to pull with the panel. Probably not much, but it was worth a try.

Before leaving the shed, he used what wood was available to start a small fire in the cast-iron stove. He needed it good and warm inside for his plan to work.

Returning to the cabin, he set up the solar panel outside, facing south. Then, running its cable back through the window, he attached it to the portable battery booster. Whether it would work or not, only time would tell.

He put another log on the fire and then went back to the shed. Under the lean-to, behind the snowmobile, was a woodpile. He made three trips.

Once he had a good stack next to the stove, he used the trapper's axe to split the logs into small enough pieces that they would fit inside.

That was the easy part. Now he turned himself to the hard part, dragging the snowmobile into the shed.

If the trapper owned a shovel, Harvath couldn't find it. He looked everywhere, but there was no sign of one.

Alternating between a decrepit Russian broom and a splintered piece of plank, he cut a path through the deep snow. It was a colossal pain in the ass.

His body was already aching from everything he had been through. More exertion only made it worse.

Dragging the sled was something straight out of the Labors of Hercules. The fucking thing just didn't want to move.

He talked nicely to it. He talked dirty to it. He threatened it, cajoled it, and made it wild promises. He picked it up in back and dropped it. He picked it up in front and dropped it. Hitting it in the middle, he rocked it from side to side.

Then, all of a sudden, it slowly started to move.

The burn of snowshoeing had nothing on dragging the Yeti. Whereas that burn had been largely confined to his legs and hips, now everything was on fire, including his arms and especially his back. It was like doing all of his least favorite gym exercises—squats, rows, deadlifts—all at the same time.

With each pull on the snowmobile, he let out a loud grunt, then paused, sucked in another breath of freezing-cold air, and repeated the process all over again.

His progress was painfully slow, but inch by muscle-searing inch he got the sled to where he wanted it to be.

At the entrance to the shed, he allowed himself a moment to sit and rest. As soon as the voice in his head suggested he close his eyes for a few seconds, he got back to his feet. Throwing open both doors, he dragged the snowmobile the rest of the way into the shed.

He pulled it as close as he could to the stove and then gave up. "That's as far as I'm willing to go on the first date," he said, closing the doors and walking back to stoke the fire.

Having been exposed to a possibly long bout of extreme cold, the Yeti could have other problems beyond a dead battery. But getting the sled warmed up would make it that much easier to start.

As he loaded more wood into the stove, he wondered how visible the smoke was from its stack. With the weather starting to lift, the Russians would be itching to get search planes into the air. He was still way too close to the wreckage for comfort.

The one thing he had going for him, though, was that the storm had erased his tracks. There was no way they'd be able to track him. They'd have to send men in every single direction.

It seemed highly unlikely, but until a few days ago, so did the idea of the Russians kidnapping him on U.S. soil.

Closing the stove door, he remembered the blue tarp outside. Perhaps wood smoke wouldn't be noticeable, but a bright blue sheet of plastic had a good chance of catching a pilot's attention.

Exiting the shed, he walked around to the side and gathered up the tarp. It was there that he noticed something sticking out of the snow right next to the woodpile, something he hadn't seen earlier because he was so focused on the sled. The trapper did have a stash of vodka after all.

He bent down and pulled one of the bottles from the drift. It was a cheap Siberian vodka from Surgut, but it was still vodka.

First a snowmobile, now booze. If the GPS was operable, he had hit the better-to-be-lucky-than-good Triple Crown. But if his years in the field had taught him anything, it was that things usually got worse, often much worse, before they ever got better.

CHAPTER 26

Bouncing back and forth between the shed and the cabin wasn't very efficient, but both fires needed to be tended. Unfortunately, even with the cast-iron stove going full blast, the poorly insulated workshop remained drafty and quite cold. So cold, in fact, that Harvath was concerned about whether he could sufficiently warm the snowmobile. Without taking it apart, there was no way of knowing what if any damage had been caused by the extreme arctic air.

The battery, though, seemed to be doing better. Resting near but not too near the fireplace, its temperature had greatly improved.

Outside, the sun had grown more visible as the storm died and the clouds began breaking up. That meant good news for the solar panel. Though all it needed was daylight, direct sunlight packed the biggest punch.

Not wanting to drain a moment of energy from the booster pack, he resisted the urge to turn it on and check its meter. He figured, at best, he was going to get one shot with it. The challenge was to pick his moment. If he tried too soon, he could blow all his gains. But if he waited too long, he was going to lose precious time.

Once search aircraft were airborne, their number-one goal would be to find the crash site. As soon as the site was located, a rescue team would be launched. But until the Russians had done a thorough search of the wreckage and the surrounding area, no one would be looking for him. That meant he had time; the only question was how much.

The other person they'd be looking for was Josef. For all he knew, the man was lying dead only a few hundred yards from the plane. Not that it mattered. One man or two, the search was going to be intense. Of that, he was positive.

On his first trip back to the cabin, he had downed several cups of melted water from the pail. Shoveling snow and dragging a snowmobile, he had worked up a powerful thirst. He had also worked up a powerful appetite.

Slicing up some of the bear meat, he placed it in the saucepan with a can of carrots and some more water. It wouldn't be the best meal he had ever eaten, but he had eaten worse—much worse.

Placing the saucepan near the fire to heat, he got to work loading up the gear he'd be taking with him. It didn't take long, as there wasn't much to pack. Everything went into a sturdy canvas rucksack he had discovered in the workshop.

After zipping over to the shed to check on the fire there, he returned to the cabin, tested his "stew," and decided to pour himself a drink.

Among the kitchen items he had found was a small etched glass. No doubt the trapper had used it for the same purpose Harvath was now. Unscrewing the cap, he filled it with ice-cold vodka.

The spirit burned going down, but it was followed by a numbing warmth that quickly spread to the rest of his body. The vodka was the closest thing he'd had to a painkiller since popping the two Russian aspirins back at the wreckage.

He was covered in bruises and lacerations from the beatings he had taken. For the most part, he had been able to ignore the pain. It was when he sat down to rest that it was inescapable. The vodka, though, helped, and he poured himself another glass.

Two would have to be the limit. He was still in extreme danger. Deadening his senses any further would have been a big mistake.

Alcohol was also a depressant, and the only thing that came racing back into his moments of rest more acutely than his physical pain was his anguish.

One drink was bad enough. Two, though, and his walls would start to lower. Abetted by any more vodka, he knew it was a steep, slippery slope into a dark, emotional pit. The luxury of guilt and self-loathing was a gift he'd give himself once he made it out of Russia—and only after he gave Lara, Lydia, and the Old Man the gift of revenge.

Sipping on the second vodka, his listened to the logs crackle in the fireplace. It was a sound that often put him at ease, something he associated with home. But not here. Every snap, every hiss and pop of the wood was amplified, a reminder that sand was slipping through the hourglass.

For someone experienced in making life-or-death decisions in the heat of battle, the indecision about when to attempt his escape was an almost unbearable weight. The snowmobile, the solar charger, and the GPS unit had been strokes of unbelievably good fortune, but only if he used them successfully. If he fucked this up, he deserved whatever happened next.

As soon as the thought entered his mind, he pushed it out. That kind of thinking, fueled by his pain and exhaustion, would get him killed. He needed to stay focused. Small achievements. Small victories.

Crossing to the fireplace, he stirred the contents of the saucepan and reminded himself of every positive thing that had happened. Even after he lost everything in the river, there had been more waiting for him on the other side.

The trapper and his cabin had offered up a shotgun, dry clothes, food, and a snowmobile with the potential to get him to the Finnish border. Though it presented its own set of challenges, his situation was unquestionably better now than it had been when he had first set off from the wreckage. He was going to make it, but only if he kept his head straight. *The only easy day was yesterday*, he reminded himself.

Removing his bear meat stew from the fire, he set it aside to cool and checked the temperature of the battery. Not that it would have made any difference, but it would have been nice to know how long it had been since its last charge. When your mind was fighting to remain positive, chalking up items in the *good news* column was like piling up gold in a vault.

As he prepared to eat, he drained the vodka from his glass and set the bottle outside the door in the snow. Even though he had an almost iron will, he didn't want the temptation. Out of sight, out of mind—at least for now.

The older the bear, the gamier the meat. With his first bite, he could tell he was in old-age territory. There were a lot of ingredients that might have improved the taste—Worcestershire sauce, balsamic vinegar, even orange juice—none of which he had. But instead of focusing on the terrible taste, he tried to remain grateful for the nourishment and focus on what his next steps were going to be.

The snowmobile didn't have a full tank of gas, but he had found one jerry can of reserve. Unless there were others he had missed, it had to be enough fuel to get the trapper to civilization. If he could get the sled started, and with it the GPS, he hoped to definitively answer the question.

But civilization didn't mean redemption. Civilization represented opportunity. Depending on how far it was to Finland, he could either revert to his original idea of stealing a car, or, if he could handle the prolonged cold, steal enough gas to get him to the border. Either way, fuel was going to be an issue.

Driving up to a gas station was out of the question. It didn't matter that one of the things not lost in the river was the currency he had taken off the dead Spetsnaz operatives. He had to avoid all interactions. It took only one grocery store clerk, one hotel manager, or one gas station attendant to blow the whistle on him. His SERE trainers had been adamant: Only mix with locals as an absolute last resort. And when you do, don't mix, but rather disappear among them.

Harvath knew a few things about the Russians. They were tough and proud, more enamored of their past than their future. Their "best" days as a nation were always those behind them, never those yet to come. The desire, among the very young and the very old alike, to return to Communism was startling.

That said, there was an overall distrust of, and even a disdain for, government. It was well-placed.

Little had changed in Russia since the collapse of the Soviet Union. The country was still being run as it had been during the Cold War. But instead of a Politburo, a handful of former KGB people now controlled everything, and they used that control to line their own pockets at the expense of the Russian people.

The contempt that Russians had for their government only grew the farther you traveled from Moscow. Out in remote areas, the evidence of the Kremlin's failures was everywhere: lack of basic services, crime, corruption, and desperation. Across the country, standards of living, life expectancy, and literacy were all decreasing.

Russian President Fedor Peshkov and his cronies had grown astronomically wealthy by raping the country. It was a modern kleptocracy. They lived like royalty, and there was nothing the average Russian could do.

Every election was rigged, and those journalists, dissidents, or political opponents of Peshkov who did stand up were quickly knocked down, or worse.

In Russia, you learned not to question Peshkov or his allies. Survival existed along one path—the path of least resistance. No one in today's Russia had ever taken on the government and survived, much less won.

But as much as the citizens of Russia detested Peshkov, Harvath was under no illusion as to where their loyalties lay. Their pride came from a deep sense of nationalism, something Peshkov was expert at manipulating.

Not a week went by that he didn't accuse America of being the source of his nation's woes. It was straight out of the Soviet playbook.

An ex-KGB man himself, Peshkov was masterful at pointing the finger overseas in order to distract from his problems at home. If he didn't continually blame "capitalism" or "American arrogance" or "American imperialism" or any of the other bogeymen he laid at the feet of the United States, the Russian people might start wondering if he and his government were to blame for their crappy existence.

On the run in almost any other nation, Harvath might have been more hopeful of soliciting aid from sympathetic locals. The history of snitching, even on family members—along with the consequences for not snitching—were so entrenched in the Russian psyche, though, that it barely seemed worth considering. An American evading authorities represented only one of two things: a big reward, or a big punishment.

And even the most clueless Russian, in the deepest of the sticks, was wise enough to know what would happen if they didn't do right by the powers that be.

With that in mind, Harvath's plan was simple: stay out of sight and as far away from civilization as possible. The only exception was for supplies, and even then, his search would be limited to the very outskirts of any town or village.

Cleaning out the saucepan, he put on water for tea. While it heated, he would check the situation in the shed. There was one thing more he needed to add to his supplies before he could leave.

CHAPTER 27

The final item Harvath was missing was a length of tube or a hose—anything that would allow him to siphon gas from any vehicles he found along his way. Short of stumbling across full cans that he could just up and run with, this was his plan for replenishing fuel.

Without having powered up the GPS, he had no way of knowing how much fuel he was going to need. His goal was to stop as infrequently as possible—get in, get what he needed, and get going. That was the plan. Whether it would actually work remained to be seen.

After an extensive pass back through the workshop, Harvath found neither a hose nor any tubing. That was a problem. "Hoping" to find a siphon somewhere along the way was stupid. Hope was not a plan.

Think, he admonished himself. There had to be something. Then it hit him. He already had a length of tubing back in the cabin.

Stoking the cast-iron stove, he picked up an old water bottle he'd come across and headed back. Once inside the cabin, he opened the plastic bin and pulled out the wall cord for the booster pack. The rubber insulation was, in effect, nothing more than a four-foot-long tube.

Fully cutting off the end that plugged into the booster, he then carefully sliced through the insulation at the other end, making sure not to cut through any of the wires inside. Then he placed the plug on the floor, stepped on it, and pulled off the insulation.

It worked perfectly. He had his tubing.

Though he would have preferred a much wider pipe through which to siphon, it was better than nothing.

Opening the toolbox, he removed a sharply pointed awl, probably used to poke holes in leather. Unscrewing the cap from the 1.5-liter water bottle, he pierced a hole through it and then widened it with a screwdriver. He only needed it to be slightly narrower than the insulation tubing.

Screwing the cap back onto the bottle, he threaded in one end of the tubing and smiled. That was it. He'd done it.

In order to give his siphon a test, he placed the water pail atop the fireplace mantel. Into it he placed the free end of the tubing. Holding the water bottle below the mantel, he began to squeeze it.

He heard bubbles in the pail and then seconds later saw the bottle begin to fill with water. He couldn't believe it. It was slow, but it actually worked.

Without the water bottle, he would have been forced to suck on the tubing himself. That only ended one way—with a mouth full of gas. It wasn't necessarily fatal, but it was a level of miserable that no human being should ever have to experience. This was yet another small victory, and he was proud of it. He took it as a sign that he was going to make it, that the snowmobile was going to start and he was going to get the hell out of here.

Draining the tube and bottle, he returned the pail to where it had been and brewed another mug of tea—likely his last one for a while.

He had everything he needed at this point, and it was time to move. The storm had all but passed, and that meant planes were likely already in the sky looking for the wreckage. Half of the day's light was already gone. The sooner he got going, the better. Adding a few more items to his canvas rucksack, he began transferring all of his gear, including the snowmobile battery, to the workshop. The last thing he did was to disconnect the booster pack, coil up its cable, and retrieve the solar panel.

Before exiting the cabin, he extinguished the fire and gave the place a final inspection—a "dummy check," as they called it in the military—to make sure he wasn't forgetting anything.

Confident that he had everything, he brought the trapper's corpse back inside and placed it gently on the cot. Standing there, he thanked the man once more. If not for what he had built and stored here, Harvath probably wouldn't have made it.

Stepping outside, he made sure to close the cabin door firmly behind him. The trapper deserved to rest in peace, not to have his door blown in and his corpse turned into a carrion feast.

Back at the shed, he installed the snowmobile battery. Making sure the kill switch was firmly attached, he turned the key and hit the starter. *Nothing.*

Getting out the booster pack, he attached the jumper cables to the corresponding battery terminals. Taking a deep breath, he powered on the booster pack.

For a moment, nothing happened. Then, the green charge level lights began to cycle. *Power!*

Reaching for the snowmobile's start button, he applied pressure. Instantly, the machine roared to life.

Harvath couldn't believe it. It had worked. *All* of it. He let out a cheer.

This wasn't a small victory, it was a *huge* victory. It felt as if he had been injected with a syringe full of adrenaline. Instinctively, he grabbed for the throttle and revved the engine. The growl was music to his ears.

He sat there for several more moments, revving the engine and charging the battery back up.

Once he felt comfortable enough, he unclamped the booster, closed the engine cover, packed everything up, and opened the double shed doors.

Returning to the sled, he gave it some gas and navigated out into the snow. He drove slowly, getting a feel for the machine as he warmed up its engine and pumped life into the battery. Then came the real moment of truth.

Coming to a stop, he removed the GPS unit from inside his anorak. Plugging it into the twelve-volt outlet, he powered it on and snapped it into the holder above the handlebars.

It took a moment for the device to make satellite contact, but once it did, Harvath's chance of survival skyrocketed.

He had a topographic picture of everything around him: what his elevation was, where the river ran, and multiple waypoints selected by the trapper, which likely marked the position of his traps. But more important, as Harvath zoomed out, he could finally pinpoint his location.

He was in a densely forested area north of the Arctic Circle, more than 120 kilometers from the Finnish border. According to the GPS, the nearest inhabited area was forty kilometers away. After that, it was nothing but ice, trees, and snow for farther than the eye could see.

Marked on the trapper's digital map with what looked like the Russian word for "home," the town didn't appear to be much more than a provincial backwater. That was a good thing. Such a small, out-of-the-way location probably wouldn't have much of a law enforcement presence.

As Harvath prepared to get going, there was one critical piece of gear he hadn't been able to find in the cabin or the workshop—eye protection. Snowmobiling through the bitterly cold wind with no goggles, or even sunglasses, was going to be painful. There was also the possibility that if he pushed it too hard, he could damage his vision. But he had zero choice. It was a chance he was just going to have to take.

Though he hadn't yet seen any search planes, he could almost feel them closing in on him from above.

Hopping off the sled only long enough to extinguish the fire in the stove and close the shed doors, he hopped back on and let the GPS be his guide. The feeling of power and movement was exhilarating, but so, too, was his very real sense of fear.

He had at least seventy-five miles to go. A lot could happen over the course of those miles. He was by no means home free. Not yet. That wouldn't be the case until he had safely crossed the border into Finland. And at this point, he still had no idea how that was going to happen.

Would it be by snowmobile? If so, how much ground could he cover before it got too cold to keep going and he had to stop for the night? Was stopping for the night even an option? No matter how bad the cold was, didn't it make sense to push on? But once the Russians did start looking for him, wouldn't the beam from his snowmobile headlight, cutting through the darkness, give him away? And, if he did decide to stop for the night, what if the snowmobile refused to start again in the morning? What then? He couldn't expect to stumble across another abandoned cabin within snowmobile-dragging distance.

His best bet was to steal a car, or a truck of some sort. Actually, his best bet was to steal a car or truck that had a trailer, onto which he could load the snowmobile. He wasn't going to be crossing at any official border checkpoint. The more remote the location, the better his chances, and that meant no roads and lots of snow. Like it or not, the sled was his key to getting out of Russia.

Nevertheless, he knew circumstances, more than anything else, were going to dictate how everything would go down. It was the nature of what he did for a living. You couldn't control everything. In fact, you couldn't control most things. What made him an exceptional operative was his ability to change from moment to moment and adjust to the facts on the ground. He was an expert at adapting and overcoming. No matter what happened, no matter what was thrown at him between here and the Finnish border, he would adapt and overcome. Success was the only option.

With its wide, specially designed skis and higher-profile track, the Yeti was built for deep snow.

Hunching low, to keep as much of his face as possible behind the short windscreen, he prepared to punch the gas. But all of a sudden, he saw a flash of movement out of the corner of his eye.

Before he knew what had happened, he was struck from behind and knocked off the sled. Then a new pain began.

CHAPTER 28

The Hostage Recovery Fusion Cell was buzzing with activity. Normally, a presidential "hostage" briefing would take place at the White House. President Paul Porter, though, wanted to thank the men and women of the Fusion Cell personally.

There were fifty of them, drawn from across a broad spectrum of government agencies, working together to achieve one common goal—bringing a very important American home safely.

Each of the desks in the war room–like setting represented a different agency: Treasury, Justice, State, Defense, CIA, NSA, DHS, and others. Their job was to draw in information from their respective organizations and share it with the other team members, thereby developing the most current, accurate picture possible.

Overseeing the operation was Special Presidential Envoy for Hostage Affairs, or SPEHA, Brendan Rogers.

Rogers was a hard-charging former Navy JAG officer turned corporate attorney who had turned over his practice to his partners when the President had asked him to accept the SPEHA position. Though it was a pretty significant pay cut for a man in his late forties with a hefty mortgage and two kids in college, he had never said no when called upon by his country.

To be honest, Rogers relished the challenge. Interacting with some of the world's worst dictators and bad actors was exciting. They ran the gamut from despotic regimes to criminal cartels and terrorist organizations. Getting Americans safely back home to their families was more rewarding to him than any litigation he had ever prevailed in.

Though he went to some absolute shithole places and carried out some of the toughest, most tension-filled negotiations anyone had ever seen, he loved the job. And part of the reason he loved it so was that he was good at it. He hoped, for Scot Harvath's sake, that his winning streak continued.

Since accepting the SPEHA position, Rogers had helped secure the release of more than twenty-two Americans held in such places as North Korea, Iran, Venezuela, Afghanistan, Chechnya, and Mexico. Harvath's situation, though, was extremely difficult.

After the President had thanked everyone out on the floor, the principals adjourned to a secure conference room for the Harvath briefing.

Rogers knew the President was a detail guy who liked to ask questions, and he had prepared a detailed update.

"Mr. President," he said. "Again, let me welcome you to the Hostage Fusion Recovery Cell. I know I speak for the entire team when I tell you what an honor it is to have you here. We have some of the best, brightest, and most patriotic people working in government here. Your recognition of their commitment to bringing American hostages home safely is much appreciated."

"It's the least I can do," replied the President. "I know you all have been working around the clock. Why don't you bring me up to speed."

"Yes, sir," Rogers stated. On his laptop, he activated a piece of video and projected it on the monitors around the room. "This is security footage from the day of the attack. It comes from the neighbor across the street from the safe house on Governors Island. We've sped it up, but here you see former Deputy Director of the CIA Lydia Ryan arriving, followed later by Scot Harvath and Lara Cordero. Later that day, a black Lincoln Town Car shows up. That's where I'd like to start."

Porter nodded, and the SPEHA continued. "The Town Car was carrying a lone male passenger. He has been identified as a Polish intelligence officer working out of their embassy here in D.C. His name is Artur Kopec, and apparently he had prior relationships with Lydia Ryan and Reed Carlton. As you can see, Kopec gets out of the car, goes into the cottage for about three hours, exits the cottage, and leaves via the Town Car.

"It has been explained to me by DCI McGee that Kopec is a known Russian asset. The Russians, though, are unaware that we possess this information. Therefore, CIA wants this knowledge, and the man's identity, kept a secret." Looking over at CIA Director McGee, he sought clarification. "Is all of that correct?"

"Yes," replied McGee.

The President piped up with his first question. "Would it help if the rest of your team knew the man's identity?"

Rogers thought about it for a moment. "We're a clearinghouse for intel and analysis. That's why we exist. Is it imperative anyone outside this room know who the man is? I can't say, but the more information they have, the better they can do their jobs."

Porter looked to his CIA Director. It was obviously an invitation to chime in. "Kopec is highly valuable. However, getting Harvath back is our top priority. If we have to burn Kopec in the process, we're prepared to do that. He might, though, be able to help us."

"How?"

"We're working on it," McGee responded. "All that matters is that we don't want to burn him if we don't have to."

"But we're confident that he's the leak?" asked the President. "We're certain he's the one who revealed the location of the safe house and led the hit team there?"

"We're one hundred percent confident that he provided the information," Nicholas replied. "Whether he knew what was going to happen after providing the information is still being looked into."

Porter glanced at his FBI Director. "Where is he now?"

Militante, who had no idea, shrugged. The President then turned to McGee, who gave a quick shake of his head as if to say, *You don't want to know*.

It was Nicholas who stepped back in and ended the line of questioning. "Let's just say we have eyes on him and he's not going anywhere."

Before the President could ask another question on the subject, Rogers advanced to a new series of photos and picked back up with his briefing.

"So the team kills everyone in the house but Harvath. One of them, who may have been wearing Harvath's watch, gets in Harvath's rental car, drives to the end of the driveway, and throws Harvath's cell phone out the window, then drives off.

"Based on other cameras we were able to collect footage from, the rental car crosses the bridge from Governors Island to the mainland, makes a beeline for the interstate, and heads north on I-93. It was later abandoned near Franconia Notch State Park, about seventy-nine miles south of the Pittsburg-Chartierville Border Crossing. Which brings us to the secondary vehicle, the one we believe the hit team used."

The SPEHA brought up a new series of pictures and videos and continued speaking. "Kopec flew commercial from Reagan National to Portland, Maine, which is about ninety miles away from Governors Island.

"He was met at the Portland airport by a car service with instructions to bring him to the cottage on Governors Island. FBI has interviewed the driver, but he wasn't much help. He says the passenger was pleasant enough, but that's about all he remembers. They drove in silence most of the way there and back. The passenger made a few phone calls in a foreign language, which the driver couldn't place. He thought it sounded Eastern European."

"What about the second vehicle?" Nicholas asked.

"Panel van, rented at the Portland airport the day before," said Rogers, as he picked back up with a video feed from the counter. It showed a tall, muscular man in his late thirties. "He presented a credit card, proof of insurance, even an American driver's license—all of which, we know now, were fakes. Highly sophisticated, backstopped fakes, but fakes nonetheless.

"The next day, this panel van can be seen on multiple cameras. It begins by following the Town Car from Portland airport all the way to Governors Island. When the Town Car turns into the safe house driveway, moments later you can see the van drive past and keep going. Unfortunately, wherever it came to a stop and parked, none of the other homes there have cameras.

"Then, several hours later, as Harvath's rental car is seen leaving the island and heading north, the panel van is about ten minutes behind it. U.S. Customs and Border Patrol found it abandoned the next day, less than a mile from the border.

"At that point, the trail went completely cold. Even the Canadians were unable to generate any leads. Then they got a hit on the car rental counter footage we sent them. Two days ago, a private jet left Montréal-Trudeau International. Someone at the Canadian Security Intelligence Service decided to go back, sweep FBO security footage, and run it through facial recognition. Our car renter popped up, along with four other men. At that point, they were traveling on Finnish passports with several large pieces of luggage, a couple of which could have been used to smuggle Harvath on board. They had—"

"But no one saw Harvath," interrupted the President.

"No, sir," replied Rogers.

"Okay, continue."

"The jet's crew had filed a flight plan for Ivalo, the northernmost city in Finland. Considering the number of people on board, plus the fuel capacity, it was at right about the outer range of the aircraft. According to the Finnish government, the plane was forty-five minutes from its destination when the pilot radioed in a change. They claimed they were going to St. Petersburg, Russia, instead—but that's not where they went."

"Where'd they go?"

"A bored Finnish air defense officer continued tracking the aircraft. It ended up landing in Murmansk."

"What's in Murmansk?" the FBI Director asked.

"Lots of polar bears and terrible food," Nicholas replied.

"Do we have any satellite imagery?" asked President Porter. "Any visuals on who got off that plane?"

"No, we didn't have anything on station," Rogers answered. "Even if we had, a severe weather system was beginning to build, and it would have been difficult to get definitive imagery."

"So that's it?"

"Not exactly. After we received the FBO footage from Canadian Intelligence, we shared it with our other Five Eyes partners. MI6 came back with a hit."

"What kind of *hit*?"

"Four of the men were identified as active Spetsnaz soldiers. The fifth, though, is the most interesting," explained Rogers as he brought up a photo. "Meet Josef Ilya Kozak. Also Spetsnaz, but, more important, a colonel in Russian Military Intelligence—specifically, the GRU's special missions group."

The President stared at the man's picture. He had a drawn, gaunt face, punctuated by dull, lifeless eyes. The photo looked as if it had been snapped at the moment the man's soul had been taken from his body. He had a disturbing aura about him. It wasn't cruelty. It was more than that. The man looked evil. Everyone in the room sensed it.

"So," said Porter, "if I may?"

"Of course," replied Rogers, ceding the floor.

"We have Kopec, a known Russian asset, who was followed to the safe house by at least one, and presumably more, Russian Special Forces operatives. In the house, four Americans are brutally murdered and one goes missing. Two vehicles associated with the attack are found abandoned, one very near the Canadian border. A private jet with Special Forces operatives, including a GRU colonel, posing as Finns leaves Montréal, allegedly headed for Finland. Then forty-five minutes before touchdown, the plane claims to be diverting to St. Petersburg, but lands in Murmansk once it believes the Finns are no longer paying attention to it. Do I have that about right?"

"Yes, sir," answered Rogers. "But there's something else. It may not be connected, but considering what we know, it could be. And if it is, it's big."

CHAPTER 29

The scene from the air was horrific. The plane had torn a jagged scar through the forest and landed in three broken pieces on the edge of a clearing. There were no signs of life on the ground.

When the two black-and-neon-orange helicopters touched down, Teplov was the first off. From the moment the call had come in that the plane had been located, the hairs on the back of his neck had been standing up. He had no idea why. For some reason, his sixth sense, honed over decades in battle, was trying to warn him.

He divided his men into groups. His team took the tail section. Just before they were about to make entry through the rupture in the side of the fuselage, they found a body—or at least what was left of one.

Because of the shredded uniform, it appeared to be one of Josef's Spetsnaz operatives. The man had been torn apart, and the skin covering the top of his head was missing. Who or what had done it, he had no idea. Pulling the butt of his rifle into his shoulder, Teplov cautiously led his men into the plane.

Immediately upon entering, he saw four scalps hung along a thick piece of wire, and the hair on the back of his neck stood up even further. It was like something out of a horror movie.

Just in front of them, a cargo container appeared to have been turned into a temporary shelter. His men searched inside, but it was empty. Behind the container, though, they found two bodies.

The first was one of the flight crew. His legs had been pinned beneath the container and his pants were stained with blood. Wrapped around one of his thighs was a makeshift tourniquet. It was hard to tell if the man had fashioned it himself or if someone had done it for him. Regardless, what was apparent was that he had bled out.

Next to him was another of Josef's Spetsnaz operatives. As with his colleague outside, his scalp had been removed, but his body was still intact. Again, he was uncertain if the operative had frozen to death, died in the crash, or suffered some other fate.

Around them lay the carcasses of several wolves. They were large, but underweight.

It had been one of the longest, most brutal winters in memory. There were stories of starving wolf packs banding together in hordes to attack villages and even towns. Polar bears, unable to find food, had done the same. Throughout the Murmansk Oblast, Russians were living in fear of coming face-to-face with one of these vicious, wild creatures.

Suddenly, the radio crackled to life. From the front section of the wreckage came a report that the pilot and copilot had been found in the cockpit, burned beyond recognition.

The team in the middle section reported two corpses as well. The first was a flight crew member who had been shot. The other was a man with an apparent broken neck. He had been stripped of his clothes and his scalp had also been cut away.

Teplov didn't need to see the body to wager that it was another of Josef's Spetsnaz operatives.

Heading deeper into the tail section, one of his men found a set of empty shackles. Then, they found the body of the fourth and final soldier.

The man's face had been caved in, beaten to a congealed, bloody pulp. Looking at the blood spatters along the interior of the fuselage, it was obvious that whatever had been used to bludgeon the man, the killer had swung the weapon in wide arcs and with extreme force over and over again. It was an act of excessive violence, an act of pure rage. His scalp was also missing.

The scalps had been a message. Someone was taking revenge. That someone was Harvath.

Getting on the radio, Teplov ordered two of his best shooters to break off their search of the wreckage and get to the helicopters. Unless he was lying dead somewhere out in the snow, Harvath was already on the run. And while he might have had a head start, Teplov had both superior numbers and superior equipment. Harvath wouldn't stay hidden for long. Teplov was going to find him.

CHAPTER 30

Harvath's mind instantly went into fight mode. He had landed hard on his rucksack, with his chest and stomach fully exposed. He looked like a turtle that couldn't right itself.

The large jet-black alpha wolf had come out of nowhere. It ripped and tore at him, sinking its long, sharp teeth into every part of his body that it could.

Using one arm to fend off the massive beast, he tried to reach for the shotgun, but it was pinned underneath him. The animal seemed to sense what was happening and intensified its attack, going for Harvath's throat.

Drawing back his free hand, Harvath delivered an uppercut, punching the wolf right underneath the jaw. He followed it up with a strike to the side of the animal's head. He did it again and again and again.

He kept punching until the beast jumped off him and backed away. Harvath knew that the retreat was only temporary. It would last just long enough for the wolf to shake off the pain and then come back at him. He would have enough time to make only one move.

Getting to his feet was out of the question. He would have to fight from the ground.

In the fraction of a second that it took for him to commit to what he was going to do and make ready for the attack, the animal struck again.

On his belt, beneath the trapper's anorak, he had hung one of the dead man's best knives. It was long and incredibly sharp, and when the wolf leaped at him he drove the blade in all the way to hilt, just below the creature's breastbone.

The alpha, though mortally wounded, fought back viciously. It seemed determined to kill the man who had taken so many of its extended pack.

As the wolf slashed at him and tried to clamp its jaws around his throat, Harvath twisted the knife and drove it even deeper into the animal's chest cavity. Slicing open its left ventricle, he drove his knee up into its belly, grabbed a fistful of the scruff around its neck, and yanked its mouth away from his neck.

Rolling to his left, he pushed the dying animal off him. He was covered in blood, though whose, he had no idea. Before he could assess his injuries, he had a bigger problem to deal with—the rest of the pack.

He had been so focused on the alpha that he hadn't even noticed the others. Now that he could risk a look, he saw that they had him surrounded. Growling, their mouths dripping with saliva, they appeared ready to attack. None of them, though, were making the first move. With their alpha dead, they were waiting for a new alpha to step up and take charge. Harvath took full advantage of the situation.

Pushing himself up onto his feet, he unsheathed the shotgun, pointed it at the nearest group of wolves, and blasted away. And as soon as the first wolves dropped, he took off running.

He hadn't attached the snowmobile's kill switch cord to his clothing, nor had he wrapped it around his wrist. When the wolf had attacked, he had been revving the gas. When he had gotten knocked off, the sled had rocketed forward.

That was both a blessing and a curse. It was a curse because now he had to struggle through deep snow to get to it, but it was also a blessing, in that he could hear it was still running.

Turning, he cycled the shotgun and fired, then pumped and fired again, killing two wolves that were right behind him and practically biting at his heels.

As the animals fell, Harvath turned back and jumped onto the sled. It had come to a stop with its nose jammed against a tree. Throwing it into reverse, he backed up and fired again at the wolves. Then, tucking the hot shotgun beneath his leg, he turned the Yeti's skis, slammed the gear selector into forward, and pinned the throttle.

He risked one look over his shoulder. The issue of who would be the new alpha seemed to have settled itself. Another enormous black wolf was leading the chase after him. It was unbelievable how fucking fast they were. Harvath gave the snowmobile even more gas.

Eventually, they receded into the distance. But even then, he kept going full speed for quite some time.

When he finally felt it was safe to stop, he did so. His eyes were burning, and as they teared from the wind, the tears turned quickly to ice. It was as if somebody had sprayed bleach in his face. It hurt like hell.

He needed to assess his injuries, which was difficult because he had so much of the alpha's blood on him.

In addition, he knew the wolf had punctured his clothing several times and had succeeded in injuring him. The question was, how badly.

Reloading the shotgun and laying it over the handlebars, he removed his anorak and examined his new wounds. They were bad.

He had bite wounds to his chest and abdomen, as well as a gash along his upper left arm that was bleeding heavily. He attended to the bleeding first.

Dousing the wound with vodka, he selected the cleanest piece of clothing in his rucksack and used it as a bandage, securing it in place around his arm with duct tape.

Next he focused on the bite wounds. The first thing he did was to gently press on them to encourage bleeding. It was counterintuitive, but bites from dogs and wolves were often highly infectious. Encouraging the punctures to bleed was supposed to help flush out the bacteria.

As he had with the gash on his arm, he then cleansed the wounds with vodka and covered them with small pieces of cloth, which he held in place with duct tape.

By the time he carefully put the anorak back on, his body was trembling with cold.

He helped himself to a long slug of the multipurpose vodka before returning it to his backpack and securing the shotgun where he could get to it quickly if he needed to.

Off in the distance, he thought he could make out the sound of a helicopter. It was hard to hear over the noise from the Yeti's engine. He didn't dare shut it off, though, for fear that he wouldn't be able to start it again.

If there were helicopters in the area, that meant they had likely found the crash site. And if they had found the crash site, they had found the dead Spetsnaz operatives and everything else he had left behind. If they weren't already looking for him, they would be soon, and a helicopter would all but guarantee they'd find him—unless he could get out of sight.

He needed to get to that town on the GPS, find someplace to hole up, and figure out how he was going to get across the border.

He also needed antibiotics. Eight hours was the window. If he waited any longer than that, the risk of infection multiplied.

If he got stuck hiding someplace, even out in the wilderness, while waiting for a search party to pass and he got sick, he could die before he ever saw Finland and freedom.

Fuck, he thought to himself. Siphoning gas was risky enough. Stealing a vehicle was even more dangerous. But trying to get his hands on medicine? That was a whole other set of problems he didn't need. He had a serious decision to make.

Hitting the gas, he decided to wait until he got to town to settle on a plan.

CHAPTER 31

He stayed in the trees as much as possible. Using the thick tree cover, he hoped to hide himself and the snowmobile's tracks. He also made sure to keep the sled's light off. Whenever he thought he heard a helicopter nearby, which was happening more and more often, he would seek cover and come to a full stop. Nothing attracted the human eye like movement. The harder he could make it for the search teams, the better.

When the helicopters were out of range, he would gun the snowmobile, covering as much distance as possible as quickly as possible. As he arrived at the outskirts of the town, the sun had already begun to set.

It was bordered by a wide river, which wasn't iced over. There was one bridge on the southernmost edge of the town. He could either hide his snowmobile in the trees on this side or take it across and try to find someplace on the other side. He chose to take it across.

As the light faded, the already frigid temperatures continued to drop. On one of the streets up ahead he saw the headlights of a passing vehicle. Other than that, the only visible lights were from inside houses where locals were preparing dinner.

Harvath assumed that, as in Alaska, in such a remote area, a snowmobile passing through town didn't even warrant a second look. And even if someone did glance outside, they wouldn't have been able to see much of his face, bundled up as he was in the trapper's fur outerwear.

As he moved past houses, he kept his eyes open for opportunity—

cars left running, dwellings that were uninhabited, as well as gasoline and other supplies. He also kept his eyes peeled for anything resembling local police or military.

Not only did the fading light provide him a certain level of camouflage but it also helped hide the bloodstains covering his anorak. One good, clear look at him would have raised a ton of questions. Better no one see him at all. That was the way he preferred it—especially now.

Making his way through the snow-covered back streets, he kept on the lookout for signs of a pharmacy or doctor's office—even a veterinarian's would have done the trick.

Like the surrounding landscape, the town was bleak. If hopelessness were an actual color, this place would be all fifty shades of it.

It was exactly what he pictured when he thought of life during the interminably long, dark winters north of the Arctic Circle. He was astounded by the fact that the Finns could be so close, yet so different. The Russian psyche did not lend itself to upbeat, sunny optimism. The sooner he was out of here, the better.

More important than where he could steal the antibiotics he needed was where he could stay warm and hidden for the night. Though he had kept his eyes peeled for signs of an uninhabited dwelling, he wasn't finding any. Every home appeared to be spoken for.

If the trapper had a primary residence in town, it wasn't marked on the GPS. Following the signal, it led Harvath to a sparse, central square with a rundown, kitschy, tropical-themed café. Its mascot was a pelican wearing a parka.

Behind the frost-covered windows, he could see people drinking and having a good time. Though he could barely make it out over the noise from his engine, it sounded as if there was music playing as well. No matter how bad the weather was, alcohol and other people tended to make things better. It was a comfort that he would need to remain a stranger to.

Pushing through the town center, he found what he was looking for on the other side. It was a drab, one-story building that billed itself as a medical "clinic." As best he could tell, the clinic practiced family medicine, specializing in infants to senior citizens, and also handled "minor" dental emergencies. There was a number to call for appointments, as well as one for after hours. Harvath drove his snowmobile around back.

There had been no vehicles in front, nor were there any at the rear of the building. None of the lights were on, either. It looked as if everyone had left for the evening.

Figuring he could hike back to the café and steal a car if he needed to, Harvath decided to shut off the snowmobile's engine. Erring on the side of caution, though, he broke out the spare jerry can and filled the sled's gas tank. The needle had been hovering just above empty since he arrived. *Be prepared* was more than just a motto in his book. It was a way of life. There was no telling what kind of an exit he might have to make out of town. Better to do it on a full tank of gas.

After tucking the GPS and its power cord into his rucksack, he did a quick sweep of the building for alarm sensors. Not seeing any, he knocked on the back door. When no one answered, he raised his boot and kicked it in.

The frame splintered and the door gave way. Pushing the pieces of wood back in place to hide the damage, he gathered up his rucksack and shotgun and then hurried inside, carefully closing the door behind him.

For several moments he stood and listened. There was no one there but him.

The heat must have been turned down for the night. It was quite chilly inside. Locating the thermostat, he turned it way up. Somewhere, an old furnace groaned noisily to life. The place reeked of antiseptic.

There were two examination rooms, a small procedure suite, a break room, a waiting room, and a front office. Starving, Harvath hit the break room first. He helped himself to a yogurt and a bottle of Sprite Cucumber he found in a small refrigerator.

In a cabinet above the sink were tea, coffee, sugar, and two tins of cookies. He grabbed all of it and stuffed it into his pack. Then he headed for the procedure room.

Careful not to alert anyone outside to his presence, he kept the lights off and used only the dull-beamed flashlight he had taken from the trapper's cabin. It was enough to see by, and that was all that mattered.

Along the near wall was a medical storage cabinet. He gave the handle a try, but it was locked. Removing a screwdriver from his rucksack, he pried it open and shined his light over the contents.

Reading the contents of canned goods or IRPs was the absolute outer limit of his Russian vocabulary. That meant deciphering the Cyrillic names of medicines was completely out of the question. He didn't have a clue what he was looking at.

The last thing he wanted to do was ingest or inject himself with something that not only wouldn't help but could very well make things worse. There had to be some way to figure this out. Picking up the shotgun, he headed toward the front office.

It was an enclosed space that sat behind the counter facing the waiting room. It looked like any other doctor's office or minute clinic he had ever been to. And like those places, it had a computer.

As backward as it was, Russia had a high level of connectivity to the Internet, even in some of its most remote areas. If he could get online, he could not only search for the correct spelling of the drugs he needed but also send a covert message back to the United States for help.

The moment he sat down at the computer he realized that he was out of luck. The keyboard was completely in Cyrillic. *Damn it.*

Leaning back in the chair, he tried to come up with a plan. He knew how to read a handful of words only because he had memorized them, not because he had learned the Cyrillic alphabet. But maybe, like a Rosetta stone, it might be enough. He had to give it a shot.

Pressing the Power button, he waited for the decades-old computer to boot up.

Once it had, he was greeted with another disappointment—a password request.

He tried 0000 and 1234, neither of which worked. He turned the keyboard over, hoping to find a sticky note with the password. There was nothing there. He opened the desk drawers. Nothing still. He ran his hand under the desk and came up empty.

It was a doctor's office, albeit a Russian one, so he shouldn't have been surprised that they took computer security seriously. He was going to have to figure out another plan.

Standing up, he walked over to a long bookshelf and, aided by his flashlight, studied the titles. In the era of Google Translate, the likelihood of finding an English-Russian dictionary to help with translating medical articles was basically zero.

His pessimism was proven correct. Every book, textbook, journal, and manual was in Russian. There was only one other thing he could think to do.

Unlike clinics back in the United States, this one still relied on paper charts. Opening one of the many office file cabinets, he grabbed a stack of charts, carried them over to the desk, and set them down.

There was a particular word he knew the Cyrillic for. His friend Nicholas, who had grown up speaking Russian, used it all the time: собака. Dog.

The only reason he could imagine the word appearing in a medical file would be because a patient had been bitten. Nine out of ten times, oral antibiotics would be prescribed. Only in cases where it wasn't known if the dog had been vaccinated would a course of rabies injections be necessary. He felt confident that if he could find one dog bite case, or, better yet, two, he could figure out the name of the medication he was looking for.

Before he started reading the files he opened a large, leather ledger sitting next to the phone. It was the clinic's appointment book. As each day wrapped up, someone had drawn a slash through the date. Based on what he could understand, the first appointment was tomorrow morning at 0800. That gave him literally all night to wade through the files if he wanted. It was more than enough time.

Taking off the anorak, he made himself comfortable. There had been a small task lamp in the break room, and he went and got it. Draping a dishtowel from the break room over it, he was able to dim the light enough that he felt comfortable using it to work by. He had no idea how much juice was left in his flashlight, nor how long his search was going to take.

Just like American doctors, Russian doctors had terrible handwriting, too. Using a blank piece of paper, he went through line by line. He was about a quarter of the way through the files when he found what he was looking for.

Two brothers had both had some sort of incident with a dog. Their charts were right next to each other. In both cases they had been prescribed антибиотики.

Harvath was pretty certain this was what he was looking for. After writing the word down on the blank sheet of paper, he headed for the medicine cabinet in the procedure room.

But when he stepped into the hallway, someone was waiting for him. And that someone had a very large-caliber weapon pointed right at him.

CHAPTER 32

W ho are you?" the woman demanded in Russian. "What are you doing here?"

She was dressed in a dark-green down parka, black snow pants, and winter boots. In her hands, she held a bolt-action hunting rifle with a large scope.

Harvath hadn't even heard her come in the rear door, probably because the furnace was so loud. Stupidly, he had his shotgun over his shoulder. At this range, if he reached for it, she'd put a hole in him so big you could drive a tank through it.

Keeping his hands where she could see them, he held out the piece of paper with the word *antibiotic* written in Cyrillic.

"Who are you?" she repeated.

"I am not a threat," he replied in his broken Russian.

"Last chance," she stated, as she took a tighter grip on her rifle. "Who are you?"

"*Menya zovut* Scot." *My name is Scot.*

"What are you doing here? Why did you break into my clinic?"

She was going too fast. He couldn't understand what she was saying. "My Russian is terrible. Please. Do you speak English?" he asked.

Moments passed as she tried to decide whether she wanted to engage with him in his language rather than hers. Finally, in English she said, "What are you doing in my clinic?"

"I'm injured."

"I can see that. You have blood all over you. Why did you break my door?"

"I'm sorry. I needed medicine."

"So you just broke in?" she replied.

"You have every right to be angry."

"Of course I do. This is *my* clinic."

"Again, I'm sorry, but—"

He had begun to lower his hands and she stiffened, applying pressure to the trigger. "Keep them up," she commanded.

Harvath put them back up. "I'm not a threat. I won't hurt you."

"Is that so? Then why don't you tell me why my uncle's snowmobile is parked outside, why you're wearing his clothes, why you're carrying his shotgun, and why you're covered in blood?"

Harvath was stunned. "The fur trapper? He was your uncle?" He could see some resemblance in her face, a hint of Sámi around the eyes—but not much.

She was blonde, with high cheekbones, a thin, delicate nose, and full pink lips. She looked more Caucasian than anything else.

"What do you mean *was*?" she demanded. "What happened? What did you do to him?"

"Nothing," Harvath insisted. "He saved my life. Unfortunately, I couldn't do the same for him."

The woman, though obviously distraught at hearing a family member had passed, kept the gun pointed right at him, waiting for him to continue.

"I was in a plane crash. The only survivor. I can't even remember how long I was walking before I found your uncle's cabin, but I was on the other side of the river. When I tried to cross, I fell through the ice and almost drowned. Somehow, I made it inside and was able to start a fire before I passed out. When I woke up, I realized he had been sitting in a chair near me the entire time, but it was only what remained of him. He had passed away days, maybe even weeks before I arrived at the cabin. I don't know what happened. Maybe it was a heart attack or something like that. All I know is that it's because of him that I'm alive."

"And the blood? Are you actually injured? Or did that come from someone else?"

"May I?" he asked, gesturing that he wanted to lift up his shirt and show her.

She nodded, and Harvath lifted up his shirt. With his free hand, he began peeling away the pieces of duct tape that had been covering his bite wounds.

Her eyes grew wide. "What did that to you?"

"Wolves."

"That explains the bite marks, and perhaps the bruising was suffered during the crash, but it doesn't explain the lacerations. They look like they were caused by some sort of a whip, like you have been tortured."

Harvath lowered his shirt but didn't respond.

When he failed to provide an explanation, she pressed him. "I still don't understand why you had to break into my clinic. The evening telephone number is written outside. You could have stopped anyone in town and they would have brought me to you. Why do this?"

It was the moment of truth. Harvath had to decide if he was going to bring her into his confidence or not. His espionage training, all of the lessons the Old Man had drilled into him, told him to lie. His gut and his hard-won experience, though, implored him to tell her the truth. He decided to go with the truth.

"Three days ago, maybe four, my wife was murdered and I was taken captive. Two other people I cared for very much were also killed. The men who did this put me in shackles and loaded me onto a plane. When we landed in Murmansk, we changed planes. It was the second plane that crashed."

The woman didn't believe him. "Something like that would have been all over the news. Whenever a boat or plane goes missing, they always ask us to keep an eye out—especially our woodsmen, the hunters and trappers."

"If your government is anything like mine, the flight would have been kept very quiet," he said. "It would have been off the books."

"Why?"

"Because sending a team to kidnap an American citizen on American soil is an act of war."

She didn't know how to respond. It was an absolutely outrageous claim, but nothing about the man's demeanor suggested he was lying. In fact, he struck her as serious. *Deadly serious.*

"What did you do that made them take such a risk?"

Harvath shook his head. "It's a long list."

"Name one thing."

"The suicide bomber that leaped the fence and detonated just outside the White House, did you hear about that?"

"Yes. It was a Muslim terrorist."

Harvath kept going. "How about the assassination of the American Secretary of Defense in Turkey?"

"Also Muslim terrorists."

He smiled. "All Muslims, yes. But they were recruited and trained by the same man. He had been a student at Beslan during the terrible school siege and hostage crisis. His father had been the principal, his mother an art teacher.

"After it was all over, Moscow had combed through the survivors. They had interviewed all of them. It was an experiment of sorts. Their hope was that the trauma those students had experienced could be weaponized. Only one child showed any promise, and he was off the charts.

"They poured everything they had into training him. He worked with all of the best Moscow had to offer—spies, Spetsnaz, everything. I heard someone refer to him as Russia's Jason Bourne. It's a bit of an exaggeration, but he was incredibly valuable to the GRU."

"What happened to him?" she asked.

"I tracked him down and then put him in a deep, dark hole."

"And so that's why you were kidnapped?"

He shrugged. "That's just one reason. There are plenty of others—things that never made it into newspapers or onto television. Like I said, it's a long list, but what connects them all is me. I have a tendency to prevent Moscow from getting what it wants."

There was a beat, and then the woman said, "Good," as she lowered her rifle.

"Good?"

"You have your reasons for not liking Moscow. So do I."

"What do you mean by that?"

"I have lost someone, too," she said, coming in for a closer look at his wounds. "My husband."

"I'm sorry."

"Don't be. He knew what he was doing."

"How did he die?"

"He was a medic for a mercenary group. He was killed fighting in Syria—a place I don't think Russia should ever have been. But the Kremlin was paying his company a fortune.

"I told him that I didn't care about the money, that I didn't want him taking such risks. He had other plans, though. He wanted us to move to Moscow. He planned to open a private security company with a couple of his friends. But he couldn't do it without the money. And now he's dead, and I'm alone."

"I'm sorry about your uncle as well," Harvath offered.

"Thank you. But back to what you're doing here," she said, changing the subject as she had him lift his shirt back up. "Your plan was to break in here, steal some antibiotics, and then what?"

Harvath winced as she touched the skin near one of the punctures. "I don't know. From what I can tell, we're not far from the Finnish border."

The woman shook her head and smiled. "In these temperatures? It may not look far on a map, but there aren't enough reindeer skins in the entire Oblast to keep you from freezing to death out there."

"It's a plan," he replied, trying to ignore the pain and smiling back. "I didn't say it was a good one."

Lowering his shirt, she took a step back and said, "You definitely need antibiotics. I'd also recommend we begin a course of rabies injections. And judging by your other injuries, I believe painkillers would also be in order."

Harvath appreciated her assistance, but there was something he needed even more. "Can you help me get to the border? If you can, I promise to make it worth your while."

CHAPTER 33

After two hours of searching, Teplov's men had found Josef. His back was broken and he was suffering from frostbite and severe hypothermia, but he was alive.

As the transport plane had tumbled through the forest, breaking apart, he had been sucked out. Unable to walk, he had clawed a trench in the snow and had used seat cushions and other debris to insulate himself. Dragging himself inside, he had done the only thing he could do at that point—he had waited for rescue.

When word of Josef's discovery broke over the radio, Teplov had rushed to his friend's location. He was relieved to see him alive, if just barely. The man, though, was hovering on the edge of consciousness and obviously in great pain.

Despite Minayev's earlier orders about the allocation of resources, Teplov redirected the cargo helicopter and two of his mercenaries to transport Josef back to the air base for emergency medical attention.

Before they took off, Teplov tried to ask him if he knew what had happened and where Harvath might be. Josef was unable to answer.

Shielding his face from the hail of crystalline snow, he stood back and watched as the helicopter lifted off and disappeared into the distance.

The revelation that Josef was still alive had only deepened his resolve to track down Harvath. A couple of hours later, they had a lead.

As the area was so heavily wooded, Teplov and his team had to be dropped some distance away and snowshoe in. But it had been worth it.

Inside a cabin, they had found the body of an old Sámi with a blanket pulled up over his face. His clothes were missing, but in a pile on the floor near the fireplace was a damp Spetsnaz uniform. Harvath had been here.

In addition to helping himself to the old man's clothes and canned food, he also appeared to have helped himself to the Sámi's snowmobile.

Blowing snow had almost completely erased the tracks—only a whisper of a trail remained. Teplov and his men followed it.

A couple of hundred meters into the trees, there was another carnage of wolves.

Several lay dead by what looked like shotgun blasts. Another—a much larger black wolf—looked as if it had been gutted with some kind of blade. The snow was covered with blood.

Marking the direction the snowmobile had taken from there, Teplov radioed one helicopter to go search, and the other, which had returned from dropping off Josef, to pick him and his men up where they had been dropped off.

As they trekked back to the landing zone, Teplov consulted his GPS unit. Harvath was headed west, likely for the border. He had a snowmobile, a shotgun, and a modicum of other supplies. Did he have enough, though, to get him all the way? What's more, what kind of shape was he in?

Considering how far he had come from the crash site and how much havoc he had caused, Teplov decided he was doing well enough to be dangerous.

The only other question he had was how long Harvath had been on the run with the snowmobile. If he could answer that, it would go a long way toward tracking him down.

Night was falling, and Teplov had no idea how much fuel Harvath had. It was going to get much colder. If he was going to resupply or rest for the night, where might he do that?

Teplov consulted his GPS. If Harvath maintained his course, the nearest habitation was a town approximately forty kilometers away.

He had to have known that he would stand out significantly from the local population. Merely putting on someone else's clothing wouldn't be enough to disguise him. The people of the Oblast could recognize an outsider quite easily. That would go double for an American.

Harvath's only chance was to stay out of sight. He would be looking for a farm, another cabin, or some sort of abandoned property where he could get warm and, if need be, get food for himself and fuel for the snowmobile.

At the very least, Teplov now knew how Harvath was traveling and in which direction. That was a dramatic improvement.

Finding the needle was the easy part. Identifying the haystack was where the challenge lay.

But now he had his haystack. All he and his men needed to do was to get out their pitchforks and rip it apart. Scot Harvath didn't stand a chance.

CHAPTER 34

The Gulfstream G650 ER extended-range jet was capable of Mach 0.925, more than seven hundred miles per hour. But, in addition to its speed, its fuel capacity had made it The Carlton Group's preferred aircraft.

Fully fueled, it had a range of seventy-five hundred nautical miles. That meant it could do Hong Kong to New York nonstop. At about half the distance, Washington, D.C., to Helsinki, Finland, was even easier.

In addition to its range and speed, the aircraft was incredibly luxurious. It boasted a premium leather couch, handcrafted oversized reclining seats, sixteen panoramic windows, designer carpeting, fold-out flatscreen displays, LED lighting, a bathroom with a shower, and a full galley with a convection oven, wet bar, and even an espresso machine.

The private plane could sleep ten people and had voluminous cargo space—key requirements when sending a high-end tactical team downrange.

"This is a joke, right?" said the voice of Tyler Staelin as he opened the oven. "Who stocks a seventy-million-dollar plane with fucking pizza?"

The five-foot-ten Staelin was a former Tier One operator from the "Unit," or Delta Force, as it was more popularly known. Hailing from downstate Illinois, the experienced thirty-nine-year-old played double duty as the team's medic. An avid reader, he never travelled with less than three books.

"I did," replied Chase Palmer. "Nobody wanted to take responsibility for catering, so I stepped up. Next time, don't ignore my texts."

A native Texan in his early thirties, Chase looked so similar to Harvath that the two were often asked if they were brothers.

He had been the youngest operator ever admitted to Delta, and his exploits were legendary—filling multiple hard drives at the Department of Defense. His teammates had loosely nicknamed him "AK," for Ass Kicker, but after he had used an empty AK-47 to bluff six enemy fighters into surrender in Afghanistan, it stuck.

"You never texted me," Staelin asserted as he pulled out his phone and scrolled through his messages. When he got to the ones from Chase, his expression changed. "My bad."

"Apology accepted. By the way, there's a warming drawer behind you. You might want to take a peek."

Staelin did, and a smile spread across his face. "Sirloins?"

"You're welcome," Chase replied.

Normally, Harvath handled this stuff. He was a detail guy, and secretly they all believed he was a bit of a control freak. He liked to act as if he didn't care about what anyone thought, but they knew better. Harvath was a good man who cared deeply about the people around him. That was yet another reason why the events of the last several days had been so difficult.

The news that the Old Man, Lydia Ryan, and Lara Cordero had been murdered came as a shock to the entire team. The fact that Harvath had gone missing and that police in New Hampshire were actually considering him a suspect made them all want to throat-punch somebody. Then, Nicholas had called them into HQ for a briefing.

At each seat at the conference table, he had placed a copy of the Old Man's succession plan. Like Nicholas, Carlton had also been a no-bullshit, detail guy.

It was unnecessary. If Nicholas had said "Reed and Lydia are gone. We don't know where Harvath is. Until further notice, I have been left in charge," the team would have believed him.

But because of his dishonorable past, Nicholas often felt unworthy

around them. He respected their courage and integrity, and worked hard
to earn their respect in return. In so doing, he committed to always being
one hundred percent transparent with them, and held nothing back in his
briefings.

After detailing Kopeć's presence at the safe house, how they believed
the murders had unfolded, and then how they suspected Harvath had
been smuggled into Canada and then out to Russia via a private jet, he
began to get into the pertinent details on their mission.

The NSA had picked up chatter about a Russian Air Force transport
plane that had disappeared in bad weather. The plane had taken off from
the same airport Harvath had landed at, shortly after his arrival. While
coincidental, it wasn't conclusive. That's where the next piece of intelligence was so valuable.

Sources in Ukraine stated that right after the plane was reported missing, Kazimir Teplov, head of the Wagner Group, hastily assembled his
best men and flew them, along with a ton of equipment, back to Russia. Specifically, they had flown to Alakurtti Air Base south of Murmansk
and, according to the Finns, were there awaiting orders to begin some
sort of operation. The kicker was that whatever these orders were, they
had to do with the missing transport plane.

"U.S. Intelligence believes Harvath was on the plane that disappeared," Nicholas had revealed. "We believe that Moscow is trying to
keep the situation as quiet as possible, so instead of using active military and law enforcement personnel, they have brought in Russian
mercenaries."

It was one shocking revelation stacked upon another.

The United States Joint Special Operations Command had a quick
reaction force known as a "Zero-Three-Hundred" team on standby in
Germany. They were SEALs from DEVGRU, ready to HAHO jump in
as soon as Harvath's location was pinpointed.

As a demonstration of how serious the President was about getting
Harvath back, U.S. F-22 Raptor all-weather stealth tactical fighters had
been moved to a base in northern Sweden, and an LC-130 Hercules "Skibird" aircraft was being repositioned from Greenland.

The LC-130 was particularly special, as it was equipped with retractable skis, allowing it to land on snowfields, ice fields, and even frozen bodies of water. To assist in slushy snow or for short takeoffs, the Skibird was one of the few aircraft in the world to be equipped with rockets.

If they had to, they were prepared to send the LC-130 into Russian air space, escorted by F-22s, to bring Harvath home.

There was also talk of having the USS *Delaware*, a Virginia class nuclear-powered attack submarine, slip into the White Sea in order to insert an additional covert operations team just off the Kola Peninsula. Everything was being considered. Nothing was off the table.

The Carlton Group's job was to employ a lighter touch. If they could get in, get Harvath, and get out without the Russians' knowing, that was the President's first choice.

Though he would have killed to be on the assignment, Nicholas's physical limitations made him a liability. Snow and rugged terrain disagreed with him.

Besides, his role as de facto head of the organization meant he had to remain in D.C. and act as a liaison with all of the other players, including the White House, the Pentagon, the CIA, the FBI, and the NSA. He was thankful Rogers was helping to coordinate efforts through the Hostage Recovery Fusion Cell.

It had been decided, almost immediately, that a kinetic operation was called for. The Russians were unlikely to give Harvath up, no matter how much diplomatic pressure was applied.

Even so, Rogers had been tasked with coordinating a parallel track. With Nicholas's help, they had come up with an aggressive strategy in hopes of negotiating Harvath's release.

In the meantime, The Carlton Group team would head to Finland and prepare to cross over into Russia.

The passengers onboard the private jet looked like something out of a hard-core action movie.

In addition to Staelin and Chase, there was the former Fifth Special Forces Group operative Jack Gage—a massive six-foot-three man who clocked in at two hundred and fifty pounds. Between his physique and thick, dark beard, he looked like a pirate on steroids, or some sort of professional wrestler. He was a slave to chewing tobacco, a habit he surprisingly hadn't picked up in the Army, but rather growing up in Minnesota, of all places.

There were also two no-longer-active United States Force Recon Marines on the team—Matt Morrison and Mike Haney. Morrison, a thirty-one-year-old from Alabama, was tall, good-looking, and always ready for a fight. His teammates liked to joke that he had been born with the looks of male stripper and the IQ of the pole. It was an unfair characterization, but as they at least recognized his superior physical attributes, he let the rest of their barbs slide.

The other Marine, Mike Haney, was never knocked for being dumb. In the field, the six-foot-tall leatherneck from Northern California was in charge of all their operational technology. Radios, drones, satellite phones—if it had a battery, Haney was responsible for it. At forty years old, with one of the longest service records on the team, he carried a wealth of experience. He was both an exceptional operator and highly skilled as a leader.

Rounding out the team were Tim Barton and Sloane Ashby. Barton had been with the Navy's elite SEAL Team known as DEVGRU, formerly called SEAL Team Six. If Gage was built like a professional wrestler, Barton was built like a college wrestler. He was short—only five feet six—but barrel-chested and absolutely fearless. Whenever the team needed a volunteer, the redhead's hand was always the first to go up. Somewhat OCD, he preferred everything to be in its place—a trait that earned him regular but good-natured ribbing from his teammates.

Sloane Ashby, like Harvath, had been handpicked by the Old Man. The moment he had met her, he knew he had to have her for The Carlton Group. As she was a very attractive blonde in her late twenties, most people never saw past her looks. She had graduated top of her class at Northwestern University, was an accomplished athlete, and had paid her own way through college via the ROTC.

When she enlisted in the Army, she had done so only on the guarantee that she would see combat. She was an amazing soldier. In fact, she had racked up so many kills in Afghanistan that she reached a certain a level of notoriety. The Taliban and Al Qaeda put a price on her head, and a popular magazine did an unauthorized feature on her. As soon as that happened, the Department of Defense pulled her from combat.

She fought to be allowed to go to Iraq, but the answer was an emphatic *no*. Instead, she was sent to Fort Bragg, where she helped to train Delta Force's elite all-female unit known as the Athena Project. It was a waste to put such an exceptional operator out to pasture. When Reed Carlton offered her a chance to get back into the thick of the action, she jumped at it.

Sloane could kick doors with the best of them, and that was precisely what she did. Joining The Carlton Group was one of the best decisions she had ever made. From the moment she signed on, it had been everything the Old Man had promised it would be, and more. She was doing exactly the kind of work she had been born to do.

As the jet raced toward Finland, the team members wandered in and out of the galley to grab food, energy drinks, or cups of coffee. Some slept, some read books, and others watched movies or listened to music.

While there was much of the good-natured back-and-forth they had developed as a team, there was also something missing—*Harvath*.

He was their leader, and it felt not only odd not having him along, but it was also somewhat unnerving. The idea that he, an apex predator who had killed, they liked to joke, more people than cancer, could be captured was difficult to swallow. It meant that he was fallible, human.

He had been Superman to them. But Superman had been captured. And if Superman could be captured, none of them were safe.

They had to get him back—not only because he was their leader but because he was their brother. And because you didn't let the fucking Russians, of all people, kidnap Superman. That wasn't how things worked. Not in their world. If he was still alive, they were going to find him and bring him home.

CHAPTER 35

"**M**r. Ambassador," said SPEHA Rogers as he strode across the office and shook the man's hand. "Thank you for seeing me."

"I'm sorry for putting you off," replied Egor Sazanov. "I didn't want you to come all this way and not have answers for you."

"I practically live at the State Department these days, so I'm not that far away."

The Russian Ambassador smiled. "How about a drink?"

"I'd love one. Thank you."

Rogers and Sazanov had previously worked together when a young American had been taken hostage by a Muslim terror organization in Chechnya. The SPEHA had found him to be a good partner, honest and diligent. He was charming and had an excellent command of English. Rogers could see him as Russia's Foreign Minister or maybe even its President one day.

The Ambassador's office was filled with heavy wooden furniture and dark, sky-blue Kuba rugs from Azerbaijan. Tiny flourishes of gold leaf could be seen along the ceiling. As worldly as the Ambassador was, there wasn't a single book anywhere in the room.

He showed his guest to a seating area and gestured for his assistant to leave them alone and close the door behind him.

Sazanov was a fan of high-end bourbons and still had the special bottle Rogers had given him as a thank-you.

"Ice, correct?" he asked as he uncorked the Pappy Van Winkle's Family Reserve 20 Year.

The SPEHA nodded.

Usually he drank his neat, but he knew that the Ambassador was an ice aficionado.

In addition to his love of American bourbons, the Russian had become quite enamored of the huge pieces of crystal-clear ice served at upscale bars around D.C. He had made it his personal mission to learn how to do it himself. He quizzed every bartender, bought every silicone mold they suggested, and tried every kind of water, from bottled to boiled.

The end product was a perfect cube that looked as if it had been laser-cut from a pristine glacier.

As a Sinatra fan as well, Sazanov had ordered custom rocks glasses with the faux country club logo Frank had designed himself.

It seemed a waste to pour one of the best bourbons in the world over a huge chunk of ice, but Rogers was the consummate diplomat. He thanked his host, they clinked glasses, and each took a sip.

The Ambassador savored it and closed his eyes. "You need to tell me where you found this. I want to send some bottles back to Moscow."

Rogers chuckled. "You don't find Pappy like this. It finds you. Kind of like being struck by lightning."

Sazanov opened his eyes and smiled. "Please. How did you find it?"

The SPEHA decided to give up his secret. "The Vice President knows a private collector. After you were so generous in helping get our citizen back, I asked him to make a call."

"The Vice President of the United States?"

"The man himself."

"I did not know. That is an incredible honor."

Rogers took another sip and said, "If you can help us with our current situation, I think we can help find a lot more Pappy for you."

Instantly, the expression on the Russian's face changed, and he lowered his glass. "I am sorry, Brendan. I went to the very top. We don't have him. No one at the FSB, the GRU, or the Kremlin knows anything about his disappearance."

The SPEHA believed him. More specifically, he believed that's what the Ambassador had been told. In fact, he had expected it.

Taking another sip of bourbon, he set his glass down on the table, removed a folder from his briefcase, and handed it to Sazanov.

"What's this?" the Russian asked.

"A glimpse into what we've been able to piece together so far. I think you should take a look at it."

The man did, starting with a detailed executive summary of what the Americans believed had happened to their operative, Scot Harvath. It was followed by a series of photographs. Attached to each was a short bio. The Americans had identified four Spetsnaz operatives as well as a GRU colonel.

Unless the Americans were lying to him, it appeared his own government hadn't told him the truth. "How did you come by all of this?" he asked.

"I'm sorry, Mr. Ambassador," answered Rogers, "but I am not authorized to discuss sources and methods."

Sazanov closed the folder. "What *are* you authorized to discuss?"

"We'd like to find an immediate and peaceful resolution to this matter. I'm authorized to discuss any steps that might get us there."

"I'm listening."

"Get Harvath back to us in the next twenty-four hours, and we won't ask any questions. Maybe he was taken by a terrorist organization. Maybe he was taken by the Russian mafia. As long as he's returned, we won't challenge the story.

"And just so we're clear, if you want to use a third-party nation— Germany, China, Syria, Belarus, or even the Iranians—we don't care. We just want Harvath back. In fact, President Porter will publicly praise any third party and give them credit, if that's the route you choose to take."

The Ambassador looked at his watch. "I am going to have to make another round of phone calls."

"I understand," said the SPEHA. "But before you do, there's something else I need to share with you."

Withdrawing another folder from his briefcase, the SPEHA handed it to his host. "Your President has approximately forty billion dollars in personal assets hidden outside of Russia. As of twenty minutes ago, half of them have been frozen. Inside that folder, you'll find a full list.

"If Harvath is back to us within twenty-four hours, we'll unfreeze everything. If he's not, your President will never see that money again. What's more, we'll go public so that the entire world, but especially the Russian people, see the extent to which he has pillaged your country."

Sazanov's temper flared. "This is blackmail."

"This is business," Rogers said, stone-faced. "Nothing more. Nothing less. And, to demonstrate that we're not completely unreasonable, if your government provides us with proof of life within the next eight hours, we will unfreeze five billion of your president's assets."

"You don't understand how Russia works. I'm going to get blamed for this."

"You're not going to get the blame. You're going to get the credit. As far as anyone is concerned, unfreezing the five billion in exchange for proof of life was your idea."

The Ambassador shook his head. "Don't throw me your bones. I don't want them."

"Egor, you're a good man. The kind of man Russia needs."

"Excuse me?"

"We think you're someone we can work with."

Sazanov held up his hand. "Wait. What are you talking about?"

"If you help make this happen, the United States will be in your debt."

"In my debt *how*?"

Rogers smiled. "You have a long political career ahead of you in Russia. We want to help you be successful."

"*You* want to help *me*. That's interesting. Okay, I'm listening."

"We can work out the details later, but suffice it to say that there's a laundry list of items your government wants from the United States. Some of which we'd be willing to agree to. We would make sure the press covered you coming and going from the White House. Maybe you and a key cabinet member would be seen golfing. Then you—"

"I don't like golf," the Ambassador replied. "I prefer sailing. Like your President Kennedy."

"That's perfect. The Treasury Secretary loves to sail. The fact is that we could help promote you not only as a diplomat Americans trust but also as someone who helps get results for the Russian people."

Sazanov shook his head. "The Foreign Minister, much less the Russian President, would never allow me to steal their thunder. I could never take credit."

"I agree," replied the SPEHA. "But the best part is, you wouldn't have to. Based on the press reports alone, people would recognize that it was you who was doing the heavy lifting. Your best course of action would be to downplay your involvement, show humility. Let the American President declare how much he appreciated your role in bringing Russia and the United States together.

"We will help see to it that you are recognized as one of the most successful Ambassadors to have ever served Russia. Believe me, being seen as a diplomat whom America respects and listens to can go a long way for you back home."

The Russian took another sip of his bourbon. He liked what he was hearing. It was an interesting proposition.

It was also fraught with incredible danger. If President Peshkov developed the slightest suspicion that he was cooperating with the Americans, he was as good as dead. Diplomats, journalists, dissidents—no one was safe. That was how Russia, at least under its current President, operated. Sazanov had everything to lose.

He also had everything to gain. An offer like this, the backing of the world's most powerful nation, wouldn't come around a second time.

Still, the Russian was wise enough to not jump too quickly. "I appreciate the confidence your nation has in me," he said. "Let me think about it."

Rogers understood.

Draining the rest of the bourbon from his glass, he stood and extended his hand. The two men shook.

"Just don't take too long," the SPEHA said. "If you do, both of our nations are going to regret it."

CHAPTER 36

Harvath was on edge. He disliked not having a plan. As the doctor thoroughly cleaned and dressed his wounds, he tried to build rapport by asking her questions.

Her name was Christina. She had attended medical school in the city of Archangel at the Northern State Medical University. As part of her training, she had studied abroad in London. After returning home, she had taken over the clinic.

The town, known as Nivsky, had been founded in 1929 as a settlement for laborers building a nearby hydroelectric plant. Not much happened in Nivsky. Its people were proud, worked hard, and hoped for better lives for their children.

Christina and her husband had met at medical school, where he was studying military medicine. They had no children.

She was about ten years younger than Harvath, and in addition to being very pretty, she was also very athletic. In the winter, she did a lot of snowshoeing and cross-country skiing. The rest of the year, when the Oblast wasn't frozen solid, she was into hiking and mountain biking.

The rifle she had been carrying was a Russian-made Molot-Oruzhie. Though they were far enough from the ice not to worry about polar bears, the wolves had been a big problem. Everyone in town was carrying some sort of firearm. Considering how much drinking went on in Nivsky, Christina expressed surprise that there hadn't been any "friendly fire" incidents yet.

Harvath smiled at her joke. She hadn't responded to his request to get him to the border, and he wasn't going to push her—yet. He knew she was thinking about it.

"When was the last time you ate?" she asked.

"Besides the yogurt I found in your fridge?"

She nodded.

"I had some of your uncle's smoked bear meat and a can of carrots earlier today."

The woman shuddered. "Are you hungry?"

Harvath nodded. He was ravenous.

Christina walked up to the front office, returned with a paper takeout menu, and handed it to him. It was from the bar and café he had passed on his way through the center of town. His inability to read Russian was negated by the fact that there were pictures of everything.

"Is this for real?" he asked, pointing at one of the items.

"The cheeseburger?" she replied. "It's actually quite good. Even better if you get it with bacon."

"Perfect. I'll take two of them. And a slice of the chocolate cake."

The woman laughed. "And to drink?"

"A Diet Coke."

"Because you're concerned about calories."

Harvath smiled. "Obviously."

She shook her head, walked over to the phone on the wall, and dialed the number.

He paid attention as she placed the order, alert for any sign that she was giving him away to the authorities. There was nothing, though—not in the way she spoke or in what she said—to give him any concern.

"Twenty minutes," she stated as she hung up the phone and turned back to face him.

One of the few things he had not lost when he plunged into the icy river was the money he had taken off the dead Spetsnaz soldiers. He peeled off several bills and handed them to her. "For the food and the medical care." Then, peeling off several more, added, "And for the damage to your door."

Christina accepted his offer, and then took the rest of his money as well. "If I'm going to help get you to the border, we're going to need additional supplies. I think it's better if I do the shopping. Your Russian really is terrible."

Harvath was incredibly relieved. His odds of escape had just improved dramatically. He wanted to throw his arms around her. Instead, he maintained his professional composure. "Thank you," he said.

"Don't thank me yet. Wait till we're at the border."

Once again, he smiled. "Fair enough."

Over the last several days he had endured physical, psychological, and emotional torture. He hadn't thought he'd ever be able to smile again. Now, he'd done so twice in less than five minutes.

"What can I do for you in return?" he asked.

"I don't know," she replied. "Maybe nothing. I haven't thought that far ahead."

"How far ahead *have* you thought?"

"Dinner, as well as hiding my uncle's snowmobile before people start wondering why he's back and no one has seen him."

Good point. "What can I do?"

"First, I'm going to give you an antibiotic injection," she replied. "Then I'm going to give you day one of your rabies vaccination, which is one dose of rabies vaccine, plus a one-time shot of rabies immune globulin, which loads rabies antibodies into your system."

"What about follow-on shots?"

"You'll need three more rabies shots—on the third, seventh, and fourteenth days from exposure. I'll put together everything you need, so you can take it with you. I assume you're not afraid of injecting yourself?"

"I can handle an injection."

"Good, because if the wolf that attacked you was rabid and you did nothing, it would be a death sentence. Rabies is over 99 percent fatal. By the time a victim notices symptoms, it's too late."

"Then I'm glad I found your clinic."

"And how lucky for you my door was *open*."

Before he could respond, she had swabbed his left arm with an alcohol-soaked cotton ball and jabbed him with the antibiotic shot. There was no preamble. There wasn't even an "On three" where she tricked him and pricked him on "two." She just jabbed the needle into his arm as if she wanted to pay him back for kicking the door in, and also, maybe, as if she wanted to see if he could take it.

"I hope I didn't bend your needle," he said, flexing the muscles in his arm after she withdrew it.

Taking his joke in stride, Christina examined it and replied, "I think we can still use it for your next two shots. I'll just rinse it under some water."

For a second, Harvath thought she was being serious. Then he saw her discard it into a sharps container and prep two more syringes.

"When was the last time you had a tetanus shot?" she asked.

"I can't remember."

"Within the last ten years?"

Harvath thought for a moment. "I'm not sure."

Christina prepared an additional shot and then brought everything over on a tray and set it next to him.

She started to prep his right arm for the rabies vaccination, but he stopped her. His right arm was his dominant arm, and he didn't need it getting sore. He was in bad enough shape already.

"Can you inject that someplace else?" he asked. "I want to keep that arm as functional as possible."

"The rabies vaccine has to go into a deltoid, but I can use your left arm again," she replied. After swabbing the area, she gave him the shot.

"You're getting better at this," he remarked. "That one didn't hurt at all."

"Make sure you leave a five-star review," she quipped before motioning for him to remove his leggings and roll over onto his stomach.

He did as she asked and she swabbed his left butt cheek. "This is the tetanus injection."

"Give it your best shot," he replied.

She rolled her eyes, administered the medication, and then prepped the fourth and final syringe, along with another cotton ball soaked in alcohol.

"This is the immune globulin, and it's going to hurt," she said as she swabbed a spot on his right cheek.

"Seriously?" he asked, turning his head to look over his shoulder at her.

"I'm only kidding," she replied as she gave him the injection. "Hopefully, there's no more pain in your future."

It was a nice sentiment, but Harvath feared that there was a lot more pain to come. In fact, the closer they got to the border, the more dangerous things were going to get.

CHAPTER 37

There was nothing subtle about Teplov. He always wanted to make a big statement. *Step in. Scare the shit out of people. Take charge.* That was how he rolled.

So instead of landing the helicopters on the soccer field outside of town, he had them land right in the middle of the town square.

The thunderous, beating blades of the enormous birds sent tremors through buildings for blocks around. Their rotor wash pelted cars with shards of ice and frozen snow. The men of Wagner had arrived.

Hopping out of his helo, Teplov immediately began barking orders. He wanted his men and cargo unloaded immediately.

The patrons inside the Frosty Pelican, their faces pressed up against the windows, couldn't believe what they were seeing. They watched as one of the giant helicopters disgorged soldiers who were dressed from head to toe in winter camouflage. The other helicopter spat out snowmobiles and crates of equipment. It was like a scene out of the American movie *Red Dawn*. It was as if they were being invaded. And in a sense, they were.

Shortly before touching down, an encrypted call had come in from Minayev. After isolating it to Teplov's headset, the two had conducted a brief conversation, with the GRU General doing most of the talking. President Peshkov had put an eight-hour window on finding Harvath. He not only wanted him found, he had demanded immediate, verifiable proof of life.

When Teplov asked what had caused the increased urgency, Minayev had snapped at him. Reminding him who was in charge, he had told him to do his "fucking job" or else.

Something had gone wrong. And, as shit always rolled downhill, Teplov had the unenviable position of being at the very bottom.

Before Minayev hung up on him, Teplov had asked if there were any restrictions on him and his men. Specifically, was there anything the Kremlin wouldn't allow, as long as they tracked Harvath down? The General's answer was succinct and to the point—*Do whatever it takes*.

For all intents and purposes, the town of Nivsky now belonged to Teplov. If Harvath was here—and he had good reason to believe he was—his mercenaries would find him.

But to do so, he was going to need to enlist the locals. Judging by the number of eyeballs watching him from the Frosty Pelican, he had found the perfect place to start. Whistling over a handful of his men, he headed toward the establishment.

Like the Nazi SS, whose strategies he not only studied but revered, Teplov was a voracious consumer of data. Via a quick Internet search on the way in, he had learned how much the average citizen of the Oblast earned, how much they saved, and how much they carried in debt. Establishing a bounty on Harvath had been simple.

Fifteen thousand American dollars was more than twice the average annual salary. The townspeople would be cutting each other's throats to find Harvath and turn him in.

In addition to motivating the locals, they would block the roads in and out, while teams went house to house conducting searches.

During World War II, SS troops worked with Italian fascist units to root out American spies and saboteurs who were hiding in the snowy forests and Alpine villages near the Brenner Pass. The exercises were called *rastrellamento*—Italian for "raking up."

Though each *rastrellamento* covered a much greater area and involved far more soldiers, Teplov was confident that the same concept would work in Nivsky. It came down to offering a very big carrot, backed up with a very big stick.

As he entered the bar, the customers fell silent. Teplov pulled out a picture of Harvath and held it up so everyone could see it.

"We are looking for a man—an American spy—who has murdered four Russian soldiers and at least one Russian Air Force member. He was on a plane that crashed approximately seventy-five kilometers east of here. We have reason to believe he is now traveling via snowmobile and headed for the border.

"The Russian government is offering a reward of fifteen thousand U.S. dollars—that's nearly a hundred thousand rubles—for information leading to his capture. This man is armed and considered very dangerous. If you see him, do not approach him. My men and I will be staying in your town until we find him.

"We will be conducting house-to-house searches. If anyone is found to be sheltering this man, they will be prosecuted as an accomplice to murder and an enemy of the state. If anyone so much as gives him a crust of bread, they will also be prosecuted as an accomplice to murder and an enemy of the state.

"If you suspect that your neighbor or someone you know is aiding this American, you must report it to me or one of my men immediately. Failure to do so will result in the harshest of punishments.

"At both ends of town, we are establishing checkpoints. It will be necessary to provide your government-issued identification when entering and leaving. We are also creating a registry of vehicles.

"To that end, let's begin with the five SUVs parked immediately outside. Will the owners please identify themselves by raising their hands?"

Teplov waited until the hands went up and then sent his men to collect the keys from four of them. The man with the worst vehicle would be allowed to keep his. He would function as a chauffeur for the others.

Immediately, the men began to protest. One even refused to hand over his keys. Teplov used that as an opportunity to teach the townspeople a lesson.

When he nodded his head, two of his men dragged the resister out of the bar and beat him in front of the windows for all to see. They left him bloody and unconscious in the snow.

Returning inside, they commandeered the Xerox machine in the office and made hundreds of copies of Harvath's photo. They made sure everyone in the place had one before leaving with tape, staple guns, and the rest of the copies.

As they exited, Teplov kept an eye on the crowd until his men were safely out the door. If anyone was going to do something stupid, like throw a bottle, this was when it normally happened. No one did.

Once the Wagner men had moved away from the entrance, several of the patrons rushed outside to retrieve their beaten friend. Christina, who had been there to pick up her order, rushed outside with them.

Careful to make sure his head and neck were supported, they carried him back inside, laid him down, and covered him with a coat to help warm him up.

Everyone was aghast at what the soldiers had done. "This isn't the Soviet Union," one said. "They cannot do that to us," said another. "We have our rights!" exclaimed a third person.

Christina, though, knew differently. "Rights" were whatever the oligarchs in Moscow decided they were. They could be given and they could be taken away at a moment's notice.

She also knew that those men were not soldiers—not in the traditional sense. They weren't current members of the Russian Army. They were mercenaries. She had recognized the patch they were all wearing on their parkas. It was just like the one her husband had worn as part of his uniform. They belonged to Wagner.

And if Wagner was here in Nivsky, it could mean only one thing—the Kremlin was keeping the hunt for Harvath a secret.

Why they would do that she didn't know. She also didn't care. She had seen the condition of Harvath's body. She had also just seen the brutality they were capable of firsthand.

The Wagner men were dangerous. They were also about to close off the town and begin a house-to-house search. With four SUVs and several snowmobiles, they would be able to cover a lot of ground in a short time. She needed to get back to Harvath as soon as possible.

But with all eyes on her as the town's doctor, she first needed to tend to the man who had been so savagely attacked.

CHAPTER 38

"Get your things," said Christina as she burst through the back door of the clinic and began gathering up supplies. "We're leaving. Right now."

"I heard the helicopters," replied Harvath, already dressed and ready to go. "What's going on?"

"They know you're here. They're passing around your photo and are closing off the town."

He implored her to take a breath. "Who knows I'm here?"

"Mercenaries. Wagner, the company my husband worked for."

Harvath was familiar with them. Most were ex-Spetsnaz. "How many did you see?"

"Around twenty. Maybe more."

"How were they equipped?"

"White uniforms. Helmets with night vision. They were carrying rifles. And pistols, too."

"How do they plan to close off the town?"

"They are blocking the road at both ends. Anyone coming in or going out will be checked. They are offering a reward for your capture."

"How much?"

"Fifteen thousand dollars, American. That's a lot of money around here."

He didn't doubt it. He knew enough about Russia to have an idea what the average person earned, especially someone who didn't live in Moscow or St. Petersburg.

"How are we going to get out?" he asked.

It was a good question—one her mind had been working overtime on. "Driving is impossible," she replied. "I'm afraid the snowmobile is, too. We'll have to figure something else out, but we can't stay here. They're right behind me. We need to get going. *Now*."

The "*Now*" kicked Harvath into high gear.

Christina had struck him as a calm, very competent medical professional, someone capable of staying cool under pressure. When she intimated it was time to haul ass, he took it seriously.

Having upward of twenty, and possibly more, former Spetsnaz soldiers on his tail wasn't something he relished. He had made it this far because of good training, good luck, and one hell of a head start.

The head start was now all but gone. All he had left was his training and whatever good luck ended up in his path.

Before she had left to pick up the food, he had asked her to help him send a message back to the United States. Without revealing completely how the process worked, he had assured her that it couldn't be traced back to her and that there was no risk.

Knowing how the Russian Internet was used to hunt down anyone who opposed the Kremlin, it didn't sound safe to her. Nevertheless, she had said she'd think about it and they could discuss it when she got back.

Now, as Harvath asked her again, she looked at him like he was crazy.

"It'll take two seconds," he said.

"Do you want to get caught?" she asked. "Because I don't. They made it very clear what will happen to anyone who is discovered assisting you."

Of course Harvath didn't want to get caught. He wanted to get to the border. But he also wanted to summon the cavalry.

Knowing the best-trained, best-equipped military on the planet was speeding to his rescue wouldn't necessarily improve his odds in the short run, but it would be a hell of a morale booster. It also meant that all he had to do was stay alive until they could get to him. They would handle getting him out.

As Christina turned on her heel and headed out the back door, he abandoned any hope of hopping on her computer. No matter how little time he thought he needed to transmit his message, he couldn't do it without her help.

Outside, her tiny 4x4 was idling in the cold. Before hopping inside, she pointed to a shed and said, "It's unlocked. Put the snowmobile in there."

Harvath did as he was told.

Fortunately, the machine fired right up and he didn't need to drag it. Not that he could have if he had wanted to. His entire body was aching. He would have set the fucking thing on fire before dragging it into a shed to hide it.

Throwing his rucksack into the back of the 4x4, he hopped into the passenger seat with the pump-action Baikal and literally rode "shotgun."

"What's the plan?" he asked, scanning the street in both directions as she pulled away from the medical clinic.

"You're a bit like cancer," she said, handing him his takeout. "The Wagner mercenaries know the town has it—they just don't know where exactly to look for it."

"Okay," Harvath replied, unwrapping the first bacon cheeseburger, not sure where she was going with her analogy.

"When doctors begin to focus in on where the cancer is, they start to get excited. It makes sense. They can't kill it until they've located it. So once a location makes itself known, all attention goes to that one point."

"So?"

"So I think we should give the mercenaries a location."

"What do you have in mind?" he asked as he took his first bite.

"If they're any good, which I'm assuming they are, my clinic is high on their list of places to check for a fugitive who survived a plane crash. Once they get there, they'll see my back door has been kicked in and the heat has been turned up. They'll find bloody gauze pads, as well as fresh sterile wipes in the garbage. It won't take long for them to put two and two together.

"Expanding their search, they'll find the snowmobile in the shed. They might not get to it right away, but at some point someone will tie it to my uncle. When that happens, they'll start connecting dots. The cabin you stayed in was, obviously, within walking distance of the crash. If they haven't already, they'll search his home here, on the outskirts of Nivsky."

"And that's what you want to give them?"

Christina shook her head. "At some point, very soon, they're going to check it out. When they do, I want to leave a false trail. I want them to think you were there, but have gone in a completely different direction."

She was a strategic thinker, and he appreciated that about her. Setting up some sort of red herring at the uncle's house could buy them valuable time.

"What are you thinking?" he asked.

"I don't know yet. Finish eating. We can talk about it when we get there."

Harvath, who had been chowing through the first burger as quickly as he could while continuing to scan for threats, took out the Diet Coke and drained half of it in one long sip.

It reminded him of some low-rolling death-row inmate's last meal. He just hoped it wouldn't be his.

CHAPTER 39

The trapper's home was nothing like his cabin. It was a modern, orange brick structure clad with red roofing tiles. Wrought-iron railings bracketed a set of three concrete steps in front, which perfectly matched the house's glossy black gutters. An artsy piece of metal sheeting was bolted above the door to provide a modicum of protection from the elements when people were entering or leaving.

Inside, the rooms were small but cozy—probably just the right amount of space for an older man who lived alone and was often gone. It smelled like potting soil and old newspaper.

There were books, a television set, and even a record player. Framed family photos lined an entire bookshelf; many of them included Christina.

"I'm sorry again about your uncle," he said.

"It's how he wanted to die—out there in the wilderness. We were the only family each other had left. I think if it hadn't been for me, he would have sold this place, gone into the woods, and never come back."

"Are these your parents?" he asked, pointing to one of the pictures.

"Yes. And my aunt. They're all deceased now."

"I'm sorry," Harvath repeated.

The woman shrugged. "Life in Russia is tough. Life in rural Russia is even tougher. They all smoked and drank way too much. None of them, except for my uncle, ever got any exercise."

She sounded cold and detached, but Harvath could see the emotion in her eyes. It wasn't easy being the only one left. Harvath could relate.

Off the living room was a small kitchen. Stepping away from him, Christina ducked inside and began inventorying supplies.

As Harvath continued poking around the living room, she suggested he start a fire in the fireplace. "Not too big," she cautioned. "We want to make sure it's burned down by the time anyone gets here. Let them think we have a bigger head start than we do."

It was a good idea. After he got the fire going, he called out to her and asked what he could do next.

"My uncle was a vain man who colored his hair. There should be a kit in the bathroom. Leave any packaging in the trash, but flush the actual coloring down the toilet, after you spill some at the sink. They'll think you're trying to change your appearance. Run the shower and leave towels on the floor. If you want to shave, do it quickly. I'll grab some extra clothes from the closet."

The woman was a natural. Not everything she had suggested would work, but every time their pursuers were forced to stop, scratch their heads, and evaluate, it was an additional moment they fell behind.

Hitting the bathroom, he decided against the shave. Instead, he invested ninety seconds in a hot shower. It was one of the best showers he could ever remember taking.

With hot food in his stomach and hot water on his skin, it was the first time since the plane crash that he had felt truly warm. He had a feeling it wasn't going to last.

Climbing out, he quickly dried himself off and then wrapped the towel around his waist, below the bite wounds.

He had taken off his bandages before getting in the shower. All of them were bloodstained. Christina hadn't sewn him up. Part of healing from a wolf attack was leaving the wounds open so they could seep. That meant no stiches and no staples.

He was just about to put his bandages back on when Christina knocked and pushed open the bathroom door.

"Leave those," she said, stepping inside with her bag. "I brought more. I don't know how smart those Wagner assholes are, but I like reinforcing that you're injured. Leaving more bloody bandages will continue to make them think they have the upper hand."

After she had redressed his wounds, she placed two pain pills next to the sink and stepped out so that he could finish up.

Searching for the hair dye, he found a brand new toothbrush and brushed his teeth. It was another terrific feeling, something he had long taken for granted.

After leaving a few drops around the sink and dumping the dye chemicals down the toilet, he cast aside the packaging and swallowed the pills.

Getting dressed, he walked back out to the living room and found Christina, hands on hips, slowly scanning the bookshelves.

"What are you looking for?" he asked.

"Bread crumbs to help create that false trail we discussed in the car."

Finally, she found it. Removing a large atlas of the Murmansk Oblast, Christina carried it to the dining room table, beckoned Harvath over, and began flipping through its brightly colored pages.

When she got to the map she wanted, she stopped and tapped it with her finger. "This one."

Harvath examined the image. It showed Russian rail lines as they ran along the western edge of the Oblast.

Reaching for a ballpoint pen, she picked a spot on the border with Finland, about three hundred kilometers northwest of Nivsky, and circled it.

"Why there?" he asked.

"Because we're going in the other direction," she replied, as she tore the page out of the atlas and tucked it in her pocket.

He then watched as she returned the book to the shelf, though not as neatly as he had found it. Once more, he was impressed with her thinking.

"For somebody who's not sure how smart those Wagner assholes are, you're giving them a lot of credit."

"You don't think it will work?" she answered.

"I think it's a long shot. First, they have to find the atlas. Next they have to notice the page is missing. Then they have to source another copy of the same atlas. I'm assuming it's popular?"

The woman nodded. "Practically everybody in town has one."

"Okay," Harvath went on. "Next, someone has to notice the impression left behind by your pen. If this person knows anything, they'll lay a piece of paper down and rub it with a pencil. That'll let them know where you made your circle on the missing page. They marry that up with an intact atlas, and the wild-goose chase is on. Did I miss anything?"

Christina smiled at him. "Very well done."

"You know that's not normal."

"What are you talking about?"

"The way your mind works. Most people don't think two steps ahead, much less three."

"Well, I'm definitely not normal, and absolutely not like most people."

Harvath smiled back. "There is one problem, though. The snowmobile."

"What about it?"

"There's no way I could have covered the distance from the crash site to here so quickly—not on foot. I am assuming they found your uncle's cabin and the snowmobile tracks, which explains why they're here. This was the closest town.

"I am also going to assume that they know I have a GPS device and that's how I got here. Their proof will come when they find the snowmobile in the shed behind your clinic. There's an attachment on the handlebars for it."

Christina hadn't considered that. "You could leave the GPS unit here. Then the missing page from the atlas would be believable. Let them think you are going completely off the grid."

"Or, better yet, that I believe the grid will completely be going off."

Now he had her completely confused. "I don't understand."

"Your uncle's GPS device isn't a tracker. It doesn't send out a signal telling people where it is. Therefore, there'd be no reason for me to get rid of it. It's too valuable. But if the GPS system stops working, then it's worthless. At that point, I *would* need a map."

"I still don't understand. When was the last time the GPS system ever stopped working?"

"Last year. During NATO training exercises in Scandinavia, Finland accused Russia of jamming the GPS signal in their northern airspace. If I was concerned that they'd do it to prevent me from escaping, or from being rescued, I'd want a paper map as a backup."

"So then my plan is good."

"It is," replied Harvath. "I think we can make it better."

"How so?"

"With an Internet search of the same area. Does your uncle have a laptop or a tablet in the house?"

She shook her head. "He didn't like technology. Didn't trust it. The GPS device was as far as he would go."

"Then we'll have to run the risk of overplaying our hand," he said as he walked over to the shelf, pulled the atlas back out and then placed it on the table next to the ballpoint pen. "I don't want to take any chances that they miss it."

She didn't disagree.

"So what's the plan?" he asked.

"There's a Sámi village about twenty kilometers west of here."

Harvath did a rough conversion in his head. *Twelve miles.* "But if the roads are shut down, how are we going to get there?"

"That depends. How much stamina do you have left?"

"Don't worry about me. I'll be fine."

"Good, because we're going to have to ski."

"Downhill or cross-country?"

She smiled at him again. "If it was all downhill, I wouldn't ask about your stamina."

"What about there not being enough reindeer skins to survive in this weather?"

"That was when we were talking about you going all the way to the border. Right now, all we have to do is get you to the village."

Back out in the open, in the freezing cold, at night. Harvath wasn't looking forward to it. "And then what?"

"I'm working on it."

"What about gear? Skis?"

"You can use my husband's equipment. It's all here, in the garage," she said, leading the way through the kitchen to a door in the back. Turning on the light, she pointed to some boxes and some things hanging on the opposite wall. "My uncle didn't think it was healthy for me to be holding on to his things."

"Where are your skis?"

"At my house, but there's no time. I'll show you on the GPS where you're going and whom to ask for. Sini speaks English. She'll take care of you."

"You're not coming?"

"I'll be there as soon as I can. First I need to deal with those Wagner assholes. If I'm right, they're going to be calling me any minute about a break-in at the clinic."

"Before I go, I need you to promise me you'll do something," he replied.

"We've already wasted too much time. You need to hurry up and get out of here."

"I'm not going unless you promise me."

She couldn't believe this guy. Two dozen former Russian Spetsnaz soldiers with helicopters, snowmobiles, and stolen SUVs were all looking for him, yet he wasn't going to flee until he got a promise from her. She couldn't decide if he was incredibly brave or just incredibly insane.

In the interest of getting him moving, she agreed. And while he geared up, she created a route on the GPS and wrote down everything he needed to do.

Then, standing outside in the snow, he handed her a small, folded piece of paper. "This is all you have to do."

She looked at it. "Are you serious?"

"As serious as cancer," he said, as he turned and skied off into the woods.

CHAPTER 40

A litany of things had been flying through Christina's mind as she maneuvered home. She had to remind herself not to speed. Though they were a tight-knit community, loyalty wasn't guaranteed—not with soldiers in town offering rewards for information and beating people who resisted.

It reminded her of the stories her grandparents used to tell of life under communism. The most dangerous people weren't the apparatchiks or the secret police. The most dangerous people were your neighbors, your coworkers, the babushka who swept the street. The reign of communist terror was successful at preventing another revolution because it was impossible to organize. You didn't know who you could trust. Every person on every corner was a potential informant. Christina needed to be very careful.

She left the car outside, so the engine would cool more rapidly. She didn't want to give away that she just arrived. When the Wagner thugs came calling, she wanted her alibi to be airtight. She had worked late, called in a takeout order, and had gone straight home.

Gathering up Harvath's takeout containers, she brought them inside and spread them out across her kitchen counter. The meal had come with fries, which he had neglected, so she helped herself as she downed two quick shots of vodka to steady her nerves.

If anyone came calling, it was important that she appear to have been home, alone, drinking.

She had just poured a large glass of wine, from a half-empty bottle, when her bell rang. There was little doubt in her mind who it was.

Fries in hand, she walked up to the front door and opened it. Standing outside were three Wagner mercenaries. Front and center was the man in charge—the one from the bar who had held up Harvath's picture and had given all the orders.

He was tall, with blond hair and several prominent facial scars. "Doctor Volkova?"

"Yes?" she replied, a half-eaten French fry in her mouth.

"My name is Colonel Kazimir Teplov. I am sorry to disturb you. May we come in?"

"What do you want?"

"It's somewhat cold outside. If you wouldn't mind I'd rather do this inside."

Taking a moment to finish chewing her French fry, she then stood back and allowed the men to enter.

The rifle Teplov had been carrying at the bar was gone. From what she could see, he had only the sidearm holstered at his thigh. The two goons behind him, however, were not only carrying rifles, but appeared jumpy, ready to fire if anyone so much as sneezed.

"Thank you," said Teplov, as he and his men stepped into her home. "As I said, my name is—"

"Kazimir Teplov. I know. I was in the bar when you and your people arrived."

"Is that so?" he asked.

"It is so. By the way, the man your soldiers beat unconscious, were you aware that he served honorably in the Russian Navy? And that he is also our auto mechanic."

"I did not know that. I'm sorry. It was a most unfortunate incident."

Christina despised this guy and was having a very hard time disguising it. "So, Mr. Teplov, what can I do for you?"

"It's Colonel Teplov."

"Is it?" she asked, pointing at the patch on his shoulder. "Because I didn't know that Wagner mercenaries retained their rank from prior service in the Russian Armed Forces."

Teplov smiled. "You know who we are."

"Oh, I know all about you."

"And how did you come by this knowledge?"

Walking over to her kitchen counter, she picked up her wine, crossed her arms just as she took a long sip, and said, "Because I'm a Wagner widow."

For a moment, Teplov's mask slipped. He was genuinely surprised. "Who was your husband?"

"Demyan Volkov," she responded. "He was killed in Syria. Latakia Province."

"I'm very sorry for your loss."

"So am I. What is it you want, Mr. Teplov?"

He looked at the food containers. "Did I interrupt something?"

"Why do you ask?"

He walked over and read the receipt taped to the top of one of the containers. "Two bacon cheeseburgers, chocolate cake, French fries? Sounds like a lot of food for a woman your size."

"Are you accusing me of something, Mr. Teplov?"

He paused and, looking at her, replied, "Should I be?"

"That depends. If you asked the new girl what I normally order, she would tell you it's always salads. Sometimes, though, I get fish or chicken. If you ask someone who isn't new, they'll tell you the same thing, but they'll add that several times a year, I come in and order a very large, very unhealthy meal.

"When that happens, it tends to be on a significant anniversary—the day I met my husband, the day he died, the day we got married, or the day we had our first date, which today happens to be the anniversary of."

"Again, I'm truly sorry," said Teplov. "I didn't know."

Extending her wineglass in a mock toast, she then brought it back in and took an even longer slug. "What they won't tell you," she said, once she had swallowed, "because none of them know, is that after I bring the food home and eat it, I drink way more than I should—usually several bottles. The next day I am pretty useless."

He had no reason to doubt the veracity of her account, so he decided to cut to the chase. Taking out the photo of Harvath he had shown around the bar, he presented it to her. "Have you seen this man? We believe he may be hiding somewhere here in town."

"I have not," she answered.

"Would you mind if my men took a look around your house? As I explained in the bar, the American is armed and very dangerous."

Christina raised her palms. "I don't know why he'd be here, but go ahead. Be my guest."

Teplov nodded and his men commenced their investigation. Turning his attention back to her, he said, "We were concerned you might be in danger."

"In danger? Of what?"

"During our search for the fugitive, some of my men passed by your clinic. Were you aware that the back door had been kicked in?"

"Kicked in by whom? When?"

"We don't know. We assume it was the American and that it happened within the last couple of hours."

"Was anything stolen?" she asked, trying to appear concerned.

"We found some bloody gauze pads in the trash as well as an empty antibiotic vial, plus two for rabies. Have you had cause to treat anyone for rabies recently?"

Christina shook her head. "I have not."

"Interesting."

She had no idea if he believed her or not, but the alcohol had emboldened her. "Where would your fugitive have been bitten by a dog?"

Teplov held up his index finger. "Not a dog. Wolves."

"Jesus," she replied.

"You don't like wolves," he said with a smile.

"Can't stand them. They've been preying on people in the Oblast all winter. None of us go anywhere without a rifle. So far, though, they haven't attacked people in Nivsky. Where did this happen?"

"A hundred kilometers east of here."

"Wonderful. In addition to a murderer, we also have killer wolves on our doorstep," she said, before changing the subject. "How bad is the back door to my clinic. Was there any other damage?"

"None that my men have reported."

"Anything stolen? Besides the things you found in the trash?"

"They couldn't tell," he responded. "It sounds like some sort of cabinet used for storing medicines was broken into."

"Damn it," she cursed. Then, downing what remained in her wineglass, she grabbed her parka, which had been hanging over one of the kitchen chairs.

"What are you doing?" demanded Teplov.

"What does it look like I'm doing? Someone broke into my clinic. I need to know how bad the damage is."

"I don't think you should be driving."

"Pardon me, but who's the soldier and who's the doctor?" she asked.

"Fair enough," said Teplov. "But you're part of the Wagner family. It's our duty to look out for you. The American could be anywhere."

There was no point in arguing with them. She would accept an escort, but she wasn't going to get in a car with them. "I'm okay to drive. You can follow me to the clinic if you wish. Are your men ready to go?"

Teplov called out to his men. Moments later, they materialized and gave him the thumbs-up. They hadn't uncovered any sign of the American. The house was clean.

Locking the door behind them, Christina hopped into her 4x4 and headed back to her clinic.

She drove fast, but not too fast. She was well aware that if Teplov was the top man, and he had come out to her house, then she was his top lead. That meant that every moment she kept him and his men tied up was another moment that helped Harvath get farther away.

She just hoped that she had understood Harvath's directions correctly.

CHAPTER 41

HOSTAGE RECOVERY FUSION CELL
WASHINGTON, D.C.

"Hit!" Nicholas exclaimed from the desk he had been given in the center of the room. "Hit! Hit! Hit!"

His dogs, which the FBI Director had allowed in the building as "service animals," leaped to attention. Growling, they scanned for threats until Nicholas commanded them to lie down.

"What do you have?" the SPEHA asked as he rushed over. "Is it Harvath?" After his meeting with the Russian Ambassador, he could use some good news.

Nicholas had a smile on his face that stretched from ear to ear. "It's his rescue protocol. And the code is one hundred percent his," he said, pointing to his screen.

On it was an Instagram account with only a few thousand followers, all of them fakes. It had been set up as a digital dead drop.

The Carlton Group paid a trusted source in Iceland to update it with posts about makeup, fashion tips, and celebrity gossip. When Harvath, or someone operating under his authority, popped up and commented on the most recent entry, Nicholas was overjoyed. Rogers, on the other hand, was pragmatic.

"I know you're excited," he said. "Slow it down for me, though. What are we looking at?"

Nicholas was all too happy to explain. "Like the CIA, The Carlton Group has developed situation-dependent communication protocols. They run the gamut from transmitting SITREPs while under surveillance in friendly nations, to an operative transmitting a distress signal from inside a hostile country. We just received the latter from Harvath."

"You're positive it's him?"

Nicholas nodded. "No question. It's his authentication code and everything."

The SPEHA stared at the Instagram comment. "You can be absolutely sure, just from this?"

Nicholas nodded again, emphatically. "Harvath set all of this up himself. Using Instagram was his idea, as were all the code words. He also built in a way for us to immediately know if the message was being sent under duress."

"Under duress?"

"That someone was forcing him to write it," Nicholas explained. "That doesn't appear to be the case here."

"So what do we have?"

"First, he's alive. He's *fucking* alive. Thank God."

"And next?" Rogers asked.

"He posted from Russia. Specifically Nivsky, a town in the Murmansk Oblast. But he's on the move."

"On the move where?"

"West," stated Nicholas. "He's trying to get to the border with Finland."

"That's fantastic," said the SPEHA. "How do we get in touch with him?"

Nicholas looked up from the screen. "He doesn't have access to a means of secure communication."

"Then how do we pinpoint his location?"

"We can't. All we have is his last known location. I can only imagine what it took to get this message out to us."

"Agreed," stated Rogers. "Okay, listen up, people," he called out to the Fusion Cell. "According to what we just learned, we may have found our man. He does appear to be in Russia. He's on the run. Our starting point is a town called Nivsky, in the Murmansk Oblast, heading west. All hands on deck. I want to fix his precise location. Start pulling SIGINT, geospatial, all of it. I'll be damned if the Russians are going to beat us. Let's move!"

CHAPTER 42

Seven kilometers in, all Harvath wanted to do was puke his guts out. Part of it was the cheeseburgers, but another part was how fast he was moving. He wanted to get as far away from the mercenaries as fast as possible.

He was pushing himself too hard. He knew that. But if he didn't make it to that village, if he got caught by a Wagner snowmobile or helicopter patrol, he'd never breathe free air again. He had to push it as hard as he could.

In addition to extra food, Christina had put medical supplies and clothing in his rucksack. Mercifully, she had also affixed a water bladder to it. Given how close the enemy was there could be no stopping to melt snow into water.

The temperature tonight felt worse than anything he had experienced since the crash. Christina, however, had assured him he could make it. He was wearing her husband's winter gear and was insulated from head to toe. Even his eyes were protected by a set of goggles.

The pace he was keeping, though, had him sweating. He could feel the rivulets of salty perspiration rolling down his face and down his back.

Whenever his mind suggested that he stop, if only for a moment to catch his breath, he redoubled his efforts and pressed forward. Now wasn't the time. Stopping equaled capture.

Fortunately, he hadn't heard any helicopters overhead. Perhaps Wagner was convinced that he was holed up in one of the houses in town and had decided to give them a rest. If so, that was a good thing.

Nevertheless, he made sure to stay in the woods and to use the tree cover to full advantage. Wagner likely had access to thermal imagers that could pinpoint him based on his body heat. There was no reason to make things any easier for them than he had to.

Pushing through the deep snow, he slowed only to take quick sips of water and to check his GPS.

From time to time, he had trouble getting a signal, and when that happened, he had no choice but to ski back out toward the edge of the woods where he could get a good view of the night sky and reconnect with the satellites.

But as soon as he had reestablished the signal and had confirmed his heading, he skied back into the trees.

Even with the small course adjustments, the trip felt as if it was taking a lot longer than Christina had said it would. He knew that was just his fatigue talking, though—the unhelpful part of his brain that always spoke up when he was exhausted and wanted to sabotage his progress.

As he had done with his guilt and grief over losing Lara, he slammed an iron door shut on that part of his psyche and pressed on.

Movement and concealment were all that mattered. He needed to get to that village.

When he reached the ten-kilometer mark, he paused for the world's shortest rest. He was only one-third of the way there.

He believed that if he sat down, even with the help of his poles, he wouldn't be able to get up. So, he contented himself with leaning against a tree. Almost instantly, his legs began to cramp.

Bending down to massage them, he took his weight off the tree, which released a pile of snow from the boughs high above. *Somebody* was trying to tell him something. Stopping was a bad idea.

He took a long drink of water, hoping to ease the cramps. After clearing the snow from his pack, and his shotgun, he pushed on again.

To fuel his trek, he allowed himself to tap into an emotion he had been trying to hold at bay—his rage.

He knew behind which door it hid and he didn't just crack it, he kicked it wide open. Instantly, it crashed into his bloodstream like liquid lava, taking him over.

It was the darkest energy from the darkest part of his soul. More addictive than any drug, more powerful than any other emotion, rage lay beyond reason, beyond any sense of right or wrong. Rage was primal. And though he had been taught to never let it take control, he gave himself over to it, fully.

He saw everything from the cottage in New Hampshire unfold once more in his mind's eye. He saw the brutal executions and the lives leaving the bodies of the people he loved. He saw the men responsible. He saw his own role—unable to stop any of it—and pure, toxic hate rose within him once more.

His mind shifted to the Spetsnaz soldiers at the crash site—those who had already been dead and those he had killed. He saw himself taking their scalps and stringing them along a piece of wire—his small and unsatisfying act of revenge. Carving off pieces of those men was an end-zone dance. Hanging those scalps up was a "fuck you" to the men who would eventually come upon them.

The only real sense of satisfaction he would get would be when he tracked down the men who were ultimately responsible for what had happened. It didn't matter if it took him days, months, or even years. All he knew was that he wouldn't stop until he had found them and had taken from them just as much as if not more than they had taken from him.

With the molten rage pumping through him, he pushed his way through the snow.

He eventually developed a rhythm. Kilometer after kilometer fell away behind him, until the terrain began to angle upward.

It wasn't a very steep ascent, but it was agonizing, reengaging many of the muscles he had torn down while snowshoeing. There wasn't enough rage left in his tank to propel him at the clip he had been going.

And as the rage started to ebb away, it was replaced by something else—fear. *He wasn't going to make it.*

Each push of his skis came at greater cost—each required more energy, each was more painful, and each carried him over a shorter distance. He had gone from moving feet to moving only inches. And whether or not it was a trick of his exhausted mind, the incline felt as if it were growing.

If ever he needed his rage to spur him on, it was now, but he couldn't summon it. Leaning forward, he used his poles to drag himself up the hillside.

Millimeter by millimeter he climbed, refusing to give up. He could feel the muscle fibers tearing in his back and shoulders, arms and legs. His body, already badly broken, didn't have much left to give.

Once again, the voice of the saboteur came to him, urging him to drop his pack, to stop, rest, give up. He tried not to listen, but the voice only grew louder, its arguments more convincing. There was nothing he could do to close it off. He was too weak to fight. So, he did the only thing he had left in him—he negotiated with it.

He cajoled and bargained, but never stopped moving. He allowed the voice to run wild, to persuade him why it was right and he was wrong. Eventually, he succumbed.

He was almost at the top when he realized that he had lied to Christina. His stamina was for shit. The stress of being on the run, the bitter arctic cold, the grueling physical exertion, had eaten it all away.

He couldn't go any farther. This was it. He needed to rest, maybe even to sleep, if only for just a little while.

Planting his skis, he stuck his poles in the snow, unslung his shotgun, and dropped it alongside him. He followed with his pack, but as he tried to get out of the straps, he stumbled.

He landed with his legs twisted beneath him and one of the skis missing. He didn't care. All he wanted to do was to close his eyes. It would be a death sentence, however, to fall asleep out here in the cold.

A feeling of warmth was spreading across his body. Along with it whispered the voice of the saboteur, encouraging him to give in.

It felt so good to be still, to be off his feet. Through breaks in the snow-covered trees he could see an occasional star. They were the same stars he had pointed out to Lara while sitting on his dock back home in Virginia.

He had begun to teach Lara's son, Marco, the names of the constellations, the same way his father had taught him. It was in those small, simple moments that they had come closest to being a family—the thing Harvath had wanted more than almost anything else.

Now, lying here in the snow, he had a reason to stay put. He had convinced himself to keep staring up into the night sky—that once he had seen enough stars to identify a constellation, he would start moving again. It was an homage to Lara, a eulogy of sorts. No matter how cold or how tired he got, he wouldn't move until he had done so.

"Sit up," a voice suddenly said.

It was hard to hear it over the wind.

"Sit up," it repeated.

It was Lara's voice.

"Stop playing games. Get moving."

He ignored her. He knew her voice wasn't real. He was losing his mind again.

Maybe, he thought to himself, *things would make more sense if I just closed my eyes for a little bit.*

And so, despite every rational circuit in his brain telling him not to, he gave in to the saboteur and allowed his lids to close.

CHAPTER 43

Christina made a big deal about the back door to her clinic having been kicked in, letting loose with several choice words not necessarily befitting a doctor.

Teplov, who had been on her bumper the entire way from her house, had followed her inside. He watched her, closely, to see what she did.

After bitching about the damage in back, she went straight to the room with the cabinet where the drugs were stored.

It was obvious it had been broken into. Inventorying the contents, she appeared relieved.

"What is it?" Teplov asked. "What do you see?"

"I see my narcotics. Fortunately, none of them were taken."

"Anything else?"

"As you mentioned, a vial of antibiotics is missing, along with the first two doses of a typical rabies vaccine, plus the follow-ons."

"The *follow-ons*?"

"Yes, the doses that would be need to be given on the third, seventh, and fourteenth days from exposure."

"Interesting," mumbled Teplov, lost in thought.

"Why? Because your American understands what a course of rabies vaccination entails?"

"No," said the mercenary, coming back around. "What's interesting is that he stole the entire course. Either he's planning on hanging around for the next two weeks, or he's concerned with how soon he might be rescued."

Christina was nonplussed. "That's your problem. I want to know who's paying for the damage to my back door and the stolen medicines."

"I hope you have insurance."

"Exactly what Wagner told me when my husband was killed."

Without waiting for the man to respond, she left the room and went to check the rest of the clinic.

"Doctor Volkova," he called out after her. "Doctor Volkova."

She turned and faced him in the hallway. "If you cooperate with us, the Kremlin has a 'Heroes' fund," he said. "Perhaps we can get your husband recognized as a hero of the Russian Federation. It comes with a modest stipend."

"Fuck you," she replied.

"Excuse me?"

"You heard me. *Fuck you*. I am here. I *am* cooperating. And regardless of what Wagner or the Kremlin says, my husband *is* a hero."

Teplov was taken aback. "I didn't mean to suggest that he—"

"I don't want to talk about it anymore. Do you understand me?"

The mercenary nodded and Christina continued her search.

In one of the examination rooms, she pointed out the bloody gauze pads. Then, in the office up front, she drew Teplov's attention to the fact that the computer had been left on. Something, she explained, that clinic staff never did.

Looking through the break room, she noted that there were several small food items missing. The more honest she was, the quicker she believed Teplov would lose interest in her.

It was trending in that direction when one of his men entered the clinic through the back and asked to speak with his boss in private.

When they were done, Teplov rejoined her.

"I wonder if you could come outside with me for a moment," he said.

"What for?"

"It won't take long. There's something I need you to identify, please."

It didn't sound like she had a choice. So, as the man stood back to let her pass, she zipped up her parka and walked toward the back door.

Outside, a couple of the Wagner men had opened the shed and discovered the snowmobile.

"Do you recognize this?" Teplov asked.

Ever since she'd had Harvath put the machine in the shed, she had expected the question. "I do," she replied. "That's my uncle's snowmobile. But what's it doing here?"

"Doctor Volkova, when was the last time you saw your uncle?"

She took a moment as she tried to remember. "It has been at least three weeks."

"And how was his health?"

"Why do you ask?"

"Just answer the question, please," the man commanded.

"He had emphysema and an irregular heartbeat. What is his snowmobile doing in my shed? If you know something, *tell* me. Where is my uncle?"

Teplov was a soldier, not a clergyman or a counselor. His bedside manner was sorely underdeveloped. "Doctor Volkova, I'm sorry to have to tell you this, but your uncle is dead."

"Dead? How?"

"We don't know."

"What does this have to do with my clinic being broken into? Is the American you're looking for connected to this? Did he murder my uncle?"

He held up his hand. "We don't know."

"Well, what the hell *do* you know?"

Teplov tried to calm her down. "Your uncle was a fur trapper and had a cabin, correct?"

She nodded.

"We think the American, Harvath, found your uncle's cabin and may have stayed there for a short time. We believe he helped himself to clothing and other supplies and then used your uncle's snowmobile to come here."

"But did he *murder* my uncle?" she repeated.

"We found your uncle in his bed, with the blanket pulled up over his head. We couldn't find any signs of trauma."

"Then how did he die?"

Teplov shrugged. "We don't know."

"So he stole my uncle's snowmobile, rode into Nivsky, and just happened to break into *my* clinic? How is that possible?"

"We assume that he either found a map, or judging by that," Teplov said, pointing at the bracket mounted to the handlebars, "a GPS device. Do you know what your uncle used for navigation?"

"GPS," she replied, telling the truth. "All of the hunters and trappers use them."

"That confirms what we thought."

"But how did this Horvath—"

"Harvath," he stated, correcting her.

"How did this *Harvath* make the connection between me and my uncle?"

"There's likely no connection at all. Just coincidence. He's injured and needed medical supplies. That's why he came here."

"So where did he go? I'm assuming your men searched the clinic."

"They did and he isn't here. I have other men searching the nearby buildings."

"Do you think he might come back?"

"To your clinic?" asked Teplov. "No. I think he got what he came for."

"Rabies vaccine, a couple of tins of cookies, coffee, tea, and sugar?"

"He's a fugitive. They tend to travel very light."

"Whatever you say," she replied. "Can I work on getting somebody out here to fix my door?"

"Not yet," said the mercenary. "First we need to talk about where Harvath may be headed."

CHAPTER 44

An escort sat in the car with Christina while Teplov and several of his men swept her uncle's house. Once they had deemed it safe, they had her come inside.

"Was he here?" she asked as she was escorted into the living room.

Teplov nodded and held his hand over the coals in the fireplace. "It looks like it."

"Sir!" one of the mercenaries called out, as he emerged from the bathroom carrying the hair dye kit and handed it to his boss.

Teplov examined it and said, "Spread the word that we believe the subject has changed his hair color to . . . midnight raven."

"Sir?" the operative replied.

"Black," he growled. "Harvath has changed his fucking hair color to black."

As the soldier stepped away and took out his radio to pass the word, Teplov looked at Christina. "Same question as at the clinic—what do you see?"

"I see my uncle's house," she replied, playing it as cool as possible.

"Yes, but is anything missing? Is anything out of place?"

It was now that she was especially glad she'd had the two shots of vodka. Teplov didn't know what he was looking for. As a result, he was asking her.

Whatever she told him, as long as she was believable, would dictate where his search went next.

"Is it okay for me to look around?" she asked.

"Absolutely."

She headed for the bathroom and Teplov followed.

Pointing at the wet towels and bloody bandages, she remarked, "It looks like your American was trying to clean up."

"What can you infer about his injuries?"

She told the truth. "You don't suture canine bites. You let them ooze. Your fugitive seems to be doing that, which suggests he definitely has medical training."

"Anything else?"

She shook her head and stepped out.

Leading Teplov into the bedroom, she looked through the closet, the dresser drawers, and the nightstands before declaring them untouched. She did the same thing in the kitchen. In the dining room, she paused.

"What is it?" asked Teplov.

"Nothing," she replied.

He had seen what she was looking at—a pen on the dining table. He walked over and picked it up.

"Why did this catch your eye?"

"Look around you. My uncle was a neat freak. It's an insufferable character trait."

"You disapproved?"

"He's my elder, my uncle. I don't get to approve or disapprove. But it was a source of tension between us. His need to have everything in its place bordered on unhealthy."

It was a lie. Her uncle wasn't a "neat freak." He was just an older man with few possessions who kept his home in order. The neat freak label was useful, though, in pointing the mercenary in the direction she needed him to go.

"Interesting," said Teplov, as he picked up the pen, walked it over to the desk near the bookshelves, and placed it in the leather cup with the others. "What else do you see?"

She took her time looking around. She absolutely wanted to draw his attention to the atlas, but of all the cards she had to play, this one was the most critical.

After a protracted search, she walked back into the kitchen, pulled a small, etched glass from the cupboard, and took a bottle of chilled vodka from the freezer.

As Teplov watched, she poured a tall shot and knocked it back. When it looked as if she was setting up a second, he stopped her.

"We're almost done here. Why don't you wait until you're back home?"

Christina glared at him. "My uncle's dead, but at least you're consistent. That's exactly the level of empathy I'd expect from Wagner."

He didn't know what she wanted and he was running out of patience with this woman.

While driving to the clinic, he had contacted his offices in Moscow and had verified that she was who she said and that her husband had died while employed by his company. Even so, there was something about her that bothered him. He didn't trust her.

Nevertheless, for the moment, he had to humor her.

"I'm sorry. Is there someone I can contact for you?"

She put on an all-too-obvious fake smile and shook her head. "There's no one to contact. You and President Peshkov killed my husband. And now, somehow, the two of you have figured out a way to kill the only other family member I had left."

Teplov didn't know what to say.

"Okay if I have one more?" Christina asked as she poured another shot and, without waiting for his response, tossed it back.

Setting the bottle down, she left the kitchen and walked back into the living room. She looked through her uncle's desk and then, with her hands on her hips, she stood staring at the bookcase.

Teplov was watching her. As with the pen, he again noticed that something had caught her eye. What, though, he couldn't tell.

Before he could ask her what it was, she pointed to a large atlas covered in green fabric. It was out of place, its spine unaligned with its neighbors, as if someone had failed to properly put it back.

Teplov stepped forward and removed it. Casually, he flipped through several pages and then tossed the book on the couch.

Damn it, Christina thought to herself.

"Did I miss something?" Teplov suddenly asked, returning to the book.

It was as if he had read her mind. Nevertheless, she needed to play dumb. "You asked me to look for things that were out of place."

"Interesting that you chose this atlas."

"Why is that interesting?"

"I don't know yet," he said, as this time, he flipped through the pages much more carefully. When he got to the part where she had removed one of the maps, he stopped.

Christina felt a bad feeling growing in the pit of her stomach.

"There appears to be a page missing," Teplov declared. "That doesn't seem like something a neat freak would do, much less a man who owned his own GPS."

He looked at her and Christina stared right back at him. The alcohol was continuing to embolden her.

"Doctor Volkova," he asked, "why would your uncle pull pages out of such a beautiful atlas?"

Christina shrugged. "He was an old man. They do weird things."

"I agree," said Teplov, as he produced the missing page and held it up. "My men found this buried between the seats of your car."

She wanted to curse, but the words wouldn't come. Despite the circumstance, all she could think of was Harvath. She had failed him, but she knew that as bad as things now were, she still might be able to buy him a few more minutes with which to escape.

But before she could say anything, Teplov approached her, drew back his fist, and punched her in the stomach, knocking the wind out of her.

As she doubled over in pain, he grabbed a fistful of her hair and painfully jerked back her head.

"Out of respect for your deceased husband, I'm going to give you one, and only one, chance," he hissed. "Where the fuck is Harvath?"

CHAPTER 45

We heard from Harvath," Nicholas explained as The Carlton Group jet was about to land at Helsinki Airport.

"Thank God," replied Sloane Ashby, who had taken the call over the plane's encrypted satellite phone. "Where is he? Is he okay?"

"What's going on?" Chase asked.

"Harvath made contact," she answered as she put the call on speaker and everyone moved closer. "We're all listening now. What do we know?"

"There's not much," Nicholas replied. "Apparently, he was in the Russian town of Nivsky, headed west."

Haney pulled up a map on his laptop. "Nivsky. Got it," he said, projecting the image onto the screens in the cabin. "About 250 kilometers south of the city of Murmansk and, as the crow flies, about eighty kilometers due east of the Finnish border."

"In other words," stated Staelin, "deep in Indian country."

"What else do you have?" asked Barton, as he adjusted the pitch on his seat so it matched the seat across from him. "Is he traveling by car? On foot? Is he injured?"

"That's all we know," said Nicholas. "The message came in as a comment on Instagram using one of our prearranged codes. It was posted from an account belonging to a doctor in Nivsky—Christina Volkova. She appears to be in charge of a medical clinic there. If she's helping Harvath, it might explain why there wasn't a lot of detail. He'd want to protect her and limit her exposure."

"What's the plan, then?" asked Matt Morrison, as the plane eased out of its descent and began to climb.

"We're diverting you to Lapland Air Command in Rovaniemi. There, you'll meet up with a representative from the Ministry of Defense who will travel north with you to Sodankylä."

Haney found it on his map. "It's practically a straight shot from Nivsky—just an additional eighty klicks after crossing the Finnish border."

"It's also," Nicholas added, "home to a battalion of the Finnish Army's Jaeger Brigade."

"Those guys are badass," stated Gage. "We trained with them when I was in Fifth Group."

"So did we," said Haney, pointing at himself and Morrison. "They know their stuff when it comes to arctic warfare and equipment."

"That's why President Porter has asked for their help," Nicholas continued. "The Finns, though, are skittish about supporting an incursion into Russia. They don't want to provoke a confrontation, which means the scope of their involvement is still being worked out. Be ready for a lot of last-minute decisions.

"Now, to give them top cover, this is being treated as a downed pilot exercise. The Zero-Three-Hundred team is being moved to Luleå in northern Sweden, where they will be on call with the Skibird and F-22 Raptors."

"The Finns wouldn't allow them in?" asked Sloane.

"Like I said, they're skittish. And on this issue, the President agrees. The Russians have a lot of eyes in Finland, particularly when it comes to movements of military equipment. While we can hide some SEALs from DEVGRU, we can't hide F-22s and a Skibird. Moscow would know something was up. It's much better for our purposes if we slide in under the radar."

"How exactly are we going to slide into Russia?" asked Barton.

"That's Jaeger's area of expertise. First, we have to pinpoint Harvath's location. Best-case scenario, he makes contact again and is able to give us his precise coordinates. In the meantime. we're working on getting a satellite overhead.

"The Finns have also stepped up. As the most forested country in Europe, their 832-mile border with Russia is notoriously difficult to patrol. They have invested a lot in new drone technology and are going to make some of their best equipment available to us."

"So in the meantime," asked Morrison, "we just wait?"

"Negative," replied Nicholas. "Our goal is to get you outfitted and inserted into Russia ASAP. We don't want to wait for Harvath to come to you. We want you to go to him."

The team was in agreement and there was a chorus of "Roger that," which resonated through the cabin.

Being one of the older, most experienced team members, Staelin was one of its most pragmatic. In his estimation, this operation was going to either be a stunning success or an unimaginable failure that would be taught throughout the Special Operations community as a "what not to do."

Though they were paid handsomely to take on high-risk, short-notice assignments, this one gave him a really bad feeling.

Normally with hostage scenarios, you found out where the subject was being held and you inserted a spotter team. While they kept 24/7 watch on the location to make sure the hostage wasn't moved, an exact replica of the target was constructed back in the United States. There, a takedown team rehearsed until they knew every door, window, stairwell, and flagpole on the property.

When it came time for the assault, the operators were as familiar with the location as they were with their own homes.

They also knew that hostage-takers often were under orders to kill the hostage if any rescue attempt was made. It created an added layer of danger, and stress, but that's what made them the best. They were completely focused, high-end professional athletes, able to turn on a dime and adjust to real-time changes on the field. Nobody did these kinds of things better than they did.

Nevertheless, this kind of operation was nothing but wild cards. With each unknown, the odds of failure rose exponentially. To say what they were about to do was exceedingly risky would be a gross understatement.

Haney felt the same way. In fact, he had pulled Staelin aside, shortly after takeoff, to share his reservations.

As the senior operatives, the mission planning and decision-making would come down to them. It was a tremendous responsibility, but one they were more than capable of taking on.

With all of the unknowns, there was one thing they did know, one thing they agreed on: that no matter how dangerous, no matter how bad the odds, Harvath would risk it all to come for them. He was one of them, their brother. They weren't going to leave him behind enemy lines.

"So," said Nicholas, wrapping up. "Does anyone else have any questions?"

Staelin leaned in toward the phone, wanting to make sure he was perfectly heard. "Just one thing," he said. "What are the rules of engagement?"

"There aren't any."

"So weapons free?"

"*Weapons free*," Nicholas confirmed, granting approval to engage any target with lethal force. "The only thing that matters is bringing Harvath back."

CHAPTER 46

Harvath was delirious. He couldn't remember if he'd heard the dogs first or had felt the rough hands as they yanked him to his feet. They were carrying guns.

He did remember someone making a big deal about his shotgun and snatching it up so that he couldn't reach it.

In a sense, he was relieved to have been captured. He hoped they'd put a bullet in his head and just be done with him, but in the back of his mind he knew that wasn't likely.

His brain was foggy and his eyesight was almost nonexistent. It was nearly impossible to tell what was going on.

One of the men, yelling in Russian, slapped him around. He had suffered worse in his SERE training. The more the man yelled, the more the dogs barked. Someone patted him down. They then took off his skis and tied him up. After that, he had blacked out.

When he awoke, he could still hear the dogs. They were someplace close. Did Wagner even have dogs? It was possible, he supposed. Plenty of military units used them. But dogs meant any escape was next to impossible. It sounded as if they had a lot of them.

His vision was slow to return. He attempted to move his arms and to his surprise, he was no longer tied down.

When his eyes adjusted to the darkness, he could see that he was in a cabin of some sort. It smelled like clay and chimney smoke. A fire crackled in the fireplace.

Most of his clothing had been removed. He was lying in a bed, with a compress laid across his head. A fire burned warm and bright nearby.

At a small table, an older woman sat with her back to him, humming. Next to a leather satchel were what looked like plastic Ziplocs filled with dried herbs. He had no idea where he was or what had happened.

His head felt as if it had been split open with an axe. He tried to sit up, but that only made it worse. Closing his eyes, he fell back against his pillow.

When he opened them again, the woman was standing over him. A large cup was in her hand. "Drink," she said in English, offering it to him.

Seeing the distress he was in, she set the cup aside and propped him up. Then, she held the cup up to his mouth so he could drink.

It was a broth of some sort. "*Spaseba*," he said, after he had finished.

"It's okay. I speak English."

"Where am I?"

"In the woods."

"*In the woods* where?"

"Outside the village of Adjágas," she replied. "You're safe here."

Adjágas, though, wasn't the village he was supposed to be in. "I need to get to Friddja," he said, trying to get up.

"Relax," she responded, easing him back down. "Everything is going to be okay."

"You don't understand."

"I think I do," she said, removing the note Christina had written and handing it to him. "I'm Sini."

"Where'd you get that?" he asked, taking a better look around the room. Near the front door he could see his rucksack, along with his shotgun.

"The men who found you in the snow, they were trying to figure out who you were. They searched your pockets."

"Why did they bring me here?"

"They're from Adjágas. They were on their way home from a hunt. Their dogs were tired. It was better to come here and then send word to me in Friddja."

"I remember being tied up."

Sini nodded. "You were in bad shape. They wrapped you in blankets and secured you to one of their sleds so you wouldn't roll off."

She had a kind, craggy face and a gentle voice. Harvath reached for the cup and she held it to his lips again so he could drink.

When he had finished, he asked, "What about Christina? Have you heard anything from her?"

Sini shook her head.

He looked at his watch and tried to figure out how long it had been since he had left Nivsky. "I can't stay here."

The Sámi woman smiled. "It's late. It's also very cold outside and you are in no condition to travel. Let's wait until morning. Maybe Christina will be here. We can discuss everything then."

Harvath didn't have the will to fight. He also didn't have the strength to charge back out into the snow—not tonight at least. So he gave in.

"May I?" Sini asked, pointing at the blanket that covered him.

He nodded and she pulled it down in order to reexamine his wounds. Slowly, using the items on the table, she began replacing the poultices she had applied to him earlier.

"Are you a doctor, too?" he asked.

"No," she replied. "In my language, I'm called *noaidi*, a healer."

"Your English is very good. Where did you learn it?"

"I grew up in the Swedish part of Lapland. We all studied English in school."

"How did you end up in Russia?"

"It was part of my calling as a *noaidi*. I'm originally from here. We left because of communist persecution. Eventually, I felt compelled to come back."

"And Christina? How do you know each other?"

"The Sámi people embrace both traditional and modern medicine. Christina has always been good about coming out if there's a situation I can't handle. I guess you could say that we began as colleagues, but now are close friends. She's a very special person."

Harvath agreed. Christina was special.

Pulling his blankets back up, Sini removed his compress and walked into the kitchen to prepare another, along with a special kind of tea.

Returning with the new compress, she laid it across his forehead. "Your body has absorbed a lot of punishment. It needs rest. This will help you sleep," she said, as she raised the cup, now filled with tea, to his mouth.

Harvath was grateful for the broth, the poultices, and especially the rescue. He knew he was not one hundred percent and that his body needed repairing. He also knew that he couldn't stay here. He needed to get moving. For the moment, though, he'd gladly take anything she offered that would help him recover.

"Is there anything else I can do for you?" she asked.

He looked around the room once more. "Is there a computer or a cell phone? Maybe a radio of some sort?"

The Sámi woman smiled and shook her head. "We still do things the old way here. Word travels fast, but it travels by foot."

Pointing at his shotgun, he asked, "Would you please bring that to me? I dropped it in the snow and need to clean it."

"It will be fine until tomorrow. Like I said, you're safe here. Nothing is going to happen to you."

He didn't doubt her sincerity, but she had no clue about the two dozen mercenaries who had landed in Nivsky and were actively hunting him. He needed to get across the border. But it wasn't going to happen tonight.

At best, he'd be well enough to strike off in the morning. And while he didn't like having to operate during daylight hours, if Sini and her friends were willing to help him, he might be able to make it to the border. Already, a plan was beginning to form in his mind.

Tomorrow, though, was a long way off. There were still many hours of darkness to go. And under the cover of darkness was where some of the worst things were known to happen.

CHAPTER 47

Teplov had dragged Christina out of the house by her hair. He didn't care who saw. The more the better as far as he was concerned. Just as at the bar, it would send a message. She had lied to him, repeatedly, and in so doing had only made things worse for herself.

As intelligent as she was, it baffled him that she never thought they would check her vehicle. She should have burned the page she tore from the atlas, not shoved it down between the seats.

It didn't matter. All that mattered was that Teplov and his men knew where Harvath was headed and that they had been saved from a massive wild-goose chase.

Now, they were going to get a chance to drag her through the center of town before putting her on one of the helicopters. Seeing their beloved Doctor Volkova dealt with so sternly would help solidify any cooperation they might need going forward.

And God help her if they needed it. If she had lied to him again, the beating she had received inside her uncle's house was nothing compared to what would be coming. If they went through all the trouble to load the bird and fly out to Friddja, only to find no one had even seen Harvath, there'd be hell to pay.

Teplov had radioed ahead. He knew whom he wanted with him and how to make the biggest spectacle in order to draw the most attention.

He planned on leaving a sizable stay-behind contingent, just in case

Doctor Volkova had lied again. The contingent would continue search-ing for Harvath in and around town.

The fresh ski tracks they had found outside the uncle's house, though, were a good sign. They led in the direction of the village he was allegedly headed toward.

He had sent his men to follow them, but with the wind and blowing snow, the tracks had quickly disappeared. Their best hope now was to fly overhead and catch Harvath en route, or to isolate him on the ground in Friddja and capture him there.

The moment they arrived at the town square, the cargo helicop-ter came alive. As its engine began to roar and its rotors started to spin, townspeople, including all of the patrons inside the bar and café, were drawn to the windows around the square. He had their attention.

They had previously witnessed the beating his men had doled out to the bar patron who had refused to cooperate. Now they would see their doctor, beaten and bloody, dragged out of a vehicle, placed in the helicop-ter, and flown away.

It was yet another SS tactic he found useful. You always dealt harshly with those who showed initial resistance. Afterward, it was often necessary to make an example of a highly respected member of the community—someone whom people looked up to and who was seen as being above reproach.

Pulling up outside, he saw all the patrons, just as before, glued to the windows. He parked his SUV right in front and had his men remove Doctor Volkova.

She refused to comply as they tried to parade her forward. Teplov or-dered his men to let her be.

When they stood aside, he walked over and punched her in her lower back. Her knees buckled and she fell to the ground, where she spat blood into the snow.

People inside the bar and the café gasped. It was barbaric, what was hap-pening outside. None of them, though, dared to react. They had no doubt that the soldiers would shoot them dead on the spot. Instead, they did the only thing they could do. They cowered inside and watched it all unfold.

Teplov grabbed Christina by the hair and pulled up her head so everyone inside could see her face. Several of them turned away in horror, unable to watch what was happening.

Letting go of her head, Teplov stood and commanded his men to walk her to the helicopter. If she refused to walk, she was to be beaten until she complied.

Christina had suffered enough. When the soldiers helped her to her feet, she did exactly as she was told. With a man holding each of her arms, she allowed them to guide her forward and then up the ramp.

Once Teplov and his people were all present and accounted for, the spinning of the rotors increased and the helicopter lifted off, throwing snow and ice in all directions and pelting all the vehicles parked around the square.

It banked to the north, hovered briefly over the uncle's home, and then made its way west toward the Sámi village of Friddja.

As the helicopter slowly flew, the crew scanned their instruments for any signs of Harvath. Attached inside, heavy black ropes sat coiled on the floor, ready to be kicked out the doors if the Wagner mercenaries needed to rappel down and grab him.

When out of the darkness the village appeared up ahead, the men checked their weapons and prepared their night vision goggles.

As with the Nazi SS, to be a member of Wagner, recruits not only had to have been tops in their previous military units, but they also had to have "pure" Russian blood. They had to have demonstrated obedience and an absolute commitment to Russia, the Russian President, and the Russian people.

The Wagner motto was identical to that of the SS: *My honor is loyalty*. Teplov led the men in a recital of their oath. "We swear to you, O Russia, fidelity and bravery. We solemnly pledge obedience to the death to you, and to those named as our leaders."

Inside the helicopter, the men exploded in the Russian battle cry, popular since the days of the Imperial Russian Army, *"Ura! Ura! Ura!"*

If Harvath was down there, Teplov had no doubt that his fired-up, highly disciplined, and highly experienced men would find him.

CHAPTER 48

Harvath hadn't been asleep that long when he heard the helicopter pass. Instantly, he shot straight up in bed.

Sini, who was sitting nearby and watching her patient, had heard it, too.

"What is it?" she asked.

"Bad news," replied Harvath. "Very bad news."

The letter from Christina had explained that he was in trouble, but that it wasn't his fault and that he could be trusted. Her only request had been for Sini to see to his injuries and to keep him safe until she could get there.

The Sámi woman saw Harvath eyeing the shotgun. This time she didn't argue with him. Walking over to the door, she picked it up and carefully brought it to him.

"What else do you need?"

"A rag," he replied. "And some oil if you have it."

Sini hunted the items down and carried them over to Harvath. She watched as he unloaded the weapon and expertly took it apart, examining each piece, rubbing some with the cloth, and applying small drops of oil where necessary.

Then, as quickly as he had broken the shotgun down, he reassembled it, loaded the rounds, and racked one into the chamber.

His confidence with the weapon spoke to a certain level of expertise. The injuries to his body, as well as his detached demeanor, suggested to her a man all too familiar with violence. His concern over the helicopter suggested he was being pursued by the state.

"That helicopter is looking for you," she said. "Isn't it?"

Harvath nodded.

"And you think they will come here?"

"I know they will."

"Why?" she asked. "What happened?"

"I don't have time to explain. How far are we from Friddja?"

"You think that is where the helicopter is going?"

It had to be. There was no other reason he could think of for it to be out here.

But, if it was heading for Friddja, that could only mean one thing—Christina had given him up. There was no way they could have tracked him through the snow. Any trail he left was quickly covered over. It had to have been Christina.

Though he barely knew her, he doubted she had given him up willingly. The soldiers from Wagner had proven their brutality outside the bar in Nivsky. It wasn't a stretch to believe they would have beaten Christina as well if they thought she had information they needed.

"The men in that helicopter are mercenaries. They beat a man back in town unconscious because he refused to give them his vehicle. If they are headed to Friddja, it's because they figured out Christina was helping me and they forced her to talk. When they get there, and can't find me, they're going to come here. We need to get moving. Now, how far away is Friddja?"

"*Poronkusema*," she replied. "One *poronkusema*."

"I don't know that word," he said, as he removed the poultices and began pulling his clothes on.

"In this area, we herd reindeer. Reindeer can't walk and urinate at the same time. They have to stop. A *poronkusema* is the average distance between stops," said Sini as she tried to come up with an equivalent he would understand. "Somewhere between nine and ten kilometers. We'll say nine and a half."

It was way too close. "Who knows you're here?"

"My husband, of course. Why?"

"Who else?"

"No one. Just him."

"What did you tell him?" he asked.

"I didn't tell him anything," she said. "Jompá, one of the brothers who rescued you, put together a new dog team and came to get me. When he arrived, he showed me the letter they had found in your pocket.

"He told us the story of how they had found you in the snow. He asked me to come back to Adjágas with him. That was all. I told my husband to send Christina as soon as she arrived."

"Are we in Jompá's home right now?"

She nodded. "He is at his brother's."

"Okay. Listen to me very carefully. All of you are in danger because of me."

"We could hide you until—"

"You can't hide me. These men can smell a lie from a mile away. And once that happens they will hurt you. All of you."

"So what are we supposed to do?"

"Tell them the truth, all of it—that they found me in the snow, that you gave me medical attention, and that when I heard the helicopter, I fled."

"But Christina asked me to take care of you, to keep you safe."

"I am very grateful for all that you have done," he said, lacing up his boots, then putting on his coat and zipping it up.

"I'm sorry," Sini replied. "I wish there was more that we could do. I know Jompá and his brother will feel the same."

"You need to go be with them. Please tell them that I said thank you. You saved my life."

"Where will you go? It's freezing out there."

"I'll figure something out. Where are my skis?"

"Just outside," she said, "along with your poles."

Removing the bladder from his rucksack, he handed it to her. "Can you fill this for me please while I put them on?"

Sini did as he requested. Then, putting on her own coat, she stepped outside and handed it to him.

He thanked her and asked one last question. "Which way is Friddja? That's the way they'll be coming from."

She raised her arm and pointed. "That way," she said. "Through the trees. You can't miss the path." She then watched as he skied off in the opposite direction.

It was completely black and only took a matter of seconds before he was swallowed up by the darkness.

In her heart, Sini wanted to believe that he would make it, but in her head she knew that wasn't going to happen. A man in his condition, alone in the bitterly cold wilderness, hunted by mercenaries with a helicopter, didn't stand a chance.

The woman, though, didn't know Scot Harvath.

CHAPTER 49

As smoke rose from the chimneys and stove pipes of Friddja's snow-covered houses, the arctic helicopter touched down on the edge of the village, spooking a herd of reindeer kept in a pen nearby.

Squeezing the back of Christina's neck, Teplov pushed her out the door and ordered her to identify the dwelling where she was supposed to meet Harvath. She resisted until the pain became unbearable. Only then did she point it out.

After two snowmobiles had raced down the helicopter's loading ramp to secure the perimeter, Teplov ordered his men to move in and encircle the house.

Just as in Nivsky, residents had gathered at windows and even more had poured outside to see what all the commotion was about. Sini's husband, Mokci, made the mistake of opening his door just as one of Teplov's goons had stepped up to kick it open.

For his trouble, Mokci caught a rifle butt in the mouth and was shoved back inside. He fell to the floor as the assault team spilled in searching for Harvath.

Standing outside, Teplov took satisfaction in the villagers' shocked and indignant reactions. He, along with several more men, watched and waited for someone to make the mistake of picking up a rifle, but none of them did. *Mission accomplished.*

Moments later, the assault team leader stepped back outside and signaled the all clear. Harvath was not inside.

Trying to keep his anger under control, Teplov marched Christina up to the house and pushed her through the door.

When she saw Mokci sitting in a chair, blood gushing from his face, her professional instincts kicked in and she rushed to help him. Teplov didn't stop her.

She found a clean towel and had him hold it to his mouth and apply pressure. In the meantime, she asked and was granted permission to retrieve a piece of ice from outside. When she came back in, she wrapped it in another clean towel and had Mokci hold that against his wound.

He was almost an identical male version of his wife—small, but sturdy with a kind, weathered face, dark hair, and brown eyes.

"What is wrong with you people?" Christina demanded as she turned to face Teplov. "That was completely unnecessary."

"Shut up," the mercenary ordered, as he grabbed the Sámi man's face and examined it by twisting it from one side to the other. "He'll be fine."

"You might have broken his jaw."

"I told you to shut up," he barked, focusing on Mokci. "Where's the American?"

"What American?" Mokci blubbered through a quickly swelling and still bleeding lip.

"The one Doctor Volkova sent here. The one who was supposed to meet with your wife."

"I don't know what you're talking about."

Teplov could tell by the way the man refused to make eye contact that he was hiding something. Drawing his cupped hand back, he aimed for his left ear and slapped him as hard as he could in the side of the head.

The blow was so intense, it knocked the Sámi out of his chair and down onto the floor, where he screamed in pain.

"Stop it!" Christina shouted. "First you try to break his jaw and now you're trying to rupture his eardrum. He said he doesn't know."

Teplov spun on her and grabbed her by the throat. "I'm not going to tell you again. Shut. Up."

Casting her aside, he nodded at his men, who picked Mokci up and placed him back in his chair. Tears were streaming down his face.

"I haven't done anything wrong," the man pleaded.

"That wasn't what I asked you," retorted Teplov. "I asked you where the American is."

"I told you. I don't know what you're talking about. I have not seen any American. No American has been here."

Teplov, scanning the main living area, demanded, "What about your wife?"

"What about her?"

"She is a *noaidi*, is she not?"

Mokci nodded.

"Where is she?"

"Adjágas," he replied. "A village not far from here."

Teplov looked at one of his men, who located it on his map and showed him. "Why?"

"Someone was ill."

"*Someone* who?"

"I don't know."

Teplov raised his hand to strike him again.

Mokci cowered and told him everything he knew. "A man named Jompá said he and his brother had found a man, more dead than alive, in the snow. They brought him back to Adjágas and then Jompá came here to get Sini. That's all I know. I am telling you the truth."

"How long ago?"

"Several hours at least."

"And do you know what house in Adjágas belongs to this Jompá?"

The Sámi man hesitated and that was the only confirmation Teplov needed.

Over the radio, he sent the two snowmobiles on ahead. Before they boarded the helicopter and took off, he wanted to conduct a search of the village. He had too much riding on this to lose Harvath just because the

Sámis had heard the helicopter coming and were smart enough to have hidden him in another house.

It wouldn't have been the first time something like that had happened. It wouldn't matter, though. He would turn over every rock, look under every branch, and search every house in the Oblast until he found him. There was no way Harvath was going to make it to the border.

CHAPTER 50

Once out of sight of Adjágas, Harvath cut into the woods. Because of all of the heavy snow, there were broken pine boughs scattered around.

He skied in circles, joined back up with his tracks on the main trail, then returned to the woods where he removed a length of rope from his rucksack and tied it around his waist.

Spotting the perfect pine bough—wide, but not too heavy—he tied it to the other end and dragged it behind him in an attempt to partially cover his tracks.

On a scale of one to ten, the results were a four, but it was better than nothing. He hoped that, in the dark, it would be enough. He only needed a little head start.

Soundlessly, he moved through the trees, making his way back toward the village as quickly as he could. The only hope he had of being successful was via the element of surprise.

His mind was moving as fast as, if not faster than, his skis. There were a lot of unanswered questions, vital equations, he was trying to solve.

First and foremost, *How many men were on that helicopter?* Had the full two dozen been sent, or had some been left behind to continue searching for him in Nivsky? If Harvath had to wager, he'd be willing to bet that they had left some behind. That still didn't fully answer his question, though.

His next question was, *What was his objective?* Obviously, it was making his escape. But what was that going to look like? There was no way to know until the opportunity revealed itself.

He couldn't outrun their helicopter. And if they had brought snowmobiles along, which they probably had, he couldn't outrun those either.

That meant that he was either going to have to convince them that he was no longer running, or make it so they couldn't chase him.

At the very least, he'd do enough damage to force them to fall back, regroup, and be very nervous about coming after him.

They would, of course, come after him, but if they did so with trepidation, he would have secured the upper hand.

Injecting fear into the hearts of battle-hardened special forces soldiers, Russians or otherwise, was no easy feat. It was quite a tall order, but one that—if he was lucky—he might just be able to pull off.

For that to happen, though, a lot had to take place between now and his eventual escape. And all of it had to go right. One single screwup on his part would mean either death or capture, which he was certain were pretty much the same thing.

Arriving back in Adjágas, the first thing he did was to ditch the pine bough. He followed that up by hiding his skiing equipment in a crawl space beneath one of the cabins.

Now, his only liability was his boots. They left very distinct prints. But as he had done when trying to disguise his ski tracks, all he could do was hope that in the chaos of the moment, with loads of adrenaline pumping through them, that none of the mercenaries noticed.

Hope, though, wasn't a plan. In fact, he needed to do everything he could to make sure his tracks would not stick out.

Staying away from fresh snow, he trod only where the villagers themselves had walked, altering how he placed his feet so as not to leave a full print.

The boots were rigid. They not only hurt his feet, they also slowed him down. Nevertheless, it was worth it. He hadn't come this far to leave a trail that would lead right to him. The element of surprise, right now, was the only thing he had going for him.

Arriving at Jompá's cabin, he peered into one of the windows. Sini was nowhere to be seen. Coming back around, he tried the door and, as he had expected in such a small village, it was unlocked.

Stepping inside, he closed the door behind him, removed the flashlight from his pocket, and set it on the floor so as not to draw attention from anyone outside.

Unshouldering his rucksack, he pulled out the box of shotgun shells he had taken from the trapper's cabin and made a tough decision—how many could he part with? He settled on half.

Giving up ammo, especially when you didn't know how many of the enemy you were facing, normally wasn't the best idea. But in this case, the rounds could end up acting as a force multiplier.

After retrieving a glass jar he had seen earlier in the kitchen, he took out his knife and began opening the shells, making sure all of the powder went inside and that all of his buckshot was accounted for.

It took him several more minutes to complete his improvised explosive device, but when it was done, he felt confident that it was more than up to the task. The only problem remaining was where to place it.

He lacked the materials necessary to create a fuse with a delay. If he set it up at the front door, it would go off the minute someone set foot inside and only affect the first person through. To be worth it, it had to kill, or at the very least injure, as many of the Wagner mercenaries as possible. He decided to set it up farther inside and use the bed as bait.

Christina had been right about playing up his injuries. The more blood and bandages they saw, the more their confidence grew that he was weak and unable to put up a decent fight. If he was lucky, a booby-trap would be one of the last things they'd be thinking about.

All of Sini's supplies were still scattered about. After setting up the bed to make it look as if someone was sleeping in it, he placed other items nearby so that to anyone entering, it would appear that he was in even worse shape.

By the time they got close enough to realize that the bed was empty, it would be too late. They would have already hit the trip wire.

At least that was the plan. He had constructed several IEDs in his day that had worked, as well as several that hadn't. It seemed that the more he needed them, the greater the odds were that they would fail. He hoped that tonight, that wouldn't be the case.

After doing one last sweep to make sure everything was perfect, he backed out of the cabin and closed the door. Far in the distance, he could hear snowmobiles.

All of a sudden, he got another idea. Slinging the rucksack and his shotgun, he ran off toward the trail Sini had pointed to earlier, the one that led to Friddja.

And as he ran, he said a silent prayer that not only were the snowmobiles taking that route, but that he could get to the right spot before they did.

CHAPTER 51

Harvath ran as fast as he could up the trail. He didn't care if he was leaving footprints in the snow or not. All that mattered was speed.

As he ran, he kept his eyes peeled for the ideal place to set his trap. Finally, he found it.

The two trees were thick enough and were positioned perfectly on either side of the trail.

Rummaging through his rucksack, he pulled out the second spool of wire he had taken from the trapper. It was a heavier gauge than he had just used to set the trip wire for his IED. Because of the amount of force it was going to have to withstand, it needed to be.

While he would have loved to have been equipped to kill multiple birds with one stone, he knew that wasn't going to happen. The trail was too narrow for the mercenaries to be riding in anything other than single file.

Harvath only had enough wire for two traps. The best he could hope to do was to take out the men piloting the first and second snowmobiles. After that, he'd be reliant on his shotgun.

He worked quickly, guesstimating where precisely to set the first wire, and then making sure it was as secure as humanly possible. Clipping the wire, he ran about five meters farther down the trail, where he set the second trap. This one was even more difficult.

Based on what Christina had seen while picking up his dinner in

Nivsky, he knew the mercenaries would be wearing night vision goggles. That meant he would have to camouflage himself. He couldn't arm the second trap, though, until the first snowmobiler had raced past, and even then, he had to remain hidden. He needed a spring, something he could activate from his hiding place without revealing his presence.

He found exactly what he needed in the shape of a younger, more pliable tree, which even in the deep arctic cold he was able to bend. He tied it down using a piece of cord and an adjacent tree trunk.

With his wires set, he stashed his rucksack and then dug a place in the snow, which he covered with several pine branches. Holding his knife in one hand and the shotgun in the other, he made ready. He could hear the snowmobiles. They were close, almost there.

He was about to lose his only advantage—the element of surprise. Once the first rider hit the first trap, the mercenaries would know they were under attack. The tricky part for him would be timing the leap from his hiding spot. Fortunately, he had a halfway decent view of the trail and would be able to make that call on the fly.

Straining his ears, he tried to discern how many snowmobiles were approaching. It was an impossible task. All he could tell was that it sounded like more than one. He had no way of knowing how many men he was about to face.

Lying there in the snow, he would have given a decade's worth of paychecks for a few claymores or a box of hand grenades. There was precious little cover available beyond tree trunks. If this turned into an all-out gunfight, he was going to be in trouble.

He had to win it before they could get in it. That meant he had to be fast as hell and on the money with each shot.

Reminding himself of the old maxim for coming out on top in a gunfight, he repeated, "Slow is smooth and smooth is fast."

The snowmobiles were hauling ass. He could hear the whine of their engines as they raced toward him. That was a good sign—the faster, the better.

They were seconds away now. Ten. Maybe twenty.

Extending his knife out from under the cover of his hide site, he let it hover just above the taut cord that would spring the second trap. His heart was pounding and he took several deep breaths in order to help it calm down.

When the first snowmobile came blazing past, he slashed the cord. The young tree did exactly what it was supposed to do, pulling the wire wrapped around a much sturdier tree taut. What Harvath hadn't been expecting, though, was that the second rider would be following so closely behind the first.

There was a loud *twang* as the snowmobiler hit the wire, which was hung across the trail like a clothesline at chest height, and he was instantly decapitated.

His sled went sailing into the woods, hitting several trees before landing mangled and upside down.

The lead rider must have noticed something had happened—maybe, out of the corner of his eye, he had seen the beam of his colleague's headlight as it bounced off into the forest—because just as his machine drew even with the other trap, he turned and looked behind him.

Either Harvath had set it too low, or this guy was too tall, because instead of having his head sliced clean off, the wire cut off his arm and sliced into his torso.

He was thrown clear of the snowmobile, which managed to stay on the trail until it glided to a stop.

Harvath looked and listened, but there were no other snowmobiles. Leaping from his hide, he ran from the woods and up to the trail to the mercenary who lay bleeding out in the snow.

He could have shot the man from where he was, but he was unsure how far the sound would carry and how close the rest of them were. Instead, he slung his shotgun and closed in on him with his knife.

Even before he drew even with the man, he knew there was no saving him. Not even a tourniquet would have made a difference. In addition to losing his arm and slicing open his chest, the wire must have snapped up as he was thrown from the snowmobile and cut into his neck, severing a major artery. He was spurting blood like an out-of-control sprinkler.

Harvath made sure to not get too close and kept one eye on the man's hands. The mercenary, though, didn't attempt to reach for his weapon.

Under the glow from the night vision goggles, Harvath watched as the life left the man's eyes. There was no need to plunge his knife into him. The job had already been done. Harvath's challenge now was to figure out what to do next.

He didn't bother to wait for the good idea fairy to strike. Instead he raced back to retrieve his rucksack and stripped the two dead mercenaries of anything of value to his survival. In that category, there was a ton.

He helped himself not only to their weapons, but also to their ammo-packed chest rigs, four fragmentation grenades, the decapitated man's winter coveralls, which, because of how his body had landed, had only minimal bloodstains, and best of all, one of their helmets rigged with night vision goggles.

In almost any other situation, he would have booby-trapped the bodies with the frag grenades. He was afraid, though, that one the villagers might come along and get hurt. So leaving the dead soldiers where they were, he gathered up the rest of his equipment and ran down the trail to the remaining snowmobile.

He secured the gear as best he could and was preparing to take off when he heard a sound that shook him to his core.

The helicopter was coming.

CHAPTER 52

It was make or break time. When that helicopter landed, he had no idea how many men would be pouring out of it or how they'd be equipped. Would they be on foot? On skis? Or all on snowmobiles? There was no way of knowing.

What he felt certain about, though, was that they had located Sini's house in Friddja. That meant either Christina had described it to them, or more than likely, they had brought her along to make the identification in person.

Once they had found Sini's, they had probably found her husband, which was why they were inbound to Adjágas.

And just as he suspected that Christina had been dragged along, the Wagner mercenaries had probably brought Sini's husband as well. His job would be to help them identify Jompá's cabin.

What the mercenaries planned to do with their hostages was anyone's guess. Harvath knew they were not going to let Christina go—not after she had aided his escape. This left him with a serious problem.

Either they were going to hand her over to the GRU, who at best would throw her in prison, and at worst would execute her, or the mercenaries would rape and then beat her to death, leaving her body for the wolves. None of those were acceptable outcomes in his book.

She had helped him and he needed to help her. He just prayed to God that she was on that helicopter. He didn't want to have to go back to Nivsky to find her.

Based on the possibility of hostages being among the mercenaries, his mindset flipped from ambush to rescue. That didn't mean, though, that he couldn't kill every last Wagner soldier on that helo, it just meant he had to make sure no harm came to Christina and, if he was present, Sini's husband.

If he knew exactly where the helicopter would land, he might have been able to find concealment nearby and, using the night vision goggles, catch a glimpse of who, and how many, got off. But as it stood, he had no clue.

All he knew was that they would search Jompá's cabin first. That's where they expected to find him. With the bird coming in fast, he kicked it into high gear.

He hid the snowmobile and his rucksack at the edge of the village, covering them with broken pine boughs. Then, he strapped on as much gear as he could carry, shouldered all the guns, and rushed toward the cabin.

He knew where he was going to end up, but before he got there, he needed to establish several alternative positions—places where he could predeploy weapons and ammunition.

Moving through the shadows behind the cabins, he picked his spots carefully. He wanted to be able to quickly access the gear, but also to remain hidden. And, if he found himself in a running gun battle, he wanted at least some cover.

With everything set, he moved to his final position.

Each cabin in Adjágas was different, but most of them were built with crawl spaces underneath—similar to the one where he had hidden his skis.

One of them was rather dilapidated, but had an excellent view of Jompá's. Even better, it was uninhabited.

Clearing some of the snow away, he was able to dig a hole wide enough to allow him to squeeze underneath. It was only then that he realized how structurally unsound the cabin was.

The floor above had rotted through in places and it sat on beams atop short, stacked stone pillars. He had the sense that just bumping one could bring the entire cabin crashing down on him.

The space was so small, he had to balance the AK-15 rifle on his forearms and belly crawl to get into position. Had he been even the slightest bit claustrophobic, it would have been impossible.

At the far end of the crawl space, he set his rifle aside and pushed away enough of the snow to be able to see Jompá's. The range was perfect and there was nothing obstructing his view. The only drawback was going to be his muzzle flash. As soon as he started firing, it was going to be obvious where it was coming from.

Backing up, deeper into the crawl space, and firing from there was out of the question. As he backed up, his line of sight became impaired and he couldn't fully see the target. He was going to have to risk shooting from where he was and follow the three Bs: be fast, be accurate, and be the hell out of there.

He hoped there'd be enough chaos that he could get in all the shots he needed. But he knew better than to think like that. Murphy, of the eponymous law, always found a way to screw things up.

For his own good, he needed to resist becoming greedy. Staying one second too long in that crawl space could mean death. If at all possible, he had to be on the way out before they even began shooting back at him. It wouldn't be easy, but he didn't get to choose the circumstances. He only got to choose how he was going to react to them.

Outside, he could hear the *thump, thump, thump* of the helicopter's blades as it arrived and hovered somewhere overhead. The rotor wash sent snow and ice flying in all directions as it illuminated its powerful searchlight and lit up Jompá's cabin. Even at his distance, the light was practically blinding for Harvath.

Shielding his eyes, he was able to watch as ropes were dropped and a team of six operators in total rappelled down.

This wasn't what he had planned for. He had expected them to set down someplace and come in on foot. *Fuck*, he thought to himself. *Now what?*

There was only one thing he could do—what he was trained to do: *adapt and overcome*.

Though he hated to do it, he backed up, turned around, and scrambled back in the direction from which he had entered the crawl space.

He didn't need to see them to know there were snipers onboard providing overwatch for the operators. The moment he started firing, they'd be putting rounds all over him. The deadly difference, though, was that they'd be shooting from above, through a rotting floor, rather than trying to skip rounds off the ground and maybe hit a target hidden in a crawl space.

The presence of the helicopter was a game changer. It also provided a potential opportunity.

Harvath had less than a minute, thirty seconds at best. The moment the mercenaries triggered his IED, all bets were off.

Moving as fast as he could, he popped out of the crawl space, flipped up the night vision goggles on his helmet, and leaped to his feet. It was critical that he time his next move precisely.

Based on the searchlight, he knew exactly where the helicopter was. He made sure to keep the corner of the cabin between him and the snipers. They couldn't shoot what they didn't even know was there.

Already, the fire selector on the battle rifle he had taken from one of the dead Wagner snowmobilers was set to semiauto. Wrapping the sling around his arm for stability, he didn't need to double-check that the weapons were hot. He had already chambered rounds in all of them.

The enormous helicopter continued to blast the village with whirling sheets of ice and snow, as its searchlight illuminated Jompá's cabin with its white-hot beam.

Harvath had done countless entries over his career. Though he was tempted to stick his head out and see what was going on, he stayed right where he was.

There was only the front entrance, nothing in back. They would have seen that as they had flown over and before they had rappelled down.

Right now they'd be lining up in a stack, ready to kick in the door. After which they would charge in, searching the room for threats, their weapons sweeping left and right when . . .

BOOM.

The explosion wasn't the loudest Harvath had ever heard. But it was significant.

While all attention in the helicopter was on the IED that had just gone off inside Jompá's house Harvath swung out from behind the corner of the dilapidated cabin facing it and began firing.

He focused on the helicopter's searchlight, and it took him a total of four shots to knock it out.

The instant the light went dark, he swung his barrel and dumped four more of the 7.62x39 rounds into the door area, where there was indeed a sniper.

After killing the sniper, he shifted to the pilot's window, fired four additional rounds, and then targeted the bird's engine with the rest of the ammunition in his mag.

If Christina was onboard, he prayed that she was strapped in. Having run the weapon dry, he ejected the empty magazine, and pulling a fresh one from his chest rig, rammed it home and cycled the bolt.

But before he could reengage, the helicopter banked hard away from him. Smoke was billowing from its exhaust and it was losing altitude. Harvath didn't need to see any more to know the big Mi-8 was going down.

Snapping his eyes to Jompá's house, he saw two Wagner mercenaries, each dragging an injured comrade out of the burning cabin.

He didn't give his next move a second thought. Taking aim, he pressed his trigger and lit all four of them up.

Changing magazines, he heard a clap of thunder as the helicopter snapped through the trees of the forest beyond the village and slammed into the ground.

It was a bad crash, but based on how low the helo had been, he knew it was survivable.

Disguised in Wagner winter whites and carrying a Wagner-issued weapon, he flipped down the night vision goggles on his helmet and went to finish what they had started. His first stop—Jompá's.

As the villagers slowly popped their heads out to see what had happened, Harvath waved them back inside. He didn't need them making this any more dangerous than it already was.

Out of the corner of his eye, standing outside one of the cabins, he saw Sini. And she saw him.

Harvath didn't need to ask for her help. She understood what was happening. Immediately, she began shouting in Sámi and gesturing for people to get back inside their homes.

The killing had only just begun.

CHAPTER 53

Slinging his rifle, Harvath pulled the pistol he had taken off the dead snowmobiler and quickly approached Jompá's cabin.

The minute he was in range, he head-shot every Wagner mercenary he saw—just to be sure. He wanted to be absolutely certain that they were dead.

After he drilled the four at the door, he took a quick peek inside. Blood and pieces of flesh from the other two operatives were splattered everywhere. The IED had done its job. Nevertheless, each of the bodies inside received a head-shot as well. Now, he needed to get to the helicopter.

Taking a quick peek outside to make sure no one was lying in wait, he stepped through the doorway, helped himself to fresh magazines and extra frag grenades from the dead men.

One of the mercenaries had been carrying two incendiary grenades and Harvath grabbed those as well. They were used for destroying equipment and could burn at four thousand degrees for forty seconds.

As he had with the snowmobilers back on the trail, he decided against booby-trapping the bodies.

Shoving everything into his pockets, he left the bodies alone and ran for the snowmobile. Along the way, he picked up his other guns and ammunition. There was no telling what he was going to encounter at the downed chopper.

After tossing away the branches, he secured his rucksack and equipment, fired up the snowmobile, and took off.

He had a general idea of where the crash had happened, but didn't know what the terrain was like or how close he was going to be able to get to it.

Using his night vision goggles to see by, he kept the headlight turned off. It was bad enough that the loud whine of the engine would give away his approach—he didn't intend to add a visual beacon on top of it.

About half a klick into the forest, he began to see light in the distance. It had to be coming from the downed helicopter. He kept going, getting as close as he felt comfortable, then killed the engine and went in the rest of the way on foot.

The snow, as it was everywhere else in this godforsaken country, was deep and he struggled to push through it. If he never saw a single flake of it again, it would be too soon.

As he moved, he made sure to take advantage of the natural camouflage of the trees. There was no telling who had survived the crash. Any number of them could be headed his way, or worse, preparing an ambush.

Every few yards, he stopped and listened. But even as he closed in on the chopper, he didn't hear anything. It was still—deathly still.

Cresting a small rise, he saw the helicopter beneath him. It was down in a gulley, lying on its side. All around, the tall pine trees had been snapped like toothpicks. The helo's rotors had been shorn off and there were pieces of wreckage strewn everywhere. Using a tree for cover, he crouched down. For several moments, he watched and waited.

No one moved. No one made a sound. He had a bad feeling that Christina might be dead. He wouldn't know, though, until he got down there.

Picking the route that provided the most protection, he slowly descended into the gulley.

It reminded him of an operation he had conducted in Norway, on similar terrain and in similar conditions. There had been an ambush and it had turned into a bloodbath. Gripping his rifle, he kept his eyes open, stopping every few feet to listen.

The only sounds he heard were the last gasps of the helicopter's mechanical and electrical systems, punctuated every so often by the hiss of hydraulic fluid as it spat from a severed hose somewhere.

Once in the gulley, he carefully approached the helo from its nose. Peering through the shattered cockpit windscreen, his AK-15 up and at the ready, he could see the pilot and copilot. They were both dead.

It was hard to see any deeper inside—some piece of cargo was obstructing the view. He kept moving.

With the bird lying on its side, the helicopter's porthole-style windows were pointing either up toward the sky or down toward the ground. He'd have to climb on top of the helo if he wanted to look through the windows. He decided to make a complete loop of the aircraft and quietly slid around to the back.

The tail had been sheared off coming through the trees and tossed somewhere in the woods. From where he stood, he couldn't see any sign of it, nor its rotor.

The rear cargo doors, mounted at the back of the fuselage and underneath where the tail had been, were still intact, but badly damaged and partially ajar.

Harvath didn't like it. Even though they looked as if they had been forced open because of the crash, he proceeded with caution.

Sneaking a glance under one of the hinges and not seeing anything, he risked a look around the door itself. There was no one inside—at least not anyone alive.

Cargo lay scattered everywhere and there was a strong smell of spilled gasoline. Unlike jet fuel, which needed to be aerosolized first, gasoline was highly flammable. The presence of frayed electrical wires, some of which were actively sparking, was bad news.

Off to the side, he saw multiple jerry cans—likely for the snowmobiles—that had ruptured. What he didn't see was any sign of Christina. Climbing over and around all the debris, he moved toward the cockpit.

At the forward doors, wearing harnesses, he found the two Wagner snipers on either side of the chopper. One of them was the one he had been shooting at. Judging by the man's wounds, he had hit him at least three times. The other looked as if he had died on impact.

It appeared that Christina hadn't been brought along after all. That could only mean that they were holding her back in Nivsky. *Damn it.*

Shoving the large container aside that had earlier blocked his view, he quickly went through the cabinets near the cockpit. He didn't want to leave anything behind that could be of value.

Gathering what few things he had found, he walked them to the rear, tossed them out the cargo doors, and then examined the jerry cans. Most of them were in bad shape.

Only two of them were salvageable, so, slinging his rifle over his shoulder, he picked them up and carried them outside.

When he did, he saw Christina standing there waiting for him. Next to her was a Sámi man, his face badly beaten. And behind both of them, holding a gun, was a very large Wagner mercenary. Based on the description Christina had given of him earlier, this had to be the one from the bar—the one who was in charge.

"Hands up," Teplov said, pointing his gun right at him.

This time, Harvath didn't have a pistol hidden under a blanket he could use. There was no choice for him but to comply. Setting the cans down, he did as the man instructed.

CHAPTER 54

Tero Hulkkonen, from the Ministry of Defense, had met The Carlton Group jet on the tarmac at Lapland Air Command in Rovaniemi. He had an NH90 tactical transport helicopter, its rotors hot, standing by. As soon as the team had transferred their equipment, they lifted off and headed for the Jaeger Garrison 125 kilometers north-northeast in Sodankylä.

The helo landed in a heavily fenced area on the far side of the base. It reminded Chase, Sloane, and Staelin of the Delta Force compound at Fort Bragg. In fact, it was the first thing they mentioned when they hopped off the bird and began unloading their gear. Alternatively, the first thing Haney, Morrison, and Barton remarked on was how "fucking cold" it was.

The base commander, Colonel Jani Laakso, had set them up in a private barracks contiguous to their ops center. Once the team had stowed their gear, they met up with the Colonel and their MoD liaison in one of the op center's secure conference rooms.

A few trays of hot food had been brought over from the mess hall. There was coffee and bottled water. None of The Carlton Group members bitched about dietary restrictions. They were professionals and had been trained to show respect to their hosts, especially when forging a relationship. What's more, they had all been subjected to significantly worse cuisine. Finnish food was absolutely gourmet compared to meals they'd had in places like Somalia, Pakistan, Mozambique, and Yemen.

Everyone loaded up a plate, grabbed a coffee or water, and sat down at the long wooden table. After their flight, they were wiped out, and not in the mood to do much talking. The team was relieved when a reconnaissance specialist was shown in, the lights were dimmed, and a briefing began on a flatscreen at the front of the room.

The specialist brought them up to speed on everything the Finns knew about the terrain, Russian capabilities, and continuing efforts to pinpoint Harvath. It was nothing they didn't already know from their own experience, as well as the work they had done on the plane.

When the presentation was complete, Colonel Laakso thanked the specialist and then asked if anyone had any questions. There were none.

The Colonel promised that if there were any developments, someone would come get the team leader, whom the team members had all agreed on the plane would be Haney.

They thanked the Colonel for his hospitality and, as he and the specialist left the room, Hulkkonen from the Ministry of Defense took over.

He had just finished reading a message on his phone, and now tucked the device into his pocket. "So, the position of the Finnish government, and thereby the Finnish Defense Forces, remains that we can help you up to the border, but we cannot violate sovereign Russian territory."

"We wish your position was different," Haney replied, "but we understand and we appreciate any and all assistance you can give us. Obviously, our one and only goal is to get our teammate safely home."

"Have you had any updates?" Hulkkonen asked. "Any more specific idea as to what route he is traveling, other than west from Nivsky?"

Haney shook his head. "Not yet. We're hopeful, though, that we'll have something soon."

"Us, too. In the meantime, here's the plan. You try to get some rest. At 0600, we'll serve breakfast in this room while we conduct another briefing. Then, we'll go over potential mission parameters and get you outfitted with cold weather gear, skis, and whatever else you may need."

"And after that?"

"We plan to move you up to one of our border outposts. There's a 'hole' of sorts that the Russians are unaware of. It will allow you to get across the border without raising any alarm."

"The plan is for us to ski eighty klicks into Russia?" Staelin asked, a bit taken aback.

"No, not the full eighty. I'm working out the details now. I'll have more for you by tomorrow."

"What about access to Finnish airspace? If we want to HALO a team in?" Haney asked, referring to a High Altitude Low Opening parachute jump and thinking about the Zero-Three-Hundred team on deck at the Luleå Air Base in northern Sweden.

"That request is looking better. I haven't heard of any final approval yet, but from what I understand, as long as your aircraft remains within our airspace, we do not have a problem with that. This is a 'downed pilot' exercise, so it would be natural to rehearse airborne reconnaissance.

"If, during this rehearsal, a door opened and 'items' were separated from the aircraft, we'd prefer not to know about it. Does that sound fair to you?"

"Very," Haney replied.

"Okay, then. I will be staying here on base as well and will see you all at 0600. If you need anything in the meantime, you have my cell phone number."

They said good night to Hulkkonen and, after finishing their food, shuffled back to the barracks.

The building was divided into a series of rooms with private bathrooms. As the lone female on the team, Sloane got her own. The rest had to double up. Not a single person bitched. Not only was there central heating and indoor plumbing, they all knew that Harvath was having a much rougher night.

Haney encouraged everyone to grab a shower and get to bed. While he waited his turn, he typed out a quick SITREP and sent it to Nicholas back in the United States. There wasn't much to report, but it was a policy the Old Man had set himself. Even if there was no news, he still wanted to regularly hear from his people in the field. And if you failed to report in, there had better be a damn good reason for it, or there was going to be hell to pay. As a result, they all had become compulsive report writers.

The word "compulsive" was exactly what sprang to Haney's mind as Barton exited the bathroom in a towel and a pair of flip-flops.

"You remembered to bring shower shoes?" he asked.

"You didn't?" replied the former SEAL, shaking his head.

Haney had pounded so much ground as a Marine that his feet resembled a Hobbit's. He wasn't concerned.

Powering down his laptop, he grabbed his dopp kit and headed for the shower.

Once in the bathroom, he closed the door and got undressed. Pulling back the curtain, he saw the shower was not only spotless, but had a head that could be adjusted to pulse and give you a massage.

Haney turned on the hot water full blast, but then changed his mind. Out of a sense of solidarity with Harvath, he flipped the temperature selector to cold.

It was good not to get too comfortable in the field. That's when complacency set in.

Freezing his ass off, Haney took one of the shortest showers of his life. It reminded him of how bitterly cold it was outside and what Harvath was going through right at this very moment.

When he hit his bunk, he was thankful for the blanket, which he pulled up tight under his chin.

Before he drifted off to sleep, he said a prayer for Harvath. He vowed that if God would keep him alive, he and the rest of the team would do everything it took to get him out.

It wasn't the first time Haney had made a deal with God. Often, in his life, there was blood, bullets, or both, but God had never let him down. And he didn't believe that God would this time either. The only thing he needed was a sign.

CHAPTER 55

The "sign" came a few hours later when Haney's encrypted cell phone awoke him. He knew who it was just by the ring. They all had ringtones for each other. Partly as a joke, but partly because he respected him as one "bad motherfucker," his ringtone for Nicholas was the theme song from *Shaft*.

Before even opening his eyes, he had grabbed his phone, activated the call, and pressed it up against his ear.

"Haney," he said, blinking at his watch to see what time it was.

"I think we've got a fix on Harvath," the little man stated.

"Where?" he asked, throwing back the blanket and getting out of bed.

"What's up?" asked Barton, his head still on his pillow.

"We may have a fix on Harvath," he replied.

"The National Reconnaissance Office had a satellite searching the area over Murmansk Oblast. They picked up something outside Nivsky."

"They've got Harvath?"

"If it's not Harvath, then the Russians have got another very big problem on their hands."

"What did you see?" Haney asked.

"I'm transferring the imagery now. Hulkkonen and the Colonel are going to meet you in the ops center," Nicholas answered. "We'll pick back up via conference call there."

Haney hung up and quickly got dressed. As he exited the room, Barton was right on his heels. Haney wanted to tell him that it might be nothing and that the operator should go back and get some sleep, but he knew it was no use. If their positions had been reversed, Haney would have insisted on coming along as well.

When they got to the operations center, the Colonel was already there. One of his techs patched in Nicholas via a secure video link and put his image up on one of the large screens on the opposite wall. He looked like a giant and Haney told him so as Barton brought over cups of fresh coffee.

As soon as Hulkkonen had arrived, Nicholas explained what the NRO believed it had picked up.

After the message had come in from Harvath, they had worked like crazy to get a satellite over Nivsky. The presence of the two helicopters in the town square told them the Russians were onto him.

From there, they started looking for vehicles traveling west. There were only a handful, but nothing definitive. There was also one person traveling via what had to have been skis, and even a couple of dog teams in the area. Again, there was nothing definitive.

"That," said Nicholas, as he switched from the still images he had been feeding to the op center's screens to infrared video, "was when this happened."

They all watched as there was a commotion in the square and people and equipment, including two snowmobiles, were loaded onto one of the helicopters and it lifted off.

The satellite followed the bird as it traveled toward a speck of a village Nicholas identified as "Friddja," about twenty klicks west.

There, the bird touched down and disgorged the two snowmobiles and all the people who had gotten on in Nivsky. One person, it appeared, was being dragged, or at least forced, by the presence of figures on either side.

A handful of other figures then got into a stack formation and made entry into one of the houses. Moments later, several more followed.

A short time later, they emerged with an additional person.

As the snowmobiles raced off, several figures went house to house. Then, all the figures got back onto the helicopter and flew to the next village, ten klicks over.

This, Nicholas explained, was another indigenous Sámi village, called Adjágas.

They watched as the snowmobiles approached, only to have both of their riders knocked off and a mysterious figure appear out of the woods.

"That's got to be Harvath," exclaimed Haney.

"Like I said," replied Nicholas. "If it isn't, then the Russians have another *very* big problem on their hands. Keep watching."

All eyes were glued to the screens as the rest of it unfolded. They sat riveted as six figures rappelled out of the helo only to hit a house and have something explode inside. Then as the survivors were dragging out their injured, they were all engaged by sniper fire from the same mysterious figure, who moments later began firing at the helicopter and caused it to crash.

The footage began getting crackly and then went dark as the satellite passed out of its window.

"That is definitely Harvath," Barton stated.

"We agree."

The Colonel had one of his people pop up a map. "Adjágas is close, only about sixty kilometers from the border."

Haney recalled Staelin's complaint about potentially having to ski eighty kilometers. He wondered if he'd feel any better knowing it had been cut to sixty.

Turning to Hulkkonen, he said, "Based on this new information, I'd like your government's permission to scramble our aircraft out of Luleå Air Base in Sweden and for it to enter Finnish airspace."

"As part of our joint training exercise," he responded.

Haney nodded and the man pulled out his cell phone, walking away so he could converse with his superiors discreetly.

Looking back at Nicholas, and careful not to implicate the U.S. President directly, even in front of an ally, he asked, "Has the White House seen this?"

"He has. They want final approval over whatever the plan is, but you're the ones on the ground, so you get to set the board."

Haney looked at the Colonel. "Mr. Hulkkonen mentioned that there's a hole, a blind spot of some sort, we can exploit at the border."

"That is correct."

"He also said we'd have to go in via foot, or at least on skis, but perhaps not the entire way. What did he mean by that?"

The Colonel looked at the Ministry of Defense representative and then returned his attention to Haney. "We have an asset in that area. Someone who might be able to help."

"Someone who can provide transport?"

"Yes, but it's complicated."

"It's *always* complicated," Haney said.

"But in this case, even more so."

"Why?"

"Because," said the Colonel, "the asset hates Americans."

CHAPTER 56

*A*ll this? All the cold, all the pain, and all the miles just for this? Just to get captured? Harvath was pissed. He was pissed at himself. He was pissed at his circumstances. He was pissed at everything. In fact, he was more than pissed. He was *fucking* angry.

And his anger was calling up something deeper, something much more deadly. His anger was calling back up his rage.

"Very slowly," Teplov ordered, well aware of the type of man he was dealing with. "Let the rifle fall to the ground."

Reluctantly, Harvath did as he was ordered.

"Now the chest rig."

His rage building, Harvath unclasped it and tossed it to the side.

"Remove the whites. And your coat. *Slowly*."

Trying to come up with a way out of this, Harvath did as the man instructed and let them drop to the ground.

"Now turn around," the Russian commanded.

As Harvath turned, the intense, bitter cold bit through his remaining clothes and into his flesh. And though his eyes should have been fixed on the Russian and his gun, he couldn't help but glance at Christina.

He wanted to convey to her that everything was going to be okay, that he would protect her, but she couldn't see his eyes. They were hidden behind the night vision goggles suspended over his helmet.

Somehow, as if Teplov could read his mind, the Russian commanded, "Take off the helmet."

Flipping the goggles up, he unfastened the chinstrap and tossed the helmet aside. He didn't like losing his edge, but now they were on even ground. The Russian wasn't wearing night vision either.

As his eyes adjusted, he quickly shifted them to Christina. She looked terrible—beaten, defeated. The Sámi man standing next to her looked even worse.

But they had survived the crash. And they hadn't survived just to be killed now. Harvath had to do something. But what? He needed to buy himself more time, so he attempted to engage his captor.

Apropos of nothing, he raised the issue that had been burning him up, "After my plane went down, there was one person I couldn't find—a man named Josef."

Teplov smiled. "He made an impression on you, did he?"

"A big one," Harvath stated, the hatred revealing itself across his face. "In fact, I promised him that I'd be the last person he ever saw before he died. Did I succeed?"

"We found him in the woods, beyond the wreckage. His back was broken, and he was suffering from hypothermia, but he is still alive. So it looks like you failed."

"For now."

The Russian's grin broadened. "On your knees."

Harvath held out his arms as if to say, "Cuff me."

Teplov, though, was too smart for that and not in the mood for games. "Mr. Harvath," he said. "It's quite cold and we all know how this is going to end. Let's not drag this out. On your knees."

Harvath refused to move.

Adjusting his pistol, Teplov fired into the ground just next to him.

"On your knees," he repeated. "Or I'll put my next shot *in* one of your knees."

Disabling Harvath would make it difficult to get him out of the gulley and back to the village, but something told him the Russian wouldn't care. Harvath had no doubt that he'd shoot him. So, with no other choice, he began to bend his knees.

Just as he did, there was an enormous explosion as the fumes from the ruptured gas cans inside the helicopter ignited.

The force of the blast threw Harvath more than twenty feet away, almost impaling him on a piece of severed rotor blade.

Leaping to his feet, he spun and saw his captor. Teplov had also been thrown a considerable distance and appeared to have come into violent contact with a tree. He was much slower in getting up. Christina and the Sámi man were lying nearby. Neither one of them was moving.

Harvath scanned for a weapon, but didn't see one. Knowing he wasn't going to get another chance, he put his head down like a running back and charged.

Hitting Teplov was like running into a wall. The man was a good half a foot taller and weighed at least seventy more pounds. As he struck him, the big Russian just absorbed it. Then Teplov began to rain down his own blows.

Fists, knees, and elbows flew. Harvath couldn't believe how fast the man was. Every time he thought he saw an opening, the Russian closed it and struck him again.

Harvath could taste blood. Whether it was coming from his mouth or his nose, he had no idea. It was probably both.

What he did know was that he couldn't keep going for much longer. He didn't have the strength.

He managed to land a decent jab, cross, hook combination, but the Russian wasn't even fazed. He just kept coming.

Harvath angled to take out one of Teplov's knees, but every time he did, the man seemed to sense what was coming and got out of the way. And as he did, Harvath would catch another elbow, often to the head, in the process.

He was bleeding, short of breath, and almost completely out of energy. He needed to end this fight, *now*.

Pretending he was going for Teplov's knee again, he stopped halfway through the move. The Russian, though, had already set in motion the changing of his footwork and couldn't pull it back. He had left himself wide open.

Stepping in, Harvath delivered an absolutely searing kick to the man's groin. The big Russian doubled over in pain. And as he came forward, Harvath met him with the biggest uppercut he had ever thrown.

There was the sound of breaking bone and he didn't know if it had come from his hand or Teplov's jaw. The Russian's head was so hard that it was like hitting a cinderblock.

Harvath's punch was followed by a spray of blood from Teplov's mouth as his head snapped back.

He couldn't have timed or delivered the strike any better than he had. It should have been a knockout blow. But it wasn't.

Teplov's eyes looked unfocused and he must have realized that he had almost been rendered unconscious, because out of nowhere, he pulled a knife.

Harvath leaped back, but barely in time, as the blade sliced through his clothing, just missing his skin.

With blood pouring from his face, Teplov advanced.

From the way he was holding and moving the knife, it was apparent he was very skilled.

He came at Harvath fast, thrusting and slashing. It was everything Harvath could do to fend off the blows and not get cut.

He was at a serious disadvantage. Teplov was driving him backward, through the wreckage-strewn snow, and he couldn't see where he was going.

With his long arms, the Russian was able to keep the knife out well in front of his large body. It was absolutely impossible for Harvath to land any blows to the man's head or body. His only options were to either trap the knife and wrench it away, or create another feint, and this time actually drive his boot into one of the Russian's knees.

Considering how skilled and how fast Teplov was with the knife, Harvath decided to go for the man's knee—the right one.

But no sooner had he made the decision than he hit a piece of debris and stumbled. He tried to catch himself, but only caught a handful of air as the knife sang past and sliced off the top of his glove, missing his index finger by a millimeter.

As he fell backward, the Russian kept coming, lunging for him and incorporating himself into the fall.

Harvath hit the ground with the taller, heavier, and considerably stronger Teplov right on top of him.

The Russian switched the knife into his left hand and wrapped his right around Harvath's throat and began to squeeze.

Harvath tried to summon every grappling and ground fighting technique he had ever learned, but none of them worked

As he struggled in the snow, the Russian increased the pressure of his choke on him. Harvath was starting to see stars—little points of light—as his vision dimmed. Then he saw the man pull back the knife and raise it into the air.

There appeared to be a glint in the blade. Maybe it was light from the burning helicopter, or perhaps it was a trick caused by the oxygen being cut off from his brain. But he thought he saw something. Movement.

Before he brought the knife plunging down, Teplov increased his impossibly tight hold on Harvath's throat even further.

With the last ounces of strength he had remaining, he attempted to drive his knee up and into the Russian. The moment he did, he heard a crack—and everything went black.

CHAPTER 57

L ike a bungee jump in reverse, oxygen filled his body and Harvath was snapped back up onto the bridge of his consciousness.

Upon opening his eyes, he found himself staring right into the same face again. But something was different. Teplov's eyes were lifeless.

He was no longer straddling Harvath, trying to plunge the knife into him. Instead, he had fallen partway to the side. Harvath pushed him the rest of the way off and rolled away from him.

As he did, he could see that a piece of the back of the man's head was missing. *What the hell had happened?*

Scrambling away from the body, he struggled to get to his feet.

"Easy. Go slow," a voice said. It was Christina's.

Turning, he saw her walking toward him, his AK-15 in her hands. The crack he had heard wasn't from bones or cartilage snapping, but from the rifle. She had shot Teplov and in so doing had saved his life.

"Are you okay?" he asked.

"I'll be fine," she replied. "We need to get moving, though. The co-pilot put out a distress call. Reinforcements are coming."

Harvath had gotten lucky bringing down the first helicopter. He didn't expect to get that lucky again. What's more, he had lost the element of surprise. The second Wagner helo would be coming in hot and probably shooting at anything that moved. They needed to be gone before it arrived.

He found his helmet, with the night vision goggles still intact, but there was no sign of his coat, so he stripped Teplov of his and put it on, along with the man's gloves. While he did, Christina went to get Sini's husband, Mokci.

The man had taken some shrapnel in the explosion, but he was conscious and fully ambulatory.

Joining them, Harvath asked Christina to translate that Sini was back in Adjágas, that she was unharmed, and that there was a snowmobile nearby. They would all ride back together.

As Mokci nodded, Harvath accepted the AK-15 from Christina. He then pointed the way out of the gulley and told them he would catch up.

"Why?" asked Christina. "What are you doing?"

"Just go," he insisted, not wanting her to see. "I'll be right behind you."

Once they were out of sight, Harvath scalped what was left of Teplov's head and used the Russian's own knife to nail the bloody trophy to the nearest tree. He wanted the rest of those Wagner fucks to know who was responsible for killing their boss.

It would also, like the scalps he had left at the airplane crash site, add to their fear of him. Fear slowed people down. It made them pause and think twice. Even the shortest of pauses might make the difference between capture and escape.

The final thing he did was to make an exception to his "no booby-trap" rule. They were far enough from the village, and he knew the mercenaries would be on-site shortly. The gulley was narrow and, as he rigged Teplov's facedown body with multiple frag grenades, he hoped to kill or injure as many of them as possible.

When everything was set, he chased after Christina and Mokci and reached them about halfway to the snowmobile.

It was difficult to move in the deep snow, but he urged them to pick up their pace. They needed to hurry.

With each step, he pushed himself to come up with a plan. Where would Teplov's men be drawn first? To the downed chopper? Or, would they do a quick overflight of the village and see the bodies of their dead colleagues outside Jompá's cabin and start there?

Either way, it didn't matter. Not counting Teplov and the pilots on the first helicopter, Harvath had taken out eight Wagner mercenaries. If they really had arrived in Nivsky with two dozen, there could be as many as fourteen more speeding their way toward him.

They had enough men to drop ropes and rappel teams down at both Jompá's and the crash site, while still keeping men in reserve. The helicopter could then fly a safe distance away and await further instructions.

If there was a way to create a diversion, it wasn't springing to mind. His brain was all but spent. There had to be something else, though. Yet the only thing he could think of was the warning Lara had yelled to him outside the safe house in New Hampshire: "Run!"

But where was he going to run? The border? There might be enough gas in the snowmobile to make it. He still had his GPS. It was only sixty kilometers, give or take based on the terrain. It might be worth a try. If anyone with Wagner figured it out, though, he was as good as dead.

It didn't matter whether they had a team on board who could rappel down. All they'd need would be a single sniper. They could pinpoint his heat signature with thermal imaging and that would be that.

His thoughts then turned to Christina. She was as good as dead if she stayed behind. He had to take her with him. How he'd get *both* of them out, though, was unimaginable at the moment. He just knew he had to do it.

Suddenly, something bubbled back up in his mind. When Sini had been taking care of him, he had begun to formulate a possible way to escape—*if* she and her friends might be willing to help. Now, the plan seemed to take a more definite shape. They would still need some sort of diversion.

Arriving at the snowmobile, Harvath told Christina to sit behind him with the extra weapons. Mokci would sit behind her and wear his rucksack. He had just picked it up and was about to hand it over when he saw the Sámi man already had a bag.

"Where'd that come from?" he asked.

Christina asked and translated his response. "He said it belonged to Teplov. After the crash, he had gone back inside the helicopter to bring it out. It seemed rather important."

Harvath asked to see the bag and Mokci handed it over.

Inside, wrapped in plastic, were stacks of currency—including U.S.

dollars—probably designated as petty cash to be used for bribes, as well as the reward promised at the bar in Nivsky for Harvath's capture. There had to be at least $100,000 worth.

He continued to dig. In addition to a few chocolate bars and personal items, he found a weatherproof notebook, detailed topographic maps, and a small SERE kit containing a signal mirror, stormproof matches, tinder, chem lights, a handcuff key, razorblade, lock picks, and a small compass like the one he had taken from the plane. The real payoff, though, came next.

Rapidly searching the outer pockets, he found a med kit, Teplov's GPS device, and in the last pouch, hit the jackpot—a satellite phone.

Closing it all up, he put the backpack on over his chest, fired up the snowmobile, and when they were all on board, hit the gas and raced as fast as the sled would carry them back to the village.

• • •

On the outskirts of Adjágas, Harvath killed the engine. They left the snowmobile in the woods and crept the rest of the way on foot. It was better if no one knew that they were there.

The Wagner thugs were going to turn every house inside out. They were also going to sweat the inhabitants—hard.

With their boss and so many of their comrades dead, anyone holding out on them was going to get a severe beating and possibly worse. The mercenaries could get out of control and end up murdering everyone in the village and burning every house to the ground. Harvath couldn't let that happen.

As he had warned Sini earlier, you couldn't lie to these mercenaries. You had to tell them the absolute truth. If they did that, they might be able to escape any brutality. That meant he had to give them a good story—a true story.

He also needed to leave a trail that would take the mercenaries away from the village and, if possible, throw them off his scent. In other words, he needed a distraction. But first, he needed help.

They snuck up behind the cabin of Olá, Jompá's brother, and stopped.

Peering around the corner, he scanned the area with his night vision goggles. There was no one to be seen. The bodies of the dead mercenaries still lay in the snow. No one had touched them and according to Mokci, no one would. The Russians would have to claim their own dead. The Sámis, partly out of superstition and partly out of not wanting anything to do with what had happened, wouldn't go near them.

That was good news for Harvath. Pulling Christina aside, he told her what he needed her to do and handed her Teplov's backpack full of cash. Then, as she and Mokci slipped inside, he headed for the Wagner corpses.

Without having to worry that one of the villagers might roll one of the dead mercenaries over, he was able to set additional traps. Using frag grenades, he booby-trapped them all. No matter which body was touched first, it was guaranteed to be a deadly result.

Though he couldn't see them, he could feel the villagers' eyes on him. After he was done, he disappeared into the woods and rigged the corpses of the dead snowmobilers, before doubling back to the cabin where he had left Christina and Mokci.

Peering through the rear window, he waited for her signal. When she flashed him the thumbs-up, he pulled out Teplov's satellite phone, extended the antenna, and powered it up.

"Please work," he said under his breath, knowing this might be the only chance he got.

As he waited, he pulled out his GPS device courtesy of Christina's uncle and powered that up as well. The clock was running out. Everything now depended on the groundwork being laid inside the cabin.

CHAPTER 58

"Quiet!" Nicholas yelled to the room, as he stood on top of his desk to get everyone's attention. Instantly, the dogs were on guard and he had to give them the command to relax.

The room fell silent instantly and when it did, he returned his attention to his phone. "Say again, please?" he asked. It was a terrible connection and kept going in and out.

"Norseman," Harvath repeated, using his call sign, as was their protocol for this type of emergency transmission.

A series of coded challenge questions and answers then went back and forth, ending with, "Tim has a metal roof. I repeat. Tim has a metal roof."

"*Tim has a metal roof.* Good copy," said Nicholas, acknowledging the final coded response. "*Would you like to hear the specials?*"

"Negative. My wife and I are ready to place our order."

Nicholas looked at SPEHA Rogers, who had appeared at his desk, and pantomimed for the man to grab a pen and paper to take down the following information. Harvath had authenticated that it was him, that he was calling on comms he couldn't trust, and that he was going to need to get pulled out plus one—a woman.

"I'm ready," said the little man.

Harvath rattled off two strings of letters and numbers, which Nicholas repeated back to him. Rogers wrote them down and was about to race over to the NSA desk, which was coordinating with the National Reconnaissance Office, when Nicholas stopped him.

"Subtract one from the latitude coordinates and add two to the longitude."

Rogers nodded and headed off.

There was a lot that Nicholas wanted to ask, but for Harvath's sake, he had to keep things as short and to the point as possible. "Have you eaten with us before?"

"Twice."

Harvath was being professional, delivering the coded information calmly, but Nicholas could sense a distinct underlying tension in his voice.

"Are you free to take a quick survey about that experience?"

"Negative," said Harvath. "A lot of people want to use this phone."

"We'll get this order placed right away for you."

Nicholas was about to add, "So good to hear your voice," when the call went dead.

"Hello?" the little man said. "Hello? Can you hear me?"

Confirming that the call had indeed been terminated, he hopped down from the desk, just as the SPEHA hurried back over.

"What did he say?"

Nicholas ran through everything Harvath had relayed in their brief conversation.

"Do we know who is chasing him?" Rogers asked. "Russian military? Russian law enforcement? Both?"

"He didn't say."

"How about the identity of the woman? Do we know who she is?"

"We don't know that either, but if I had to guess, it's the doctor we saw the Instagram post from."

"What about how he's traveling? Is he on foot?"

Nicholas shook his head. "No, definitely not on foot."

"By vehicle then?"

"I think so."

"Do we know what kind? Is it a car? A truck?"

Once again, Nicholas shook his head. "He could have given me a code, but he didn't. All we know is that whatever it is, he and the woman are traveling separately."

"Why? What purpose do you think that would serve?"

"Maybe there are checkpoints and one has to act as a decoy or something. I don't know. He didn't say."

Rogers could tell Nicholas was getting frustrated with him. "I'm just trying to help. Don't worry. We'll get to work on what we have. Did he say when he'd be back in touch?"

"No. The call went dead."

The SPEHA put his hand on the little man's shoulder. "I've never met him, but based on what everyone has told me, he's going to make it."

Nicholas agreed. If anyone could beat the odds, it was Harvath. But if there was one thing he had learned in their business, it was that if you weren't cheating, you weren't trying.

They needed to make sure that they were doing everything to stack the deck in Harvath's favor. It was time to go all in.

CHAPTER 59

T ell him that I'm freezing my balls off out here and that if he doesn't open the door and let us in, I'm going to burn his fucking house down," said Haney. *"With him in it."*

The Jaeger soldier, whom the Finns had reluctantly sent along, relayed the message in perfect Russian, though with just a little added tact.

"Fine," the asset agreed, "but make sure they hide their equipment around back. I don't want anyone to know they're here."

The Finn translated, and while Haney and Staelin stood guard in front, the rest of the team went around back and shrugged off their gear.

Once they had all deposited their equipment, Barton and Gage offered to take first watch.

Haney had been instructed to get right to the point. And once inside, he did just that.

He spoke slowly so the Jaeger soldier could translate and, because the subject matter was somber, he made sure to adopt a respectful tone.

"United States President Paul Porter extends his deepest condolences to you and your family. He hopes you will accept my country's sympathies for what happened to your brother during the Soviet-Afghan War. We deeply regret that it was an American weapon, provided by the United States to the mujahideen, which caused his death."

Haney, along with the rest of The Carlton Group team, studied the older man's visage, searching for any hint of softening, or of forgiveness.

He was a stone-faced, flinty bastard, well into his seventies if he was a day. His hate for the United States oozed from every pore. The only country he hated as much was Russia, which was why he had agreed to work against it, in the service of the Finns.

His codename was Pavel. That was all the Jaeger commander was comfortable sharing. Haney was fine with that. He wasn't here to make friends. He was here to rescue one.

Both the United States President and the Secretary of State had given Haney permission to make the in-person apology. "Just don't gild the lily," the Secretary of State had warned him.

Haney didn't care. He would have told Pavel that the U.S. had faked the moon landing if it meant securing the Russian's cooperation. As the team saw it, there really was no way to pull this off without him.

Upon confirmation from Nicholas that Harvath was alive and they had a location for him, the team had been flown to the border on Army Aviation MD500 "Little Bird"–style helicopters.

The Jaegers had sent one of their intelligence specialists, Aleksi, along to help manage the meeting with Pavel and to make sure that the Americans didn't "screw it up."

Pavel was one of many cooperators the Finns had within Russia. They functioned not only as human trip wires, alerting Finland to Russian troop movements, but also as guerilla fighters ready to harass the Russian military and provide assistance to Finnish soldiers and intelligence officers should war ever break out.

Pavel, though, was more than just a prized agent-in-place for Finland. He had highly specialized training that made him invaluable in the effort to recover Harvath. It was training the United States was willing to pay top dollar for.

And to that end, Haney opened his backpack and removed multiple bricks of U.S. currency and set them on the table. "In addition to President Porter, we also bring salutations from another notable American, Mr. Benjamin Franklin."

The Russian and the Jaeger soldier watched as Haney continued pulling money out and stacking it on the table.

"He wants to know how much that is," said Aleksi.

"Two hundred and fifty thousand dollars," Haney replied. "He gets half now and the other half when we get back."

It was a fortune, especially in this part of Russia, and the old Russian's face lit up as the Finn translated. He had his hands around the throat of a golden goose that could lay diamond-encrusted eggs. He wasn't about to let go.

"Two hundred and fifty thousand dollars for his help," the Jaeger soldier translated. "How much in reparations? For the loss of his brother at the hands of an American shoulder-fired missile?"

Haney had known that was coming, and he smiled. "Please explain," he stated, "that my country doesn't pay reparations in situations like that."

As soon as the words had been translated into Russian, Pavel began to put on a show of shock and dismay. His lousy acting was akin to that of a soccer star who had been tapped by another player's foot and who fell down on the field, writhing in phony agony.

"But," Haney continued, "because we value his cooperation and want to have a good relationship, we're willing to negotiate something."

"How about we don't kill him?" Staelin asked, so that only Haney could hear. "How about that for a counteroffer?"

Staelin hated dealing with people like this. It was part of the job, but he had never liked it. The moment you opened your wallet, they wanted everything and more from inside. The fact that they were negotiating with the United States only made people greedier. They figured the U.S. could afford to give them whatever they asked for.

Aleksi listened to Pavel and then said, "He wants $10 million for the loss of his brother."

Haney had been ready for an opener like that and simply replied, "No." He didn't offer a counter.

The old Russian sat there trying to figure out what to do. If he wasn't careful, his golden goose would slip out of his grasp and leave him with nothing.

He dropped quickly down to "$5 million" and passed the request on through Aleksi.

Haney continued smiling and tried to keep his tone respectful. "Mr. Pavel, I am authorized to offer you an additional $250,000. It will be delivered to you once we are safely out of the country. That's my best offer."

The Russian listened to the translation and stared at his American counterpart long and hard. Finally, he blinked, and the blink was followed by a smile.

He leaned over and spoke to Aleksi, who replied, "He'll take it."

Pavel then got up from the table and walked over to his kitchen. Assembling a tray, he returned with glasses for everyone and a bottle of vodka.

Haney looked at the Jaeger soldier. "Should we be doing this?"

Aleksi shrugged. "It's tradition. It's how they seal the deal. Plus, he's a pretty serious alcoholic."

"He's what?" Haney asked, taken aback. That was a part of Pavel's history that hadn't been shared by the Finns.

"Alcoholism is quite common in Russia, especially in Murmansk Oblast. If you attempt to stop him from drinking, it could blow your entire operation."

"Are you nuts?" he asked, careful not to raise his voice. "The American government can't agree to pay some drunk $250,000."

"It just did," replied Aleksi. "And before you start having second thoughts, let me remind you that not only did you ask for this, but you don't have any choice. This is the best way to get to Harvath."

To get to Harvath, though, they were going to have to survive the trip. And as he watched Pavel pour a tall shot of vodka, that was now one of his biggest concerns.

CHAPTER 60

"Here," Christina said, as she pointed at a spot on Teplov's topographic map. "Jompá and his brother Olá were just out there yesterday. They said the wind has been so strong that the surface is completely swept clean. The lake looks like a black mirror."

Harvath prayed they were right. The only thing that could possibly give them away would be footprints. But as long as there was no snow on top of the ice, they might just make it.

He had to give Christina credit. She had been an exceptional saleswoman. Jompá and Olá had every reason to say no, but using the money from Teplov's backpack and leveraging her relationship with their village, she had convinced them to say yes.

As instructed, she had left Sini and Mokci out of it. In fact, as the husband and wife had been reunited, a plan was hatched to get them on their way, unseen, back to their own village.

The Wagner thugs were mercenaries, not detectives. They'd be anxious to pick up Harvath's trail. Retracing their colleagues' footsteps back to Friddja, hoping to find a witness to interrogate, was too much work.

Harvath quickly studied the map and asked, "Where's the rendezvous?"

She placed her finger on a spot, up a river, two kilometers inland. "It's a small hunting camp, part of a chain, shared by the Sámi. Jompá and Olá will meet us there."

Memorizing the map, Harvath fired up the snowmobile. He needed to let Nicholas know where they were headed, but more important, he needed to get the hell out of there before the Wagner assholes arrived. The call would have to wait.

As soon as he felt Christina wrap her arms around his waist, he hit the gas and took off.

Driving a car under night vision, even down a gravel road, was tough enough. Navigating a snowmobile, at high speed, through a forest, though, was like playing Russian roulette.

Harvath clipped so many trees along the way that he was positive that the Audubon Society was going to put him on a hit list.

The sled's fiberglass body got beat to shit. The rest of it, thanks be to the "escape gods," remained in working order. Nothing critical was damaged.

Just as he had done when he had fled the trapper's cabin, whenever he hit an open piece of ground, he pinned the throttle.

The sled screamed beneath them and raced forward. As its skis jerked and bumped over the frozen terrain, the frigid air smelled to him like freedom. Suddenly, all he could think about was home.

Every atom in his body ached to be free, to be back in America, and to be back among the people he loved.

Making himself more aerodynamic, he dropped his shoulders, put his head down, and leaned over the handlebars, urging the snowmobile on. They couldn't get to their destination fast enough.

Soon, the ground began to slope downward, and through the trees up ahead, he could see it. Through his night vision goggles, it looked like an oblong, asphalt parking lot.

As he sped out of the forest, he made sure to leave plenty of visible tracks along the shore before speeding out onto the ice. There, he flipped the goggles up so he could see the surface unaided. It looked like a piece of polished black marble.

Flipping the goggles back down, he cruised to the other side of the small lake, being careful to avoid the thinner ice, and found the perfect spot to unload Christina and their gear.

Here, the woods came right down to the shore. As soon as they set foot in the snow, they'd be in the forest and their path would be difficult if not impossible to detect.

After unloading everything and making sure Christina was safe, he got back on the snowmobile.

"Be careful," she warned him.

"I've already been swimming once on this trip," he replied. "I don't plan on doing it again."

Hitting the gas, he spun on the ice, got control of the sled, and then steered toward what looked like the most logical spot.

Several streams, two of which were quite wide, fed the little lake. They came together and pushed fresh, warmer water underneath the ice. That was where he intended to carry out his diversion.

Bringing the snowmobile to a halt, he pulled out his satellite phone, extended its antenna again, and powered it up. He had no idea if the Russians were tracking its calls or not.

Speaking quickly, he delivered another coded message to Nicholas, which relayed his location as well as how he and Christina planned to make their escape.

Then, after turning off the phone and putting it back in his coat pocket, he pulled out the two incendiary grenades.

He had gone over the plan several times in his head. The most important part was the placement of the devices. At four thousand degrees each, he needed to be extremely careful how he used them.

Snapping a chem light, he tied its lanyard to the back of the sled, activated the snowmobile's headlight, and then, with the incendiary grenades right where he wanted them, he pulled the pin of the one in front and then the one in back, before moving backward on the unstable ice so as not to be sucked in.

He knew better than to look at the bright light from the burning phosphorus, which could damage his retinas. Turning his head away, he shot an indirect glance to the side as the white-hot thermite rapidly melted the ice around the snowmobile.

There were loud cracks, like windows being broken, as the ice beneath the snowmobile began to melt rapidly.

In less than a minute, the sled had fallen through, swallowed up by the cold, black water.

Harvath had never used an incendiary grenade to melt ice before and was impressed by how fast it worked.

Retreating to the shore, he stood with Christina for a moment, watching the eerie glow of the snowmobile's headlight beneath the surface.

"How long do you think that will last?"

"In these temperatures?" he replied. "Not very long. That's why I tied the chem light to the back. That won't be much better, but it was worth a try. Ready to go?"

When she nodded, they shouldered their equipment and headed upstream toward the camp.

It was a rough push. The snow was deep, it was bitterly cold, and they were both tired and in pain. But they kept going.

She was in excellent shape and Harvath admired her. Anyone else would have slowed him down. Not once, though, did he have to encourage her to hurry up.

Every several minutes, they paused and listened. But all they heard were the sounds of the forest. Water rolled beneath the iced-over stream. Wind blew through the trees, shaking their boughs.

It was getting stronger, and he suspected another storm might be coming. Foul weather could work to their advantage, providing cover, but if bad enough, it could also hamper their progress.

Approaching the camp from the south, Harvath dropped everything but his rifle and had Christina hang back in the trees. He wanted her to wait there until he had made sure it was safe to come out.

It only took him a few minutes to clear the camp and determine that there were no threats.

Rejoining her, he helped pick up their gear and then pointed out where he wanted them to go.

There wasn't a lot of shelter to choose from, but right off the bat he crossed the traditional tents off the list.

Made of reindeer skins, they were probably decent for keeping warm, if you lit a fire inside. They, though, weren't going to be lighting any fires.

Instead, Harvath steered them toward a small shed with a metal roof.

Known as a *banya*, the freestanding sauna was the perfect place to hide, especially if what you were hiding from was thermal imagining.

Once the two of them had piled in with all their gear, he closed the door, and they tried to get warm.

Pulling out the heavy blankets Jompá had given them, he wrapped one around Christina and one around himself.

He looked longingly at the sauna's rocks, which sat atop a rudimentary stove. There was nothing he would have loved more than to have loaded it with wood and dropped in a match. The little structure would have heated up in seconds. So, too, though, would the stovepipe.

Out in the middle of nowhere, its heat signature would have been the equivalent of slicing through the night sky with a Hollywood movie premiere searchlight. Until Jompá and Olá had arrived, he wasn't going to take any risks.

They were both shivering. Christina opened her blanket, pulled him close, and pressed her body against his in an attempt to conserve warmth.

Her touch sent a jolt of electricity through him, but right behind it came a crashing wave of guilt.

Christina was an extremely attractive woman. She was also lonely, and in part vulnerable—like him. No doubt, if they had both agreed, they could have had each other right there. But that wasn't what Harvath wanted. He wanted Lara and she was gone.

He stood with Christina for several more minutes until they both started to warm up. Then, he gently stepped away. Things were complicated enough without adding to the confusion.

The only thing he wanted to be thinking about was getting them both out of Russia alive.

CHAPTER 61

Not in the dark," Aleksi translated. "Not on a lake he has never landed on before. We have to wait until morning. In the daylight, he can conduct a flyover and inspect the area to make sure there are no obstructions."

Haney had worked with plenty of bush pilots. He knew the drill. That didn't mean he liked it.

Harvath was so close. They could be on top of him in less than half an hour of flight time. The old Pilatus airplane the Russian pilot kept in the hangar outside was capable of carrying their entire team. It was outfitted with skis so that it could land on ice or snow, exactly like the Skibird the United States had repositioned from Greenland. The Pilatus, though, was much smaller and classified as a STOL—Short Takeoff and Landing—aircraft, which meant it needed even less runway.

Even so, based on the new coordinates Nicholas had provided, the lake Harvath was at now was too small. There was another, longer lake a few miles away that would work perfectly. Harvath, though, would have to get there. That's what Haney and the rest of the team were worried about.

"So what are we going to do?" Staelin asked, as he and Haney stepped to the other side of the room to talk.

"We wait."

"*Wait?* That's bullshit. We need to get moving. Now."

Haney looked at him. "You're the guy who was bitching about skiing all the way to Nivsky."

"But we're not going to Nivsky," he said, pointing at the map. "We're linking up with Harvath here. If we leave now, we can be there in two hours. Two and a half tops."

"If you were skiing hard, over flat terrain and minimal snowpack—none of which you would be. Then there's Wagner and their Mi-8. The minute you get picked up on any sort of imaging system, it's game over."

"They'll be too busy looking for Harvath. They won't expect us to come in from the west."

Haney shook his head. "Wouldn't you be expecting us? Don't underestimate these guys. They're good. The only reason Harvath is still alive is that he's better.

"Then there's the problem of the Alakurtti Air Base. We could almost hit it with a nine iron from here. Wagner wouldn't need to waste any manpower. Their pilot could simply call it in—a column of heavily armed skiers, moving through the nearby forest, under cover of darkness. I'm guessing they'd send someone to check that out. What do you think?"

"I think it would probably get a pretty substantial response," replied Staelin.

"Which is why we're not doing it."

"I understand, but we can't just sit here."

Haney appreciated his doggedness. They all felt the same way about Harvath, and part of what made them all so good at their jobs was never taking "no" for an answer. They were always pushing back, always looking for different and better ways to achieve their missions. Never had it been more important for any of them than right now. But Haney's job was to examine their list of options and select the best one.

"Waiting sucks," Haney agreed. "I get it. It's even worse knowing that Harvath is so close. For the moment, though, he's okay."

"*For the moment*," the former Delta Force operator stated.

"Listen, the best thing we can do for him is to get some rest and be ready for wheels up before first light."

Staelin wasn't done yet. "What about the Zero-Three-Hundred team?"

Haney consulted the most recent message he had received. "Finland has agreed to open their airspace. The Zero-Three-Hundred team, along

with U.S. aircraft, is being spun up in Sweden right now. But in all likelihood, we're going to get to Harvath first. If we do, then we pick him up,
we get him out, and no one's the wiser."

It was a solid plan, but even the most solid of plans could go sideways.
"What's our contingency?"

"I'm working on it," said Haney. "We should have another satellite on
station shortly. Once we get a look at the latest imagery, we'll be able to
make some more decisions. In the meantime, why don't you grab a piece
of floor with everyone else and try to get some shut-eye."

Staelin knew he'd be no good to Harvath, or anyone else on the team,
if he wasn't at his best, and so he gave in.

But it was more than just being at his best for the team. He didn't
know why, but he had felt apprehensive ever since they entered Russia.

Something told him that he was going to need everything he had to
get through this assignment.

CHAPTER 62

Nicholas and SPEHA Rogers had made the short drive from the Fusion Cell at FBI Headquarters to 1600 Pennsylvania Avenue together. This was the first time the little man had been on the White House grounds, much less inside one of its buildings. It was difficult for him not to feel a sense of awe.

President Paul Porter met them in the dining room, just beyond the Oval Office and his personal study, as he was wrapping up his dinner. "Can I get either of you anything?" he asked, knowing how hard they had been working.

"No, thank you," the pair replied.

"How about some coffee?" he then asked. Before the men had answered, he rang for the steward and placed the request.

They made small talk until the steward arrived. Once he had cleared the President's dinner dishes and had left the room, they got down to business.

"So how soon until we pick him up?" Porter asked.

"If all goes well," Nicholas replied, "a few hours. But that's only half the battle. Then, the team will need to get him back over the border and into Finland."

"Do we have a plan for that?"

"Yes, sir. Several actually. Per our agreement, the ultimate call will be made in conjunction with the team leader on the ground."

"Understood. What's the weather looking like?"

"Not good," said Nicholas. "It's going to get rough again. The question is whether we can beat it."

"When will you know?"

"Unfortunately, not until we're right up against it. A few minutes on either side might end up making all the difference. We're going to need to move fast."

"And you want to run the operation out of the Situation Room downstairs, correct?" asked Porter.

"Yes, sir. As I said, this is going to come down to fast decision-making with only minutes or seconds to spare. We believe it's critical that it be done here and that you be in attendance."

"Without question. We'll set it up."

"Thank you, sir."

The President then turned to Rogers. "Now, tell me about this grand fallback plan in case everything goes wrong."

Rogers cleared his throat and spent the next five minutes laying out his proposal. Porter listened intently, interrupting only a handful of times when he thought his SPEHA was being too vague, or too optimistic. Each time he did, though, he was impressed by the thoroughness of the man's reply.

When Rogers had finished laying everything out, the President picked up his coffee cup and leaned back in his chair. It was a lot to ponder—especially as it was packed end-to-end with risks, not the least of which was an all-out war between the United States and Russia.

It was also an offer the Russian President might not be able to refuse. When they had gone after Harvath, they realized how valuable he was. What they hadn't realized was what it would ultimately cost.

Could they crack the diplomatic door enough for the Russian President to save face? If tossed a quiet lifeline, would he take it?

There was no telling. Time and time again, Peshkov took stances and pursued courses that, by all accounts, were completely against Russia's, as well as his own, self-interest.

And time and again the United States had struck back in response to his aggression. Yet, in one form or another, the aggression had continued.

It was as if the Russian President had a screw loose. But even that was too simple a metaphor.

For years, the brightest minds in U.S. intelligence had been trying to figure him out, and for years they had been continually frustrated. The man simply defied any profile they came up with. He was the enigma of all enigmas.

This time, though, they were trying something different. It was simple, and perhaps, that's what had been missing in all of their past engagements.

Porter hoped that his visitors were correct, that their plan was as well thought through and airtight as it appeared, because the alternative was almost unthinkable.

"All right," he said, leaning forward and setting his cup down in its saucer. "We're going to move forward with this plan. I want to be perfectly clear, though. We all need to be prepared for what happens if it doesn't work. So, if you're not fully confident—if there's some other idea you've been holding in reserve—now's the time to get it on the table. Once we pull the trigger, there's no putting this bullet back in the gun."

He paused to let his words sink in. Slowly, he looked at Rogers and then Nicholas. Neither of the men seemed eager to offer any alternative.

"That's it then," the President decreed. "Let's start calling everybody in. In the meantime, I'll make sure they get you everything you need."

"Thank you, Mr. President," Rogers said as he stood and shook Porter's hand.

Nicholas followed suit.

As he watched the men leave the room, the President was gripped by a singular thought. What they were about to launch would go down as one of the most courageous rescues in history, or it would be viewed as one of America's greatest mistakes.

Either way it would be pinned to him and to his legacy. He wouldn't lose sleep over that, though. That wasn't why he had accepted this job. He had accepted it because someone needed to be willing to stand up and do the right thing for the nation, no matter what the personal cost. All he cared about was getting Harvath home.

He prayed to God that they had made the right decision.

CHAPTER 63

Harvath had stood at the door listening, his blanket still wrapped around him, while Christina had curled up on one of the sauna's benches and fallen asleep.

Standing still went against everything he had ever been taught. All of his training had hammered into him that the key to escaping and evading enemy forces was to keep moving.

Waiting for Jompá and Olá to show was beginning to feel like a mistake. So much so, that part of him wanted to take his chances in the snow, to wake up Christina and run for the Finnish border. The other part of him, though—the rational, sane, experienced part—told him to stay put, take a deep breath, and relax.

He needed to dial his anxiety down, to think of something else that would move him off code red to at least code orange, or maybe even code yellow.

Normally on an operation, he didn't allow his mind to wander. He had become an expert at compartmentalization, and could remain focused, no matter how badly his mind wanted to wander. But for a few moments, he allowed himself to wonder what he might do once he made it out.

He knew one thing for sure: whatever he did, it wouldn't involve snow and it definitely wouldn't involve cold. There was a little hotel he liked in the Florida Keys. He had taken solace there before. Maybe that's where he would go—warm sand, warm water, and a bottomless bar bill.

He couldn't go home, at least he couldn't stay there—not for long.

Home was Lara. Her clothes were hanging in the closet, her makeup in the bathroom, her fancy teas all organized in the kitchen.

At some point, he would have to make his peace with what had happened, but not until he had settled the bill. It would happen on his time, and only when he was ready. There was no other way it would work.

Leaving the sound and smell of the ocean, he brought his mind back to the here and now.

As the sauna had no windows, he had felt okay snapping a couple of chem lights and using them to dimly illuminate the tiny space.

He looked at Christina. She had been through a ton. He had been trained for this kind of grueling exhaustion, she hadn't. It was good to see her sleeping. The more rest she could get, the better. The biggest push was still ahead.

He knew she could handle it, though. She was amazingly resilient. When he had explained all of the risks that faced them, she had smiled and simply said, "Let's go."

It wasn't hard to understand why, but she had explained it to him nonetheless.

There was nothing left for her in Nivsky, nothing left in Russia, except pain. She had made up her mind to go with him the moment she had agreed to help him. He was an answer to a question she didn't even know she had.

It didn't matter what lay ahead. All that mattered was that she keep moving forward and put Russia behind her.

She knew all too well how her country operated. Everything good came at a heavy price. It was why so many of its people were so miserable. Nothing good ever really happened to average Russians, there were just shades of "less worse."

Living abroad had given her a taste of what could be. She just hadn't had the courage then to stay abroad. And while England wasn't the United States, she had gotten a taste of Western culture and understood what it meant.

The United States was still a land of opportunity. The only limits there were the ones you placed on yourself. Whatever she wanted to do, she could do it.

In Harvath's opinion, she had nailed it. In fact, she had nailed it in a way that only someone who didn't have those advantages and freedoms could. It eased his mind that involving her had been the right thing to do. Somehow, all of this seemed destined to have happened.

That said, they still had much to do before they could consider themselves free.

Looking at his watch, he tried to anticipate how much time remained before Nicholas would be able to see him again via satellite. Several times, he had heard the distant rumble of what sounded like the Wagner helicopter, but it had yet to make it this far out. In a way, that was a victory. And despite its being small, he knew he should celebrate it. So far, so good.

Christina must have had incredible hearing, because at the first, far off barking of the dogs, she stirred and sat up.

"Jompá and Olá?" she asked, rubbing her eyes.

"It sounds like it," he replied, picking up the rifle. "We should get ready to move."

Together, they packed up their gear except for a little bit of food, which they split between them.

They ate quickly and in silence. By the time the dog teams pulled up outside, they were ready to go.

With Christina translating, Harvath showed Jompá and Olá the spot on the map where he wanted them to be taken to.

The men nodded. The lake was known for its fishing and there was another Sámi village not far from there. Two Sámi coming to trade shouldn't be an unusual sight. All that was left was to load Harvath and Christina onto the sleds.

Pulling back the reindeer hides, the brothers exposed the large slabs of frozen moose meat they had brought with them. They would be uncomfortable to hide beneath, but they would effectively shield them from any thermal imaging.

Harvath's initial plan had been to purchase from Jompá and Olá two live reindeer that were scheduled for slaughter, have the brothers hollow, or "cape," them out, and for him and Christina to be transported to the rendezvous inside those.

It would have been a warm, but somewhat disgusting way to travel.

The weight, though, the brothers had explained, was too much for the dogs to pull, so they had settled on their current solution.

To help insulate their passengers from the cold, they had brought extra reindeer hides along.

Laying Harvath and Christina down, they helped bundle them up and then lowered the moose meat down over them.

Fortunately, there was a small, wooden framing system atop which the slabs set, but it didn't leave a lot of room. Both Harvath and Christina had to turn their heads to the side or tuck their chins into their chests to avoid their noses pressing directly against the meat.

Once everything was set, Jompá and Olá called out to their teams, the dogs started barking, and the sleds lurched forward.

Over thousands of years, the Sámi had built up an amazing tolerance for the cold. Whereas Christina had warned Harvath that there was only so much distance he could travel before succumbing to exposure, Jompá and Olá could far outlast him. The dogs also moved a hell of a lot faster than a man on skis or snowshoes.

While he hated not being able to see what was going on, Harvath tried to relax and enjoy the ride. If everything went according to plan, they'd be across the border and into Finland in a matter of hours.

By the same token, he knew that very seldom did everything go according to plan. In fact, the better things seemed to be progressing, the greater the likelihood that something bad was right around the corner. It was how Murphy worked.

He gripped the rifle a little tighter. In addition to the shotgun lying on his other side, he also had a pistol. Christina had a pistol, too, as well as a rifle.

Doing a quick mental inventory, he tallied up how many frag grenades he had left and then how many rounds of ammunition they had between them.

In the end, he hoped they wouldn't need any of it, but if they did, he prayed that it would be enough.

CHAPTER 64

Pavel, the bush pilot, made his money chartering his old plane to anyone capable of paying. Mostly, he flew hunters and fisherman. Occasionally, he got an arctic research team or a group of mining company executives. No matter who the client was, the seats were removable and the cabin could be reconfigured to handle the load.

It was a tight fit, and would be even tighter on the way back with Harvath and the woman, but they had managed to get themselves and all of their gear loaded.

Haney's concern over the pilot's drinking remained. Though Aleksi had convinced him to lay off the booze, when he rose to do his preflight check of the aircraft, he didn't appear to have sobered up much. He probably kept a bottle in his bedroom, the bathroom, or both. In fact, Haney was willing to bet there was one aboard the plane as well.

"Did you remember to pack a parachute?" Staelin joked, as they watched the wobbly pilot walk around the Pilatus, manually testing the flaps and rudder.

"I did," Barton deadpanned, as he slid past carrying bladders full of fresh water.

Haney chuckled. Sipping on a fresh cup of coffee, he stomped his boots in the snow and tried to warm up. "You ready for this?"

"As ready as I'm going to be," answered Staelin. "What's the latest on Harvath?"

"Everything's on track. NRO is monitoring two dog sleds heading toward the LZ."

"What about the weather?"

"We're going to have to move fast," Haney replied. "The front is already closing in and visibility is dropping."

Staelin used his chin to gesture toward the pilot. "Can we rely on this guy?"

"Aleksi says yes, but I don't trust anyone I don't know. That's why I'm riding up front with him in the copilot's seat."

"Have you ever flown a plane before?"

Haney nodded. "Just haven't done any takeoffs or landings."

"That's reassuring."

"Relax. We're going to be fine."

"I'll relax when we've got Harvath and we're out of Russia," Staelin replied. "Speaking of which, what do we know about those mercenaries who are after him?"

"As far as we know, they're still looking. The last report I received was that the helicopter had landed at Alakurtti for refueling and probably a crew change."

"So we've got no idea if they've given up or are still in the hunt?"

"They're still in the hunt. There are men on the ground at and around the village where the other Mi-8 went down."

"And our rules of engagement still stand?"

Haney nodded. "They still stand. Weapons free."

"Roger that. When do you want to do the final briefing?"

Looking at his watch, the team leader said, "Let's gather everybody up and do it now."

It took several minutes, but once Staelin had pulled the team together, he handed the floor over to Haney. He reviewed the mission parameters, the rules of engagement, and all the latest intelligence. He then opened it up for questions. There were none.

After a comms check, he gave the team the ten-minute warning and grabbed Aleksi to have a final chat with the pilot.

The Finnish soldier would not be coming with them. His government had forbidden it. They had no desire to be part of an act of war on Russian soil, no matter how justified.

Haney didn't like not having a translator along. Pavel didn't speak a word of English. Even though they were asking for trouble, it was the hand they had been dealt. They were lucky the Finns had gone along with them this far. As long as the Russian and his plane could fly, they'd take everything else as it came.

Anxious to be gone before sunrise as well, Aleksi bade the team good fortune, clamped into his bindings, and skied back into the forest toward the border.

As he did, the first flakes of snow from the storm began to fall. Haney and his crew were now on their own.

CHAPTER 65

With the Wagner disaster, as well as President Peshkov breathing down his neck for proof of life on Harvath, General Minayev hadn't gotten any sleep, which only served to make him more disagreeable than usual. When the Mi-8 flared and touched down, he was already outside, waiting impatiently on the tarmac.

As soon as Teplov's second in command, a man named Garin, hopped out, Minayev grabbed him and dragged him to the operations center at the back of the restricted hangar.

Once there, he cleared everyone else out and then began shouting. "What the fuck happened? Thirteen dead. *Thirteen!* Including Teplov! And he took down a Russian Air Force helicopter! One *fucking* man did all of this?"

"Yes, sir."

"And he's scalping people? *Scalping?* What is he, a fucking maniac?"

"Apparently."

Minayev waited for him to expound, to provide a little additional insight based on what he had seen, but the man didn't offer anything further.

"Damn it!" the General shouted. "Fucking damn it!"

Garin knew Minayev's reputation for biting the heads off his subordinates. It was better to give the shortest answer possible and not to step out on a rhetorical limb. Speak when spoken to, and always keep your opinion to yourself around him, even when he asked for it.

"Where is Harvath now?" the General asked. "Right this very second."

"We don't know."

"Where do you think he is?"

"I'm sorry, sir. I don't have enough information at this time to answer your question."

"Damn it, Garin! Don't play games with me. Where the fuck do you think he is? Answer me. That's an order."

At this point, the Wagner mercenary had no choice but to obey. "He's either dead or on his way to the border with Finland."

Minayev wanted to put a bullet in him. "That's the dumbest fucking answer I have ever heard. Did you come up with that on your own?"

"Sir, let me explain."

"This had better be good."

"Harvath stole one of our snowmobiles. We believe that is how he was able to get away from the village before we could get there.

"We found tracks near the helicopter crash. It looks like he parked the snowmobile and came in on foot. After shooting and scalping Colonel Teplov, he hiked back to the snowmobile with two other people. We think it was Dr. Volkova from Nivsky and the husband of the healer she was supposed to meet in Friddja."

"He only has a snowmobile, but *you* have had a helicopter. So where the fuck is he?"

"The reason we think he may be dead is that we followed a set of fresh tracks to a lake southwest of the village. There was a hole in the ice— one big enough that the snowmobile could have fallen through—and we could see some sort of light under the water."

"So he fell through? Are you positive?"

"No, not at all."

"Then why is there light coming from the bottom of that fucking lake?" Minayev demanded.

Garin remained composed, hoping his calm might prove contagious. "It could be intentional. Meant as a diversion. Maybe he wants us to think he fell through. Until we get a cold-water dive team out there, we can't be sure."

"I will requisition one."

"Thank you."

The General then locked his eyes on him. "And if it *is* a diversion?"

"Then we need to be focusing all of our attention on the border," said Garin. "That's where I believe he will be going."

"The border is over thirteen hundred kilometers long. Just where exactly are we supposed to fucking look?"

"Not *where*, sir," the mercenary replied. "But rather, *for what*."

"Okay," Minayev responded. "*For what* are we looking? And before you answer, understand that I'm out of *fucking* patience. This had better be informed. *Very* informed."

"Yes, sir," said Garin, confident that his information was just that. "We have been interrogating the villagers. Apparently, two brothers were returning from a hunt when they found Harvath unconscious in the snow. They brought him back to one of their cabins—the one that ended up being booby-trapped. And while the owner stayed with Harvath, the other brother went and collected the healer woman from Friddja, the next village over."

This was good information indeed. The General removed a cigarette and lit it. "And what did the two brothers have to say about all of this?"

"Nothing. We can't find them. They're gone."

"What do you mean *they're gone*?" he stated, exhaling a cloud of smoke.

"When we went to question them, they had already left."

"Meaning they just walked into the woods and vanished? Or maybe they fell into your fucking ice hole and are down there swimming around with Harvath, the snowmobile, and all the fish."

Garin ignored his sarcasm. "According to the villagers, whenever the brothers have a successful hunt, they keep some of the meat and the rest they go and trade."

"Go and trade *where*?"

"With any number of other Sámi villages."

Minayev took another puff of his cigarette as he tried to recall how many indigenous villages there were in the Oblast. There were more than a few. Nevertheless, he couldn't figure out how this information was useful, and was just about to say so, when Garin continued.

"While we may not know where they're traveling," he said, "we know how. This is where the *what* comes in. The two brothers are using dog teams. As soon as we can get the helicopter refueled and get a new crew assigned, that will be the focus of our search. They may be helping Harvath."

The General smiled. This he could work with. The Kremlin would be pleased. "New crew or old crew, as soon as that helicopter is refueled, you're lifting off. Is that clear?"

"But General Minayev, the—"

"Is that clear?" he barked.

"Yes, sir," said Garin.

"Good. Now get the fuck out of here. And don't come back without Harvath—even if you have to chase him into fucking Finland."

CHAPTER 66

Jompá and Olá stopped only once to rest the dogs and check their heading. Hearing no sound of helicopters, they lifted the frozen slabs of meat to allow Harvath and Christina a chance to get out of the sleds and stretch their legs.

It was snowing and the wind was blowing even harder than before. With the rifle slung over his shoulder, Harvath removed the satellite phone from his pocket and dialed Nicholas as he walked.

They kept the call short. Harvath provided him with an update on their progress and Nicholas confirmed their location via the live satellite footage they were watching in the White House Situation Room.

Nicholas also let him know that the plane with the team was airborne and that there was no sign of any Russian activity in his immediate area.

Good news, thought Harvath. *For the moment*.

After he and Christina had climbed back into the sleds, Jompá and Olá replaced the slabs, covered everything with reindeer hides, and then mushed their dogs toward the landing zone.

Harvath's senses were on fire the entire way. As close as they were to escaping, there were still so many things that could go wrong.

Some of the most intense battles he'd ever been in were en route to an extraction. They were all-or-nothing scenarios. The bad guys knew it was their last chance to take you out. You knew that if you didn't succeed, you weren't going home. Both sides had everything to lose and winning came down to who fought the hardest.

Even so, you could fight like hell and still lose. Sometimes it was nothing more than a numbers game. That was always the biggest risk when you were fighting on someone else's territory. Better to get in and out without being seen and without engaging the enemy.

That was Harvath's biggest concern right now—getting out without being seen. He'd been able to stay one step ahead almost the entire time he had been in Russia. If he could just continue that streak a little longer, he'd be home free.

He hadn't asked to come here. He hadn't asked for Lara, Lydia, and Reed to be murdered. He hadn't asked for any of it. All he wanted now, after everything he had been through, was to get across that border. But as he had spent a lifetime learning the hard way, circumstances often seemed to conspire against him.

As the sled sliced through the snow, he forced himself to relax as he breathed deeply. *Stay calm*, he repeated in his mind. *Almost there*.

But as he said those last two words to himself, he knew that it was a lie. He wasn't *almost there*. In fact, he was far from it.

At the moment that thought entered his mind—as if he had the power to conjure up the worst possible demon to come and torment him even further—he heard something. He heard it over the barking of the dogs and the creaking of the sled. Though it was faint, he knew exactly what it was—a *helicopter*.

"Fuck," he whispered, as the sound of its rotors grew louder.

He had no doubt that it was Wagner, and within moments, it was hovering almost directly overhead. Jompá and Olá, though, kept going.

Harvath heard the helicopter change position and hover out in front of them. The pilot was sending the mushers a message: *Stop*.

Jompá and Olá had no other option. That's what they did.

The frozen slabs of meat should have hidden their presence from any thermal imaging. This had to be about something else. Someone in the village had talked.

Harvath, though, had expected that. What he hadn't expected was that the Wagner mercenaries would devote time and resources to scouring the countryside for a couple of Sámis known to be gone at odd hours and for days at a time, hunting and trading with other villages.

Sinking the snowmobile had been meant to throw them off his trail, but maybe it had ended up leading them right to him.

He didn't have time to figure out what had happened. He needed to make a plan to deal with this threat—right here, right now.

The helicopter was too loud for him to yell back to Christina. It was almost too loud for him to communicate with Jompá. Almost.

Though Harvath's Russian was pretty bad, he knew enough to get what he needed in this situation.

"*Shto ty vídish?*" he shouted. *What do you see?*

"*Odin vertolet,*" the man shouted back, so that Harvath would be sure to hear him. "*Dva verevki.*" *One helicopter. Two ropes.*

This wasn't a reconnaissance. It was an interdiction. They were going to have a team rappel, inspect the sleds, and question Jompá and Olá.

Harvath planted his feet and brought his knees up against the slab of meat. "*Skol'ko soldat?*" *How many soldiers?*

"*Chetyre.*" *Four.*

Two for each sled, Harvath thought to himself.

He tried, in vain, to listen for the approach of footsteps. But between the roar of the helicopter blades and the dogs barking, it was impossible.

Suddenly, though, he could hear the helicopter ascend and then move off to the side. It was still close, but not directly in front of them, nor immediately overhead. The mercenaries were obviously concerned about what they were about to face. And having already lost one helo, they didn't intend to lose another.

As the Wagner men neared his sled, they began yelling at Jompá in Russian.

"*Dva ostalos,*" the Sámi said for Harvath's benefit. "*Dva verno.*" *Two left. Two right.*

With his face hidden behind the ruff of his anorak, the mercenaries couldn't see him feeding one last clue to Harvath. It was the last thing he was able to utter before the men were right on top of them.

Harvath gripped his weapons as an icy calm settled over him. Now that trouble had arrived, he was in his element.

His challenge was to affix in his mind, without having seen them, where all the players were—the four mercenaries on the ground, the helicopter and its likely snipers, Christina, Jompá, and Olá.

He was about to engage in an incredibly dangerous gamble, but there was no alternative. It was kill or be taken prisoner, and he had already made it quite clear where he stood on that proposition. He was going to kill whoever got in his way, and he would keep killing until he had escaped. He was going home and *nobody* was going to stop him.

Though the clouds had dampened its first rays, the sun had begun to rise. To his left and to his right, Harvath was able to see beneath the edges of the reindeer hides covering the sled.

He could make out two pairs of legs. Both were wearing the same winter whites as all the other Wagner thugs.

Once he had both his weapons in place, he said a quick prayer, exhaled, and pressed the triggers.

CHAPTER 67

Using his legs to upend the frozen slab and the reindeer skins, he let them fall to the ground as he came out shooting.

He put two more rounds into the injured men on either side of his sled, killing them both, and then quickly rolled to his left to engage the men behind him before they could get to Christina.

As he did, the snipers in the helicopter let loose with a withering barrage of fire. Jompá, who had crouched down behind the sled for cover, fell bleeding into the snow.

Harvath kept his attention on Olá's sled and the two men there. One of them had his weapon pointed right at him. Harvath fired before the man could get off a shot, double-tapping the mercenary in the chest and putting an additional round underneath his chin and up into his brain.

Before the man had even hit the ground, Harvath had his colleague in his sights and was already lighting him up.

He ripped a zipper of lead from the man's left rear buttock, up through his ribcage, and into the back of his head, splattering brain, blood, bone, and bits of helmet everywhere.

All the while, the snipers continued to fire, unable to get an accurate fix on him. Curtains of snow obstructed their view, as powerful gusts of wind buffeted the helo.

Rolling back behind the sled, Harvath ejected his magazine, slammed home a fresh one, and dragged Jompá closer, hoping to save him. There was nothing Harvath could do for him, though. The man was dead.

Popping up from behind the sled, and using the oblong slab of moose on the other side for concealment, he went full auto and emptied his magazine into the cockpit of the helicopter, before disappearing back down again.

Doing another magazine change, he scanned his surroundings. They were out in the open, which was an absolute death sentence when dealing with a helicopter. They needed to get to the trees.

He called out to Christina and Olá, but neither of them replied. He prayed it was only because they couldn't hear him.

Rising into a crouch, he popped up once more and began firing as he ran back to the second sled.

Sliding in next to it like a baseball player stealing home, he ejected the magazine from his AK-15 and rocked in another.

"Christina!" he yelled over the sound of the helicopter as it swung around in an attempt to provide its snipers with a better angle. "Christina!"

Peeking behind the sled, he saw Olá lying facedown in the snow, bleeding. Harvath didn't need to roll him over to know that, like his brother, he was also dead. The snipers had taken both of them out.

"I can't get out," Christina shouted. "The slab won't move. It's stuck."

Lifting up the reindeer hide, he peered underneath and saw the problem. The edge was jammed between two of the bed's supports.

"I'm going to lift it. When I do, roll toward me as fast as you can. Okay?"

Christina nodded.

"On three," yelled Harvath, as he planted his boots and leaned into the slab. "One. Two. *Three!*"

It was incredibly heavy, just like the one he had hidden under. He was only able to raise it a few inches, but it was enough for Christina to get out, pulling her rifle behind her.

Before she could even thank him, she saw Olá. She tried to go to him, but Harvath stopped her.

"They're both dead," he said. "We need to get to the trees."

"How?"

"You go first and I'll cover you. Ready?"

Christina nodded and once again, Harvath counted to three and yelled for her to run.

As she took off, he popped up from behind the sled and began firing, successfully putting several rounds into the side of the helo, forcing it to swing away from them.

Once he saw that she was safe, he pointed at the helicopter and instructed her to start shooting. The moment she did, he ran back to Jompá's sled. He needed his rucksack.

Sliding again to safety, he reached inside and pulled it out. Now, all he had to do was make it to the trees.

The helicopter, though, had shifted into a new position, one that was going to make it very difficult for Christina to engage from her position.

He was getting ready to jump up and fire at it himself when she stepped out from behind the trees and began shooting.

It was an incredibly courageous move, and one that he didn't waste. Hopping to his feet, he ran faster than he could ever remember having run in his life.

He got to her just as her weapon ran dry and together they bolted into the trees as the snipers began to return fire.

The bullets tore off pieces of bark and sent snow flying all around them. Up ahead, Harvath could see a small rock outcropping. He pointed at it and shouted for her to keep running. "No matter what, don't stop!"

She did as he ordered and didn't notice until she got there that he had stopped to return fire on the helicopter.

It seemed like a suicide mission to her. Hovering above the trees, the snipers rained down bullets, slicing through the branches and coming very close to hitting, and likely even killing him.

Harvath, though, was equally dangerous to the helicopter. He not only found his target, but also put no fewer than two rounds through its belly.

Whether those rounds penetrated into the cabin and took out any of the mercenaries on board, he couldn't be sure. What he did know was that he had burned through precious ammo, but once again had succeeded in beating the helicopter back and forcing it to break contact.

As the helo temporarily disengaged, Harvath rushed for the outcropping.

"We're not going to have long," he said, as he changed magazines and tried to catch his breath.

"They can't get to us here, can they?" Christina asked.

"Not with the helicopter. They'll come in on foot. At least one group from uphill, so they can shoot down on us. Another will come in on one of our flanks."

"What are we going to do?"

"We're going to fight," he replied, pulling the few magazines he had left from his rucksack and handing one to her.

"But I don't know how," she insisted, and for the first time, he saw the fear written across her face.

He stopped what he was doing and looked at her. "Listen to me," he said. "I'm not going to let anything happen to you. Do you understand?"

She believed him and, slowly, she nodded.

Turning his attention back to his preparations, he pulled the satellite phone from his coat pocket, extended the antenna, and powered it up.

He waited for several moments, but the device failed to acquire a signal. There was too much tree cover. He had no way of giving Nicholas an update on their situation.

As he powered the device off and returned it to his pocket, he heard the helicopter stop and hover up the slope from where they were. The pilots must have found a big enough break in the trees, through which men could rappel.

After inspecting and reloading Christina's rifle, he handed it back to her. "Get ready," he said. "They're coming."

CHAPTER 68

I don't care what's going on down there," Haney said, his face a steely, don't-fuck-with-me mask. "You land this plane right now."

When Pavel refused to comply, Staelin, who was sitting right behind him, pulled out his H&K pistol and pressed the barrel right up against the back of the bush pilot's head.

During his initial flyover to check for obstructions on the ice, they had passed over the top of the Wagner helicopter and had seen shots being fired. It had frightened Pavel enough that he was now trying to abort the landing.

But as Haney and Staelin were making perfectly clear, despite the language barrier, they weren't aborting anything.

Resigning himself to what he was being forced to do, the pilot swung the plane around, decreased its airspeed, and prepared to land.

The Pilatus touched down with only a light skip of its skis on the snow. It was one of the best landings any of them had ever experienced. Pavel might have been a terrible alcoholic, but he was a terrific pilot.

When he tried to pull back on the throttle to slow down, Haney put his hand over Pavel's and pushed it forward, forcing him to speed up.

With his free hand, Haney pointed at the very end of the ice. Bullets be damned, that's where they were headed. He wanted the team dropped off as close to Harvath as possible. The bush pilot did the only thing he could do—he obeyed.

When they were almost at the shore, Haney allowed Pavel to finally slow the aircraft down. He even allowed him to turn it around, so that it was ready for takeoff when they returned.

As the team raced to unload their gear, Haney gave the Russian a final warning. Whether the man could understand his English or not didn't matter. He could understand his tone.

"Don't you fucking go anywhere," he ordered, poking his finger into the man's chest. "Remember, we know where you live."

The look on the bush pilot's face made it clear that the message had been received. Reaching over, he killed the plane's engine and held his hands up in mock surrender.

Hopping onto the ice, Haney slung his large pack, clicked into his ski bindings, and hailed the tactical operations center of the Joint Special Operations Command at Fort Bragg in North Carolina as they raced toward the woods.

To limit the number of cooks in the kitchen, JSOC had been assigned to coordinate this phase of Harvath's rescue.

Haney engaged in a very quick back-and-forth. He let them know that they had landed safely and were inbound to Harvath. JSOC let Haney know what Harvath's last position was and what kind of force was arrayed against him.

Everyone else on The Carlton Group team was listening to the report over their headsets. There was no need for Haney to repeat any of it.

On point, Sloane Ashby had a wrist-top computer strapped to the outside of the left sleeve of her winter whites. The technology had gotten to the point where she didn't need to peel off her gloves and punch in Harvath's location. It was being done for her by JSOC via satellite. Her job was to lead her team to him.

It was a good piece of technology to have, especially as the snow continued to fall and visibility worsened. The only downside to it, though, was the very real possibility of losing the link due to heavy cloud cover.

Knowing that Harvath was under fire, they all pushed themselves at top speed to get to him.

The plan had been for the dog sleds to transport him and the woman to the forest at the edge of the frozen lake. Once the plane had landed, the team would jump out, link up with them in the woods, and escort them back to the aircraft. They would then fly back to Pavel's and disappear across the border. That was the best-case scenario.

The list of worst-case scenarios was endless. It included everything from Harvath and the woman being injured and needing to be carried, to Harvath being recaptured and the team needed to go inland to break him out and bring him back. The one thing they had all agreed on was that they were absolutely not leaving Russia without him.

Up at the front of their column, Sloane continued setting a blistering pace. But then something happened.

From somewhere out in front of them, they began to hear gunfire. And all at once, they took an impossibly hard pace and kicked it up. *Way up*.

CHAPTER 69

In the SEAL teams, Harvath had had a good buddy from Texas. On a long deployment, when they were mind-numbingly bored, he had made the mistake of asking him what he thought the greatest state in the union was. He should have known what the man's answer would be.

The SEAL held forth for well over an hour about how Texas, hands down, was the greatest state in the Union.

Texans were a special breed. In fact, they were some of the toughest warriors Harvath had ever encountered. As a glutton for punishment, Harvath had followed up by asking his friend what he thought the second-greatest state in the union was. The answer had surprised him.

"Tennessee," the SEAL said.

"Why?" Harvath had asked.

"Because if it wasn't for Tennessee there'd be no Davy Crockett and if it wasn't for Davy Crockett, there'd be no Texas."

Crockett, of course, had been part of the Texas Revolution and had been killed by Mexican troops at the Battle of the Alamo.

A student of military history, Harvath had always wondered what it must have been like to have been at the Alamo, to have been completely surrounded, and to have fought against such overwhelming odds.

He assumed it must have been akin to the three hundred Spartans who had held back the Persian army at the Gates of Thermopylae, or even the Allied forces that had landed on the beaches of Normandy and had pushed the Nazis all the way back to their downfall in Berlin.

The point was that some of the most important battles in history had been won not by those with the greatest number of troops, but rather those with the largest commitment to winning the fight.

And now, low on ammunition and sitting in what was shaping up to be his own Alamo, Harvath was determined to show the same commitment.

The overhang above them made it impossible to see who or what was coming downhill. Only when they pressed themselves against the rocks to either side could they even grab a partial glimpse of what was happening. And, if anyone ran up toward them from below, they were completely exposed and vulnerable.

Having warned Christina that the mercenaries were incoming, he picked up his rifle and made ready.

As he had done earlier, he once again did the math. Four dead Wagner operatives at the sleds meant there could be ten left—eight if they had maintained their two snipers aboard the helicopter.

Either way, those were bad odds and Harvath knew it. It was also the kind of battle a true warrior wished for. Only against an overwhelming force could you ever really prove that you had what it took.

The one thing about Harvath, though, was that no matter how many times he had proved it, he always felt as if he had to prove it again.

Maybe it was a hangover from his SEAL father, who never seemed happy with anything he had done. Maybe it was something else.

Maybe, like his father, Harvath was always trying to push himself just a bit further than anyone else was willing or able to go.

Whatever the answer, it didn't seem to matter much as he saw the first mercenary approach and he readied his rifle. Then, when the shot presented itself, he took it. And the moment he did, everything around them exploded.

The Wagner mercenaries had done an excellent job figuring out exactly where he and Christina were taking cover. As their rounds slammed into the overhang and the large rocks that acted as its wings, sharp chips went flying in all directions, hitting both Harvath and Christina in the face. It was like standing behind a revved-up jet as someone dumped a box of razorblades into one of the turbines.

Sticking the barrel of his weapon through a space between the rocks, he pressed his trigger and sprayed his assailants with a ton of lead.

It forced the mercenaries back, but only for a moment. Before he knew it, the barrage was back on and he and Christina were dodging bullets and more flying pieces of stone.

He was beginning to grow concerned about their ability to battle their way out of this. He could fight, but he could only kill what he could see. Their position provided only a few vantage points. And Christina, as tough and as willing as she was, didn't have the training to go up against ex-Spetsnaz soldiers. At best, she might be able to hold them off by firing in their direction, but only until her ammo ran out.

The mercenaries were incredibly adept at using the trees for cover. Harvath had yet to put one down. Every time he actually caught sight of one and took a shot, his target disappeared—and not the way he liked, as in a spray of blood. Nevertheless he kept shooting.

With Christina keeping an eye on their flank, he worried about being overrun from above. He couldn't pop his head out to look uphill without possibly getting it blown off.

At the same time, he knew what he had heard. The Wagner helicopter had hovered up the slope and it hadn't done so to admire the view. Any second, men were going to pour over the overhang—or worse, they were first going to send a grenade.

Seeing movement again in the trees to his right, he fired and blew through the last two rounds in his magazine.

Letting the spent magazine drop to the ground, he inserted a fresh one and called Christina over to him.

"I need to poke my head out and look uphill," he said. "When I do, I want you to spray all of the trees over there. Just swing your barrel back and forth and keep shooting. Can you do that?"

Christina nodded and when Harvath gave the signal, she stuck her rifle out and began firing.

As she did, Harvath peered over the overhang and risked a look up the ridge. It was a scene straight out of a nightmare—multiple Wagner mercenaries were quickly closing in on them.

Without proper cover or concealment, there was no way Harvath would be able to repel their attack.

They couldn't stay here. As dangerous as it was to move off into the trees, it was more dangerous to stay put and wait for their position to be overrun.

Helping Christina swap out magazines, he explained to her what they needed to do and prepared her for how to make it happen.

He would give her the biggest head start possible and hold them off as long as he could.

He told her to run, and not to stop running until she couldn't hear the gunfire anymore.

"What about you?" she asked.

"I'll be right behind you."

She knew that wasn't true. He was going to stay and fight in order to buy her time to get away. She was afraid he wouldn't make it. She didn't want to let him do that.

"We can both run," she said.

"No," Harvath replied. "There isn't time. You need to go. Now."

Another volley of gunfire tore up the rocks around them. Harvath spun and fired back.

When he turned back around, he said, "We'll do it like before. When I count to three, I want you to run."

He was just about to start counting, when a pair of mercenaries appeared atop the overhang behind him.

"Look out!" Christina screamed.

CHAPTER 70

One moment the mercenaries appeared on the overhang and the next moment they fell down dead at Harvath's feet. Neither he nor Christina, though, had killed them. Somebody else in the forest had fired the shots.

What's more, they had come from suppressed weapons—something Harvath was intimately familiar with.

Tier One operators used them not only to dampen noise and help reduce muzzle flash, but also to know which gunshots were being fired by their teammates.

The sound was unmistakable and hearing it now could only mean one thing. There were friendlies close by.

Scrapping his plan to abandon their position, he warned Christina not to shoot anyone, unless she was absolutely certain she was targeting Wagner mercenaries.

She asked how she would know the difference, when all of a sudden there was a flash of white behind one of the trees below them. It was followed by another and another.

A small force, carrying suppressed rifles, was quickly working its way up toward them.

Their winter whites were more sophisticated and less splotchy than Wagner's.

Harvath was just pointing out the difference to Christina when several of them raised their weapons, pointed them in their direction, and began firing.

Instinctively, Harvath and Christina dropped to the ground. As they did, two more dead Wagner mercenaries dropped over the edge of the overhang.

The force then split into three teams, two of which branched off to the sides, forming a perimeter as they continued to engage the enemy, while the third headed right for them.

When the leader turned his head and revealed the muted American flag on his helmet, Harvath felt flooded with a sense of both relief and overwhelming pride. He wanted to wrap the man in the biggest bear hug he had ever given. Even before the operative had pulled down his face-mask, he knew exactly who it was.

"Friendlies!" Haney called out.

Harvath helped cover them as they hurried up to the outcrop.

"Somebody here order a pizza?" Staelin asked, pressing himself against the rocks next to Christina.

"Hours ago," quipped Harvath, who was so glad to see them. "What took you so long?"

"Traffic was terrible."

Harvath couldn't wait to hear all about it. Patting Staelin on the helmet, he ran his gloved hand over its American flag patch.

"We've got a plane waiting," Haney stated, as he kept his weapon up and continued to scan for threats. "It's a couple of klicks away. Are you both capable of walking?"

"Affirmative," answered Harvath.

Haney was attempting to call in a SITREP to JSOC when all around them a tidal wave of bullets crashed down and showered them with more sharp pieces of chipped rock.

"What the fuck?" Haney angrily demanded. "How many more of those assholes are out there?"

"Can't tell," Staelin responded, as he looked for targets to fire on. "Harvath picked the one spot in the entire Oblast with zero lines of sight."

"I was in a hurry," Harvath said in his defense, subtly giving his colleague the finger. "But I counted four on our flank."

"Plus the four above you," Haney stated, unshouldering his backpack. "Whom we neutralized."

"What's the plan, boss?" Staelin asked.

Unzipping the pack, Haney withdrew a two-foot-long, olive-drab-colored tube and said, "I'm going to need some cover fire in a moment."

"Roger that. Just say when."

Harvath pulled Christina closer to him. The back blast from the M72 Light Anti-Tank Weapon, or LAW, could be pretty intense. You didn't want to be anywhere within its path.

The LAW was a one-time-use, shoulder-fired, 66 millimeter, anti-armor rocket launcher that weighed five and a half pounds. It was, essentially, a mini bazooka.

Pulling the retaining pin from the back, Haney removed the rear cap and then the one up front. Extending the collapsed tube to its full, locked length—causing the front and rear sights to automatically pop up—he slid the safety forward. The weapon was now armed and ready to fire.

"Going hot," said Haney, as he checked to make sure no one was behind him in the exhaust area. Placing the weapon on his shoulder, he called out, "Back blast area clear?"

"Clear," Harvath and Staelin responded.

"Cover fire in three. Two. *One.*"

Harvath and Staelin trained their rifles on the trees from where the Wagner mercenaries had been firing and unleashed a storm of lead of their own. As they did, Haney leaned out from behind the rocks, sighted in where he believed the Russians to be, and fired the LAW.

The projectile erupted from the rocket launcher and went screaming through the trees.

When it connected with its target, it exploded, sending snow, bark, and body parts in all directions.

Haney looked at his buddies and said, "First rule of a gunfight? Bring a Marine with an antitank weapon."

"Oorah," Staelin replied, grunting the USMC battle cry.

"If we're done fucking around," asked Harvath, "can we go now? I'd kind of like to get the hell out of here."

"No matter what I do for you," said Haney, rolling the spent launcher tube in the snow to cool it off, before putting it back in his pack and zipping it up, "I never get a thank-you."

"You'll get my thank-you when we're on the plane."

As Chase, Sloane, and Barton hung back to cover their six o'clock, Morrison and Gage led the march downhill, while Haney and Staelin stayed in tight with Harvath and Christina.

Not a single gunshot was heard. The LAW had done its job. If any of the Wagner mercenaries had survived, they hadn't been in any shape to give chase or to fight back.

At the bottom of the hill, where the trees started thinning out, and just within sight of the dog sleds and the dead Sámis, Haney was finally able to get a satellite signal.

As he relayed a quick SITREP back to JSOC, he watched as Christina said something to Harvath. Nodding in agreement, the pair walked cautiously into the open. It took him a moment to realize what was going on, and then he saw it. The dogs were still harnessed to the sleds.

One by one, Harvath and Christina unfastened them. But instead of running off, back to the village, they lay down next to Jompá and Olá and refused to move.

"What are we doing, Harvath?" Haney asked, as he walked up behind them, his report to JSOC complete.

"The dogs don't want to leave."

"Guess what?" the Marine replied. "*I do*. In fact, I never even wanted to come to this godforsaken place. But I did it, for you. So, you'll forgive me for not caring about a bunch of fucking dogs. When they get hungry enough, they'll go home. As for us, we need to get moving."

The Marine wasn't wrong. The dogs could make up their own minds. Harvath had made up his.

"Let's go."

As the team clicked into their skis, Sloane and Chase each unstrapped a pair of snowshoes from their packs and handed them to Scot and Christina.

"Snowshoes," Harvath groaned. "Love these."

Sloane, who loved to bust Harvath's balls, was about to tease him, until they all froze.

Coming in fast over the trees was a Wagner helicopter.

CHAPTER 71

Reinforcements!" Garin yelled into his headset to Minayev back at Alakurtti Air Base. "He's escaping! Send *everyone*."

As the helicopter made a pass over the scene below, the Wagner commander was stunned to see at least nine individuals, all of them armed. Somehow, a rescue team had made it to Harvath. He was furious.

Turning to his snipers, he ordered, "Stop them. And if you can't stop them, kill them. *All* of them."

The snipers nodded and as the helicopter came around again, they fired repeatedly, chewing up the snow near Harvath and his rescuers, who dove for cover.

As the helo banked above the trees to swing out and prep for another pass, they saw one of the figures—a man dressed in Wagner winter white whom Garin assumed to be Harvath—get back to his feet and raise a defiant middle finger as they flew out of view.

• • •

"How many more LAWs do you have in your backpack?" Harvath demanded, as he lowered his finger.

"One," said Haney, as he got back onto his skis.

"I want it."

"For the helo?"

"You're damn right *for the helo*," Harvath replied.

The Marine was reluctant. "How many fingers am I holding up?"

"How many fingers *am I* holding up," replied Harvath, raising his middle finger again and directing it at Haney.

"I guess you've earned it," said the Marine as he handed him his backpack. "But what if this doesn't work?"

"Then you'd better have a hell of a Plan B in place. For right now, let's get everybody out of sight."

The team did as he asked, moving deeper into the trees. Harvath remained up front, concealing himself as best he could.

When the Wagner helicopter returned, it came in low and fast with its snipers hanging out the windows, itching to unloose their weapons on anyone they saw.

The problem, though, was that there was no one to see. Everyone had vanished, likely into the woods.

The helicopter was just about past when a lone individual suddenly materialized. Garin spotted him, his defiant middle finger raised high once more.

"It's him!" he shouted. "Right there! That's him!"

Pulling back on the speed, the pilot aggressively banked the helicopter in an attempt to line the snipers up for a shot.

It was exactly what Harvath needed.

Sighting in the cabin area behind the cockpit, he gave it just enough lead, depressed the Fire button, and sent the projectile skyward. It couldn't have been a more prefect shot.

Upon piercing the Mi-8, the warhead detonated and the helicopter exploded in a roiling fireball.

As it came crashing to the ground, the team cheered.

Harvath, though, knew they weren't safe yet. They still had to make it back to the plane—and even then, he wouldn't feel completely relieved until they were out of Russia.

Rapidly organizing the team, Haney had Sloane return to the point position and lead them toward the lake.

With just his first steps in the snowshoes, Harvath was reminded of how much agony his body was in.

He could have asked Staelin, who functioned as the team's medic, for a painkiller, but he didn't want to slow them down. It could wait until they got to the plane. Or at least, that's what he had thought.

Out of nowhere, they heard the sound of an engine coming to life, powering up, and then speeding away.

Harvath didn't need to ask what they were hearing. The look on Haney's face said it all.

"Is that our ride leaving?" Harvath asked.

"That motherfucker," the Marine cursed. "I knew we shouldn't have trusted him."

"Who's *him*?"

"Pavel," Haney replied. "A local alcoholic and chickenshit bush pilot who's an asset of the Finns."

"You left a foreign asset sitting there with a fully functioning aircraft? You didn't even pull the master fuse?"

"I had no idea how quickly we'd need to take off. I didn't want to screw around with his plane."

"So what are we going to do now?" asked Harvath.

Without missing a beat, the Marine stated, "We're walking out. It's just a little over fifty kilometers."

"I knew this was going to happen," said Staelin.

"That's enough," replied Haney as he looked over at Sloane and said, "Pick the nearest spot the Finns told us we'd be safe to cross the border and plot us a course."

"Roger that," she replied, punching her ski poles into the snow and turning her attention to her wrist-top GPS device.

In the meantime, Haney transmitted a new SITREP to JSOC and told them to stand by for the updated route information, which was slow in coming.

"Sloane," he said. "What's taking so long?"

"All of a sudden, my GPS is all wonky," she responded.

"What do you mean *wonky*?"

"Wonky meaning it's not working."

"Is it the weather?" the Marine asked.

"I don't know."

Harvath, though, did know. "It's not the weather. The signal is being jammed. And if the signal is being jammed, that means Russian military is inbound."

"Wait," said Haney. "How do you know?"

"The Russians have been perfecting their GPS jamming. During the last set of NATO training exercises in Norway, they turned everything upside down."

"If that's what's going on here, how do you know they're inbound?"

"Because the system has a particular radius. The jammer is usually mounted on a ship or a vehicle of some sort. As we're not close enough to the water and there are no passable roads anywhere near us, I'm guessing it's on a plane or a helicopter."

"We're not far from Alakurtti Air Base," said Haney. "They're known for their helicopter regiment that specializes in electronic jamming."

"There you go," replied Harvath. "So what's Plan B?"

As team leader, the Marine rapidly weighed their options.

But when he didn't answer right away, Harvath began to feel uncomfortable. "There *is* a Plan B, right?"

"There's *one hell of* a Plan B. But the President needs to sign off on it."

Pretending his hand was a telephone, Harvath lifted it to his ear and said, "Then you'd better get hold of him fast because the Russians aren't going to stop at killing our GPS. They're going to flood this area with troops and either capture or kill all of us."

CHAPTER 72

When JSOC relayed Haney's request to the President, Porter immediately turned to Nicholas and SPEHA Rogers. "Are we officially out of options? Because as we discussed, this has the ultimate downside risk."

Rogers looked at Nicholas and then back to the President. "The team on the ground has maps. They know where they are and can attempt to land nav to the border, but . . ." he said, as his voice trailed off.

Porter raised an eyebrow. "*But* what?"

"But there's a reason the Russians are jamming their GPS," stated Nicholas. "They want to slow them down, so they can capture them. Not only will they have Harvath, but seven more Americans who will be accused of espionage and God knows what else. At this point, we're out of options. We need to pull the trigger on Plan B."

"Do you agree?" the President asked Rogers.

"Yes, sir," the SPEHA replied. "I do."

With his mind on everything that had gone wrong in the failed Iranian hostage rescue of the 1980s, Porter looked to the Chairman of the Joint Chiefs. "Can we successfully execute in this kind of weather?"

"We won't be able to have the Zero-three-hundred team parachute in. It's too dangerous. Everything else, though, we can do," the Chairman replied.

"Show of hands," the President then called out, addressing the rest of the national security personnel seated around the long mahogany table.

Every single hand went up.

Turning his attention back to the monitor with the live feed from JSOC, the President transmitted his order. "Launch Operation Gray Garden."

After confirmation from JSOC, it was time to start the next phase of their plan.

"We have a total of three calls to make," said Porter. "Who goes first?"

"I do," replied Nicholas. "Once Matterhorn has the information, he will transmit it directly to Moscow."

"Then," said Rogers, "I will reach out to the Russian Ambassador and communicate our offer, which he will also transmit directly to Moscow."

"After which, I will call President Peshkov and ask him for his answer," stated Porter.

"Yes, sir," responded the SPEHA. "At that point, the ball will be completely in his court. It's his call."

"And if he says *no*?"

"If he says no," Nicholas answered, "Then we buckle up, because things are going to get very bumpy."

CHAPTER 73

If the Russians were coming, Haney had decided it was better to dig in and make a stand than to try to outrun them.

Retracing their path to the lake, they chose the spot they had originally marked out for Harvath. Unlike the outcropping where they had found him, this location provided excellent fields of fire and could be much better defended.

With Harvath and Christina running on fumes, it took twice as long to get there as Haney had expected. Once there, he told Harvath to stand down. The man had been through enough. He didn't need to now man a post.

Staelin saw to both of them—Christina first, because Harvath insisted. When it came to his needs, he refused to take anything stronger than Ibuprofen and Tylenol. Until they were safely out, he didn't want anything fogging up his head.

And as for laying his rifle down and not manning a post, there was no way that was happening either. This was his fight and he was going to see it through until the very end.

When Haney had explained "Plan B" to him, he admired not just its audacity, but also its cleverness. If it ended up working, he owed Nicholas and whoever SPEHA Rogers was the best steak dinner in D.C.

As the wind and the snow continued getting worse, his concern began to grow. It was bad enough that he was surrounded by seven teammates who had all risked their lives to save him, but to add to their ranks? He didn't like all of this being done on his behalf. Upping the risk and enlisting more lives to save his felt wrong.

He was the one who was supposed to risk everything to go in and get people out. Not vice versa.

With all of his experience and all of his training, he should have been able to handle this. It was who he was. He should have been able to get himself and Christina across the border without risking anyone else's life—just as he should have been able to save Lara, Lydia, and the Old Man.

Now, Jompá and Olá, the men who had pulled him from the frigid snow, were dead. Theirs were just another two entries on a long list of people who had died because of him. Why, he wondered, was he still alive? What possible purpose could his life even serve?

He was slipping down a razorblade-threaded rabbit hole of survivor's guilt when Chase Palmer signaled for everyone to be silent. He had heard something.

Harvath listened but didn't hear anything. His ears had been around a little longer than Chase's and had been subjected to a lot more explosions and gunfights.

In a couple of moments, though, he began to hear it as well. *Helicopters*—plural.

"Everybody grab some ground," Haney ordered.

The team was huddled together where part of the forest had eroded, behind several fallen trees.

As they all lay down, Haney added, "Everybody stay frosty."

"Seriously?" Staelin remarked, as he blew a cloud of warm breath into the air.

"One more peep out of you," whispered the Marine, "and you'll be walking all the way home. Are we clear?"

"Good copy," the Delta Force operative acknowledged, shooting him a smile and a thumbs-up.

No one moved a muscle as the sound of the helicopters grew louder.

Gage, the Green Beret, had the best view of what was headed their way. "Fuck me," he said. "I'm looking at two Mi-8s, plus a pair of Mi-24 helicopter gunships."

"Fuck *us*," Sloane responded.

"There'll be no *fucking*," Haney sternly responded, "unless it's *us* fuck-ing *them*. Is that understood?"

"Oorah!" Staelin grunted while everyone else joined in a chorus of "Roger that."

"Got any more tricks up your sleeve?" Harvath asked.

"Nope. I'm all out," said Haney.

"So what's the plan?"

"The plan," the Marine explained, "is that we hold our position and wait for extraction."

Harvath looked at Christina and saw that the fear from earlier had re-turned. Reaching over, he put his gloved hand reassuringly on her arm. "Everything is going to be okay," he said.

She didn't speak. She didn't even try to force a smile. She gave him one quick nod and that was it.

He let his hand linger for a moment longer and then turned his atten-tion to his rifle. Drawing back the charging handle, he made sure a round was chambered and that the weapon's safety was off.

Around him, the other operators quietly conducted similar drills.

"Hey. About that *no fucking* rule?" Gage asked, breaking the silence.

"What about it?" Haney replied.

"Things are starting to get romantic."

Crawling over to see what he was talking about, the Marine peered through a space between the downed tree trunks and watched as the Mi-8s touched down.

"Jesus," he muttered as the helicopters disgorged their occupants.

"What's going on?" Harvath asked.

Haney waved him over to see for himself.

As Harvath stared at the troops massing in the snow, Haney turned and addressed the team.

"Okay, listen up," he said. "In addition to the two heavily armed Mi-24s, the Mi-8s just vomited up an entire platoon of soldiers. By my count, there are at least thirty of them. And if they're dropping here, that probably means they suspect we're nearby. So stay alert and stay ready."

"Only thirty?" Morrison mused, as he made sure the rounds were seated in all of his magazines. "That'd be a pretty short gunfight."

Though Harvath appreciated his sense of humor, the thirty Russian Army soldiers from Alakurtti Air Base had them outgunned by more than three to one. They also had four helicopters, two of which could blast the piles of logs they were hiding behind into matchsticks in the blink of an eye. It would be a short fight all right. In fact, it'd be a slaughter.

"What are the rules here?" Barton asked, his extra mags unpacked and stacked neatly in front of him.

"We're still weapons free," Haney confirmed, as he went to call in an update to JSOC. "But let's not start anything we can't finish."

They all made sure to remain on the ground. If they popped any part of their bodies above the logs, their heat signature could be detected by one of the helos, or by one of the soldiers on the ground if they were carrying handheld units.

"Shit," said Haney. "I'm having trouble getting a satellite signal again."

"Is it the Russians?" Harvath asked. "Do you think they're affecting our comms as well?"

"Our system is antijam. I think it's the weather—too much cloud cover. We'll have to go old school and hope our ride's in range," he said. Pointing at Chase, he began relaying instructions. "Power up the Falcon and see if you can reach Hurricane Two-Two on any of the designated frequencies. Let them know we need assistance ASAP."

"Roger that," Chase replied, as he reached for his backpack and removed the Multiband Multi Mission Radio he was lugging as a backup. Hurricane Two-Two was the call sign for their ticket out.

As Chase set up the radio, Haney kept trying to get a satellite signal on his device. And while they worked on comms, Harvath and Gage attempted to keep an eye on the Russian soldiers. But with the weather, it was becoming increasingly difficult to see what they were up to.

All of the soldiers were on skis, were wearing whites, and were carrying an array of weaponry. They divided into eight four-man fire teams and then began skiing off in different directions. One was headed right for them.

"Hurricane Two-Two, this is Nemesis Zero-One," Chase said into the handset. "Do you copy? Over."

He waited for a reply and then tried again.

"Hurricane Two-Two, this is Nemesis Zero-One. We need immediate extraction. Do you copy? Over."

When, through the static, a faint voice finally replied, it sounded weak and far away—as if it was coming from the bottom of a well.

"Nemesis Zero-One, this is Hurricane Two-Two. We read you. What is your status? Over."

After letting Haney know that he had established contact, Chase had a back-and-forth with Hurricane Two-Two, answering some questions and giving a quick SITREP.

"Acknowledged," said Hurricane Two-Two when Chase had finished. "Nemesis Zero-One, stand by. Over."

"Roger that," said Chase. "Nemesis Zero-One, standing by. Over."

Peering through his rangefinder at the approaching Russian soldiers, Gage provided an update. "Two hundred meters and closing."

"Good copy," said Haney, acknowledging the information. "Two hundred meters."

Gage was an exceptional distance shooter and carried an H&K 417 rifle with a twenty-inch barrel. Its effective range was eight hundred meters—more than four times the distance of the approaching threat.

"Are we going to let the air out of these guys?" he asked.

"Negative," Haney replied. "Hold."

"Roger that. Holding."

"What's the status of Hurricane Two-Two?" Haney then asked.

Chase held up the handset. "I'm still standing by."

Harvath didn't like how long this was taking.

"One hundred seventy-five meters," Gage reported.

"Copy that," replied the Marine. "One hundred seventy-five meters."

"Still nothing," Chase stated.

Harvath needed to remember that this wasn't his team right now. It was Haney's. And as such, Haney was in charge. Nevertheless, he couldn't help but wonder if they should have tried to make it out on foot.

"One hundred fifty meters," announced Gage.

"Roger that," Haney replied. "One hundred fifty meters."

"Heads up," said Sloane. "We've got activity just south of us. One of the other fire teams has changed direction and is now coming up this way."

"Range?"

"Approximately one hundred meters."

"I've got clean shots here," Gage stated.

"Me too," replied Sloane.

"Negative," Haney ordered. "We hold."

Harvath looked at him, but the Marine had already shifted his focus to Chase. "Tell Hurricane Two-Two right now that—"

But the young operator held his hand up and cut him off as he listened intently to the voice on his handset.

A fraction of a second later, he said, "Roger that, Hurricane Two-Two. Good copy. Nemesis Zero-One out."

Then, turning to his teammates, he declared, "Angels inbound. Thirty seconds."

No one spoke. No one moved. Lying on the frigid ground, they watched the approaching Russian soldiers and strained their ears for the telltale sound of their rescue.

Ten seconds passed. Then twenty. At exactly thirty seconds, a pair of F-22 Raptors flew in incredibly low and blisteringly fast. Hitting supersonic, they broke the sound barrier.

The boom was so powerful, the earth trembled and snow was knocked off trees for as far as the eye could see. It sounded as if a rip was being torn through the fabric of the sky. All of the Russians dove for cover.

If the intent had been to scare the hell out of them, it had worked. Even with the reduced visibility, Gage and Sloane could tell the nearest fire teams were calling their superiors, asking what had happened and awaiting instructions as to what to do next.

Collectively, Harvath and the rest of the team held their breath. This was the moment of truth.

President Porter had proven he was willing to violate Russian airspace. President Peshkov now had to decide whether he was willing to let it stand.

In the last five minutes, Peshkov would have received intelligence through Artur Kopec's handler that the Americans had a team on the ground and had recovered Harvath. Egor Sazanov, his Ambassador to the United States, would have phoned the Foreign Minister and shared the good news that the entirety of Peshkov's frozen assets was poised to be thawed.

Then, just before the American jets had crossed into Russia, the U.S. President himself would have called. He would have explained what he wanted and, more important, what he was willing to do to get it. The choice after that was up to Peshkov.

And it became apparent, very quickly, that he had made it.

CHAPTER 74

arvath and the team watched as, one by one, the Russian troops turned around and returned to the ice.

There, covered by the Mi-24 gunships, they climbed back aboard their Mi-8 helicopters and took off.

All the while, the F-22 Raptors stayed on station, circling overhead, ready for anything they might be called on to do. Never once did a single Russian intercept aircraft appear to address the incursion. Whatever word had come down from on high, Peshkov had made it clear that no action was to be taken.

As a SEAL, Harvath had been inside more C130s than he cared to remember. But never had one sounded as sweet as the one that came roaring in on approach, landed, and taxied to the edge of the frozen lake.

The propeller engines on the Hercules aircraft were known as the "Four Fans of Freedom," which couldn't have been more appropriate than at this moment.

They continued thundering as the rear cargo ramp dropped and the Zero-Three-Hundred team raced out onto the ice, riding cold-weather ATVs.

When they got to him, Harvath insisted on snowshoeing the rest of the way to the aircraft. Despite all that had happened, he wasn't going to leave his teammates. He encouraged Christina to accept a ride, which she did.

When they reached the ramp, a pair of Air Force Pararescue Jumpers, more commonly known as PJs, was waiting. They stepped forward to give Harvath a hand, but he waved them off. He didn't need any help getting on the aircraft.

C130s were essentially enormous cargo planes. There was the cockpit, a bathroom, and maybe a galley. After that, it was just open space configured for the mission.

In the Skibird, the center aisle was about ten feet wide and reserved for cargo. Along the sides, suspended from bright orange nylon webbing, were seats made from the same material, which flipped down.

At the far end, an enormous American flag had been hung. Upon seeing it, Harvath was filled with emotion.

The PJs were the medical component of the operation and they tried to steer Harvath and Christina to two stretchers upfront. Once more, he told the PJs to assist Christina and promised that he would join them in a moment. Until everyone was on board, he wasn't going to stand down.

Popping out of their skis, Haney, Staelin, Chase, Sloane, Morrison, Gage, and Barton climbed into the aircraft and stowed their gear.

They were followed by the DEVGRU SEALs of the Zero-Three-Hundred team. Once their ATVs were lashed down and everyone was ready, the Skibird's loadmaster radioed the pilots that they were ready for takeoff.

Before the engines were even powered up, one of the PJs had already started an IV on Harvath with a saline drip. It was standard procedure and would make administering any meds much easier. There was also the concern, after everything he had been through, that Harvath was severely dehydrated, which the IV would help to reverse.

Taking seats alongside the stretcher, his friends sat down with him.

"We did it," said Haney. "It's over."

Harvath understood what the Marine was trying to say, but it wasn't over. Not for him. And not by a long shot. The only thing he could think to say was "Thank you."

"Don't thank us until we're out of here," replied Staelin, as they felt the big LC-130 shudder as it turned and set up for takeoff.

"Fuck that," joked Barton. "I'll take my thank-you now."

"Me too," added Gage. "Do you have any idea the amount of shit I had to rearrange to be here?"

"I didn't even want to come," replied Chase.

"At least they told you the truth," snarked Sloane. "They told me that I'd be rescuing the President."

Harvath didn't think he had it in him, but he smiled nevertheless. He then looked at Morrison. "What about you?"

"I can't lie," said the younger Force Recon Marine. "I came for the vodka."

Harvath raised the arm with the IV and pointed toward his rucksack. "Open it," he said.

Morrison did and inside found the remainder of the bottle of vodka Harvath had found at the trapper cabin. Pulling it out, he held it up. The team cheered.

"First drink goes to Christina," Harvath ordered. "That belonged to her uncle, and the two of them saved my life."

Morrison handed the bottle to one of the PJs, who unscrewed the cap and handed it to Christina.

Sitting up on her stretcher, she smiled and held it aloft. "*Za Vstrechu*," she said, taking a swig. *To our meeting.*

The bottle was then handed to Harvath. This time, he had no difficulty finding words. "To those who are no longer with us," he said, as he took a drink and passed it along.

Each of his teammates repeated his toast as they took a sip. Outside, the thrum of the engines increased as the throttles were pushed forward.

"I've got an idea," said Haney, just as the brakes were being released. "How about we ask our new pilot to swing by Pavel's house so we can kick his ass?"

Once again, a cheer rose from the team.

Harvath had always loved his teammates, but he had never really known how much until right now. They had all fought and bled together. But when he had been dragged into hell, they had rushed in to drag him back out.

It wasn't about money, medals, or fame. It was about loyalty, friendship, and honor.

Even if no one ever knew what had happened here, *they* would know. They would know *what* they had done and *why* they had done it. Integrity was all the reward any of them would ever need.

Harvath only wished that his own integrity had been enough to prevent his wife and two of his dearest friends from being murdered.

Before he could get sucked into that line of thinking, the huge aircraft lurched forward and began racing down the ice.

When it seemed it had reached its maximum speed, yet still couldn't achieve lift, the rockets on the sides kicked in and the nose of the plane began to rise. As the LC-130 became airborne, another cheer went up.

The F-22 Raptors accompanied the plane out of Russia and into Finnish airspace, and then all the way back to Luleå in northern Sweden.

Along the way, it was Christina who convinced Harvath to accept something more than he had already taken to deaden the pain of his injuries.

He had agreed, but on one condition. Turning to Haney and Staelin, he had made them promise that as soon as they landed in Luleå, they would all board The Carlton Group jet and head straight home. No detours to Landstuhl or any other overseas medical centers for treatment. They would fly directly back to the United States and Christina would be coming with them. Haney and Staelin had immediately agreed.

Unbeknownst to Harvath, those had been their specific orders.

CHAPTER 75

Death was never easy. It was messy and complicated on the best of days. On the worst of days, it was tragic, heartbreaking, and incredibly unfair.

After arriving in Sweden, Harvath had spent almost the entire plane ride back to the United States asleep, or pretending to be. He wasn't in the mood to talk. What's more, his body desperately needed the rest.

When the jet touched down at Andrews Air Force Base, instead of Dulles International, it wasn't hard to guess who was waiting for him. The amount of security alone gave it away.

Inside the hangar, an enormous American flag had been hung to welcome Harvath and the team home.

Harvath took his time pulling himself together, allowing his teammates to deplane first. He had no idea how many of them, if any, had met the President of the United States before. Finally, when he couldn't wait anymore, he led Christina down the air-stairs.

The small receiving line was composed of President Paul Porter, CIA Director Bob McGee, Nicholas—minus his dogs—and a fourth man whom Harvath didn't recognize.

Starting with the President, Harvath shook hands and introduced Christina.

"On behalf of the United States," Porter said to her, "I want to thank you for helping bring Scot home."

"It is my honor Mr. President," she replied, a bit awestruck that the President of the United States had come to meet them personally.

"It's good to have you back," Porter then said to Harvath.

"Thank you, sir. It's good to be back."

That was all Harvath had in him. The President wasn't offended. He realized how much the man had been through. The fact that he had walked off the plane under his own power was a testament to how tough he was.

Graciously, Porter passed him off to McGee, adding, "You and I will catch up soon."

"Yes, sir," Harvath replied, as he thanked the President once more before shaking hands with the CIA Director and introducing him to Christina.

"Welcome home," said McGee, to both of them.

Next up was Nicholas, who greeted Harvath warmly before engaging Christina in Russian.

Harvath waited a couple beats and when the little man didn't break off his chat, he reached out and introduced himself to the last man in line.

"Brendan Rogers," the SPEHA said, shaking hands. "Very glad to have you back home."

"Thank you for everything you did to make it happen," Harvath responded. "I owe you and Nicholas a steak dinner at some point."

"You don't owe me anything. I was just doing my job. Although I would like to be able to chat with you about your experience, if that would be okay."

"Now?"

"No," Rogers said, with an exaggerated shake of his head. "You work on getting acclimated. We can talk when you're ready."

"Thank you."

As Nicholas continued to speak with Christina, Rogers explained what they had arranged for her.

He had come not only to welcome Harvath home, but also to personally escort Christina to a farm in Virginia where she would be looked after while all of her paperwork was being processed. For her role in helping

Harvath escape, she was being given full U.S. citizenship, as well as a substantial reward.

"Start-up funds," Rogers said. "With which she can begin her new life."

They chatted for a few more minutes before Nicholas finally broke off and introduced her to the SPEHA.

Once they had met, Harvath said to her, "I don't think I can ever repay you."

"You don't have to," she replied.

"I do, though. You gave up everything to help me."

"I'm going to be all right."

"I know you are," he said, as they hugged.

As their hug ended, she smiled at him warmly.

"For your safety," Harvath continued, "Rogers and his people are going to keep you out of sight for a while. As soon as I can, I'll come see you. Okay?"

"That sounds nice. I'd like that. And for *your* safety, don't forget to get the rest of your rabies shots."

With that, the SPEHA led Christina over to the Diplomatic Security Service protective team that would be taking care of her. Once those introductions were made, they all exited the hangar together to a pair of waiting SUVs.

Turning around, Harvath watched as President Porter posed for pictures with the team, eventually waving him over to join in. There, in front of the giant red, white, and blue American flag, they commemorated their successful mission.

After shaking hands with everyone once more, Porter was whisked away by his Secret Service detail.

As the team pulled their gear from the plane, Harvath pitched in and helped. One by one, he thanked them.

Once they had completely unloaded, Nicholas directed them toward the vehicles he had waiting. Harvath, though, wasn't included. The CIA Director had other plans for him.

"We'd like to get you to the hospital and have you looked over," said McGee. "After they run some tests, we can—"

"I'm fine," Harvath interrupted. "I don't need a hospital. I'd rather just go home."

"I understand. Unfortunately, we can't do that. Not yet. I need to debrief you first."

A debriefing was the absolute last thing he wanted to do. What he wanted was to be left alone. He wanted to go home, get drunk, and not talk to anyone for a week—or maybe forever.

But while he didn't like the idea of a debriefing, he knew why it had to happen. He had been under the control of and interrogated by a hostile foreign power. The CIA and the President needed to know what questions he had been asked and, more important, what he had said in response. He didn't have a choice. Better to get it over with.

"Okay," Harvath said, giving in. "Where? Back at Langley?"

McGee shook his head. "We'd like to make you a little more comfortable than that."

•   •   •

"More comfortable" than Langley turned out to be an Agency safe house a short helicopter flight away on Maryland's Eastern Shore.

It had a nice view of the water, was tastefully decorated in a nautical motif, and smelled like steamed crab. There Harvath, McGee, and a CIA psychiatrist named Dr. Levi, spent the next four days, watched over by a small security contingent.

The home had a large, comfortably furnished den, which was well lit and had been wired for both sound and video. While someone else might have been self-conscious about being under such scrutiny, Harvath didn't care. He had long lived by the maxim from Mark Twain—as long as you told the truth, you didn't have to worry about remembering anything.

He answered every question that was put to him and asked many of his own.

McGee and Levi drilled down on everything, endlessly circling back and asking him to repeat details he had provided minutes or even days before.

Both men were impressed that Harvath had held out as long as he had. Everyone, though, breaks. Harvath had been close, but had had the presence of mind to feed them falsehoods that they wouldn't be able to verify until they were back in Russia. The crash of the military transport plane had turned out to be a blessing in more ways than one.

Beyond learning what techniques the Russians used and what intelligence they had wanted Harvath to reveal, they were deeply interested in his ordeal and how he had survived. No doubt, he was going to end up as a case study at the Agency, as well as in all of the SERE schools.

The questions they continued to ask ran the gamut from his relationship with Kopec and what had happened at the safe house in New Hampshire, to how he had discovered the trapper's cabin, what he had done after breaking into Christina's clinic in Nivsky, and why he had chosen to assault the Wagner mercenaries the way he had.

As someone uncomfortable with praise, he was even more uncomfortable with talking about himself. Many times he couldn't give them a *why*. He did what he did because it was either the way he had been trained or the only option he saw available. There wasn't necessarily a lot of high-level thinking going on. In fact, a lot of it was gut-level.

The worst parts were when McGee stepped out of the room and left him alone with Levi. The man loved two things—golf and cars. He used both in an attempt to build a rapport with Harvath. Harvath wasn't interested.

When the doctor couldn't get him to open up, he took more direct routes—literally asking Harvath how he was feeling, what regrets he may have had, and what he thought he was going to do moving forward.

It was pretty intrusive stuff and frankly none of Levi's business. He worked for The Carlton Group, not the CIA. If he chose to throw his hat in the ring for any future contracts, they could discuss his fitness then. Wanting to pick apart his current "emotional well-being," as Levi put it, was a nonstarter. He made it clear that there was a bright line and that Levi better back up off it.

The only saving grace of the debrief was that one of the men on McGee's detail, a guy named Preisler, was a hell of a cook. Steaks, pasta, all sorts of breakfasts, it seemed there was nothing he couldn't pull off. For a former door-kicker, he was a formidable chef.

The other thing Harvath had appreciated was that when the debrief was done for the day, it was done for the day. There were no prohibitions on Harvath's having a couple of drinks. As long as he wasn't under the influence when they had him on the record, they didn't care what he did. In fact, they went out of their way to give him his space and leave him alone.

Though Levi likely had a hand in it, you didn't need to be a shrink to realize that after everything Harvath had been through, he was going to need some time to be by himself. He was even allowed to leave the house and walk down to the water without anyone accompanying him.

While he would have preferred his own house, his own dock, and his own slice of the Potomac, the view of the Chesapeake from here wasn't terrible. And though he had to put on a coat, at least there wasn't any ice or snow.

On their last night, Levi walked down lugging a cooler and dropped it on the dock next to Harvath. After helping himself to a beer, he sat down and looked out over the water. Harvath waited for him to say something, but the man didn't make a sound.

They sat like that for a good ten minutes before Harvath broke the silence. "What else is in the cooler?"

"I wasn't sure what you were drinking, so I put a little bit of everything in there," the doc replied.

Leaning over, Harvath flipped up the lid and grabbed the bourbon, plus a couple of fresh ice cubes. He dropped them into his glass and then poured himself several fingers.

"Cheers," said Levi.

Harvath raised his glass without looking at him.

"Scot, right now we're off the clock. None of this is official and nothing is going into my notes. Okay?"

Harvath sipped his drink.

"You've been through some unbelievable trauma," the shrink continued. "In my experience, people tend to go in either of two directions from here. They quit and usually fall into a life of substance abuse, which often ends in suicide, or they allow themselves time to grieve, time to heal, and they come back better, stronger."

It was an observation, not a question, so Harvath didn't feel compelled to respond.

"With just the little bit I know about you from your file," offered Levi, "and what I have seen of you here, I think you can come back much stronger. It has to be your choice, though. That's why if there's anything you want to talk to me about, anything at all, I want you to know that you can."

Levi might have been a nice guy, but Harvath wasn't here to make friends. There was nothing he needed to "get off his chest." All he wanted to do was to be left alone. In furtherance of that goal, he remained silent.

• • •

Walking back up to house, Levi found McGee sitting on the porch, smoking a cigar.

"It didn't work, did it?" the CIA Director stated.

The doc shook his head. "No, it didn't."

"I told you it wouldn't. That's not how a guy like Harvath operates."

"And I'm telling you, you have a malfunctioning weapon on your hands. If you let him go, I won't be held responsible for what he does."

"His wife is being buried the day after tomorrow. We can't keep him here. We have to let him go."

"At least put a surveillance team on him; follow him—for his own good."

Not a chance, thought McGee as he blew a cloud of smoke into the air. "Anything else?"

"No. I'm driving home tonight. My report will be on your desk in the morning."

The CIA Director nodded, turned back toward the water, and took another puff from his cigar. His concern wasn't that Harvath was "malfunctioning." In fact, based on everything he'd seen, Harvath, all things considered, was functioning better than anyone would have assumed.

No, his concern ran deeper, to something more visceral.

Inside every human being was a very dark, very cold place. Sealed behind a heavy iron door, the cold dark was populated by the worst demons known to man.

But crack that door—even just an inch—and out all of the demons would fly. And once they had escaped, there would be no bringing them back until they had fed.

What they would feed upon was what worried McGee the most. In the case of Harvath's demons, only one thing would satiate them.

Revenge.

CHAPTER 76

Harvath didn't know what was harder, facing Lara's parents and explaining how they had secretly gotten married at Reed Carlton's bedside, or facing Lara's little boy and not being able to explain to him why he couldn't save his mom.

The service was gut wrenching. It was a full-on police funeral, where Harvath was highly disliked and seen as the guy who had convinced Lara to leave the force and move to D.C. In everyone's mind, he was the reason Lara was dead. And while they knew next to nothing about the details, which only served to piss them off more, they were right. It was his fault that she was gone.

No matter how long he lived, he would never be able to escape that fact. It was another link in the heavy chain of guilt he carried over women who had been killed or injured because of who he was and what he did.

While meant as a slight, it was actually a blessing that Harvath wasn't invited to speak. Instead, he sat quietly with Lara's parents, holding Marco's hand when the little boy had reached out for his.

The Brits had a term for what he was feeling—gutted—but it didn't go far enough. Harvath was absolutely hollowed out.

The night before, he had stood outside the funeral home for hours in the rain. No matter how hard he tried, he couldn't summon the courage to go inside, not while the viewing was going on.

Lara's colleagues loved her dearly and he could tell by the amount of drinking that was going on in the parking lot that if he had shown his face inside, there would have been trouble. This was Boston after all. They were proud, profoundly decent people with a deep sense of right and wrong.

He didn't blame them. Each of them wanted to believe that had they been there, regardless of what had happened, they would have made a difference. That's who they were. They were cops, warriors. It was grossly unfair to them that Lara was gone and Harvath was still here. They couldn't willingly fathom a scenario in which he lived and she died. In their minds, it had to be a failing on his part. If only she hadn't left Boston. If only she had chosen a cop over whatever secret-squirrel bullshit Harvath did for a living.

Once all the cars had departed, once the funeral director and his staff had gone home for the evening, Harvath had disabled the alarm and had let himself inside.

They had done an amazing job. Lara looked beautiful. Pulling up a chair, he placed his hand atop hers.

For an hour, all he did was sit there. He didn't have the words, much less the breath, to speak.

This was the woman he was going to spend the rest of his life with. After putting off marriage for so long, he had finally taken the leap, only to have his bride ripped away from him.

The family he had put on hold so he could pursue his career had been within his grasp. He and Lara and Marco had been a perfect fit. She had lost her husband and Marco had lost his father. Harvath had arrived at the point where he was ready to take on both of those roles. But now it was all gone.

She was so smart, so beautiful, and so funny. What's more, she had understood him. More important, she had understood why he did what he did and why it was so important. In short, she not only loved him, but she allowed him to be who he was.

Gripping her hand, he let it all come out. He let her know how much he loved her, how much he missed her, and how sorry he was that she was gone and that he had not been able to save her.

And as he did, the iron door to the dark, cold place swung the rest of the way open.

. . .

Still exhausted, he fell asleep in the chair next to her.

It was just before dawn when her voice came to him, and told him that it was time to wake up.

He lingered for a moment in that halfway place between sleep and wakefulness, hoping she would say something more, that maybe she would tell him that everything was going to be okay, that she forgave him. He waited, but no further words came.

Looking at his watch, he saw that he would have barely enough time to make it back to his hotel to change before meeting up with Lara's parents at their apartment.

As he had been at the safe house in Maryland and wanted to catch the first available flight to Boston, Sloane had been kind enough to go to his house, pack him a bag, and bring it to him at the airport.

Though she had taken creative license on similar errands in the past, this time she was incredibly respectful—white shirt, black shoes, black tie, and black suit. She had even included a black overcoat, as well as a couple extra days' worth of subdued clothing.

She had also been thoughtful enough to include a heartfelt note of support. Everyone on the team, including Nicholas and even McGee, loved Lara. She was someone very special. All of them would have made the trip to Boston to be there for her funeral, but Harvath had asked them not to. Out of respect for him, they had all stayed back in D.C.

Upon arriving at Lara's parents' house, Marco had thrown his arms around Harvath and hadn't wanted to let go. There was a spark of his mother in him and it felt better than Harvath could have ever imagined to hold the little boy close.

After the burial, when they arrived at the hall where the wake was to take place, Harvath looked out the window of their limo at the steady stream of strangers parading in.

These were people Lara and her parents knew. None of them knew who he was. If the looks he had gotten at the mass and at the burial were any indication, he was not going to be very warmly received here either. On top of that, this was going to be wrenching for Marco.

Pulling his father-in-law aside, Harvath asked if he could take the little boy out to get something to eat and promised to bring him back to the apartment later. Lara's mother and father had both agreed.

After the grandparents had exited the limo, he had the driver take them to a little Boston breakfast place Lara had loved.

Seeing the pair dressed in dark suits and ties, the hostess must have intuited where they were coming from, because she waved them over and found them a table ahead of the other people who had already been waiting. Harvath tried to give her a tip for her kindness, but she refused to take it.

Looking at the children's menu, Marco had trouble deciding what to eat. Harvath told him that on a day like this pancakes were the right choice. He didn't know why, other than that when his father had died, one of his father's SEAL buddies had taken him for breakfast and had suggested the same.

After they had eaten, he asked Marco what he wanted to do. The little boy wanted ice cream, so that's what they did. They then went to the Lego store, a bookstore, and a spot on the banks of the Charles River where he liked to feed the ducks. All too soon, it was time to go home.

The limo had already gone back to the hall, so he and Marco had been walking and taking cabs. Instead of taking one all the way back to the apartment, he had them dropped off a few blocks away. He wanted to walk a little bit more.

Sensing that their time was growing short, Marco reached out and took his hand again as they made their way up the street.

Harvath, as tough as he wanted to be, was doing all he could to hold it together. He wasn't the only one who had lost the chance at a family—so had Marco. Both his mother and his father were gone.

Nearing the apartment, he dreaded saying good-bye. More to the point, he dreaded the question he knew was coming, "When will I see you again?" or worse, "Why can't you take me with you?"

But those weren't the words the little boy used. Instead, after squeezing his hand exactly as Lara always did, he looked at him and said, "I love you."

"I love you, too," replied Harvath as he kneeled down and gave the boy a long hug. "Be good for your grandparents. I promise I will see you soon."

Marco smiled, gave Harvath one more hug around his neck, and then disappeared inside.

He was a good boy and Harvath meant what he had said. He loved him, just as much as he had loved Lara.

It took him several blocks to find a cab to take him to the cemetery. He wanted to spend time at Lara's grave before flying back to D.C.

Unlike at the funeral home where he had spent his time apologizing, this time, he remembered to be thankful.

In particular, he remembered to thank Lara for coming to him when he had been at his weakest in Russia. Whether he had imagined it, or whether it had actually been her, didn't matter. She had saved him and for that he was grateful.

After his time at her grave, he returned to the hotel to pick up his bag and then head out to the airport. He had two more funerals to attend in D.C.

Once those were over, the reckoning would begin.

CHAPTER 77

With distinguished careers in the intelligence world, Lydia Ryan and Reed Carlton shared many of the same friends and colleagues.

In order to make it easier for those flying in from across the country and from around the world, it was decided to hold both services on the same weekend.

Lydia's would be on Friday and the Old Man's would take place on Sunday. Saturday was scheduled as a day off, so that people could rest their livers and recover from all the drinking.

The Ryan family organized a sedate viewing, followed by a tasteful Catholic mass and burial. That night, a block from Union Station, they rented out the entirety of the Dubliner for one of the most raucous Irish wakes Washington, D.C., had ever seen.

It was packed with personnel not only from the CIA, but from allied intelligence agencies as well. As a courtesy, and as a precaution, Metro D.C. Police had closed down the street outside. They also brought out SWAT and K-9 units just to be safe. This kind of guest list was a terrorist's wet dream.

Poster-sized pictures of Lydia had been placed on easels around the bar. In every photo she was either laughing or flashing her bright, beautiful smile. The message from her mass was reinforced at the wake: *Life is short. Love who you are. Love what you do. Make every day count.*

Her family couldn't have picked a more perfect encapsulation of who she was. Still aching from his trip to Boston, Harvath was glad to be among his teammates—all of whom made sure he was not left alone.

Between the funeral and the wake, Harvath ended up seeing CIA personnel he hadn't seen in years. Among them were Rick Morrell and three of his teammates, DeWolfe, Carlson, and Avigliano. Harvath had gone into Libya with them years ago hunting the heirs to Abu Nidal's terrorist organization.

They traded stories for a while until everyone drifted off in different directions to refresh their drinks and catch up with other long-lost friends.

It was after midnight when Harvath pulled Sloane aside and let her know he was going to leave.

"All right," she said, "I'll gather everybody else up."

"No. I'm good. I'm going back by myself."

"Are you sure?"

"I'm sure," he replied.

"How about I swing by tomorrow and just check in? Help you box stuff up?"

By "box stuff up" she meant boxing up Lara's things.

"Let's see how you feel in the morning," he said, nodding at the new drink she held in her hand. "Text me."

"You going to be okay to drive?"

Harvath nodded, "I'm fine. I'll talk to you tomorrow." And with that, he had quietly slipped out.

The next morning, Nicholas showed up at his place bright and early. Along with the dogs, he had brought with him the fixings for breakfast.

He had chosen to avoid the Dubliner for health reasons. A crowded room full of staggering drunks wasn't a good environment for a person his size. And the fact that he suffered from easily broken bones only compounded the potential risks.

Nicholas had, though, attended both the mass and the burial. His presence had sent whispers racing among the foreign intelligence operatives who had no idea that "The Troll" had received a full presidential pardon for his past deeds and had taken up residence in the United States.

Harvath was certain that while Nicholas couldn't be at the wake, he

had raised a glass of good whiskey in Lydia Ryan's honor and had helped
to send her off in style.

"You look better than I expected," the little man said, as he placed his
shopping bags on the bench in the kitchen. "How late did you stay?"

"I slipped out sometime after midnight," he replied. "Coffee?"

"Tea, please," said Nicholas, nodding at Lara's tins.

"What kind?"

"What was her favorite?"

"Lapsang Souchong," he stated, pronouncing it proudly.

"That's what I'll have then."

After petting the dogs for several moments and putting down bowls of
water for them, Harvath put a kettle on.

While he did, Nicholas clambered up onto one of the chairs at the
dining table, opened his messenger bag, and laid out everything he had
brought with him.

"Chase says you owe him 10 percent," said the little man.

"Ten percent of what?"

"Of whatever comes of this."

Harvath looked over as Nicholas held up the journal Harvath
had taken from Teplov back in Russia.

When The Carlton Group jet had landed at Andrews, Harvath had
slipped it to Chase with a request that he quietly pass it on to Nicholas.

Harvath had assumed, correctly, that he would be immediately taken
into loose custody with an offer for medical attention, which he had de-
clined, followed by transport to a secure location for his debriefing. Had
he been carrying the journal, McGee and his people would have found it
straightaway.

"I just want to say two things before we start," Nicholas declared.
"First, I have a lot of respect for you and what you're planning to do. Second, I think you and your plan are fucking crazy."

"Good to know that I haven't lost my touch," Harvath replied as he
prepared the cups and then brought everything over to the table when it
was ready.

As he poured the hot water, Nicholas explained what he had learned
from the journal. Not only did they have a full name and background for

Josef, they also learned who had selected him and had coordinated everything from the murders of Lara, Lydia, and Reed Carlton to the hiring of
the Wagner mercenaries once the plane had gone down in Russia. It was a
General out of the GRU named Minayev. And Minayev had been operating on direct orders from Russian President Peshkov.

When Sloane called early in the afternoon, sounding very hungover,
Harvath told her everything was okay and that there was no need for her
to drop by. Nevertheless, she insisted.

It wasn't until he put the call on speakerphone and she could hear
Nicholas's voice that she believed he was there.

Nicholas seemed an odd choice to help box up Lara's things and decide what should go to her parents and what should go to charity, but if
that's what Harvath wanted, she wasn't going to go against his wishes.

Telling Sloane that he would see her tomorrow at the Old Man's service, Harvath had disconnected the call and gotten back to his work with
Nicholas.

They had a lot more to do before he infiltrated back into Russia.

• • •

Technically, Reed Carlton's service hadn't been a funeral. It had been a
"memorial."

The Old Man's last will and testament had been specific. And as executor, Harvath had followed his wishes to the letter.

Cremation. Ashes to be placed into a cut-down, silver-coated 75 mm
artillery shell—a crazy gift from some Raja whom Carlton had befriended
decades ago while working at the CIA's station in New Delhi.

The memorial service at his local church had been followed by a re-
ception at Carlton's home, complete with a "well-stocked" bar. Food had
been permitted, "but don't go overboard." And no "goddamn vegetables," he had instructed.

That had made Harvath smile. Even in death, the Old Man had remained a detail guy.

There had been a lot of particulars to go over. Some were obvious,
such as Harvath being tasked with taking over the organization. Other

details had been less obvious, though a letter from Carlton explained that in time, they would be.

His guest list was a who's who not only of global intelligence personalities past and present, but also of American politicians and foreign leaders. The security alone was a sight to behold.

Though he didn't want to, Harvath worked all of the events, introducing himself and shaking hands. The Old Man had been very clear that he expected Harvath to assume control over his business, as well as his network of contacts.

Whether he ended up going the management route or staying in the field didn't matter. To have this many powerful, connected people in one place was an opportunity he needed to take advantage of.

Unlike Lydia's wake, the Old Man's wasn't one he could sneak out of. He was the heir apparent and everyone wanted time with him. So he had stayed till the end and till every last guest had left.

Wandering the empty house felt strange. It was hard to believe Carlton was gone. He had been a legend *and* an institution, someone people both turned to and aspired to. They had broken the mold when they had made him.

Harvath walked into the study. It was like a mini museum, filled with reminders of the Old Man's exploits, many of which most Americans would never be aware of. For a long, long time, he had been the person the nation had quietly turned to in order to solve its most pressing and dangerous problems.

That era, though, had passed. Many politicians, as well as many citizens, were willing to trade liberty in exchange for security. But as Ben Franklin was alleged to have said, *Those who would trade a little liberty for a little security deserved neither and would lose both*. The world was still a dangerous place, and it was growing more so.

The price of freedom had been and always would be *vigilance*. It required hard, nonstop, dangerous work. But the work was worth it.

And as long as there were men and women willing to give everything to preserve it, America could retain its freedom and continue to be the greatest beacon for hope and opportunity in the history of the world.

Deciding how to divvy up the Old Man's personal effects was going to take weeks. There were a handful of things he knew the CIA's historian would want to have, but there were others he felt should go to the International Spy Museum in D.C. It was important, in Harvath's opinion, that America be given a glimpse into what an amazing man Reed Carlton was and how much he had given his nation.

Of course, if the Old Man were still alive, he'd resist such a thing and beat Harvath to within an inch of his life for suggesting it. That was simply who he was. He believed in America and what was required to protect it.

As executor, Harvath was responsible for the entirety of the Old Man's estate—a large part of which was his legacy. He was an inspirational figure and the good he had done could live well beyond his violent death at the safe house in New Hampshire. That was Harvath's plan. But it would have to wait.

Reed Carlton would have wanted him to do something else first. And, he would have been very specific about how he had wanted it done.

CHAPTER 78

Harvath had used a combination of intelligence assets to help him get all the way to, and into, Russia undetected.

A contact of his, Monika Jasinski at Polish Military Intelligence, had met him at the airport in Warsaw, then scrubbed clean all records of his arrival and transported him to the border with Belarus.

At the border, a team of smugglers loyal to the Old Man, who had also been handsomely rewarded on a recent operation by Chase and Sloane, picked him up and transported him across the country to the border with Russia.

There, he was met by an old acquaintance. Before the murders in New Hampshire, he had been developing her as an intelligence asset inside the FSB—Russia's equivalent of the CIA. She was a patriot who loved her country, but despised its system of government.

Bob McGee, Lydia Ryan, and even President Porter had all been aware that he had slowly been attempting to bring her over. This was the one part of the plan that Nicholas hated the most. He saw Alexandra Ivanova as its weakest link—an untested pillar they would be resting all of their weight upon.

Though she and Harvath had a long history, and despite the fact that he had even killed a major Russian mafia figure in the Caribbean the previous year to help advance her career, there was no telling how she would handle his request. He was putting his neck in a noose, handing her the other end, and closing his eyes.

The hardest part for Nicholas was that, while he loved the plan in general, there was no one he could go to help him push back on Harvath and the specifics. McGee and the CIA had no idea what they were doing. And that went double for the President. This was completely off-book, and therefore off anyone's radar.

The little man had argued as intensely as he could, but Harvath's mind had been made up. There was only one thing they had agreed with each other on—if Ivanova double-crossed them and Harvath ended up captured, the Russians would go to extraordinary lengths to guarantee there would be no rescue this time.

It was a risk that Harvath had been willing to take. In fact, "willingness" had nothing to do with it. After running it through his mind a thousand and one times, this had been the only path he could see available.

He knew it had to be the right course because the Russians wouldn't see it coming, and it was also exactly what the Old Man would have done. It was a plan that required a pair of the biggest balls anyone had ever seen.

Once he had the address he had been waiting on in Moscow, he prepped an envelope and sent it on its way. Inside was a letter to Russian president Fedor Peshkov. It was signed by Harvath and explained, in excruciating detail, everything he was going to do to him. It brought chilling new meaning to the words "hate mail."

Hiding in a farmhouse near the border between Belarus and Russia, Harvath had fieldstripped, cleaned, and reassembled Reed Carlton's 1911 pistol so many times that it gleamed in the darkness.

Putting together his kit for the operation, it had seemed appropriate to carry the legendary spymaster's favorite weapon. Even if Harvath never drew it, the mere fact that he had brought it along for protection would be a profound way of honoring him.

Of course, the greatest way to honor Carlton would be to avenge him, which was exactly why he was here.

When Alexandra Ivanova finally showed up, they had a brief exchange before he climbed into the cutout in her trunk. She covered him with a custom piece of carpeting, and shut the lid.

He felt every bump, jostle, and pothole in the road. The ride was absolutely brutal. But it was also absolutely necessary.

Ivanova was one of the smartest intelligence operatives Harvath had ever met. It was one of the reasons he had labored so hard to get her to come to work for him. She didn't have ice in her veins; what she had was molten steel.

She had agreed to the operation with one caveat: Everything that happened inside Russia was her call.

Naturally, Nicholas had balked at this condition and had told Harvath that he'd be better off cutting his own throat in D.C. At least then it would save SPEHA Rogers the trouble of negotiating the repatriation of his body.

Harvath, though, had agreed to all of her demands. He trusted Alexandra. If she had wanted to burn him, she could have done so long before now. As far as he was concerned, she was someone he could trust.

Riding in the secret compartment in the trunk, he expected to feel the car slow down at some point, if nothing else then for the border. The slow-down, though, never came. She kept the pedal to the metal.

Ivanova had assured him that as long as he could make it to the border, she could get him across. And apparently, she had been right.

When she pulled her less-than-new sedan off the highway, they were halfway to Moscow.

Opening the lid and pulling back the carpet, she let Harvath out of the back.

"Welcome to Russia," she joked.

Even though he wasn't in the mood, Harvath smiled. "Thank you," he said. "I ordered an in-flight meal, but never received it."

Without missing a beat, Alexandra responded, "I'll make sure to let my supervisor know. We value every passenger attempting to sneak into our country."

"Speaking of which," said Harvath, "how is it we didn't stop at a border checkpoint?"

"I bribed the guards. On the way out, I flashed my credentials and gave them all cartons of cigarettes. On the way back, I told them I'd be coming with live lobsters on melting ice destined for the Kremlin. None of them argued. They opened a lane for me and I drove straight through."

It was a good start. Harvath hoped it would last.

They spent the first night in a suburb on the outskirts of Moscow. Alexandra had done all of the advance work. She knew the routines of each target, where they would be and when. For the first one, though, Harvath wanted to see for himself.

The next morning, after a cold shower and a bad cup of coffee, she took him to the target's apartment building. Then they watched him emerge and followed him to work.

"Satisfied?" she asked.

Harvath nodded. The real satisfaction, though, would come the next morning. That's when the rubber would meet the road and Ivanova would have to prove her commitment to the operation.

Smuggling him across the border was a good start. But helping him to scratch the first name off his list was the real test. If she proved herself fully onboard tomorrow, it would be one less thing he had to worry about.

CHAPTER 79

They had spent the rest of that day checking in on the other targets and visiting the other locations. Everything was set, or at least as set as it was going to be.

That night, they stayed in and ate takeout that she had brought back to the apartment. She asked him what had happened, and he told her, *all* of it.

Alexandra's heart, which had always had a soft spot for him, broke. It was one of the worst stories of loss she had ever heard—possibly even worse than her own.

When the words stopped coming and he could no longer speak, she offered him the bed. Ever the gentleman, he took the couch.

She slept in her bedroom, the door open in case he changed his mind.

They rose well before dawn and made ready. He had brought money for Alexandra, which she tried to refuse, but he insisted. She was taking an enormous risk. She deserved to be compensated.

There were four more envelopes, also filled with cash. She had promised that she would make sure they were quietly delivered to Sini and her husband Mokci, as well as the families of Jompá and Olá in Murmansk Oblast.

With everything cleaned up and put away, they went through the apartment once more, wiping it down for fingerprints. Harvath doubted the Russians would ever make the connection, but he didn't want to leave any proof that he and Alexandra knew each other and had ever been at the same location. She was too valuable an asset to lose.

Despite the cold, the car started right up. The moment it did, Harvath set the heater to High. He knew it wouldn't do any good until the engine had warmed up, but psychologically it made him feel better.

It was still dark as they made their way out onto the snow-covered suburban streets. Only a few cars were about, people getting a jump on the morning shift traffic.

Normally, Harvath wouldn't have involved Alexandra in this part of an operation, but he needed her language skills. It was critical that he extract absolutely unambiguous intelligence from their target. The less time he spent inside, the less chance of his getting caught.

Nicholas had been key to the entire operation. With only Teplov's journal, and what Harvath had been able to share with him, he had gone to work. It was astounding what he had been able to put together in just two weeks.

Pulling up behind the apartment building, Alexandra found a place to park and then, after she had killed the engine, they both exited the vehicle.

"Ready to go?" Harvath asked.

Alexandra pulled up the scarf, covering her face. "Ready to go," she replied.

They were using burner phones from Vladivostok. They might as well have been from Mars. Even if they were discovered, local police were never going to expend any manpower tracking down how they had come to Moscow.

Taking out his lock pick tools, Harvath unlocked the back door and waited for Alexandra to text that she was in place. Their target lived on the ground floor.

When the text came, he pressed his ear against the glass, waited until he heard the doorbell, and then let himself in.

The man lived alone and had no girlfriend that Nicholas had been able to ascertain based on his emails, texts, and social media pages. He also didn't have any pets. There was nothing else special about him other than he was about Harvath's height and weight and worked on the floor they needed.

As Alexandra fed him a line of bullshit at the front door, Harvath crept up silently on him from the back of the apartment. Once he was in range, he deployed his Taser and took him down.

Kicking his legs out of the way, Alexandra stepped inside and closed the front door.

The fluidity with which Harvath flex-cuffed him and threw a hood over his head demonstrated that he had done this before.

Grabbing a chair from the kitchen, Alexandra helped Harvath drag him into the bedroom and sit him down. There, as she pulled the barbed Taser probes out of him, Harvath tied him up.

The man couldn't see his attackers, but he could hear them. Harvath asked if he understood English. When the man claimed not to, everything else went through Alexandra.

They grilled him for over two hours until, looking at his watch, Harvath indicated that it was time to go.

After Alexandra had left the room, Harvath removed the man's hood, but only long enough to gag him and wrap several passes of duct tape around his mouth before replacing his hood.

Per Harvath's instructions, Alexandra returned with a gas can from the car and placed it beneath the chair. Even under the hood, the fumes were instantly recognizable. She explained in Russian that a bomb had been placed under him and that if he attempted to move, or made too much noise, it would explode.

She also relayed that as long as he cooperated, they would be back within twenty-four hours and would set him free. Who they were, where they were going, or why any of it involved him, they never revealed.

Going through his closet, Harvath found the clothes he needed and quickly got dressed. Then, in the living room, Alexandra handed over the man's ID badge and repeated how security at the entrance to the facility worked. Alexandra would go in first, and be nearby in case anything went wrong.

Harvath hoped that wouldn't be necessary. If there was one thing he knew, it was that nightshift workers were practically zombies once it was time to go home. The morning shift that replaced them was almost as bad, needing a lot of coffee—and most important, sunlight—before they were fully awake and functioning. It was the perfect time to make their move.

Leaving the man bound and gagged in the apartment, Harvath pocketed his cell phone and they headed out.

It was a short drive to their next stop and Alexandra parked out on the street, rather than in the employee parking lot, so that they wouldn't be impeded in making their escape.

By the time they got to the front entrance, there was already a line of employees slowly shuffling inside. Alexandra went first, followed by Harvath.

Completely wrapped up against the cold, all he was required to do was show an ID. The security guards never even asked him to show his face. Without looking at Alexandra, who had taken one of the public chairs just inside the entrance, he pressed on into the building.

Eschewing the employee locker room, he found a utility area where he dumped the man's coat, gloves, and scarf. From there, he was only one stairwell away from his target.

With his eyes downcast, he maintained the plodding, uninterested pace of the average Russian worker, while every cell inside him wanted to charge to his destination. He knew from experience, though, that sure and steady was what would win the race *and* get him what he wanted.

Because he moved the way that he did, no one gave him a second glance. He looked exactly as he had hoped he would. He looked as if he belonged there.

Arriving at the door, he took a deep breath and tried to steady his heart rate. *Breathe*, he reminded himself. So he did.

Reaching out for the cold, stainless steel handle, he opened the door and stepped inside.

The room was dark, its blinds closed. One of the things the man tied up back at the apartment had said was that upon entering, his job was to prep the room for the morning. So, that was exactly what Harvath did.

Opening the blinds, to allow the early rays of the sun to shine in, he heard something behind him. The patient was awake.

Turning, he smiled and said in English, "Good morning, Josef."

CHAPTER 80

Before the man could cry out, Harvath was on him.

Josef had been admitted to Moscow City Hospital Number 67 for a complicated spinal surgery due to injuries had had suffered in the crash. He was paralyzed from the waist down and could only move his upper body.

Stunning him with a blow to the head, Harvath disconnected his patient call button, slapped a piece of duct tape over his mouth, and then removed a syringe.

Reaching for Josef's IV, he injected it with succinylcholine and then, grabbing him by the throat, he pulled the piece of tape from his mouth.

"I told you back in New Hampshire I'd find you," said Harvath, "and that when I did, I'd kill you. So now, guess what?"

"Fuck you," gasped Josef.

"Don't talk," Harvath instructed. "Just listen. You killed my wife and you also killed two of the most important people in the world to me. You dragged me all the way over here to your shithole country to interrogate and then kill me. It didn't work, though. You want to know why? Because you're a failure. You have always been a failure. And now you will die a failure."

"Fuck you, you—" Josef began again, but Harvath choked him quiet once more.

"I just injected you with suxamethonium chloride. Also known as sux. Right now, all of your muscles are starting to give up. In about sixty seconds you will be fully paralyzed and unable to breathe, but you'll still be fully conscious and aware of what's going on. Two minutes from now, when the nurses rush in to give you CPR, it'll be a lost cause. Before that happens, though, I'm going to make sure you die as painful a death as possible."

Withdrawing his hand from around the man's throat, he straightened up and struck the Russian brutally and repeatedly in and around his chest.

Josef tried to raise his arms to defend himself, but he could not. He tried to call out for help, but he was equally unable. He could do nothing but lie helplessly and watch it all happen, much the way Harvath had been forced to witness the murders of Lara, Lydia Ryan, and the Old Man.

When Harvath had finished pounding on him, he stood back. There was no doubt he had broken multiple ribs.

Josef was not only going to die of suffocation, but as the well-meaning medical staff pushed down on his chest in an effort to revive him, they were going to be exacerbating the pain of his broken ribs and helping to puncture his lungs.

It wasn't the slow death Harvath wanted to give him. That kind of pain would have taken weeks or months. But all things considered, it was a very nasty death he was all too happy to deliver.

Placing a bag-valve mask over the man's face, he pushed the emergency call button and shouted out instructions in perfect Russian, just as Christina had instructed him, for the local equivalent of a Code Blue.

Within moments, the room filled with medical personnel, all of whom were exclusively focused on the patient.

As they fought to revive Josef, Harvath slipped out the door, walked downstairs, and left the building without anyone noticing.

By the time he made it to the corner, Alexandra was already there, in the car, waiting for him. *One down, two to go.*

Their next target wouldn't be available for several hours. To her credit, Alexandra had taken that into consideration and had planned accordingly.

In an empty office across the street, she had placed a couple of cots, food, water, and even medical supplies in case the first hit had gone sideways.

Harvath had to hand it to her, she was very good at her job.

They passed the day and into the early evening in relative silence. Had he taken her up on her offer last night, they could have found a more enjoyable way to while away the hours, but it was what it was. As night fell and the city darkened, she brewed coffee and went over the next phase of the operation with him.

She knew General Minayev only by reputation. She had never met the GRU bigwig in person. And while she understood the reasoning behind the next phase of Harvath's operation, she found it particularly distasteful. Even so, she had agreed to go along with it.

Once more, Nicholas had been the key to their planning. Three times a week, Minayev rendezvoused with his mistress at a small apartment he owned not far from the cheese shop he so loved.

If the upper echelons of the FBI and CIA had as many men cheating on their wives as Russian Intelligence did, the American Congress would have been up in arms and rightly purging them left, right, and center. The fact that Russia condoned such behavior could only be added to the list of reasons they lagged behind the rest of the developed world when it came to law, order, and trust in government.

Corruption, sadly, wasn't something to be avoided in Russia, it was something to be studied and then expertly exploited.

Aside from the unseemliness of it all, what was particularly helpful was that the lovebirds always ordered in. They did so via an app, which Nicholas had no trouble tapping into.

When the food arrived, Alexandra was standing on the chipped curb, waiting to receive it. As the driver sped off, she rang the bell, announced herself, and then sent Harvath up as the door buzzed open.

Reed Carlton's 1911 in his hand, he stepped out of the stairwell and into the hallway. Russian apartment buildings had always seemed to smell the same to him—fucking horrible. He didn't know what caused it. At its foundation, it had to be the cooking, but from there it was anybody's guess.

He waited for Alexandra to appear from the opposite stairwell and when she did, they approached the apartment door together.

After she rolled down her balaclava and took off her jacket to expose a Russian Security Services raid vest, Harvath knocked.

As they had anticipated, the mistress answered the door. There was no way Minayev was going to risk being seen here.

The woman was surprised to see a man standing at the door, when it had been a woman who had called up on the intercom from downstairs.

He put his index finger against his lips as if to say, "Shhh," and then pointed at Alexandra, who beckoned the young woman over to her.

Believing something official to be up, the mistress stepped into the hall and did as they instructed.

As she passed, Harvath slipped inside. He could smell Minayev before he even saw him.

The legend of the cheese the man ate smelling like a decomposing corpse didn't do it justice. It actually smelled *worse*. How his wife, much less his mistress, could stand to be with him was a total mystery. Both must have been suffering from anosmia.

Normally in a situation like this, Harvath would have felt comfortable drawing out the man's death. But the odor was so bad that he couldn't wait to get the hell out of the apartment.

Assuming his mistress was dealing with the delivery, Minayev sat in the living room, his back to the hall, watching TV.

Holstering his weapon, Harvath uncapped a new hypodermic needle and crept forward. With the television up so loud, Minayev never had a chance.

Harvath jammed the needle into the base of his neck, depressed the plunger, and held him down while he waited for the sux to do its work.

"Do you know who I am?" Harvath asked, as Minayev caught a glimpse of him out of the corner of his eye, before paralysis took hold.

The GRU man nodded.

"Josef killed my wife, my colleague, and my boss on your orders. Now, I'm here to kill you. But I'm not just going to kill you. I'm going to destroy your professional reputation as well. Even after your death, people will revile your name."

Harvath wanted to continue, but he could see that the man's breathing had slowed. Every muscle in his body had relaxed. He thirsted desperately for air, but lacked the ability to exercise his lungs and draw new oxygen in. Staring into his eyes, Harvath watched as he slowly asphyxiated.

Everything now came down to timing. Quickly, Harvath wrapped a cord around the man's neck, pulled it tight and dragged him with it into the bathroom.

There, he slung it up and over the door, attaching it to the doorknob on the other side.

Stripping off Minayev's clothing, he dressed him in the women's lingerie he had brought along and then scattered hard copies within reach of the child porn Nicholas had made sure would be discovered on all of his devices.

Out in the hallway, Alexandra didn't feel like talking. This was the part of it that she didn't like, the pornography. Her reaction was exactly what he was hoping other Russians would feel when the news broke.

As they left the building, he gave the okay for her anonymous source to contact the local paper.

It would not be a good day for the GRU. One of its most distinguished Generals would be found hanged, by his own hand, via auto-erotic asphyxiation and surrounded by child porn.

With two down, there was only one left to go.

CHAPTER 81

If you asked Muscovites who, on the social scene, they hated the most, privately, they would all give you the same answer. *Misha*.

Misha was the diminutive of Mikhail, and everyone knew who it referred to—Mikhail Peshkov, pride and joy of the Russian President, Fedor Peshkov.

It was said that the only thing the elder Peshkov loved more than his money and power was his son. He was his sole offspring, the only living memory of the President's deceased wife, who had also been his childhood sweetheart. The boy represented the continuation of the family bloodline, but like many only children, he had been recklessly spoiled by his over-adoring father.

The blinders the Russian President wore when it came to Misha had seen a spoiled child grow into a dangerous young adult.

Though barely into his twenties, the young man had become known not only for his gluttony and abandon, but also for his cruelty. Even the local Russian mafia despised him. Had it not been for his all-powerful father, he would have already been taken out.

But because of the elder Peshkov, he was free to run wild, free to terrorize businesses throughout Russia, legitimate and otherwise, with impunity.

He had caused grievous damage "bottling" prominent rich Russian night-club goers by slamming their heads with champagne bottles, crip-

pling and even killing prostitutes, and had pioneered a sick new form of
polo that entailed running down stray dogs with cars.

Immediately after Harvath had read the dossier Nicholas had com-
piled, he couldn't wait to get his hands on him.

This target, though, was more difficult than the others. This one was a
"twofer" and as such, it had to be executed flawlessly.

Even more than the son, Harvath wanted the Russian President to
suffer. He wanted to grab the elder Peshkov by the throat, cut his eyes
out with a penknife, and slowly lower him into a vat of acid, but that pain
would have only been temporary. That wasn't good enough.

Harvath wanted Peshkov to suffer, as he had suffered in losing Lara,
Lydia, and the Old Man. He wanted the Russian President's pain to last
for years. That was why he and Alexandra were here now.

The Federal Security Officers sitting in the cars outside Misha's loft
hated the President's son as much as the rest of Moscow did. Harvath and
Alexandra had no problem slipping past.

The officers posted inside the building were a different story.

Affixing a suppressor to the Old Man's 1911, Harvath had Alexandra
in her short skirt, dark wig, and thigh-high boots come in the front door,
while he entered from the back.

Having done presidential protective details, Harvath knew the extent
to which the United States went to keep the children of prominent politicians safe. What he saw in the lobby was stunning.

There were two security agents in total. They were both focused on the
front door, which allowed him to come in from the back unchallenged.

While Alexandra engaged Tweedledee and Tweedledum, telling them
she was supposed to meet a girlfriend there for a party in one of the lofts,
and they stared transfixed at the tops of her breasts in her low-cut top,
Harvath hit the stairs.

He had no idea if the twenty-six-year-old would be by himself or surrounded by some lowlife "posse." Either way, Harvath had a plan.

Creeping up to the top of the stairs, a pair of latex gloves on, he slowly
pulled back the exit door and looked out.

For a moment, he couldn't believe it. Then he had to remind himself
that he was in Russia. There were absolutely no guards on this floor.

That didn't mean there wasn't a guard inside the unit, but from what he had seen so far, he doubted it. The lazy perimeter security was an excellent indication of how little the guards thought of the President's son.

Walking over to the apartment door, Harvath pressed his pistol up against it and softly knocked.

Based on Nicholas's research, the man was a gamer. He spent up to sixteen hours some days on his Xbox. Harvath hoped that he was gaming now. The fact that no one had responded to his knock made him feel his hope wasn't without merit. It was also a pretty good indication that there was no guard waiting on the other side.

Removing his picks, he went to work. Like everything else in Russia, the lock was a piece of shit. Within seconds, he was inside.

He crept forward into the loft until he heard someone cursing in Russian and froze.

With the 1911 against his chest in the Sul position, ready to be thrust out into the fight, he waited. The seconds passed interminably slowly. The pause felt like an eternity.

Finally he heard Misha howl with laughter and begin taunting some unseen person all over again. *The little motherfucker was definitely on his Xbox.*

This was Harvath's opportunity, and he moved cautiously forward.

In the large living room at the end of hall, Misha sat at a sleek glass and chrome desk, surrounded by empty bags of potato chips and energy drink cans.

With his eyes focused on the screen and headphones cutting off his hearing, he had no idea Harvath was right behind him until it was too late.

He felt the stab of the syringe as it was jabbed into the left side of his neck and the cold of the liquid content as it rushed into his body.

He reached for a panic button, but Harvath pulled his chair back before he could get to it.

The sux was fast acting. It was the last thing Peshkov's hideous son was able to do before paralysis overtook him. Death was not far behind.

Removing the vials of heroin, a dirty shoelace for a tourniquet, and a new needle, he got to work. The scene didn't have to be perfect, only believable.

When everything was complete, he texted Alexandra, and backed out of the apartment.

He took the stairs down to the ground floor, unscrewed the suppressor from his pistol, and put everything in his coat pockets. Then, he exited the building the same way he had come in. The security officers remained none the wiser.

They wouldn't roll back the CCTV footage until much later. And by then it would be too late.

Meeting Alexandra two blocks down, he climbed into her car and turned up the heater.

"How did it go?" she asked, as she put her car in gear and pulled out into traffic.

"Perfect," he replied. "There's only one thing left to do. Do you have the key for me?"

"Glove box," Alexandra said, nodding at it.

Harvath opened it and withdrew a small envelope with a post office box key inside. He was pleased. "Now all we have to do is decide on the best way to get it to him."

She looked at her watch and smiled. "I think I have an idea. How about a visit to the Ritz?"

CHAPTER 82

Getting anywhere near the Russian President was out of the question. The same was true for handing him any sort of a note or package. Felix Botnik, his Chief of Staff, though, was something else entirely.

A confirmed bachelor, Botnik was a renowned man about town. He was also a creature of habit, which drove the intelligence services crazy.

It was well known that he ate twice a week at one of Moscow's trendiest restaurants—the O2 Lounge on the twelfth floor of the Ritz Carlton Hotel.

Completely enclosed in glass, the rooftop establishment was popular for its stunning views of the Kremlin and of Red Square. The views inside, though, were said to be even better.

Every night, the O2 Lounge was packed with the city's richest, most powerful, and most beautiful people—making it the place to see and be seen.

It was always wall-to-wall, and if you weren't plugged in, you weren't going to ever find a seat as every table was marked with a "reserved" placard. As Chief of Staff to President Peshkov, Botnik didn't have that problem.

Arriving at O2, his table was already waiting for him. So was a crisp, off-white, Ritz Carlton envelope with his name neatly written across the front.

Opening it, he withdrew a small, flat key that looked as if it could have been to a safety deposit box. With it was a handwritten note on the hotel's stationery.

It simply said: *To President Fedor Peshkov. From Scot Harvath.* And it included an address.

Harvath had gotten the stationery at the front desk, written the note, and then carried the envelope upstairs, where he paid a waiter $100 to make sure it would be waiting for Botnik when he arrived.

The moment Botnik read Harvath's name on the note, he knew they were in trouble. His biggest concern was that the President might be at risk. Pulling out his cell phone, he had dialed Peshkov's Chief of Security and had headed quickly for the elevator.

By the time his driver had pulled up downstairs, a plan had already been formulated and put in motion.

The drive to the main post office on Myasnitskaya took almost twenty minutes in Moscow traffic. By the time he arrived, the police had already closed off the street and an evacuation was under way. If Harvath had placed a bomb, they wanted to make sure that they kept the loss of life to a minimum.

It took an additional forty-five minutes before the bomb disposal team was on scene and could send their robot in. Opening the post office box, though, proved impossible. They needed a human for the job and suiting up one of the technicians took an additional twenty minutes. Shortly thereafter, they finally retrieved the letter.

After X-raying and testing it for hazardous materials, it was handed over to Botnik. Per its postmarks, the letter had been sent more than two weeks ago from the United States—Washington, D.C., to be specific. The sender was listed as Scot Harvath, and the return address Botnik had to look up on his phone. It turned out to belong not to Harvath, but rather to the International Spy Museum. If he was trying to be funny, the Chief of Staff didn't find it amusing.

Knowing that the President was waiting on what they had found, he returned to his car to make the call. He had his driver remain outside the vehicle.

As Botnik read the letter, his heart froze in his chest. The things Harvath was threatening to do to Josef Kozak, General Minayev, and the President's son were horrifying.

On the other end of the line, he could hear Peshkov shouting directions to his security people to check on Misha, as well as to warn Minayev, and to alert the hospital Josef Kozak was being treated at.

Botnik's eyes scanned the rest of the letter. It ended with a final warning from Harvath. The only reason he had spared the Russian President was so that he would spend the rest of his life grieving his son—just as Harvath would grieve his wife and two dear friends. If Peshkov took any steps to retaliate, Harvath promised to find him and kill him in the most horrific way imaginable.

As the Chief of Staff finished reading, he heard the President cry out in anguish.

"Misha," Peshkov wailed. "No!"

CHAPTER 83

Harvath had been tempted to park himself near the Moscow post office to watch the fireworks, but Alexandra had warned him about pushing their luck. She had been right, of course.

She had also been right about getting the PO box key to Botnik at the Ritz. It had worked perfectly. As soon as he had left the envelope with the waiter in the O2 Lounge, he had exited the hotel, and met back up with her a couple of blocks away for the six-hour drive back to the border with Belarus. Though he would have liked to have gotten some sleep, he kept his eyes open and his head on a swivel the entire way.

When they met up with the Old Man's smugglers and said their good-byes, he thanked her. She had taken a lot of risks on his behalf and he wanted her to know how much he appreciated it. Without her, this could have very well turned into a suicide operation.

Climbing into the smuggler's truck, he made himself comfortable for his next six hours of driving to the border with Poland. There, he'd at least be back in NATO territory, though he couldn't let his guard down. At least not fully.

It wasn't until he was back on The Carlton Group jet and in the air that the weight of everything he had been under started to lift. Once he was in international airspace, he got up and poured himself a drink.

Returning to his seat, he raised the glass and toasted the Old Man. He hoped that somewhere, up there, Reed was proud of him.

As he sat there, sipping his bourbon, Harvath conducted a mental after-action report. He went over every single detail, contemplating what he could have done differently, and where appropriate, what he could have done better.

Once his review was complete, he went through all of it again, looking for anything that might identify Alexandra, or tie her directly to him. Fortunately, there was nothing he could come up with to be worried about.

From Josef's hospital where she had avoided the cameras and had stayed bundled up, to the interaction with Minayev's mistress where she had worn the balaclava, and finally to the security guards at Misha's loft where she had been wearing a dark wig and heavy makeup while making sure to never face the cameras, she had been the perfect partner. Even outside on Moscow's streets, she had made sure they stayed in the shadows.

Alexandra, thinking of everything, had taken down the telephone number of the management company for the building where they had left the hospital worker tied up. She had promised to phone in either a noise complaint or some sort of anonymous tip, so that the man would be found and cut loose.

He didn't know how she planned to get the envelopes full of cash up to Sini and everyone else, but he assumed that would be done anonymously as well. The less she showed her face, the better. There was no reason, especially after the fact, for her to be tied to any of that. Peshkov, eventually, was going to sift through everything that had happened, looking for someone to punish.

Harvath, though, would be far outside his grasp, and he'd be insane to come after him again. The Russian President had gotten what was coming to him.

That left Harvath with only one loose end: Artur Kopec, whom Nicholas had gone to bat for.

While Kopec had admitted sharing information about his pending visit at the New Hampshire safe house, he claimed to have had no idea that an assault had been planned. Nicholas, who was famous for his shockproof bullshit detector, had believed him. It was why he had gone to bat for him and had asked Harvath to spare his life. He was also still an incredibly valuable asset and had played a minor role in getting Harvath out of Russia.

Harvath would need to speak with the Polish Intelligence officer himself before he would be satisfied. For the moment, he was content, albeit grudgingly, to let him live.

After a second drink and some hot food, Harvath had stretched out on the couch and closed his eyes.

He had felt sure that he'd fall asleep instantly. Sleep, though, didn't come. Instead, his thoughts had turned to Lara.

He went through all the recriminations—all the things he could have and should have done differently, all the things he wanted to tell her but never did, all of the time he had wasted taking extra assignments downrange because the jobs had sounded exciting, he went through all of it.

And then once he had steeped in it good and long, when the plane was getting ready to land, he put it all away. He packed it up in that iron box inside his mind and forced himself to look forward.

What was he going to do next? That was the question he needed most to answer, and the answer wasn't going to be easy. He hoped that taking some time off would help focus his mind.

When the jet touched down at Naval Air Station Key West, he was beyond ready to be done traveling. All he wanted to do was sit in one warm place and not move.

As the plane came to a stop and the pilot shut down the engines, the copilot opened the forward door and dropped the air stairs. Harvath thanked them for the ride and stepped outside.

He saw rustling palm trees and could smell the salt of the ocean. The balmy, humid air was nothing like what he had experienced in Russia. Closing his eyes, he stood there for a moment, feeling the sun on his skin and soaking it all in.

Soon enough, the roar from a pair of F/A-18 Hornets shook him from his reverie. There'd be plenty of time for kicking back once he got to the resort.

Nicholas had arranged for a car, which was parked just outside the base commander's office. The keys had been left inside the gas cap as promised. It had that new car smell, overheated by being left in the sun, that reminded him of vacations he had taken as a kid.

Driving out through the main gate, he headed north twenty-five miles up US-1 to Little Torch Key. At Pirates Road, he pulled into the parking lot for Little Palm Island Resort. He checked in at the thatch-roofed welcome station and was put on the next motor launch for the island. He was the only guest aboard.

He had always loved Little Palm Island, because the only way to get there was by boat or seaplane. Sitting on the rear deck of the launch, he once again closed his eyes.

Suddenly, he felt a lot more charitable toward those SEALs who had foresworn cold winters for more tropical climes. Cutting through the open water, sea spray on his face, this was something he could see himself getting used to.

A pretty young crew member, tan, blonde, and in her twenties, appeared from the wheelhouse and brought him a freshly made rum concoction on a silver tray.

Thanking her and settling back with his cocktail, he looked out at the setting sun as it began its slow descent toward the horizon. This was definitely something he could get used to.

When the boat pulled up to the dock at Little Palm Island, he was met by one of the staff, who welcomed him back and led him to his West Indies–style bungalow, all of its doors and windows open wide to the breeze. Harvath recognized it immediately. It was the same room he had stayed in last time.

An ice bucket with a bottle of champagne had been placed on the coffee table. And even though his reservation had been for one, there were two glasses.

It seemed sad being in such a beautiful spot all alone. That must have been what the waiter had thought as he or she was setting everything up. One glass was sad, final. A second glass offered promise, possibility.

Removing the foil and unwinding the cage, he opened the champagne and poured himself a glass.

Sitting upon the luggage rack at the foot of the bed was the suitcase Sloane had been kind enough to pack for him and ship down. He opened it, interested to see what she had packed, but it was empty. The staff had already hung his clothes and put everything away.

Crossing to the closet, he opened the doors and looked inside. As with his clothes for the funeral, she had been kind, packing good, conservative staples. She had also packed his running shoes, and in the dresser, he saw that she had included his workout clothes.

He was about to take his champagne out to the terrace when he noticed a large padded envelope sitting on the desk. There was nothing written on it, but he assumed that it had been among the items the staff had unpacked for him from his suitcase. Setting his glass down, he opened it.

For a moment, he couldn't believe what he was seeing. Inside was the framed, silver picture of Lara from his bedroom back in Virginia.

There she stood, on his dock, in her sundress, with a glass of white wine in her hand.

It was the same image of her that had come to him after he had fallen through the ice in Russia. Lara, in that same sundress, with that same glass of wine, had beckoned him to the safety and life-saving warmth of the trapper's cabin.

Looking at it now, he couldn't help but wonder if she was once again trying to save his life.

Whatever it was that she was trying to tell him, he now had plenty of time to listen.

Picking up the picture, and his glass, he headed outside. The sun was almost low enough to touch the water. He wanted to watch it disappear. Then he wanted to start thinking about what he was going to do next.

ACKNOWLEDGMENTS

I want to start out by thanking the most wonderful people in the writing process—you, the **readers**. You make all of the hard work worth it. Thank you for reading my books and for telling people about them.

Next, I want to thank the exceptional **booksellers**, who not only ignite passion for reading, but also fan the flames. You are gateways to incredible adventures, and I thank you for bringing my books and readers together.

As with every novel, I save this space to thank the courageous men and women who protect and defend our way of life. They work in intelligence, in the military, and in law enforcement. Several assisted with *Backlash*, and while I cannot openly name them, I want them to know how deeply grateful I am. Any and all mistakes herein are mine and mine alone.

Robert C. O'Brien (to whom this book is dedicated) is an exceedingly good man who has given much to the country. You couldn't ask for a better neighbor or friend. I am honored to know him and deeply appreciate all that he has done for me and our nation.

James Ryan, **Sean Fontaine**, and **Chad Norberg** are three of my dearest friends. They are always there for me, especially when I need to kick ideas around. I thank them not only for their help with the book, but also for their continued dedication to doing what is right, no matter how hard, nor how dangerous.

Rob Saale, FBI (ret.) provided some incredibly helpful background for the book. Thank you for everything, but especially for your service to our great nation.

Michael Maness, CIA (ret.) was very generous with his time as I assembled the research for the book. Hopefully, by the time this goes to print, I will have taken him for a proper steak dinner and thanked him face-to-face.

Kristian J. Kelley, Deputy Chief, Gilford Police Department, could not have been kinder or more professional. As he is a graduate of the FBI's National Academy, I was impressed both with his experience and his commitment to his community. Thank you for your help.

U.S. Navy SEAL **Jack Carr** (ret.) was once again incredibly helpful with details for this book. He also continues to be one hell of a thriller author. If you haven't checked out his books yet, do it. You'll love his writing. Thank you, Jack.

U.S. Navy SEALs **Pete Scobell** (ret.), **Marcus Luttrell** (ret.), and **Paul Craig** (ret.) were also very kind with their time. Getting the details right is important to me, and I appreciate their help. Thank you, gentlemen.

John Barklow, U.S. Navy (ret.) has trained some of the most elite warriors on the planet in cold-weather survival. His discussions with me early on helped frame what Harvath would be facing and what he'd need to do to get out alive. I really appreciate all of his insight and exceptional expertise. Thanks, John.

Carey Lohrenz, U.S. Navy (ret.) and **Kenneth Johnson** are two impressive aviators who were incredibly helpful with all things airplane-related. Thank you.

My thanks as well go to my longtime friend **Patrick Ahern** for his digging into foreign snowmobiles for me. Hopefully, sometime soon, we'll get the chance to retrace some of our favorite routes via sled.

I have been with the outstanding people at **Simon & Schuster** since my very first thriller and want each and every one of them to know how much I value what they do for me, and how much I enjoy working with them.

Captaining the ship is the incomparable **Carolyn Reidy**. An author couldn't ask to work with a more respected, talented, and committed pro. Thank you for everything.

My magnificent publisher and editor, **Emily Bestler**, is what an author dreams about when they imagine a career as a writer. She is not only an incredible editor, but also an unfailing champion of her authors and a stellar publisher. She and her team at **Emily Bestler Books** blow me away with each book we do together. Thank you, all!

Atria publisher **Libby McGuire** and Associate publisher **Suzanne Donahue**, thank you for all of your incredible support!

Kristin Fassler and **Dana Trocker** in marketing, your enthusiasm, hard work, and fresh ideas are so appreciated.

Tons of work goes on behind the scenes in order to bring a book to market. To that end, I want to also call out and thank the amazing **Gary Urda**, the remarkable **Jonathan Karp**, and the unparalleled **John Hardy**. I couldn't do it without you.

Jen Long and the entire crew at **Pocket Books** are nothing short of fantastic. Thank you for your continued commitment to excellence and going the extra mile. I deeply appreciate all of you.

The **Simon & Schuster audio division** is composed of some of the coolest, most creative people you will ever meet. I extend my deepest thanks for another record-setting year to the phenomenal **Chris Lynch**, **Tom Spain**, **Sarah Lieberman**, **Desiree Vecchio**, **Karen Pearlman**, and **Armand Schultz**. You all are the best.

Speaking of the best, I want to give a BIG thank-you to the outstanding **Atria**, **Emily Bestler Books**, and **Pocket Books sales teams**. They knock it out of the park every single day. Without you, nothing else would be possible. Thank you a million times over.

David Brown, my sensational publicist, continues to crush it. From planning my elaborate tours, to handling all the wonderful media requests that come in, he tackles everything with exuberance and style. It is a pleasure to work with someone who is so good at what he does and takes such joy in doing it. Thank you, David.

Cindi Berger and the **team at PMK-BNC** are absolutely stupendous. The added PR wizardry they bring each year is simply incredible. Thank you for continuing to knock it out of the park.

One of my greatest joys of being at Simon & Schuster is being able to work with some amazingly talented people. These astonishing folks work tirelessly, and I want to express to them how grateful I am for everything they do for me. My thanks to the remarkable **Colin Shields**, **Paula Amendolara**, **Janice Fryer**, **Adene Corns**, **Liz Perl**, and **Lisa Keim**. In addition, I have to thank the exceptional **Gregory Hruska**, **Mark Speer**, and **Stuart Smith**. Thank you, all.

While I'm calling out stellar members of the Simon & Schuster family, I also want to recognize the fantastic **Lara Jones** at Emily Bestler Books. You do tons for me all year through. Thank you. I really appreciate you.

One of my favorite people at Simon & Schuster is also one of its hardest working, the unparalleled **Al Madocs** of the Atria/Emily Bestler Books Production Department. Al, I value your eagle eye more than you will ever know. Thank you for everything.

Thank you to the out-of-this-world talents, especially **Jimmy Iacobelli**, at the Atria/Emily Bestler Books and Pocket Books Art Departments. The stunning visuals you help to create truly set us apart.

Once again, I'd like to thank the fabulous **Saimah Haque**, **Sienna Farris**, **Whitney McNamara**, and **David Krivda** for another amazing year. Thank you for all that you do for me.

My beloved agent **Heide Lange** of **Sanford J. Greenburger Associates** is simply spectacular. Our partnership, as well as our friendship, continue to be two of my proudest accomplishments. My gratitude for everything that she has done for me knows no bounds. Thank you, Heide, from the bottom of my heart.

Heide is assisted by her world-class team, including **Samantha Isman** and **Iwalani Kim**. All of you at **Sanford J. Greenburger Associates** are like family to me, and I cannot thank you enough for another fantastic year!

Yvonne Ralsky—you are nothing short of superb. Every year, we set the bar higher and you keep coming up with new ways to leap over it. You know how much I value you, but I always enjoy putting it down in writing for everyone else to see. Thank you for everything.

They don't get any better than my marvelous entertainment attorney, **Scott Schwimer**. Handsome, humble, and wicked smart, I could neither have written a truer a friend, nor a fiercer advocate into my life. Thank you, Scottie, for being you.

Finally, I get to say my biggest thanks of all. To **my absolutely fantastic family**—thank you. Thank you for all of your love, your support, and the never-ending joy you bring me. Writing novels is a deeply satisfying career, but it would mean nothing without all of you. I love you more than I can ever put into words.

SODANKYLÄ •

• ROVANIEMI

LULEÅ •

SWEDEN

FINLAND

NORWAY

OSLO •

• HELSINKI

STOCKHOLM •

ESTONIA

LATVIA

LITHUANIA